D1191054

VENGEANCE
OF THE
IRON DWARF

THE LEGEND OF DRIZZT

Follow Drizzt and his companions on all of their adventures
(in chronological order)

The Dark Elf Trilogy	*The Hunter's Blades*
Homeland	The Thousand Orcs
Exile	The Lone Drow
Sojourn	The Two Swords

The Icewind Dale Trilogy	*Transitions*
The Crystal Shard	The Orc King
Streams of Silver	The Pirate King
The Halfling's Gem	The Ghost King

Legacy of the Drow	*The Neverwinter Saga*
The Legacy	Gauntlgrym
Starless Nights	Neverwinter
Siege of Darkness	Charon's Claw
Passage to Dawn	The Last Threshold

Paths of Darkness	*The Sundering*
The Silent Blade	The Companions
The Spine of the World	*(Book 1 of The Sundering)*
Sea of Swords	

The Sellswords	*The Companions Codex*
	Night of the Hunter
Servant of the Shard	Rise of the King
Promise of the Witch-King	Vengeance of the Iron Dwarf
Road of the Patriarch	

R.A. SALVATORE

VENGEANCE OF THE IRON DWARF

D&D

VENGEANCE OF THE IRON DWARF

©2015 Wizards of the Coast LLC.

Published by Wizards of the Coast LLC. Manufactured by: Hasbro SA, Rue Emile-Boéchat 31, 2800 Delémont, CH. Represented by Hasbro Europe, 2 Roundwood Ave, Stockley Park, Uxbridge, Middlesex, UB11 1AZ, UK.

Printed in the U.S.A.

Cover art by: Tyler Jacobson
First Printing: September 2015

9 8 7 6 5 4 3 2 1

ISBN: 978-0-7869-6570-0
ISBN: 978-0-7869-6582-3 (ebook)
620B2368000001 EN

Cataloging-in-Publication data is on file with the Library of Congress

Contact Us at Wizards.com/CustomerService
Wizards of the Coast LLC, PO Box 707, Renton, WA 98057-0707, USA
USA & Canada: (800) 324-6496 or (425) 204-8069
Europe: +32(0) 70 233 277

Visit our web site at **www.DungeonsandDragons.com**

PROLOGUE

IT WAS A SOLEMN GREETING AT THE UNDERGROUND WESTERN GATES OF Citadel Felbarr, on the first day of the second tenday in the eleventh month of Uktar. The first snows had fallen in the Upper Surbrin Vale, and the white coating already reached low among the Rauvin Mountains above the dwarven fortress. But if the orc hordes now controlling what was left of once-mighty Sundabar, or those in sacked Nesmé, or besieging mighty Silverymoon, or camped around the dwarven citadels of Mithral Hall, Felbarr, and Adbar had any intention of packing up and returning to Dark Arrow Keep, or to anywhere else within the accepted boundaries of the Kingdom of Many-Arrows, they didn't show it.

Nor were the vast networks of Upperdark tunnels clearing of invaders, as the procession from Mithral Hall discovered on their journey to the planned council at Citadel Felbarr. For nearly the entire month of Marpenoth and into Uktar, the legion of battle dwarves surrounding King Connerad Brawnanvil and his distinguished entourage had fought their way from waypoint to waypoint, regions the dwarves of Mithral Hall and Felbarr had strongly secured, heavily fortified and well supplied, in their long underground journey to the halls of King Emerus Warcrown.

Emerus himself was there to greet the dwarves of Mithral Hall. They were a tenday overdue. That had all been explained, and the actual arrival announced well in advance, thanks to the cunning dwarves of the Silver Marches, who had set up elaborate messaging systems through their connecting tunnels. Side-slinger ballistae would hurl messages rolled and tucked into hollow darts down long tunnels to be retrieved at the next guard post and there loaded again and sent flying along. Unless a section of the secured tunnels had been

1

overrun by orcs and their allies, a message from King Connerad to King Emerus could be sent the two hundred miles in just a few days.

"Well met, King Connerad!" Emerus said as he wrapped his peer in a great hug, to cheers from his fellows gathered at Citadel Felbarr's gate. "Ah, but we been concerned, me friend."

"Aye, the vermin are learnin' o' our main boulevard, and poking and prodding all about," Connerad replied. "Me and me boys had to stop and help along the way—or might be that our warriors down there didn't need our help, but we just wanted to punch a few orcs, eh!"

That brought a cheer from dwarves of both groups.

"Aye, but the meetin' ye asked for can wait until a few orcs're killed!" Emerus agreed. "Ye surprised meself and the dwarves o' Adbar in callin' it, with such grim news dancing all about."

Connerad nodded and pulled off his metal gauntlets. "Bringed some fellows with me ye might be knowing," he explained. "And when ye're seein' the truth, ye'll know why I called us all together."

Emerus nodded, putting a curious look on his face as he glanced past Connerad to the group of newcomers still out in the hallway, just beyond the immediate torchlight. Connerad followed his lead and glanced around. With a knowing grin, King Connerad waved the rogue drow, Drizzt Do'Urden, forward.

"Aye, I expect ye're knowing this one, then," Connerad said as Drizzt stepped up and bowed before the old King Emerus.

"Drizzt Do'Urden," Emerus remarked, nodding. "It has been many years since ye've been seen in the Silver Marches, old friend o' King Bruenor."

"Too many, it would seem," the drow answered, and extended his hand, which Emerus clasped and shook warmly. The curious manner in which Emerus had spoken of him, as a friend of Bruenor, surely didn't slip past Drizzt or Connerad.

"These drow leading the orcs claim—" Emerus began.

"To be of my House, yes," Drizzt interrupted. "Though I beg to differ. There is no House Do'Urden, good King Emerus, or at least, there is no House Do'Urden of which I have been aware for many decades now."

"So ye deny these drow be yer kin?"

"Kin, perhaps," Drizzt replied with a shrug. "I deny any foreknowledge of this attack, if that is what you mean to ask me."

"And deny that yerself was sent here to bring about the conception o' Many-Arrows, and so, in the end, to bring about this very war?" the old

2

dwarf king asked. Still he held tight to Drizzt's hand. Tighter even, squeezing as if the handshake was as much a test as this blunt line of questioning.

"Bah, but shut yer mouth!" roared a familiar voice from behind—one familiar to Drizzt and Connerad, and also to King Emerus and the dwarf named Ragged Dain, who stood behind the king of Felbarr. All glanced that way to see a young dwarf with a fiery reddish-orange beard hopping out from among the others.

"Little Arr Arr!" Ragged Dain cried, both in surprise and to scold the impetuous young warrior.

The dwarf came forward, looking very much like he would put his fist into King Emerus's old face—until Connerad stopped him with a shout. "It is not time for this, Mister Reginald Roundshield!"

The young dwarf paused and put his hands on his hips. He looked to Drizzt, who nodded, and grumbled as he went back to the group to stand beside a fair-haired human woman.

Ragged Dain continued to glower at the fellow, though he whispered to the others around him, "Ye be at yer ease, Mister Do'Urden. None outside o' the human cities're thinking bad o' King Bruenor and his old friends."

"Bring yer boys in," Emerus bade Connerad. "All of 'em. We'll show ye to yer rooms and show ye proper Felbarr hospitality, don't ye doubt."

"Show me boys to their rooms," Connerad replied. "For meself and a few others, show us to the gatherin' at yer table. I've much to tell ye, and it's not for waitin'. Get King Harnoth and his boys, and let's get to talking!"

King Emerus shook his head. "King Harnoth didn't come," he explained, and Connerad's eyes went wide.

"I begged ye all . . ."

"His seconds're here," King Emerus explained. "And we'll collect them for yer talk." He looked to Ragged Dain and nodded. "Take Connerad and them he wants aside him to the table."

Huffing and puffing, Franko Olbert stumbled up against the thick trunk of a tree. He dared a glance back across the snowy field to the distant wall of the town that had been his home for most of his life.

3

But though the skyline of Nesmé was surely familiar, Franko could not look upon that blasted and cursed place as his home. Not since the orcs had come. Not since the drow had come.

Not since Duke Tiago Do'Urden had come.

He started away once more, determined to get to the Uthgardt tribes, to raise an army, to find some way to repay the monstrous scum. His mother was Uthgardt. He knew their language, their ways, their pride. The proud barbarians would not suffer the orcs and dark elves to hold a city so near their borders.

Franko slipped away from the tree to another, then made a short run to a copse not far from there. He paused when he saw the human form lying on the ground facedown. The fallen man was dressed in armor: plate mail, mostly, and with a full helm, like some knight from Everlund.

The escapee hesitated and looked around cautiously. There were no signs of a struggle, other than the clear implications that this man was quite dead. He wasn't moving at all, set in the snow in an awkward and broken pose, with the stillness Franko had seen all too often since the monstrous horde had poured over Nesmé.

Seeing no one around, the escapee inched his way toward the fallen knight. He gingerly grabbed the dead warrior by his arm and turned him a bit so he could look into the man's face.

He shuddered at the gruesome visage. One eye had been pecked out, with more than half the poor man's face shredded and torn. Franko dropped the corpse back down to the snow, then fell back into a sitting position, forcing some deep breaths to help steady himself.

He noted the man's sword poking out from under one hip, and he was fast to it, easing it out of its sheath. Franko was an accomplished warrior, had ridden with the Riders of Nesmé, and he knew weapons. This one was fine indeed! And so was the armor, he noted, and the man was almost exactly his size.

"Thank you, brother," he said with respect, and he went to the man and began his looting.

With every piece he put on—the greaves, the breastplate, the pauldrons—Franko grew more confident. He strapped on the sword belt and breathed a sigh of relief. Even if his pursuers caught up to him now, he knew he would die a warrior, and Franko could ask for no more than that, particularly given the torturous executions he had witnessed in

Nesmé under the cruel gaze of the tyrant Duke Tiago. The city stank of bloated corpses.

"I should bury you, friend, but I haven't the time," he whispered. "Please forgive me, leaving you to the crows. Please forgive me, stealing your sword. But never would I steal your honor."

He knelt and said an Uthgardt prayer for the spirit of the dead man, then removed the dead man's helmet, gently and respectfully pulling it free of the torn head.

Before Franko had even brought it back, he understood something was amiss.

He plopped the helmet on his head and jumped to his feet, determined to be away quickly, but even as he took his first stride, he was stopped by curiosity and turned back.

Something nagged at him, just beyond his conscious recognition.

The wounds on the back?

He turned back to the corpse and this time suppressed his revulsion to take a good look at the poor man. The corpse had been rolled over in the process of looting it and that shredded face was clear to see.

"Marquen?" he gasped, and he looked closer, confirming his suspicion. "Marquen," he said, for surely this was the warrior Marquen of Silverymoon, who had moved to Nesmé a decade before. Franko's shock turned quickly to confusion. He had seen Marquen die, just a tenday earlier, as part of the executions in the open square in Nesmé.

Marquen had been tied to a pair of stakes and beaten mercilessly by Tiago's wife. Franko had watched as the vile Duchess Saribel Do'Urden had put her awful, venomous snake-headed whip to its cruel work. Again and again, the serpents struck, tearing Marquen's shirt, tearing his flesh, filling him with poisonous fire.

And there was the tattered, bloody shirt, and Franko didn't have to pull the ripped strands aside to know that the viper wounds were there in the flesh. Aye, this was Marquen, and Franko had watched Marquen die.

So how was he out here in the snow, a mile from the city, dressed in armor and carrying a sword?

"By the gods," Franko whispered, figuring it out, and he leaped to his feet and ran off at full speed.

He neared a small ravine, and didn't dare slow.

Not until he was struck blind.

No, not blind, Franko realized, as he stumbled over the ledge and tumbled down, falling out of the globe of magical darkness.

He felt his shoulder pop out as he crashed into the rocky dell, but came right up and threw himself hard into a tree, jamming his limb back in place. He ignored the waves of nausea and the dimming consciousness. He had no time for that.

Indeed, Franko had no time at all, as he learned when he spun to find a small but deadly figure standing in front of him, looking quite amused.

Duke Tiago of Nesmé.

The drow smiled and raised his gloved hands, his small, translucent buckler strapped to his left forearm, and began to clap.

"You did well, *iblith*," Tiago said. "You traveled farther than I expected. A most worthy hunt, considering my prey is no more than a pathetic human."

Franko glanced around, expecting to see some orc archers or a giant holding a boulder nearby. Or other drow.

"It is just me," Tiago assured him. "Why would I need more?" As he finished, he held out his arms.

And Franko leaped at him, sword cutting for the foul drow's head.

But up came the shield, and its edge spiraled magically as it did. With each turn, the magnificent shield enlarged, and behind it, Tiago easily ducked the blow.

And out came the drow's sword, so fast that Franko didn't register the movement, or hear the star-filled blade sliding free of its scabbard.

Franko felt the bite of the tip, though, as it pierced his thigh. He grimaced and fell back into a defensive crouch, his sword slashing out sidelong to keep his enemy at bay.

But Tiago wasn't advancing. Instead, he moved easily, circling Franko, just out of reach.

"Fight," the drow said. "There is only me. I've no friends nearby. Only me, only Tiago, standing between you and your freedom."

"You think this sport?" Franko spat at him, and he rushed and chopped with his sword, cleverly—he thought—pulling up short and breaking his momentum to stab straight ahead.

"Is it anything less?" a laughing Tiago said from back the other way, having somehow eluded Franko's attack so fully that the stabbing sword was farther from Tiago's flesh than it had been before Franko began the strike.

6

Franko licked his lips. The extent of that miss wasn't promising.

"Just me," Tiago teased, circling back the other way.

Franko, too, began to circle, studying the area to see if he might find some advantage in the uneven ground, trees, and rocks.

"Is that not a fair game, human?" Tiago asked. "I even armed and armored you, finely so! I could have struck you dead while you robbed the corpse. I could have stopped you from fleeing Nesmé—a dozen archers watched you run out. They had their bows trained upon you even as you squeezed through the crack in the wall. I held their shots. I gave you a chance. All you need to do is defeat me, and as you're nearly twice my size, that should prove simple enough."

His voice never strained, never lost its composure, even though Franko came on in midspeech, ferociously chopping and stabbing, pressing ahead, trying to simply overwhelm the diminutive drow.

"Though I admit you are a bit clumsy," Tiago added, and that last sentence was spoken from behind Franko, as the drow's sword slashed across the man's calf, tearing a painful line.

Franko turned and slashed with his blade, and staggered, hopping up on one foot as fiery agony filled his other leg.

Ahead sprang Tiago, his sword poking forward and turning subtly to avoid the desperate parry, slipping past to prod Franko in the shoulder, in the crease between breastplate and pauldron. The blade came again, stabbing a second time in the same place, and ahead yet again, and this time, as Franko wildly tried to protect that burning shoulder, Tiago shifted Vidrinath the other way, taking Franko in the crease between his right pauldron and breastplate.

The man fell back, waving his sword wildly to fend off the drow, who was not pursuing. As Franko's weight came down on his torn leg, he stumbled and fell over backward, wildly trying to right himself, slashing his blade, desperate to keep the drow at bay.

Except the drow was still standing, back where he had stabbed the man.

Franko stared at him, hard and determined, pulling himself back to his feet, hating this drow all the more. Tiago was playing with him, taunting him by refusing to press the advantage.

Supremely confident.

Franko silently berated himself. He was overplaying his hand. Perhaps it was the size difference, as Tiago had hinted. Or maybe Franko's supreme hatred of this false tyrant duke had stolen his better judgment. He knew he was a better fighter by far than he was showing against Tiago. He was a Rider of Nesmé, finely trained, and he knew better than to give in to his anger.

He told himself all of that, replayed the drow's maneuvers, and nodded quietly as he considered a better approach to engage this skilled swordsman.

He moved ahead slowly.

Tiago stood there, his left hand on his hip, his sword tip down to the ground at his right side.

Tiago's posture invited a fierce attack.

But Franko paced himself this time, eased his way forward, and kept his sword in tight, defensively. He understood now that Tiago's seemingly unprepared posture was just that, "seemingly." The drow reacted too quickly for him to hope for an open strike, and indeed, the overbalancing thrust would get him stabbed yet again.

But now he knew.

He stepped his sword ahead in a measured and balanced thrust, a lazy and meaningless attack.

Too lazy, Franko thought.

Too slow.

And his arms were too heavy.

He didn't understand. He didn't know the more common name of Tiago's sword, Lullaby, and didn't know that each strike had sent sleeping poison coursing into his body and blood.

But he knew that he was sluggish, and so he reached his sword out once more to keep the drow at bay until he could sort it out.

The drow wasn't there.

Franko heard a laugh behind him, and he swung around as quickly as he could manage, sweeping his sword.

It got halfway around but no more, met with a sudden and vicious uppercut by Vidrinath.

Franko's sword went flying away, his severed hand still gripping it. The man brought the stump of his arm in close, crying in pain and shock, hugging tight his bloody wrist.

"Run away," Tiago said teasingly, and stabbed him again, this time in his fleshy rump. "Flee, you fool!"

He stuck Franko again, and the man began his run and Tiago was close behind, poking him painfully. Then Tiago was beside him, taunting him, sticking him repeatedly, but never deeply, never a wound to kill him.

Desperate now, Franko threw himself at the drow. But the drow was too quick, and kicked out his ankles, dropping him hard to the ground.

And in came Vidrinath, and a sizable piece of Franko's right ear flew away.

He was crying, frustrated and angry and hurt, but he stubbornly got his legs under him and began stumbling away.

And again Tiago paced him.

"You, human," the drow said. "You, yes you, you fool!" His sword tapped Franko on the shoulder, but didn't cut into any flesh this time, but rather, pointed ahead.

"You see that clearing beyond the birch?" Tiago asked. "Run, fool. If you get there, I will not pursue you further!"

He ended with a hard slap across Franko's rump with the flat of his blade.

"Ah, but you are too tired," Tiago teased, pacing the man just behind, close enough to kill Franko with an easy thrust. "Your legs are heavy. Aye, you can barely stay upright! Oh fie, but then I'll have to kill you!"

He poked Franko in the rump again, and twisted his blade painfully for good measure.

Tiago's laugh chased him.

But Franko had an idea now. He felt as though he'd gained some insight into the sadistic drow. He slowed even more and staggered sideways as much as forward with every step. He didn't think Tiago would kill him until the last moment, until he reached the birch tree, and he used that knowledge to change the cadence of the pursuit.

He got stabbed again, repeatedly, but never more than superficially, never intended to inflict true damage, but always to inflict more pain. But he held his course, his ruse. The birch was close now.

Franko stumbled and started to fall, enough to look good, but he burst ahead suddenly, using every ounce of weary strength he could muster to propel him to the birch tree and past it, diving out into the clearing.

He rolled onto his back, expecting the treacherous drow to be right above him, ready to kill him. To his surprise, though—indeed to his shock—Tiago had not come out past the birch.

"Well played!" the self-proclaimed Duke of Nesmé said, and he tipped his sword in salute.

"Come on, then!" Franko yelled at him, certain it was all a cruel taunt.

9

"I am a drow of my word, fool," Tiago said. "I am a royal duke, after all. I promised that I would pursue you no further, and so I shan't. Indeed, you are free of my blade, though I expect your wounds to take you in the forest. If not, then you'll come back, of course, with some pitiful army, and I will find you again and finish my kill. Next time, I will start with your eyes, so that you will not see the next blow falling.

"Ah, but you will hear me, and that voice, my voice, will frighten you, for it will portend the fall of Vidrinath upon your exposed flesh."

And he laughed an awful laugh as Franko stumbled away across the wide field. He kept looking back, but Tiago was not pursuing.

So he turned ahead, determined to find the Uthgardt, determined—

The ground erupted in front of him, and a beast, gleaming stark white and colder than winter itself, came up from the snow.

"Oh fie," Tiago lamented behind him. "Did I not warn you that my dragon was waiting?"

Franko screamed, feeling the warmth of his own piss running down his leg when those terrible jaws opened wide, spear-like teeth closing around him. Up he went into the air, sidelong in the dragon's maw, legs hanging out one side, head and shoulders out the other.

He kept screaming, but the dragon didn't bite down, or maybe it did and he was already dead and just hadn't realized it yet. He couldn't know.

"I do find this enjoyable," Tiago whispered in his ear.

Jolted by the voice so near, Franko composed himself just enough to turn and look the drow in the eye.

And in came the sword, surgically, and Franko's right eye flipped free into the drow's waiting hand.

"Dear Arauthator," Tiago said to the dragon. "Pray do not bite the life from him. Nay, swallow this proud one whole, that he can lay pressed in your belly, your juices melting him to nothingness."

The dragon issued a long, low growl.

"He has no blade, I promise!" Tiago assured the beast.

Up went the head, tossing poor Franko inside—and down he went into the beast, helpless.

"I feel more a snake than a wyrm," Arauthator complained.

"Is he wriggling?" the drow asked.

The dragon paused in a pensive pose. "Whimpering, I think," he answered.

"Good, good," said Tiago.

"Are you done with your silly game, Husband?" asked another voice, and Tiago turned to see the approach of Saribel.

"I must find my pleasure where I can!" he said. "Would that I could fly the Old White Death over Silverymoon to drop stones on the fools within! Would that I could assail Everlund—"

"You cannot!" Saribel scolded. Tiago couldn't argue; that command had come from Matron Mother Quenthel Baenre herself.

They were to sit quietly in their conquered lands and vast encampments. "Let the folk of the Silver Marches take hope that the spring will bring relief" was Matron Mother Quenthel's command.

Tiago understood the implications all too well, as did Saribel. The matron mother was making sure that no other surface kingdoms from beyond the Silver Marches' alliance of Luruar became involved in this war. The drow incursion could inspire no terror beyond the North; they would involve none but those kingdoms they had used their orc fodder to assail.

No one would raise an army and fight here because there was no ultimate victory, no lasting gains of land and conquest, to be found here, not on the battlefield at least. The campaign had never been about that.

"We have pressed them to the edge of doom, and we will let them wriggle free," Tiago said. He turned to the dragon. "But that one will not!"

Arauthator laughed, a strange and unnerving rumble, then belched, and from deep inside, a muffled cry of hopelessness and pain accompanied the burp.

"It is not about victory," Tiago said accusatorily.

Saribel held her ground and even looked at him rather condescendingly. "Define victory," she said.

"It is about Matron Mother Quenthel securing her hold on Menzoberranzan," said Tiago.

"You would wish differently? She is our benefactor, our reason for existence. House Do'Urden is the domain of the matron mother as surely as are the halls of House Baenre you walked as a child."

Tiago muttered a curse under his breath and turned away. He was full of battle lust, craving victory and glory, and these pitiful hunting games he allowed himself with the captives of Nesmé were growing older and more boring with each tormented kill.

"We have already achieved victory," Saribel said.

"Quenthel has!" Tiago spat before he could properly voice the name, and he blanched when the whip appeared in Saribel's hand, and when Arauthator's toothy maw moved right beside him, reminding him so poignantly that the word of the matron mother, and thus, the word of her priestesses, outranked the demands of the Duke of Nesmé.

"Matron Mother Quenthel," he said and lowered his eyes. He silently told himself, though, that if Saribel struck at him with that whip, he would kill her then and there, and hopefully be done with the witch before the dragon ate him. In that event, with Saribel, the only witness, lying dead, perhaps he could convince great Arauthator that eating him would only complicate things.

But the blow from Saribel's whip did not fall.

"Be of good spirit, Husband, for we too have won!" Saribel said, and replaced the weapon on her belt.

Tiago looked up at her and growled, "We will be recalled soon."

Saribel nodded. "And even now, we can return to the city with dignity, as heroes of Menzoberranzan, victorious in the glorious campaign, and so take our place as royals of House Do'Urden."

Tiago started to respond, but paused as he considered the lighthearted, joyous tone of Saribel. His eyes widened as he figured it out.

"You expect to replace her," he said. "*Darthiir*, Matron Mother of House Do'Urden. You expect . . ."

He stopped and stared, Saribel's expression giving no indication that she meant to argue the point. And as he thought of it, as he thought of broken Dahlia, he found that he, too, could come to no other conclusion as to where all of this was leading. For Dahlia was *darthiir*, a surface elf, and her appointment as Matron Mother of House Do'Urden had been no more than a cruel joke Matron Mother Quenthel had perpetrated on the Ruling Council. An insult to the very traditions of the drow, of the unending hatred the dark elves held for their surface cousins. Quenthel had elevated Dahlia for no better reason than to prove that she could, and to prove, even more poignantly, that there was nothing the other matron mothers could do about it.

And so, yes, it all made sense that Saribel, noble daughter of House Xorlarrin, would ascend to House Do'Urden's ruling seat when the filthy Dahlia had outlived her usefulness.

VENGEANCE OF THE IRON DWARF

"Ha, but sure ye're to fit in the line o' Battlehammer kings," Ragged Dain said to King Connerad as they made their way to the Court of Citadel Felbarr, Connerad's chosen entourage in tow. General Dagnabbet and Bungalow Thump were among that group, along with Little Arr Arr and another tough, black-bearded fellow Ragged Dain did not know.

But so were Drizzt Do'Urden and a human lass.

"Never could stick to yer own kind, ye danged Battlehammers!" Ragged Dain teased. "Even when old King Bruenor went huntin' for Mithral Hall. Bah, but he was the only dwarf among that group what found the place!"

Connerad laughed the good-natured jab away, but he knew it was true enough. In the war with the first Obould a century before, Connerad's own father, the great Banak, had been overlooked as steward when Bruenor had fallen in battle. On Bruenor's orders, a halfling had taken control of Mithral Hall.

A halfling! And with an army of decorated dwarves ready to step in!

Connerad couldn't suppress a glance back at the dwarf he knew to be Bruenor as he considered the insult to his father. Banak Brawnanvil had brushed the whole incident away, mitigating the sting, and reminding his son that Regis had been beside Bruenor as friend and confidant for years and knew the old dwarf's heart better than anyone.

The young dwarf in the procession noted Connerad's glance and offered him a knowing wink, and Connerad found that his anger, what little there was, couldn't hold. Bruenor had honored his father and family in the end, elevating the Brawnanvils to the throne of Mithral Hall.

"And how 'bout yerself, Little Arr Arr?" Ragged Dain said when they entered the gathering hall. "Ye done good for yerself, so it's seemin'. So are ye meanin' to sit with the Battlehammers or with yer own o' Felbarr? And when're ye to go and see yer dear Ma, Uween? Did ye even send word to her, then? Tell her that ye've returned?"

The young dwarf nodded. "Battlehammers," he said gruffly. "That's me place above all."

"Yer Ma might not be agreein'," Ragged Dain teased.

"Me Ma's to find a lot to scramble her brain, don't ye doubt," the red-bearded young dwarf replied, and he snorted in emphasis.

The seven representatives of Mithral Hall took their seats on their appointed side of the triangular table King Emerus had constructed specifically for meetings of the three citadels. General Dagnabbet, Bungalow Thump, and Bruenor sat to Connerad's right, Athrogate, Drizzt, and Catti-brie to the young king's left.

King Emerus entered soon after and took his place, flanked by Ragged Dain and Parson Glaive, and last came the delegation, six dwarf officers from Citadel Adbar, led by the fierce Oretheo Spikes of the battleraging Wilddwarves.

After proper greetings, promises of friendship, eternal alliance, and no small amount of ale, King Emerus called the chamber to order and turned the proceedings over to King Connerad.

"What news from Mithral Hall, then?" Emerus bade his young but respected peer. "Ye promised us great tidings, and I'm meanin' to hold ye to 'em!"

"Aye, but we could all use a bit o' good news then," Oretheo Spikes added, and lifted his tankard in toast.

"Ye see that me friend here, Drizzt Do'Urden, has returned to our side," King Connerad began, and he paused and looked to the dark elf ranger.

The dwarves at the other sides of the triangular table did bristle a bit, but ultimately lifted their tankards in toast to Drizzt.

Connerad offered Drizzt the floor.

"I fought at the defense of Nesmé," Drizzt began.

"Nesmé has fallen," King Emerus interrupted, and the expressions on the faces of the Battlehammer contingent and those from Citadel Adbar showed that to be new information indeed.

"Bah!" Athrogate snorted. "But we knowed she couldn't be holdin' for long."

"A dragon arrived to bolster the Many-Arrows horde," King Emerus explained. "One ridden by a drow elf callin' himself Do'Urden."

More grumbles came from the Adbar dwarves at that, but the Felbarrans remained stoic, having clearly already digested the news.

"I can say nothing to that claim," Drizzt replied honestly. "There is no surviving House Do'Urden that I know of, but I have not been to the city of my birth in long over a century now, and have no hopes or desires to ever return."

He paused, and all eyes went to King Emerus, who nodded solemnly, indicating his acceptance of the explanation.

"My party was returning to Mithral Hall when we encountered this strange, darkened sky," Drizzt explained. "Then we encountered the western flank of the orc line camped outside of Nesmé."

"Tricked 'em good," Athrogate put in.

"Good enough for them to sack the town, so it's seeming," King Emerus said dryly.

"Bah, but it taked 'em long enough!" Athrogate roared in protest. "And know that the fields're filled with orc dead!"

"The town has fallen, so you say, and so it must be," Drizzt interjected. "It had not when my friends and I left through the tunnels of the Upperdark to get to Mithral Hall. Be assured that the taking of Nesmé was no easy task for the hordes of Many-Arrows. Thousands of goblins and orcs were slaughtered at her walls before we departed, and with the rotting stench of dead ogres and giants among them. They came against Nesmé's walls day after day, and day after day, they were slaughtered."

"This I have heard," Emerus admitted. "And yerself played a role in that?"

"Aye," said Drizzt. "As did Athrogate of Felbarr here." He patted Athrogate's strong shoulder, but the dwarf's eyes widened, and he looked up at Drizzt, seeming near panic.

"Felbarr?" King Emerus said, obviously caught by surprise. He looked to Parson Glaive, who could only shrug in confusion.

"I be so much older than I'm lookin'," Athrogate admitted. "Was here when Obould took the place. Didn't e'er return."

The Felbarr dwarves all glanced around, exchanging doubtful looks indeed.

"Not for mattering," Athrogate said. "Ain't called Felbarr me home in two dwarves' lifetimes. Just Athrogate now. Just Athrogate."

"We will talk, yerself and meself," King Emerus said, and Athrogate looked back over his shoulder and cast a sour glance at Drizzt, who just patted him on the shoulder again.

"Athrogate was a hero of Nesmé," Drizzt said, and he moved to stand behind Catti-brie, dropping his hands on her strong shoulders. "As was this woman, my wife."

"Ye seem to be favorin' human lasses with that fire hair, what ho!" Ragged Dain declared, and he lifted his tankard in toast to the woman.

"Indeed," Drizzt agreed. "And that will be explained shortly, I expect. Perhaps even by the fourth of my party who joins us this day." He stepped to the side of Catti-brie and leaned over the table, nodding down the other end of the Battlehammer line to his dear friend, who nodded back.

"Little Arr Arr?" King Emerus asked with surprise. "So ye're with this one now, then, and not with the Battlehammers?"

"With both," Bruenor replied.

Emerus gave a snort and shook his head.

"Tale's already got me head spinnin'," Oretheo Spikes said from the Adbar side.

"Oh, but ye ain't heared nothin' yet," King Connerad assured him, assured all of them, and he lifted his pack from the floor and plopped it on the table in front of him, then reverently opened it to reveal a peculiar one-horned helmet.

"Ye e'er seen one akin to it?" he asked King Emerus.

"Looks like Bruenor's own," the king of Felbarr replied.

Connerad nodded, then suddenly slid the fabled item along the table to his right, past Dagnabbet and Bungalow Thump to the waiting hands of Little Arr Arr.

"Eh?" King Emerus and several others asked together.

Little Arr Arr lifted the one-horned helm in his strong hands and rolled it around, looking it over from every angle. Then, looking straight at Emerus, he plopped the helm, the old crown of Mithral Hall, atop his head.

" 'Ere now, what're ye about?" King Emerus demanded.

"Ye're not knowin' me, then?" Bruenor asked slyly. "After all we been through together?"

Emerus wore a curious expression and turned to Connerad for an answer.

"That one there, the one ye were knowin' as Little Arr Arr, son o' Reginald Roundshield and Uween," Connerad began, and he paused and collected his breath, even shaking his head as if he, too, could hardly believe what he was about to declare.

"Me name's Bruenor," the young dwarf in the one-horned helm interjected. "Bruenor Battlehammer, Eighth King and Tenth King o' Mithral Hall. Son o' Bangor, me Da, who ye knowed well, me friend Emerus. Aye, son o' Bangor, that'd be me!"

"Ye dishonor yer Ma!" Ragged Dain scolded and came forward over the table threateningly. But Bruenor didn't blink.

"And so too son o' Reginald Roundshield," he said. "And born again of Uween, me Ma, and she's a fine one, don't ye doubt."

"Delusion!" Ragged Dain insisted.

"Blasphemy!" added Oretheo Spikes.

"Truth in tellin'!" Bruenor spat at both of them. "Bruenor's me name, the one gived me by me Da, Bangor!"

"Ye canno' believe this," King Emerus said to Connerad. He turned fast to Drizzt, though, as he spoke. "Surely yerself's knowin' better!"

"Bruenor," Drizzt said slowly and deliberately, nodding. "It is."

"Don't you know him, then, King Emerus?" asked the woman beside Drizzt. "And don't you recognize me?"

"Now, how might I be doing that?" Emerus asked, or almost asked. The last word caught in his throat as he took a closer look at this auburn-haired young woman sitting beside the dark elf.

"By the gods," he muttered.

"Catti-brie?" Ragged Dain added, just as breathlessly.

"Aye, by the gods," the woman answered. "By Mielikki, most of all."

"And with the blessings o' Moradin, Dumathoin, and Clangeddin, don't ye doubt," Bruenor added. "I been to their throne in Gauntlgrym, I tell ye. Thought I'd be drinking at their hall, but they had other plans."

"And so we're here, in this time of need," Catti-brie added.

The others started to cheer, but King Emerus cut that short. "No, canno' be," he said. "No, but I knowed ye when ye were here, I did! Little Arr Arr! I went to yer Ma and saw ye schooled in the fightin' . . ."

The King of Citadel Felbarr paused there, the memory catching him by surprise. He looked to Parson Glaive and Ragged Dain, and they each smiled and nodded, also recalling the way this young dwarf, the son of Reginald Roundshield, had toyed with dwarflings years beyond his age.

"No, but it couldn't be all a lie," Emerus insisted. "Ye was right under me eyes! Yer Da was me friend, captain o' me guard! Ye canno' dishonor him now in such a way!"

"Ain't no dishonor," Bruenor insisted, shaking his head. "I done what needed doin'. I could no' tell ye, though don't ye doubt but I wanted to!"

"Blasphemy!" Emerus shouted.

"Wait," Ragged Dain interrupted, and it seemed a fortunate coincidence that the old dwarf picked that time to slow down the momentum of King Emerus. Ragged Dain turned to Emerus and nodded an apology, and when the king bade him continue, he spun back on Bruenor. "Then ye're sayin' it was King Bruenor who threw himself at that giant in the

Rauvins? King Bruenor who gived all but his life so that his fellows could get away?"

"Seen a giant, sticked a giant," Bruenor said matter-of-factly and with a shrug, though he did wince a bit at the painful memory. "And aye, Mandarina Dobberbright?" he asked, looking to Emerus. "Know that she saved me, as did yer second there, good Parson Glaive."

Ragged Dain, King Emerus, and Bruenor looked to the high priest of Felbarr together, finding Parson Glaive standing and staring dumbfounded then, his jaw hanging open. "It's true," he whispered breathlessly.

"Aye, so I said," Bruenor replied. "Mandarina tended me, and Dain and the boys bringed me back, though I'm not for rememberin' much o' that part!"

"No," Parson Glaive said. "Yerself . . . ye're Bruenor, and ye were Bruenor then."

"Always been," Bruenor answered, but King Emerus waved him to silence.

"What'd'ye know?" the king demanded of his high priest.

"When ye waked up after the fight in the Rauvins, back in Felbarr," Parson Glaive said to Bruenor, "I told ye that ye might've been goin' to meet yer Da, and I was meanin' Arr Arr, course, as he went off to the table o' Moradin. But ye were half out o' yer wits, and ye said . . ."

"Bangor," Bruenor replied.

King Emerus blinked repeatedly, turning from Parson Glaive to Bruenor and back again.

"Even then, ye knowed," Ragged Dain whispered.

"Always knowed, from the day o' me birth."

"Always knowed? And ye didn't tell me?" Emerus demanded.

Bruenor stood and bowed. "Weren't yer worry," was all he offered.

"And was yerself that got yerself to Mithral Hall, to train with them Gutbusters, so ye said," Ragged Dain added.

"Heigh ho!" Bungalow Thump had to put in.

The three from Citadel Felbarr exchanged looks, and Parson Glaive said with complete confidence, "By the gods, but it's him."

"By the gods!" Oretheo Spikes and the rest of the Adbar contingent, King Emerus and Ragged Dain all shouted together, and they came to their feet as one, shaking their hairy heads, clapping each other on the back and crying, "Huzzah to King Bruenor!"

"Aye, but the hopes just brightened and the dark sky ain't so dark!" King Emerus proclaimed. "Bruenor, me old friend, but how is it so?" He crawled across the table to offer a firm handshake, then pushed in closer and wrapped King Bruenor in a great hug.

"Drinks! Drinks!" he yelled to the attendants. "Oh, but we'll be puttin' 'em back for a tenday and more. Huzzah for Bruenor!"

And the cheering began anew, and the attendants came rushing in, foam flying, and the somber council quickly became a cacophony of toasts and cheers. Bruenor let the celebration go on for a while, but finally begged them all to take their seats once more.

"Not much to be cheerin' if the Silver Marches're to fall," he warned.

"And ye're King o' Mithral Hall again?" Emerus asked Bruenor as soon as they had all settled back into their seats. The King of Citadel Felbarr looked to Connerad as he spoke the dangerous question.

Bruenor, too, glanced over at Connerad, who nodded. In that moment, it looked to all that Connerad would go along with whatever Bruenor decided. That subservience was not lost on King Emerus and Ragged Dain, both of whom gasped at the sight.

"Nah," said Bruenor. "Best choice meself ever made as king was giving me crown to Banak Brawnanvil, and him, to his boy Connerad. Mithral Hall's got a king, and as fine a king as she's e'er known. An ungrateful wretch I'd be if I called for me throne back now!"

"Then what?" asked Emerus.

"I been to Nesmé, and left Nesmé right afore she fell, so ye're sayin'," Bruenor answered. "Me and me friends've come to tell ye to get out o' yer holes. Now's the time, or there's no time to be found! The land's crawling with orcs, and they ain't meanin' to go back to their holes. Nah, they're taking it all, I tell ye."

"We've heared as much from the couriers of the Knights in Silver," Connerad added.

"Bah! But what'd we care for them human lands?" King Emerus spouted. "Layin' all the blame at our feet—at yer own feet, if ye're who ye claim to be and who we think ye to be!"

"I am, and so they will, and so I won't be caring!" Bruenor declared. "I'm knowin' better. Me name's on that damned treaty, aye, but was th' other kingdoms what put it there a hunnerd years ago, and yerself's knowin' the truth o' that, me friend."

19

King Emerus nodded.

"But now's no time for blamin'," Bruenor went on. "We got thousands o' orcs to kill, me boys! Tens o' thousands! All o' Luruar stands together, or all o' Luruar's sure to fall!"

"Ain't no Luruar," said Oretheo Spikes. He rose up from his seat and slowly walked around the sharp-angled corner of the table, moving deliberately for Bruenor. "Just a bunch o' elves and humans dancing about three dwarf forts. Aye, and they're to fall," he said when he got right up to Bruenor, and he began carefully looking over the strange dwarf. "All of 'em, and there ain't a durned thing we can do to stop it."

"We put our three as one and hammer them orcs . . ." Bruenor started.

"We canno' get out," Oretheo Spikes explained, and still he looked the strange dwarf up and down, once again looking for some sign that the dwarf was an imposter, it seemed.

And who could blame him?

Into the midst of a besieged and battered trio of citadels comes a young dwarf claiming to be a long-dead king, and telling the dwarves to come out of their impregnable fortresses.

"Oh, but we tried," Oretheo went on, and he started back for his seat. "King Harnoth won't stay in his hall, so full o' grief is he for his brother, Bromm, who got himself murdered to death in the Cold Vale. I seen that murder, aye, me king frozen to death by the blow of a white dragon! Aye, a true dragon, I tell ye, and then me dear king got his head cut away by th' ugliest orc, Warlord Hartusk of Dark Arrow Keep. Oh, aye, young Bruenor, if that's to be yer name," he added and looked past Bruenor to Drizzt, "and riding the wyrm was a drow elf, much akin to the one ye bringed in with ye."

He turned his eye squarely on Bruenor. "We'd lose half our dwarves and more tryin' to get out o' Adbar. Damned orcs canno' get in, but me boys canno' get out—and I ain't for losing half o' them trying. Or might that be what ye're lookin' to see?"

The thick suspicion in Oretheo's voice was not lost on Bruenor or any of the others from Mithral Hall.

And again, who could blame him?

"I'm hearin' ye," Bruenor assured him, nodding solemnly. "And me old heart's breaking for yer King Bromm. A good one, I hear, though I knowed his Da better, to be sure."

With a glance at Connerad, Bruenor leaped upon the table and stood to address them all. "And I ain't sayin', and let none be sayin', that we're to crawl out and lose half our boys. Not for the Silver Marches, nay. But we're better off by far in saving what's left o' the place and not giving all the land above us to them damned orcs."

"How, then?" asked Oretheo Spikes. "Adbar canno' get out, and the rings about Felbarr and Mithral Hall ain't any thinner."

"One's got to lead," Bruenor said. "One to break out and go to help the next in line. If we're talkin' smart back and forth, we can coax th' orcs off the next and smash 'em from both sides."

"Then two free go to the third—Adbar'd be me guess—and we're out an' runnin'," said King Emerus.

Bruenor nodded.

"Aye, but who, then?" asked Oretheo Spikes. "Who's first out? For sure that hall's to suffer like none've been punched since Obould first came down from the Spine o' the World!"

Emerus nodded grimly at Oretheo's reasoning, then slowly swung around to regard Bruenor.

"It'll be the boys from Mithral Hall," Connerad answered before Bruenor could, and all three turned to him with surprise.

"Aye," Connerad said, nodding. "I know none o' ye're blamin' Mithral Hall and me friend Bruenor for what's come crashin' down on us, but it's right that me and me boys find our way out—out and over to Felbarr is me guess."

Emerus looked to Bruenor, who shrugged and deferred back to the rightful king of Mithral Hall.

"We'll find a way," Connerad insisted, "or I'm a bearded gnome!"

Bruenor started to agree, but that last remark, once his trademark vow, caught him off guard so completely that he nearly toppled off the table. He stared at Connerad, who offered him a grin and a wink in explanation.

"Well, huzzah and heigh-ho to Mithral Hall then," said King Emerus. "And if ye're findin' yer way out and across the Surbrin, know that Felbarr'll be itchin' to get out and join ye in the slaughter."

"Ye're talkin' months," Oretheo Spikes reminded them all, "for winter's soon to be deep about us."

"Then yerself's to keep the way from Adbar to Felbarr open," King Emerus told him. "And Felbarr'll keep the way clear to Mithral Hall while Connerad and his boys get ready to break them orcs.

"So there ye have our answer, King Bruenor, me old friend," Emerus went on. "I got no love for the folk o' Silverymoon or Everlund, nor am I losin' much sleep for the folk o' Sundabar. Aye, but they've treated yer memory with disrespect, and called me own boys cowards for the slaughter at the Redrun, and now I wouldn't lose a boy to save a one o' them towns! But aye, ye're right in that we're better with them orcs chased off and killed to death. Ye get yerselves out and we'll watch for ye."

He shifted his gaze to take in Connerad as well. "But if ye canno' get out, ye won't be findin' Felbarr leading the way up."

"Nor Adbar," Oretheo Spikes warned.

Bruenor and Connerad exchanged concerned glances, then Bruenor looked over to Drizzt, who nodded.

They really couldn't have asked for more than that.

None were happy after leaving that meeting that day in Citadel Felbarr, but the whispering echoed in every hall in Felbarr soon after, as word that their own Little Arr Arr had returned with his spectacular announcement.

King Bruenor? Could it be?

Uween Roundshield was hard at work at her blacksmithing when she heard the whispers. She wasted no time in closing down her forge and heading back to her home. Overwhelmed and confused, she didn't want to discuss the startling news. She really had no idea how she actually felt about it. If the whispers were true, she was the Queen Mother of Mithral Hall, a place she had never even visited and of which she knew almost nothing.

Whatever excitement that strange and unexpected title might inspire was surely tempered, though: If this was King Bruenor, then what of her Little Arr Arr? What of the child she had nurtured? For eighteen years, he had been her boy—not without trials, certainly, but not without love, either.

But how much of it was a lie?

She thought of the last month he had been in her home, itching to be on the road to Mithral Hall. So he knew then, she realized. Possibly, he had known for all his life.

And he hadn't told her.

She dropped her thick apron on the counter in her entry hall and plopped down heavily on a chair at her dining table, feeling much older than her hundred and ten years. How she missed her husband in this difficult moment. She needed someone to lean on, someone to help her sort through this . . . insanity.

"I come home, Ma," came a familiar voice from the hallway behind her.

Uween froze in place, her thoughts whirling.

"I hope ye're to forgive me for going to King Emerus first, but I seen the war, and it's no pretty thing," Bruenor said, moving slowly toward the woman.

Uween didn't—couldn't—look over at him. She kept her head bowed into her hands, trying to clear her mind, trying to throw aside her fears and grief and simply let her heart guide her. She heard her boy approaching, and couldn't deny the flutter in her heart.

"Ma?" Bruenor said, dropping a hand on her shoulder.

Uween spun on him and leaped up from her seat, and even in the motion, she wasn't sure whether she'd punch him or hug him. She went with the hug, crushing her boy tight against her.

He reciprocated, and Uween felt the warmth, the sincere love coming back at her.

"King Bruenor, they're sayin'," she whispered.

"Aye, 'tis true, but that's a part o' me," he whispered back. "Uween's boy, Reginald's boy, I be, and proud of it, don't ye doubt."

"But ye're this other one, too," Uween said when she composed herself. She pulled back a bit to look her son in the eye.

"Aye, Bruenor Battlehammer, son o' Bangor and Caydia, and don't ye know but that I'm shakin' me head every time I'm thinking about it!" Bruenor replied with a self-deprecating laugh. "Two Mas, two Das, two lines o' blood."

"And one's royal."

Bruenor nodded. "Still got me royal blood. Been to Gauntlgrym, to the Throne o' the Dwarf Gods, and ye canno' sit on it if . . ." His voice trailed away, and Uween blushed, recognizing that she hadn't hid her disinterest well enough. She didn't care about his other Ma and Da, or this whole King Bruenor business. Nay, this was her Little Arr Arr and not some Battlehammer!

"I'm not meanin' to hurt ye," Bruenor said. "It's the last thing I'd be wanting to do."

"Then what's this craziness that's come over ye?"

"It's not. Me name's Bruenor—always been. By the grace of a goddess was I brought back from the grave."

"So someone told ye!"

"No," Bruenor said somberly, shaking his head. "No. It is not a tale needin' telling, for it's one I've walked awake."

"And what's that meanin'?" Uween started to ask, but Bruenor's expression, deadly serious and certain, clued her to another direction. "How long ye knowin' this?"

"Whole time."

"And what's that to mean?"

"Whole time," Bruenor repeated. "From me old life to me death, to the forest o' Catti-brie's goddess, to the womb o' Uween. I knowed who I was."

"From the moment ye was born again?"

"Before," Bruenor said.

Uween fell back, overwhelmed, confused, and horrified to think that she held some sentient, knowing adult creature in her womb! What was he claiming? What madness was this?

"Ye spent the better part of a year in me belly, ye're sayin'?" she gasped.

"No," Bruenor replied. "I come in as I was comin' out. At the time o' birth . . ."

"Oh, but ye're a fat liar!"

"No."

"No babe's to be knowin' that! No memories go that far back, for any of us!"

Bruenor shrugged. "I can tell ye every bit o' the day yer husband, me Da, did no' come back. When Parson Glaive and King Emerus come to yer door."

Before she could even think of the motion, Uween slugged him in the face. She gasped and brought her hands to her mouth, tears flowing freely. "Ye knew in the crib?" she asked breathlessly. "Ye knew and ye did no' tell me? What . . . what madness?"

"I could no', and ye'd not have believed me," Bruenor said. He gave a little snort. "Are ye even believin' me now, I'm wonderin'? It was me own secret and me own burden, and why I had to go."

"To Mithral Hall?" She tried to sound understanding, now that her anger had manifested itself with the strike. She had let her horror overtake her, but only briefly, she decided. Only briefly.

"Through Mithral Hall," Bruenor answered. "And all the way to the Sword Coast."

"Did ye tell 'em? Them boys from Mithral Hall?"

"Nah," Bruenor said, shaking his head. "Not till I come back now with me friends aside me—and some o' them went through death, too. That was the deal with the goddess, and I was oath-bound. And oh, don't ye doubt that the throne of our gods let me know their anger when I was thinkin' o' breakin' that oath!"

"Ye keep claimin' the gods're on yer side then."

"I know what I know, and I know who I be. And I be Bruenor, and remember all o' that other life I knew. The life afore I died."

Uween nodded, beginning to digest it all, and telling herself that she had no choice but to accept it.

"And ye're still me Ma, I'm hopin', but course the call's yer own to make."

Uween started to nod—how could she not love this one, even if he wasn't . . .

The woman froze, her face locking into an expression of pure shock. "Me own boy," she finally managed to whisper after a long, long pause. "Me own boy . . ."

"Aye, if ye'll have me."

"Not yerself! Me boy what was in there," she said, and rubbed her belly. "What'd ye do to him then? Where's me boy o' Reginald's seed?"

Bruenor sucked in his breath and held up his hands helplessly, clearly at a loss.

Uween believed him—he had no answer as to how that transformation might have occurred, of how he had gotten into the tiny body in the womb and what had been there before him. Had the child been a blank slate awaiting the consciousness of Bruenor Battlehammer? Or some other, maybe, and so expelled—was that the way it worked?

"Get yerself out o' me house, ye murderin' dog!" the woman said, trembling and with tears pouring down her cherubic cheeks. "Oh, ye doppelganger! Abomination! Ye killed me baby!"

As she ranted, she pushed Bruenor toward the door, and he gave ground, shaking his head with every step. But he couldn't deny her charges, and could only hold his hands up helplessly, clueless.

Uween shoved him outside and slammed her door in his face, and he could hear her wailing from behind the stone.

He staggered away, but had only gone a few steps before Ragged Dain caught up to him. "Come on, then, ye fool king!" the dwarf said lightheartedly. "Might be the greatest swarm o' orcs above us the world's e'er seen, but ho, we're still to drink to King Bruenor this day! The gods've blessed us—they sent ye here for a reason!" he said, dragging Bruenor along. "We'll be singin' and dancin' and drinkin' all the night, don't ye doubt!"

Bruenor nodded—he knew the expectation, of course, and would go along. But he kept looking back at the humble home he had known in this childhood, kept thinking of the woman he had left behind the stone door, broken and grieving.

They had an army of orcs camped up above them, flooding the land, sacking the towns, but anyone looking in on the celebration that night in Citadel Felbarr would never know it. For one of the most legendary dwarves of the past two centuries had returned from the grave, and while many in the Silver Marches grumbled about Bruenor's signature on the Treaty of Garumn's Gorge, the dwarves of the North were not among those naysayers.

King Bruenor was kin and kind, friend of Felbarr, friend of Adbar, and so the celebration roared.

Bruenor spent the early part of the gathering beside Drizzt and Catti-brie. He nodded and smiled, clapped tankards, and shared hugs and well-wishes with a line of Felbarran dwarves. He did well to mask his inner turmoil over Uween, and truthfully, over the whole process that had brought him back to life and back to Toril. Had his arrival in Uween's womb thrown aside a babe? Had he taken the infant's body like some mind flayer?

The horror of that notion had him rubbing his hairy face.

"I fear for them, too, my friend, but take heart," Drizzt whispered to him on one such beard-stroking. Bruenor looked at him curiously.

"Hold faith in Wulfgar and Regis," Catti-brie clarified, and she reached over and put her hand on Bruenor's forearm.

The reminder jolted Bruenor from his other concerns. He hadn't been thinking of his lost friends at all that day—too many other problems nipped at his every step. He nodded solemnly at his beautiful daughter and put his hand atop hers. "Aye, the little one's grown. With him aside Wulfgar, sure that it's them orcs we should be worrying for!"

He lifted his mug and clapped it against the flagon Catti-brie put up, and a third came in from Drizzt, and then more as another band of well-wishers bobbed over.

And on it went, with cheers and promises that the orcs of Many-Arrows would rue the day they came forth from their smelly keep, and every drink lifted repeatedly for "Delzoun!" and "Bruenor!"

On one side of the room, a chorus began, a troupe of dwarves with tones both wistful and dulcet, singing tales of war, of victory and great sorrow. As one song, a merrier melody, gathered momentum, some dwarves began to dance, and others called for Drizzt and Catti-brie to join in.

And so they did, and soon the dwarven dancers fell back and circled them, cheering them on.

Drizzt and Catti-brie had never actually danced before, and certainly not publicly. But they had trained for war together many times, sparring in mock battle, and no two creatures in Faerûn were more attuned to the movements of each other. They glided around the floor with ease, lost only in each other, moving with sympathy and grace, and not a stumble could be found.

Bruenor couldn't help but smile as he watched the couple, and surely it did his heart good to see the love that remained between the two. It brought him back to the days before the Spellplague, when at last, Catti-brie and Drizzt had admitted to, and surrendered to, their love for one another. And here it was again.

No, not again, Bruenor thought, but still.

Eternal.

He nodded and felt warm.

Then he went back to clapping tankards and sharing hugs and handshakes.

At one pause in the procession of well-wishers, Bruenor looked past Drizzt and Catti-brie, who were returning to their seats, and noted King Emerus, Ragged Dain, and Parson Glaive sitting around a small table in an animated conversation with Athrogate.

Drizzt followed his gaze, then looked back to Bruenor with concern. Bruenor nodded and held up his hands to ward off a group coming to greet him, thinking to make his way to that table and see what Athrogate might be telling Emerus.

"Ah, but there's a slap in me face," a woman's voice followed him as he took a step in that direction.

"Aye, but ain't he the king now?" another woman asked with biting sarcasm. "Too good for the likes of us."

Bruenor stopped and dropped his head to hide the smile growing within the red-orange flames of his beard, his hands going to his hips.

Oh, but he knew these two!

"Might that we should kick him in the hairy butt," said the first, and all around, other dwarves were laughing.

"Aye, and stick the one horn o' his helm up it," said the other.

Bruenor leaped around as the two dwarves charged at him, and he caught them both, or they caught him, or they all caught each other.

And he got kissed—oh, did he get kissed!—on both his cheeks and flush on the lips.

When he came up for air, Bruenor saw Drizzt and Catti-brie standing beside him, staring at him with amused expressions. He pulled the two young ladies out to either side, keeping them firmly wrapped with his arms around their shoulders.

"Drizzt and me girl, Catti-brie, I give ye Tannabritches and Mallabritches Fellhammer, two o' the toughest fighters what ever whacked an orc!" Bruenor said. He looked to Tannabritches, then to her twin sister, noting their nicknames, "Fist'n'Fury!"

"Well met!" said Tannabritches.

"And better met!" added Mallabritches.

"Glad that ye bringed us back our Little Arr Arr," said the first.

"Ah, Sister, don't ye know he's the king?" Mallabritches scolded.

"Aye," Tannabritches lamented. "King Bruenor, we're telled."

"Aye, and he ain't young. No, he's four hunnerd if he's a day, and woe to his poor old legs."

"Woe and more when we're done dancin'!" Tannabritches insisted, and she and her sister pulled Bruenor out to the floor, to the rousing cheers of all.

Delighted, Drizzt and Catti-brie took their seats and watched the show as the trio bumbled, bounced, and banged their way through it all. There wasn't much graceful about their dance—at times, they more resembled three famished dwarves fighting over the last beer—but truly, Drizzt and Catti-brie had never seen a purer expression of joy from their grumbling friend Bruenor.

And so it went, and for that night at least, the companions could forget the orcs above and their friends lost in the tunnels.

Just for that one night.

PART ONE

THE WINTER OF THE IRON DWARF

L OST AGAIN.

It has become a recurring nightmare among my companions, both these old friends returned and the newer companions I traveled beside in recent times. So many times have I, have we, been thrown to a place of hopelessness. Turned to stone, captured by a powerful necromancer, captured by the drow, even dead for a hundred years!

And yet, here we are, returned. At times it seems to me as if the gods are watching us and intervening.

Or perhaps they are watching us and toying with us.

And now we have come to that point again, with Regis and Wulfgar lost to us in the tunnels of the Upperdark. There was an aura of finality to their disappearance, when the devilishly-trapped wallstone snapped back into place. We heard Regis fall away, far away. It didn't seem like a free fall, and orcs are known to prefer traps that capture victims rather than kill them outright.

That is not a reason to hope, however, given the way orcs typically deal with their captives.

In the first days of our return, I convinced King Connerad to double the guard along the lower tunnels, even to allow me to slip out from the guarded areas still secured as Mithral Hall, out into the regions we know to be under the control of the orcs. Bruenor begged to come with me, but better off am I navigating alone in the Underdark. Cattibrie begged me to remain in the hall, and claimed that she would go out with her magic to scout for our friends.

But I could not sit tight in the comfort of Mithral Hall when I feared they were out there, when I heard, and still hear, their cries for help in my every thought. A recurring nightmare invades my reverie: my dear friends frantic and fighting to get to the lower tunnels still held by the dwarves, but by way of an environment unsuited to a halfling and a human. One dead end after another, one ambush after another. In my thoughts, I see them battling fiercely, then fleeing back the way they had come, orc spears and orc taunts chasing them back into the darkness.

If I believe they are out there, how can I remain behind the iron walls?

I cannot deny that we in the hall have much to do. We have to find a way to break the siege and begin to turn the battles above, else the Silver Marches are lost. The misery being inflicted across the lands . . .

We have much to do.

Nesmé has fallen.

We have much to do.

The other dwarf citadels are fully besieged.

We have much to do.

The lone lifelines, the tunnels connecting Adbar, Felbarr, and Mithral Hall, are under constant pressure now.

We have much to do.

And so much time has passed in dark silence. We traveled to Citadel Felbarr and back, and many tendays have passed without a hint from Wulfgar and Regis.

Are they out there, hiding in dark tunnels or chained in an orc prison? Do they cry out in agony and hopelessness, begging for their friends to come and rescue them? Or begging for death, perhaps?

Or are they now silenced forevermore?

All reason points to them being dead, but I have seen too much now to simply accept that. I hold out hope and know from experience that it cannot be a false hope wrought of emotional folly.

But neither is it more than that: a hope.

They fell, likely to their deaths, either immediately or in orc imprisonment. Even if that is not the case, and their drop through the wall took them to a separate tunnel free from the orcs and drow that haunt the region, so many tendays have passed without word. They are not suited to the Underdark. For all their wonderful skills, in that dark place, in this dark time, it is highly unlikely that Wulfgar and Regis could survive.

And so I hold out that finger of hope, but in my heart, I prepare for the worst.

I am strangely at peace with that. And it is not a phony acceptance where I hide the truth of my pain under the hope that it is mere speculation. If they are gone, if they have fallen, I know that they died well.

It is all we can ask now, any of us. There is an old drow saying—I heard it used often to describe Matron Mother Baenre in the days of my youth: "*qu'ella bondel*," which translates to "gifted time," or "borrowed time." The matron mother was old, older than any other, older than any drow in memory. By all reason, she should have been dead long before, centuries before Bruenor put his axe through her head, and so she had been living on *qu'ella bondel*.

My companions, returned from the magical forest of Iruladoon, through their covenant with Mielikki, are living on *qu'ella bondel*. They all know it, they have all said it.

And so we accept it.

If Wulfgar and Regis do not return to us, if they are truly gone—and Catti-brie has assured me that the goddess will not interfere in such matters again—then so be it. My heart will be heavy, but it will not break. We have been given a great gift, all of us. In saying hello once more, we all knew that we were making it all right to say farewell.

But still . . .

Would I feel this way if Catti-brie were down there?

—Drizzt Do'Urden

CHAPTER 1

DUKE TIAGO

HARTUSK GRUMBLED AT EVERY STEP AS HE KICKED THROUGH THE deepening mounds with heavy, wet snow falling all around him. Behind him, Aurbangras, his dragon mount, reveled in the fluffy stuff, rolling around like a playful kitten. To the mighty wyrm, the snow signaled the onset of winter, the season of the white dragons with their frosty breath.

The storm was general across the Silver Marches, piling deep around Hartusk Keep, formerly known as Sundabar, settling in Keeper's Dale and Cold Vale, burying the surface doors of the underground dwarven citadels, locking the humans in their cities.

But stopping, too, the press of battle against Silverymoon's intact, well-defended walls. And halting any march to Everlund. Hartusk wanted to go anyway, despite the storms; and the frost giants, unbothered by the winter, were ready to march. But the drow had firmly warned him against the move, indeed, had forbidden it.

The ferocious Hartusk had planned to march anyway, but then, unexpectedly, the leader of the giants reinforcing his line, a twenty-foot behemoth named Rolloki, reputedly the eldest brother of Thrym, who was god to the frost giants, had pulled back his support for continuing the campaign through the deepening snows.

Rolloki, with Beorjan and Rugmark, the other huge giants who claimed to be of the god's family, sided with the dark elves on every issue. Given their near-deity status as brothers of Thrym, Fimmel Orelson,

34

Jarl of Shining White and leader of the frost giant legions, would not go against them.

It all came back to the drow and their cautious designs.

Hartusk's grumbles became growls as he neared Nesmé's blasted gate, giants standing to either side of the broken doors, orcs lining the wall and looking down at him and looking past him to the magnificent aerial mount that had brought him here from Hartusk Keep in the east.

The giants snapped to attention as he neared, and that measure of respect from the behemoths did improve the ferocious orc warlord's mood a little bit at least.

Between them went Hartusk, ignoring the cheers that began in the guard towers and along the wall, watching the warriors who gathered in the city courtyard to formally greet him.

An orc leaped out in front of him as he crossed the threshold into the city.

"May I announce your glorious presence, Warlord, to Duke Tiago?" the guard inquired.

Hartusk stopped abruptly and stared at the orc, a formidable sort and one apparently of high rank in the Nesmé garrison if the armor he wore was any indication of station.

"To who?" Hartusk asked.

"To Duke Ti—" the orc started to answer, his words choked off as Hartusk grabbed him by the throat and easily lifted him up to his tiptoes.

"Duke?" Hartusk scoffed, mocking the notion.

The trapped orc moved his mouth as if to respond, but little sound came forth past the crushing grip of mighty Hartusk.

The war chief looked around at the many onlookers. "Duke?" he asked, making it clear that the whole notion of Tiago's self-assumed title was perfectly ridiculous, and with such amazing ease, such power, he tossed the choking orc back and to the ground.

"Do you think I need an introduction?" Hartusk asked his seated victim.

The orc shook his head so fiercely that his lips flapped noisily.

Hartusk growled again and pressed on, the crowd parting in front of him like water before a great ship's prow. Without a word of acknowledgment to the guards at the large building Tiago and the other drow had taken as their castle, Hartusk pushed through the door.

Those gathered in the foyer and small room beyond, orc and drow alike, gasped in unison when they noted the identity of the brusque newcomer, and they prudently fell aside, many of the orcs falling to their knees as their glorious leader swept through.

The two drow guarding the next set of ornate doors wisely also moved aside. One reached back to grab the door handle, to swing the door open for the great orc, but she pulled her hand back quickly as Hartusk simply bashed through, both doors flying wide.

Those in the room, the appointed audience chamber of Duke Tiago Do'Urden of Nesmé, started and turned, except for the five drow at the other end of the long, narrow room. There sat Tiago, casually draping a leg over the arm of his wooden chair, the priestess Saribel, his wife, sitting beside him. That half-drow, half-moon elf creature attended to the priestess, along with her limping and broken-down father.

Ravel was there, too, Hartusk noted—and he trusted that drow wizard least of all.

Hartusk stood in the doorway for a long while, letting the others in the room, more drow than orcs, absorb the sight of his magnificence. And he let his stare linger, long and hard, on the five at the other end: the drow nobles who served as the mouthpieces of Menzoberranzan's efforts in the Silver Marches.

The orc warlord wasn't surprised to see them all here together. He had specifically ordered Tiago that they should not all be together in this time of winter's lull, when desperate and dangerous enemies would seek ways to strike out from their besieged cities and citadels. It seemed natural that the impudent drow would ignore his commands.

He made his way slowly across the room, taking satisfaction as dark elf and orc alike eased back from his imposing march.

"Warlord, it is good to see you," Tiago said. His words rang superficially in Hartusk's sharp mind. "Do gather a flagon—a keg, I say!—and let us drink through winter's long night."

"And find whatever other pleasures as we might," Saribel added—Duchess Saribel, Hartusk presumed, though he had not heard her referred to in that manner.

"Where is your dragon, drow?" he asked.

"Where he should be," Tiago cryptically replied. "Where I asked him to be, and of no concern to you, surely."

The brutish orc narrowed his yellow, bloodshot eyes.

"Warlord, be at ease," Tiago said to him.

"Do you mock me?" the orc asked, and at that, all in the room and in the anteroom tensed, every drow and every orc taking stock of the other race, in case it should quickly come to blows.

"My, but he seems quite upset," Ravel Xorlarrin remarked, moving over to stand directly behind Tiago's chair, and never taking his eyes off the warlord.

"He is bored, nothing more," Tiago said. "He wants blood!" He braced his hands on the arms of his makeshift throne and jumped up to his feet. "Yes, Hartusk?"

He came forward. He moved close—close enough to bite.

"Does the winter settle uneasily about your strong arms, Warlord?" Tiago asked. He grinned slyly, as did the others around the royal dais—except the surface elf, Hartusk noted, that ever-scowling little creature who never seemed to take her hand from the hilt of her fine sword. She wore an expression that bore no humor, as if she was always expecting a battle to break out.

Hartusk supposed that such a demeanor was the only way she could possibly survive in the midst of this viper's nest of treachery. Hartusk needed the drow, of course. They had been central to his coup against the children of Obould, and surely pivotal in the death of King Obould.

Obould wouldn't lead the minions of Many-Arrows to war. The drow, like Hartusk, wanted war, and so their marriage of blood had been consummated.

Their marriage of Obould's blood.

That didn't mean the warlord of Many-Arrows didn't profoundly hate the dark-skinned devils—every one.

He looked hard at the young half-elf, half-drow then, challenging her with his stare as one dog might do to another. He didn't blink and neither did she, but yes, she clutched that sword ever more tightly.

Hartusk began to smile, lewdly. And it went on, and all around took notice.

"Ah, a budding romance," the wizard Ravel remarked.

"He is *iblith*!" Saribel cried, using the drow word for offal—a word Hartusk knew.

"She is *darthiir*!" Ravel countered, the drow word for surface elves and an insult far worse than *iblith*.

The dark elves all laughed at Doum'wielle's expense, even her father, though Hartusk noted that the one named Tos'un did cast a clearly uncomfortable sidelong glance her way.

"Arauthator should fly beside his son, dropping boulders on Silverymoon," Hartusk said finally, breaking the gaze. "The minions of Alustriel are miserable in their hole, and we should make them more miserable!"

"A useless exercise that alleviates the boredom for Silverymoon's vast array of wizards," Tiago immediately countered.

"Press them!"

"Bore them!" Tiago shot back, and Hartusk narrowed his eyes again and gave a growl. "Silverymoon is not like Nesmé, nor even Sundabar, Warlord. She is a city thick with magic-users. We threw stones at her—have you forgotten?"

The orc didn't blink.

"Her wizards caught them with their spells and guided them down harmlessly," Tiago reminded. "You were there, upon Aurbangras, beside me and my dragon mount. You know the truth of it."

"We will drop the stones in the night, in the dark," Hartusk argued. "The wizards will not see—"

"We cannot even ride the wyrms at night," Tiago interrupted with a laugh—and how Hartusk's eyes flared at that. "It is too cold for drow skin, and orc skin, up high in the winter night sky."

"Then send the dragons alone!" Hartusk roared.

Tiago sat back in his chair and tapped his fingers together in front of his face, staring past the waggling digits at the obstinate orc. "Leave us," he said quietly to Saribel and the others. "Clear the room."

"It is not your place to dismiss my guards . . . Duke of Nesmé," Hartusk warned, verily spitting Tiago's assumed title.

"Keep them in place as you will, then," Tiago replied with a dismissive laugh.

The drow and Doum'wielle filtered away from the royal dais, collecting all of the other drow, a pair of giants, and several orcs and goblins in their wake as they exited the room. Hartusk continued to stare at Tiago for a while, but then nodded to the remaining orcs, his personal entourage, bidding them to leave. As the last exited, Tos'un, at the entrance, closed the door.

"We would do well to ease our demands upon the dragons," Tiago said when they were alone—seemingly alone. They both knew that Tiago's wizard companion had probably already enacted spells to spy on their private discussion.

"We would do well to sack Silverymoon and take our fight to Everlund."

Tiago gave another of his annoying chuckles. "Indeed, and none would desire that more than I. But I warn you, the dragons are not to be exploited. Arauthator is older than any other in this campaign, and the Old White Death earns his name honestly."

"He was brought in to serve," the orc insisted.

"And there you err," said Tiago. "Arauthator does not serve—not the orcs of Many-Arrows, not the giants of Shining White, and not the drow of Menzoberranzan. He is a dragon, ancient and huge and ultimately deadly."

"Your wizard brought him to us," Hartusk insisted.

"My wizard?" Tiago asked dramatically, and Hartusk nearly choked on that thought.

"The old one of your city."

"Gromph, yes, who is older than Arauthator, and perhaps the only power of Menzoberranzan who could defeat the dragon in combat. But Gromph is not here, Warlord. He is home in the City of Spiders, and home he will stay."

"Recall him," Hartusk insisted.

"Better that he stay," said Tiago. "Were we to ask Gromph to command the dragon, to threaten the dragon, he would take the far easier course and destroy us both, I assure you."

Hartusk growled yet again.

"Let the dragons have their winter play," Tiago advised. "Good Warlord, patience!"

"Damn your waiting!"

"Patience," Tiago insisted. "Our enemies are going nowhere—unless they try to break free of the prisons their cities and citadels have become. We have the granaries of Sundabar, a supply line stretching back to the drow city of Q'Xorlarrin, and freedom to roam the land and hunt as we please. The winter is but an inconvenience to us, but to our enemies . . . ah, Warlord, to our enemies, it is a time of thin rations and misery, and that is the beauty, is it not?"

"Silverymoon is full of priests and wizards," Hartusk reminded him.

"Yes, Silverymoon will survive the winter well. Everlund, too, no doubt. But the dwarves, Warlord, buried in their holes . . ."

"They spend all of every winter in their holes. What foolishness is this?"

"Yes, but they trade throughout the winter with Silverymoon and

Sundabar," Tiago explained. "Alas, but they'll find no easy routes for that now! The tunnels below run thick with my people, to say nothing of goblins and orcs. The dwarves have grown fat on trade, and now they have no trade. The dwarves know how to forage the Underdark for food, but now their range is limited. They will not enjoy this winter, I assure you. As the year turns to 1485, and the winter deepens through Hammer and Alturiak, the ringing of their hammers will be replaced by the growling of their bellies, do not doubt."

"Your people have planned well."

"We always do."

"They are a tougher lot than you believe."

"I do not doubt their resourcefulness or their resolve," Tiago said with a wry grin. "But not even a dwarf can eat stone, my orc friend. Let them wither and die in their holes—perhaps they will begin to eat their dead as the old and the young succumb."

"A pleasing thought," Hartusk admitted.

"Or perhaps they will try to break free of their prisons. Any of them. Understand, my friend, that if but one of those three fortresses falls, the other two will be in a sore predicament. Adbar makes the weapons, Felbarr is the link between the three, and Mithral Hall . . ." He paused there, and now it was his turn to growl a little bit, though it sounded more like the purr of a cat about to leap upon a field mouse.

"What of Mithral Hall?"

"That is the prize," Tiago said, but he didn't elaborate.

Tiago cared nothing for Hartusk's war—Matron Mother Quenthel had already recalled some of the principles of her little excursion up here on the surface. Gromph was back home, and Tsabrak, too, had returned to the side of Matron Mother Zeerith Xorlarrin in her fledgling city to the west. Tiago didn't expect that he and the other "Do'Urdens" would remain much longer.

But long enough, he was determined, to see the end of the heretic named Drizzt, the rogue who had fled into Mithral Hall with his pathetic friends of this wretched World Above. Tiago would flush him out, or use everything at his disposal—the fodder goblinkin and giantkind, the dragons, and the drow—to knock down the doors of Mithral Hall.

"Patience," he said again to the orc warlord, but in fact, it was his own patience that was wearing thin.

"I do so wish that Tiago would lop the ugly fool's head off and be done with it," Ravel Xorlarrin said to Saribel, Tos'un, and Doum'wielle when they were out of Tiago's audience chamber and alone in a side room.

"Tiago will do as Menzoberranzan decides," Saribel answered her brother sternly. "And I do not believe that would include decapitating the army Matron Mother Quenthel has put at our disposal."

Both Tos'un and Ravel looked at the high priestess curiously at that remark.

"My dear sister, you do seem to be embracing this Baenre stature you have found," the wizard sarcastically remarked.

" 'This Baenre stature'?" she dryly replied.

"You were always the obedient one," said Ravel. "And not even to Matron Mother Zeerith alone. When Berellip spoke, Saribel listened!"

The drow priestess narrowed her gaze, but Ravel nearly laughed aloud at that.

"Quiet and demure Saribel," he teased. When her hand went to the snake-headed whip she carried on her belt, he added, "Slow with the whip, but true to her calling."

"Berellip is dead," she replied. "Perhaps she would not be were it not for Tiago's obsession with the rogue named Drizzt."

"You openly blame your husband?"

Now it was Saribel's turn to laugh. "Perhaps I credit him. It does not matter. House Xorlarrin has determined a different course now."

"Different from yours, you mean," said Ravel.

"And yours. Or have you already forgotten? You thought you would be the archmage of this new great city of the Xorlarrins. You were the one who led us to the ruins of Gauntlgrym, of course. But the designs did not play that way, did they? Nay, it was Tsabrak who was deemed more worthy than you, Tsabrak who was blessed with the power of Lolth to enact the Darkening. Tsabrak, not Ravel. Matron Mother Zeerith fought for Tsabrak in her dealings with Matron Mother Quenthel, and the matron mother conceded him the position of Archmage of Q'Xorlarrin. Him. Tsabrak, not you."

Ravel conceded that point with a bow.

"Does it disappoint you, dear brother?"

"I prefer Menzoberranzan," Ravel admitted, and he smiled cleverly as he added, "I prefer the halls of House Do'Urden."

That elicited a surprised stare from Saribel.

"Are you not pleased with your new station, Sister?" Ravel asked.

"I am a priestess in House Baenre, the High Priestess of House Do'Urden, and have a promising young noble, a weapons master, grandson of the great Dantrag Baenre, as my husband. Just a few short months ago, I was the younger sister of Berellip Xorlarrin, and little more."

"Even with the advent of Q'Xorlarrin?" Ravel pressed.

"Oh, indeed did I hope that I would find a place—perhaps I would rule Matron Mother Zeerith's academy, if she bothers to build one."

"If Matron Mother Quenthel allows her to build one, you mean," Tos'un unexpectedly intervened, and both Xorlarrins turned to him with a look bordering on shock. There it was, spoken openly, the truth about the supposedly independent city of Q'Xorlarrin, forever destined to be a satellite of Menzoberranzan, existing forever under the suffrage of whomever sat at the head of the spider-shaped table of Menzoberranzan's Ruling Council—which meant, almost certainly, forever under the gaze of a Baenre.

"And now you are a Baenre," Ravel remarked.

"No, I am a Do'Urden," Saribel corrected. "The High Priestess of the Eighth House of Menzoberranzan. And my husband is the weapons master, and you, dear brother, are the House Wizard."

"But our loyalty is truly to House Baenre, then, is it not?" Ravel asked. "House Do'Urden surely survives because of the demands and protection of the matron mother."

Saribel nodded, and both of them glanced at Tos'un as they agreed on Ravel's point.

Tos'un was not Xorlarrin, nor Baenre. Tos'un was of House Barrison Del'Armgo, the Second House of Menzoberranzan, the principle rival of House Baenre.

Doum'wielle caught those looks and turned her own concerned gaze upon her father.

But Tos'un seemed truly unbothered. "I am Do'Urden," he said.

"A set of eyes for Matron Mother Mez'Barris, no doubt?"

Tos'un laughed at the absurdity of the remark. "You are not very old, wizard. Nor you, priestess. You do not remember the first assault upon the dwarven citadel of Mithral Hall, when Matron Mother Yvonnel Baenre was destroyed by the dwarf king Bruenor. When Uthegental, the greatest weapons master of Menzoberranzan . . ." He paused and grinned, and even bowed a bit at the obvious slip up. "Unless that title was given to Dantrag Baenre, of course," he offered, speaking of Tiago's grandfather, who was Uthegental's most hated rival.

"I remember it all so well," Tos'un continued. "The utter folly. The slaughter. We came and we were beaten back, but no, we did not leave—or did not have to leave! That was the decision of those left in dead Matron Mother Yvonnel's bloody wake. We did not avenge her, or Uthegental. No, we fled.

"Drizzt Do'Urden was there, you know," he went on, and the Xorlarrins leaned in eagerly. "In Mithral Hall in the time of that battle, fighting beside King Bruenor, against his own people. So the drow fled, and Mez'Barris was no small part of that decision—indeed, she never approved of the march in the first place."

"*Matron Mother* Mez'Barris," Saribel corrected, but there was more curiosity than outrage in her voice.

"But I did not leave," Tos'un said, the boast clear in his voice. "Nay, I would not leave. And so, with my conspirators, I waited, and cultivated our opportunity. When we found that opportunity, in the form of the original king Obould, we did then exactly as this wiser Matron Mother Baenre does now. And look what we created, friends!" He waved his arms around. "The Kingdom of Many-Arrows, where the orcs bred thick, with numbers uncounted."

"You acted in preparation for this war?" Ravel asked, clearly unconvinced. "You foresaw this day? Is that your claim?"

"I cultivated the battlefield," Tos'un replied. "Do you doubt me? With a hundred thousand orc warriors at your disposal, do you doubt me?"

"You think yourself a hero of Menzoberranzan," Saribel said, and it sounded more like an accusation than anything else.

But Tos'un clearly wasn't rattled in the least, and a smile widened across his face. "I think myself a Do'Urden," he said slyly. "The patron of House Do'Urden, if I correctly recall the matron mother's demands. And I think that a good thing. It is a fledgling House, yet already seated at the Ruling Council."

"As an echo for Baenre," Saribel dared to say.

"For now, with Matron Mother Darthiir," said Tos'un. "But consider the talent assembled in that fledgling House. Consider the alliances, particularly with Baenre. Consider the glory we bring with every victory scored here in this land—a land I know better than any drow alive. Consider our ties to Q'Xorlarrin, with two of Zeerith's children serving in positions of high regard.

"And with that one," he added, and turned and pointed back to the hall where they had left Tiago. "Full of ambition, full of fire, and full of talent. A Baenre noble, a favored great-nephew of the matron mother. It is good to be a Do'Urden."

He stopped, and there ensued a long silence as the others digested his startling words.

"Perhaps it will be, one day soon," Ravel said, finally. "For now, being a Do'Urden means being trapped in this place of roofless nightmares and wind and snow. And now, worse, it means all of that without the warmth of an enemy's blood to defeat the cold, and without the dying cries of an enemy's last hopeless moments to steal the boredom."

Saribel offered a nod at that, as did Tos'un, after a moment.

"How many years did you remain here?" Ravel asked Tos'un, shaking his head to show that the question was simply a statement of disbelief.

Tos'un did not answer, and Ravel glanced around, suddenly seeming not unlike a caged animal. He turned around, nearly a complete circuit, before settling his gaze upon Doum'wielle.

"I am bored," he said, particularly to her. "Come." He extended his hand to her, and she cast a confused glance at her father.

"Pleasure me," Ravel said bluntly.

Doum'wielle felt her cheeks flush at the crude remark. Her thoughts careened from disgust to, surprisingly, a sudden notion of a path of amazing possibilities rolling out in front of her. Ravel was the House wizard of Do'Urden, a noble son of House Xorlarrin, friend to Tiago, brother and confidant to Saribel.

Perform well! Doum'wielle thought, or heard in her head, and the possibilities of acceptance and ascension in the drow ranks flittered around her subconscious, just out of reach but tempting nonetheless.

She looked directly at Ravel and noted a sly undercurrent behind his lewd smile. That turned her to her father, who seemed quite shaken.

Still, Tos'un looked at her and nodded, even slightly motioning with his chin that she should take the offered hand and go with Ravel.

Fingers visibly trembling, Doum'wielle reached for the drow hand, and Ravel pulled her away.

"My son tells me that the war chief is not pleased," the great Arauthator said to Tiago when the drow found him in a cave not far from Nesmé.

"Hartusk is angry at . . . everything," Tiago replied dismissively. "It is that very nature of the ugly beast that made him valuable to us in the first place. I would be more worried if he was contented, particularly now with the fighting in pause."

"A pause he does not want."

"What Hartusk wants matters not. He will do as we tell him or he will be replaced." The drow gave a little laugh. "Even if he does as we instruct, he is a temporary thing. We will outlast him."

"I will," the dragon replied. "I will outlast you all. When you are dust, I will call this land my domain."

"I was speaking of the years coming, not the centuries," Tiago dryly replied.

"Years?" the dragon said doubtfully. "Your people think in tendays, not years. You will outlast Hartusk if you murder him, perhaps, but else he will call Many-Arrows his kingdom when the drow have returned to their lightless tunnels."

"Not so."

"They are already going!" the dragon said, and his insistence was forceful enough to blow Tiago's hair back and chill the dark elf to the bone. "Do you deny it? Many of your people have left!"

Tiago paused and carefully considered his next words, as he could see that Arauthator was growing more and more agitated. He couldn't

45

deny the dragon's observations, particularly in that the highest-ranking drow—Matron Mother Quenthel, Gromph, and Tsabrak, in particular—had not been seen around the region in a long while, and were not expected back, ever. It occurred to him that an angry Arauthator could eat him then and there to send a statement to the matron mother and the archmage. They had enlisted the great wyrms to their cause, after all, and if Arauthator ever began to feel that he was being exploited, the result would surely be . . . unfortunate.

"My people are not accustomed to this biting cold, great dragon," he said calmly. "Or this snow!"

"My breath is colder still," the dragon warned.

"So I have witnessed from my perch upon your back," Tiago said lightheartedly.

"You admit that the winter has driven the drow from this land and from this campaign?"

"Nay!" Tiago insisted. He turned and pointed back toward Nesmé, the smoke from the hearth fires in the town visible above the rolling hills. "You have four drow nobles just beyond the rise, wintering in Nesmé, where I am duke."

"Four," the dragon muttered, unimpressed.

"Ravel of Q'Xorlarrin, sister city of Menzoberranzan," Tiago replied. "Noble son of Matron Mother Zeerith, who rules Q'Xorlarrin. And Tos'un of House Barrison Del'Armgo, Second House of Menzoberranzan. And Priestess Saribel, who is Baenre and Xorlarrin."

"And Tiago, who is Baenre no more," the perceptive dragon remarked. "You are all of this other, lesser House, are you not? Your boasts are of Do'Urden, not Baenre, not Barrison Del'Armgo, and not Xorlarrin!"

Tiago looked carefully at the wyrm. Clearly Arauthator had been doing some investigating and more than a little spying.

"Lesser?" he asked, with a dismissive shake of his head.

"Where does Do'Urden rank among the Houses of Menzoberranzan?" the dragon asked. "Where are the drow leaders?"

"I am the drow leader in this campaign, and doubt not the importance of this fledgling House—a House purposely named to dishonor the rogue who has come again to this land."

"Him again?" Arauthator did not seem impressed.

"You should take heed of Drizzt Do'Urden, my great friend," Tiago warned. "He is one of those pesky heroes whose names are sung by the bards in taverns across Faerûn. Surely you who are of dragonkind knows of this sort. The heroes who topple tyrant kings."

Arauthator began to growl, knowing where this was going, obviously, but that didn't stop Tiago.

"The heroes who slay dragons," he finished, ignoring Arauthator's growl.

The two stared at each other for a long while.

"There are more of my people about than you see," Tiago said. "In the tunnels all about the Upperdark of the Silver Marches, pressing the dwarves in their holes. It is good that Nesmé has fallen, and better that Sundabar is no more, and better still will it be when Silverymoon is crushed beneath us!"

"I will eat every captive from that wretched city," the dragon promised, for Arauthator had taken more than a few stinging magical assaults when flying around that powerful magical fortress.

"These prizes offer much," said Tiago. "Slaves and treasure, yes, but the better slaves and the greater treasures will not be so easily pried."

"The dwarves," the dragon reasoned.

"Of course the dwarves," Tiago agreed. "The humans and elves of the Silver Marches are no threat to the drow—if ever they deigned to march upon Menzoberranzan, most would perish long before they neared the city! But the dwarves . . . My people will not suffer them to thrive as they are now in the Silver Marches. When dwarves thrive, they dig deeper, and when they dig deeper, they accost my people.

"The drow are in the tunnels all about Mithral Hall and Felbarr and Adbar," he assured the wyrm. "Every day, perhaps even at this very moment, my people battle the bearded folk, and press them tighter into their holes, and stop them from gathering food beyond their dark halls. They will come out, there will be no choice for them, and then we will all know a greater victory, and Arauthator will know piles of treasure for his hoard."

The dragon growled, but it was not threatening—it sounded more like a purr. The great wyrm nodded slowly in approval. But, as was often the case with such creatures, that mood did not last.

"You will not stay," the dragon said accusingly "The great mage and the matron mother have gone, and so will the rest. If these dwarves were as important as you claim, Gromph would remain. His power mocks all that Tiago holds at his fingers."

The drow shook his head.

"You will not stay!" the dragon insisted.

"Perhaps not," Tiago admitted, "but we will leave our mark forever upon this land."

"Your scar, you mean."

"As you wish," Tiago agreed. "And it is a scar to benefit us both. Gromph has made clear our bargain, and it is one we are all more than happy to uphold. Consider this, Old White Death, as you mull the winter quiet. My people seek longer gain while the orcs are but impulsive dullards. Hartusk and all the others, perhaps, would see to your due, but some would hide those treasures away, hoping to fool you. You have known orcs through the centuries, and so you know this to be true."

"But the drow would be more clever in their cheating."

"And the drow would be wiser than to even try," Tiago replied. "We care little for the treasures you seek. Our goal here is not wealth, but power! Power for Lady Lolth, as you seek . . ."

He paused there and smiled knowingly, reminding the dragon of the source of the original deal it had made with Gromph and Matron Mother Quenthel. Arauthator and his son had joined in the war for treasure, and not simply to hoard it, as dragons will. No, the chromatic wyrms had a need for their piles of gold and gems as they prepared the way for their maelstrom goddess.

"I am doing you a favor, am I not?" the dragon said.

Tiago nodded and smiled. "Has there been any movement about Mithral Hall?"

"Just the orcs," answered the dragon, who had been spending a lot of time circling the area of Mithral Hall, scouting for Tiago. "And a legion of giants camped with war machines on the ridge above the western door and the valley called Keeper's Dale. The great bridge over the river is thick with orcs all about it. If the dwarves broke out to the east, that bridge would be dropped into the Surbrin."

"You remained up high? Far above the giants and orcs?"

"As you asked."

"Lower, then, next time, if you would," Tiago asked.

The dragon stared at him intently.

"Find their chimneys and spy holes," Tiago explained. "Find regions on the high mountain where we can put our own spies."

"The dwarves are not fools, drow," the dragon replied. "They hide their chimneys in ravines and chasms, deep in dark caves. I will fly lower, as you ask. And you will ride with me."

It wasn't a suggestion, Tiago knew, but an order. If he didn't agree, Arauthator would not subject himself to possible ballista fire or magical spells around the mountain that housed Mithral Hall. Not unless Tiago was willing to take the same risk.

Tiago nodded, and thought that perhaps it would be wise to take Ravel along, as well. The wizard could ward him from the cold winds that would buffet him on his dragon perch, and perhaps Ravel's spells would prove useful in determining more secrets about Mithral Hall's clever inhabitants.

The harder part would be convincing Hartusk to withdraw the giants and many of the orcs. Despite his claims to Arauthator, the drow in the Upperdark were not doing much to hamper and sting Mithral Hall. Of the three dwarf citadels, that one was the most self-sufficient, so they had come to recognize.

The dwarves might be able to stay in their hold indefinitely, and that, Tiago could not tolerate.

Not when his own time here might be growing short.

Not when Drizzt Do'Urden was in that hole with them.

Doum'wielle lay in the darkness on the bed in her room, staring up at the ceiling. Tears settled in her eyes, but not from the pain she felt in her jaw. Many drow males were like that. So frustrated by their subservience to the women of their race they routinely abused others, like Doum'wielle, whom they could so casually refer to as offal.

Offal. *Iblith*, they said.

She, too, was of House Do'Urden, so it had been decreed, but she would forever be *iblith*, or, worse, *darthiir*.

She thought of her mother, then, in the Glimmerwood. Sinnafein was a queen of the elves, and Doum'wielle had been a princess.

Now she was offal.

She thought of her brother, and her tears flowed more freely. She pictured the look her father had given her when Ravel had reached out to her.

She could see him so clearly again in her mind's eye, and so now she tried to decipher that curious expression.

Ravel's call to abuse his Little Doe had likely—hopefully!— hurt Tos'un, but as she recalled that visage now, Doum'wielle couldn't help but note a twinge of eagerness there. She had initially thought it a desire to go and punish Ravel for insulting Little Doe, but now, in retrospect, a different, and most unsettling, notion came to her.

Had her father been eager to give her over to Ravel or to another of the important dark elves of House Do'Urden, as a way to better secure his own standing in the House? He was Barrison Del'Armgo, after all, of the family known to be bitter rivals to both the Baenres and the Xorlarrins. In House Do'Urden, with Tiago and Saribel and Ravel, he was vulnerable.

It all began to sort out to her then. Ravel hadn't taken her to alleviate his boredom or for any carnal needs—not primarily, at least. He had used her as a test of Tos'un's loyalty.

Tos'un had warned her of the trials they would face—nothing as specific as this, of course, but he had explained in great detail to his daughter that the ways of the drow were not much akin to the ways of the wood elves. In the Glimmerwood, sensuality and sexuality were great gifts, often shared, but never taken and never coerced.

For a few moments, Doum'wielle began to truly sink then the weight of all she had done began to descend upon her like Arauthator's leathery wings. She brought her hands up into view, expecting to see Tierflin's blood staining them. She wanted her mother, above all, and almost cried out for Sinnafein.

Almost. The moments were fleeting, and a voice promising greater comfort called out to her.

Doum'wielle rolled out of her bed and padded across the room on bare feet to the chair set by the window, to the sword belt hanging on the chair.

To the comfort of her sentient sword.

"You grow impatient," Arauthator said to Tiago just a few days later. The pair had found another cave, a deep crevice actually, set far back in the mountain known as Fourthpeak. It seemed unremarkable enough, just a crack in the stones, but Arauthator's keen sense of smell had detected a whiff of smoke emanating from within. And so the dragon had pried the stones apart, and Tiago had gone in and located the hidden chimney.

The drow didn't deny the dragon's observation. "No activity?" he asked again.

"The mountain is quiet," the dragon confirmed.

"Seal the chimney," Tiago bade his godlike mount, and the drow quickly backed away.

Arauthator looked around at the stone, gauging the integrity—or in this case, the lack thereof. "On my back, young Baenre," he said, and he lowered and turned so that Tiago could climb onto the saddle.

Once Tiago was seated, Arauthator breathed into the crevice with all his strength and all his deadly cold mist, sealing the chimney top under a layer of ice. That wouldn't hold for long, the wyrm knew, given the warmth climbing up from the fires below, and so the beast attacked the mountain itself, claws rending stone, wings pushing dislodged boulders into position. The wyrm jumped atop the pile of rubble that used to be a crevice between two slabs of stone, tightening the seal.

Let the dwarves choke on their own smoke!

"Well played, my friend," Tiago said in congratulations when the wyrm was done.

"They have a hundred more vents all around the mountain, you know," the dragon replied. "Our efforts will make parts of their complex uncomfortable, perhaps, but you'll not smoke them out."

Tiago nodded. He knew. From his high perch, the drow looked down around the mountain ways, to the black camps of orcs and goblins and the line of giants with their war machines atop Keeper's Dale.

"Let us fly to Sundabar," he bade the wyrm.

"Hartusk Keep, you mean," the dragon replied with a sly look. Both of them knew the name had been offered merely to placate the stupid orc leader.

Despite his very real fears that the dwarves would outlast him, Tiago laughed.

The dragon banked away, catching the updrafts on widespread wings, soaring out to the east. It was time to convince the warlord.

CHAPTER 2

THE DEEP SKIRMISHES

THE GRIMY LITTLE FINGERS CREPT SLOWLY ACROSS THE TABLE TOWARD the plate of eel meat—the fourth such excursion for the light-fingered goblin hand.

He had drawn a curious look from one of the others, he had noted on the third theft, and so perhaps this one was ill-advised.

Or maybe he was just sick of it all.

He retracted just in time, as a cleaver crashed down upon the table, a cut that would have severed his hand at the wrist. He fell back a step to regard the orc butcher, hulking and ugly, its chest heaving in its angry gasps.

"One!" it growled at the little goblin. "You gets one! Maybe I put your arm on that plate, eh?" Others moved closer, no doubt thinking they might soon be involved in a goblin dismemberment, which ranked as one of the best pastimes of all for the orcs serving in these inhospitable Underdark passageways.

"I ate one," the goblin replied.

"And tried to steal another!"

"I have to feed my pet!" the goblin explained.

That gave the orc pause, and it stared at the goblin curiously.

"And he eats a lot," the goblin said, nodding in an exaggerated manner, big lips flapping. "So I took a second, third, and fourth, too! And would have stolen a fifth if your cleaver hadn't fallen."

The boast had the orc staring down at him dumbfounded, jaw hanging slack, and the other orcs and goblins around could hardly believe what they were hearing. This little goblin had just asked to be executed, so it seemed.

And as the cleaver came up, a growl issuing from the orc boss, they all thought they were about so see exactly that.

"My pet has to be fed," the goblin pleaded. "We mustn't anger him."

"What pet?" the orc demanded.

"There," the goblin squeaked, pointing to a dark alcove behind the orc. "There!"

The orc stared at him skeptically, glancing back once or twice toward the indicated spot. It began to back away from the goblin, never taking its eyes off the thief until it stood right in front of the depressed alcove. Then it glanced in, just in time to see the mithral head of a fabulous warhammer come diving down out of the darkness.

The orc registered that for just an instant, just long enough for its yellow eyes to widen in horror.

Then the orc detected the slightest moment of pain, and nothing more, as the hammer drove into its skull with such force that the beast's head simply exploded, sending a shower of blood and brains and flecks of bone all around the nearest onlookers.

An orc on the other side of the goblin yelped, and yelped again when the goblin produced, as if from nowhere, a magnificent rapier, and with a sudden step and thrust, drove the fine tip through the yelping orc's throat. As it fell away, out came the goblin's other hand, now holding a hand crossbow.

A second orc fell away, a quarrel in its eye.

And where the hand crossbow had been was now a beautiful three-bladed dagger, its side catch-blades shaped like delicate and deadly serpents, and the goblin wasn't a goblin any longer, but a halfling, dirty and disheveled, perhaps, but still looking rather dapper in a blue-flecked beret, white shirt, and black leather vest.

The warhammer spun past the halfling, taking out an orc and a goblin in its devastating flight. And on came the goblin-turned-halfling's pet, a huge human with golden hair, a full beard, and crystalline fire in his blue eyes.

Eyes that shined in the torchlight. Eyes that shined with eagerness as he waded into battle, even unarmed. He hoisted a goblin and used it as a club before throwing it at the feet of a trio of orcs rushing in at him.

They stumbled around, tangling up, and by the time they straightened, that hammer had somehow reappeared in the large man's hand.

A single sidelong swipe of the magnificent weapon threw the three of them aside.

Near him, circling fast, spinning and dancing, the halfling engaged and parried, turned aside a club, turned low a sword, snapping it in half with his dirk, and took a dagger from the hand of a third goblin, that fine rapier driving right through the creature's hand.

The pair worked with practiced precision, the halfling darting all around in defense, scoring hits often, but always minor ones. He hadn't the time to finish off any enemies, moving to the next instead, protecting the huge human's back and flanks.

That one, monstrously strong and deceptively quick, went for the kill, always the kill, sweeping orcs and goblins aside with abandon. A hit from his hammer shattered bones into dust and tore the victims apart under the ferocious weight of sheer power. At one point, he let the hammer fly, smashing it into an ogre who had just entered the room, and indeed, knocking it back through the doorway and into the corridor beyond.

An orc seized the opportunity and leaped in, smashing at him with its club. He blocked with his forearm, accepting the stinging hit, and before the orc could pull back for a second attack, the man rolled his arm over the club and continued up and under, catching it in his hand and yanking hard, throwing the orc sidelong.

The man's free hand clamped over the orc's face, and he pressed immediately, driving the ugly thing over and back.

"Regis!" he cried as other orcs leaped in at him, and as the ogre came back through the door. He pressed the orc backward and down with all his amazing strength—too much strength for the powerful orc to resist, and over and down it sank, its spine crunching and crackling under the relentless strain. It didn't even think about holding its weapon, both its hands going to claw at that pressing arm.

The man flung the club at the incoming orcs, and his hammer was back then, landing neatly in his free hand.

And the halfling went by him in a blur, leaping into the approaching orcs. His hand flicked once, then twice, and a moment later, two of the four brutes went flying backward and to the floor, tugged down by a leering specter that appeared behind them, holding the living snakes that had become as garrotes around their throats.

Now with a single-bladed dirk and that magnificent rapier, the halfling engaged the two remaining orcs. He went at them sidelong, rapier arm extended in front of him, dagger arm trailing behind. Subtle shifts of his forward blade turned an orc sword, then a thrusting spear.

His weight went to his trailing foot, and the halfling leaned away.

On came an orc, eagerly, thinking him in retreat.

But the halfling fencer stepped forward instead, his weight going forward, his body leaning forward, his arm suddenly extending.

So suddenly.

Too suddenly.

Then back he went, then forward again. And a third time with sudden, definitive steps.

And he was alone against a single orc so quickly, in the blink of an eye it seemed, as the orc's companion slumped to the ground, trembling hands grasping at the three holes the halfling had put into its chest, all of them in the area of the creature's heart, two of them having pierced the organ.

Behind him came the definitive crack of bone, and the barbarian dropped the shattered orc to the floor and leaped past the halfling to the side. He landed and stopped abruptly, swinging around with uncanny awareness, his hammer leading.

That mighty weapon, that mighty swing, tore the head from the pursuing goblin.

And when that head went flying free, the other orcs and goblins back there changed their direction.

"Go! Go!" the halfling cried to the big man, and the barbarian spun back and let fly his hammer into the chest of the approaching ogre, knocking it backward yet again.

The halfling's rapier rolled in a mesmerizing dance around the extended spear, the orc futilely trying to bat at the fine blade, but never quite catching up. For several rotations, the beast seemed fixated on that twirling weapon, but then, suddenly, it roared and charged ahead with a vicious thrust instead.

Exactly as the halfling had anticipated. A slight parry from the rapier and a sudden pirouette out and away from the thrusting spear rolled him right along the spear shaft toward the orc.

The orc opened wide its mouth and bit at the halfling's face.

The orc ate the blade of a dagger instead.

It leaped away, screaming horribly, thrashing and flailing down to the floor, insane with pain. The halfling rushed by and started to lower his rapier at the fallen creature to finish it off.

But he smiled wickedly instead and retracted the blade, and let the miserable creature suffer.

"Go!" the huge human yelled, and he jabbed the head of his warhammer straight out, forcing the ogre back a step, demanding its attention. Up and back over his shoulder went the warhammer, as if to begin an overhead chop.

But the halfling ran by, past the big man and right at the ogre.

And right through the ogre's legs and out into the corridor.

The dimwitted behemoth followed the halfling's movements, bending forward, grabbing at him, but too slow.

And that warhammer did not reverse and come forward in an overhead chop, but continued down and around and under and back up again in a tremendous uppercut, timed perfectly to meet the bending ogre's presented face.

How the beast straightened back up to its ten-foot height!

The man dived through its legs, rolling out into the hall, and didn't even look back as the ground shook under the weight of the tumbling ogre.

"A lot of effort for four eels," the halfling said as the two sped along the tunnels.

"The growl in my stomach thinks it worthwhile," the big man answered, but he grunted as he finished the words. The flush of battle was wearing away then, and he had to catch his warhammer in his right hand as his left fell open and weak.

He sucked in his breath, and so did the halfling as he turned to consider the sounds, then to consider the wound.

The big man's forearm, discolored and swollen, dripped blood.

It was not the first blood these two had left in the corridors of the Upperdark over the last few tendays.

And surely it would not be the last.

Many dwarven fists raised in celebration as the rout continued, the warriors of Citadel Adbar charging along the tunnels, bowling over the goblin and orc resistance, killing the monsters by the score.

"No mercy!" King Harnoth cried. "Run them through! Leave them squirming on the floor! Bah, the dogs!"

Every southern passage out of Adbar was thick with dwarves, tight in their devastating battle groups, shield dwarves in the front rank, their interlocking great shields forming a wall of metal in front of them. Those large, flat-bottomed shields were notched to support the halberds of the spearmen in the second rank, poking and stabbing at any enemy that got too close.

In the third rank came swordsmen, their blades inevitably pointed downward to stab at the squirming and trampled goblinkin that littered the floor.

Then the priests and the crossbowmen, sending their stinging bolts out before the march.

Harnoth's group came into a large chamber, the Rundberg, they had named it, vast and nearly circular and full of precious metals. Stalagmites and stalactites filled the area like so many dragon's teeth, all glittering in the torchlight with flecks of mica and veins of silvery metals.

King Harnoth nodded as they entered, glad to be back here. Citadel Adbar had been working on properly securing and laying rail in the tunnels to this very place before the upheaval, as their miners sought areas to exploit beyond the thinning veins nearer the citadel.

"Ah, but it's good that we got 'ere so quick, me king," remarked Dondago Bloodyfist, who was in command of the Wilddwarf Brigade with Oretheo Spikes off in the south at the meeting in Citadel Felbarr—a departure King Harnoth had not sanctioned, and one that was not sitting well with him now, as Uktar turned to Nightal, the last month of 1484 Dalereckoning.

"I been thinkin' them orcs'd stand taller nearer the halls!" Dondago added.

King Harnoth couldn't disagree with that assessment. He had led his dwarves out in nearly full force into the Upperdark. They couldn't break the siege aboveground, it seemed, but they needed to do so down here. For all her redundant and impregnable defenses, Citadel Adbar could not withstand this siege. Her young kings, Harnoth and Bromm, had become too reliant on trade.

That sad error was only now becoming evident as winter deepened and the tunnels out of Adbar were clogged with enemies. Citadel Adbar was the armory of Luruar, and normally the ninth month of the year would see a grand caravan traveling the tunnel ways to the granaries of Sundabar, trading the season's supply of crossbow bolts, ballista spears, and a bevy of weapons, armor, and other metalworks for enough food to keep the whole of Adbar's dwarves fat and happy through the gloom of winter.

Not this year though, with Sundabar besieged through the summer and finally falling to Many-Arrows.

They had become too dependent on their trade with the great city. Harnoth's food stores had already begun to dwindle, and before the year had even turned. He had already started the rationing, and already ordered his own farmers to reclaim large sections of the Undercity and begin their mushroom gardens. But if they could not get through now, could not reopen the ways to the south, to Felbarr and to Mithral Hall, particularly, it was going to be a thin and difficult winter.

Beside him, Dondago began ordering the widening of the front ranks, which would now fold back on both flanks as they crossed the wider ways of Rundberg. "And watch the pillars!" he yelled up and down the line. "Damned ogre could hide against one o' them and step out in the middle of us!"

King Harnoth nodded, but something seemed out of place to him, and the hairs on the back of his neck began to tingle. Dondago's first words, he realized.

They hadn't fought their way out here to Rundberg, the orcs had baited them!

"No, hold the line!" he countermanded the order. "That mound to that mound," he instructed the front rank, indicating a pair of large stalagmites, reaching floor to ceiling some twoscore strides out from the entry tunnel, and fifty dwarves apart from one another. "Anchor yer line at those stony mounds," Harnoth ordered, "and more shields back to the wall from each!"

"Ye heared yer king!" Dondago cried. "Square up!"

The dwarves hustled to get into formation, and Harnoth sent a pair of runners back the way they had come, to venture east and west along the side passages and halt the other legions. The king didn't trust this, and wanted to secure the ground all the way back to Adbar.

Part of him did at least. Another part, a very large part, wanted orc blood and ogre blood, wanted to avenge his dead brother. He had to wince when giving the order to slow the march. He would have preferred a headlong charge across the cavern of Rundberg, enemies be damned, and enemies be slain.

But Harnoth's caution saved his life, and those of most of his forces that day. Barely had the dwarves formed their square, anchored by the stalagmites, when the enemy came roaring across the cavern. Orcs centered the charge, driving goblin fodder in front of them, and with scores of ogres and ogrillons coming in behind them.

The wall of monsters hit the dwarven shield wall like an avalanche. Long halberds impaled the leading monsters, and sometimes another enemy behind the first, but when the press became too great, those pole-arms began to snap, and in such rapid succession that the echoes off the walls of Rundberg sounded like a forest of tree limbs snapping under the weight of an ice storm.

Despite the crushing weight of the horde, despite the fury of the press, the shield wall held, shield dwarves supporting each other bravely, interlocking arms as they hooked together shields, and trusting in their fellows behind to drive aside the swords that came in at them over the metal barrier.

King Harnoth's voice roared above the tumult, calling orders to his kin, concentrating crossbow fire whenever an ogre, who could reach over the front line and destroy its integrity, got too close.

They were holding. The goblinkin were dying so thick their bodies began to bolster the shield wall. And reinforcements were not far behind, so claimed the returning runners.

Then darkness fell, so complete a blackness that many of the dwarves cried out that they had been stricken blind.

When the first fireball erupted among them—unseen flames, though surely not unfelt—the dwarves knew the truth: the drow had come.

As the shouts and screams of agony made clear the magical barrage, King Harnoth wasted no time with indecision, ordering his forces into retreat, back from Rundberg and into the tunnel, back the way they had come.

Magical drow lightning slashed at the departing ranks. The frenzy of orcs and ogres continued to fight, blindly, in the darkness, as often striking an ally as an enemy.

Still, too often striking a dwarf.

The corridor beyond the cavern had not been magically darkened, and there the dwarves reformed into tighter, retreating ranks. For more than a full day, those tunnels south of Adbar became a blood-filled battleground. Hundreds of monsters died, but nearly a hundred of Adbar's finest dwarves would not make their way back home.

And back home they went, chased into their citadel, and even as the lower door of Adbar slammed shut, a lightning bolt scored it, the retort echoing within the dwarven halls and within the heart of King Harnoth.

The noose had tightened, and the larders grew thin.

And so began a series of battles in the Upperdark that would come to be known about the Silver Marches as the Deep Skirmishes. Stubbornly the dwarves sent their legions forth, trying to break out, and ever were they chased back into their fortress by the horde and the drow, for indeed, the dark elves had learned the region around Adbar well, and every tunnel was well watched, and with monsters ready to flood in and seal off any escapes.

The dwarves of Adbar took heart two tendays later, when Oretheo Spikes and his boys somehow managed to slip back into Adbar through the monster-filled tunnels, most alive, but many wounded.

King Harnoth took no heart in that, though. As glad as he was that his dear and trusted friend Spikes had survived, the dwarf's grim words about their enemy's position confirmed King Harnoth's worst fears.

***

The big man sat against the wall in the darkness, his right hand clamped tightly around his left forearm as his halfling friend tried to properly wrap the battered limb with a cloth soaked in a healing salve.

"A potion would be better," Wulfgar muttered as the tight cloth pressed in on his muscles.

"I have none to spare," Regis replied. He knelt in front of Wulfgar, pulling another long strip of soaked cloth from a pot set on the floor beside them. "Just the two potions of healing remaining, and they will be saved for when it becomes a matter of life or death."

"We have no time for this," Wulfgar warned, his voice rolling through an octave shift as Regis pulled hard to secure the bandage. "The drow grow thick about the area—word of us travels to more dangerous enemies."

"The drow have been thick about the area from the beginning," Regis replied, but unconvincingly. He too had noted fewer targets of late, and he and Wulfgar tried hard to stay away from any groups that contained dark elves. Ambushing a few orcs and goblins was one thing, even if the occasional ogre joined in, but the pair wanted no part of any fight with drow.

"Then we should already be long gone from here," Wulfgar said.

Regis leaned back to regard his friend. Wulfgar's face was more in shadow than light, the scattered glowing lichen in the region barely casting enough of a glow to show the man's features. Regis knew him well enough to understand the heaviness in his voice, though, and surely the halfling shared that weariness anyway. They had spent a month or perhaps even more—both had long ago lost track of the days—battling and sneaking around the Upperdark, seeking opportunities to get near to Mithral Hall. Their food had run out days ago, and so now they had to add raiding goblin and orc camps to their list of necessary tasks.

They fought almost every day, and Regis spent every night back in whatever hole they were using as a hiding spot cleaning and dressing the inevitable wounds.

"We'll go back to the lower tunnels," Regis offered. "I'll find more fungus and brew more healing potions . . ."

He stopped, seeing Wulfgar's shadowy head slowly shaking back and forth.

"Our friends are in there," he scolded the barbarian.

"We hope," Wulfgar reminded him, for though they had heard snippets of the escape of Drizzt and the others into Mithral Hall, they really couldn't be sure. Indeed, even if their companions had managed to get in to the hall, that was tendays ago—might they already be back out on the surface at the head of Bruenor's army?

"I am out of answers," Regis admitted with a long and profound sigh.

"East," Wulfgar decided.

"East is the river."

"Under the river, and to the east some more," the barbarian explained. "And let us hope that Citadel Felbarr is not as encircled as Mithral Hall."

Regis fell back a bit farther, his head turning to glance over his left shoulder, to the north, they believed, and toward Mithral Hall. The thought of leaving galled him, and the thought of striking out in an entirely new direction, through tunnels they did not know and a place neither of them had been, terrified him.

"Which way is east?" he asked. "Do we even know?"

"We came from the south."

"And we don't even know how to get back the way we came!" Regis replied, too loudly, drawing a "shh!" from Wulfgar as he clamped his hand over his own mouth.

"We can guess," the large man whispered a few moments later.

"And so we'll wander the Underdark aimlessly if we guess wrong."

"And so we'll be caught and killed if we remain in this region, thick with orcs and drow," said Wulfgar. "That much is certain."

Regis didn't reply. He didn't have to. They both understood the unsaid part of Wulfgar's reasoning: that they'd likely be caught and killed in the tunnels they traveled to the east, as well.

If it was even the east. They could hardly see down here—in many places, Wulfgar was fully blind—let alone determine direction.

"How deep will we have to travel to get under the Surbrin?" Regis asked.

"How deep are we now?" Wulfgar replied, and Regis could see the crease of his teasing grin in the dim light as he asked the question, for it was one, both of them knew, that neither of them could begin to answer.

CHAPTER 3

RAIDING THE GARDEN

KRUGER STONESHIELD GAVE A GREAT YAWN AND TRIED TO RUB THE cobwebs of sleep from his weary eyes. He stood on a small ledge in a tiny alcove, peering through a long tube that poked through the side of the mountain called Fourthpeak, which housed his homeland of Mithral Hall.

A few days before, Kruger had seen the dragon flying around—the huge white wing had flashed right before his startled eyes. It was his report that had explained the sudden troubles with several of the chimneys down in the Undercity.

Since that time, though, the view had been as settled as the winter snows. Kruger reminded himself to be vigilant. His people were counting on him. King Connerad was counting on him.

King Bruenor was counting on him!

"Aye, King Bruenor," he mumbled, gathering up the end of the spyglass and lifting it to his eye. King Bruenor was back, and wouldn't them orcs be a sorry lot afore long.

That thought brought a grin and chuckle to Kruger. He imagined a swarm of orcs in full flight in front of the dwarven brigades. He wanted to be on those front lines, chasing the pig-faced dogs all the way back to their holes in the Spine of the World.

He got his visual bearings when he noted the southern rim of Keeper's Dale through the spyglass, the high sun gleaming brilliantly off the long icicles jabbing down from the ledges. Like dragon's teeth, he thought.

He stood up taller, lifting the back end of the hanging scope, moving his line of sight down, down, into the bowl and the vast orc encampment therein.

For a moment, he noted the activity superficially, hardly registering the many movements of the small dark forms around the new-fallen snow. For a moment, he just figured that the orcs were clearing off their tents and weapons racks and such from the foot of snow that had fallen the night before. But as the patterns began to truly register, Kruger's eye popped open wide, and he even pulled back from the spyglass and rubbed that orb again, trying to make sense out of what he had just seen.

He went right back to the scope and began moving it methodically around the vast encampment. And then he knew. There could be no doubt, particularly given the already long train exiting the western side of Keeper's Dale . . .

The orcs were leaving.

Hands trembling, Kruger slid his field of vision over to the northern end of the dale, then climbed up the north wall. His breath fell away when he saw the partially deconstructed catapults and ballistae.

The giants, too, were pulling back.

Had this last snowstorm broken the siege, at long last? Had events in other parts of the Silver Marches, about Felbarr or Silverymoon, perhaps, demanded reinforcements?

Almost giddy with anticipation, Kruger Stoneshield hooked his boot on the metal pole on the outside of the ladder. Like all of Mithral Hall's mountain scouts, he wore shoes with a semicircular spur made of strong mithral that he could clip onto the ladder, one side and the other, so he could slide down the thirty feet to the lower chamber—the reporting chamber, as it was called, a chamber designed for messages and set with a desk, inkwell, parchment, and smooth scroll tubes. One wall was fitted with a long pipe that wound down to sentries in deeper caverns still. A scout could write a report, stuff it into a scroll tube, and send it sliding down to the waiting hands below.

With a quick last look at the giants and another scan at the departing orcs and goblins along the valley floor, Kruger let go of the spyglass and bent low to grab the ladder, clipping his second boot in place as he did. He almost began his swift descent, but only then did the last image of the frost giants truly register to him. Many of the war machines were already dismantled, or nearly so, but the last group . . .

Were they taking apart that huge catapult?

Or turning it?

Kruger scrambled back up and grabbed the spyglass, twisting it around until he locked in once more on the group in question.

"Turnin' it?" he asked, then added, "Loadin' it!"

He licked his dry lips, he stroked his beard, but he didn't blink or pull back from the spyglass over the next few heartbeats as a large load of burning pitch went into the catapult basket. The great and powerful behemoths began to crank mightily, bending back that arm.

"What in the Nine Hells're ye shootin' at?" the dwarf whispered. There were no targets out there. The dragon, perhaps?

He couldn't hear the release immediately from this great distance, and so the spreading load of flaming pitch was speeding toward him by the time the creak and whoosh of the great beam reached his ears.

Kruger squinted and had to fight hard to resist the urge to duck away as the pitch came flying in.

He felt the tremor as if hit, higher up on the mountain than his scouting position. Perhaps it was the dragon up there, and wouldn't it be grand to see the giants get into a tussle with a white wyrm!

He heard no dragon roar, however, and the giants, standing around the catapult and, along with many of their kin, shielding their eyes from the high sun and staring up at Fourthpeak, did not seem concerned.

Then the rumble began, deeper and more resonant than the impact. And so it built, and was then a thousand times louder, and the chamber, and the mountain, began to tremble violently.

Kruger's vision was stolen by a great darkness, and he could feel the power as tons of snow swept down past him from on high. An avalanche! The giants had set off an avalanche.

Now he understood. They were indeed leaving, and closing Mithral Hall's door with a mountain of snow behind them.

Kruger got a few quick glances as the snow plummeted all around him, and he scrambled up as high as he could go, taking his field of vision back into the dale, all the way down to the east, to the mountain door of Mithral Hall. Or at least, to where he would have expected that door to be had it not been buried under the avalanche.

Then he could see no more as the snow settled, leaving a thick cap above the hole at the other end of the spyglass.

Kruger Stoneshield was on the ladder in a heartbeat, sliding down so fast that he was practically falling free, so eager was he to report this startling turn of events.

***

"They must've needed 'em elsewhere," Bruenor said when the report filtered down to the throne room, where King Connerad sat with the former king and both sets of their principle advisors.

Bruenor looked to Drizzt and shrugged.

"Felbarr breaking out, perhaps?" the drow offered.

"Scouts in the east perches ain't reportin' no movement by the Surbrin bridge," King Connerad said. "The orcs'd be crossin' the bridge if they're meanin' to get to Felbarr."

"Silverymoon, then," said General Dagnabbet. "Might be that they're not waitin' for the spring melt."

"Or they are baiting us," Catti-brie cautioned.

"Won't be smart, then," the fierce Bungalow Thump was quick to interject. "Bah, but if they're lettin' us out in the open where we can put into squares and such, we'll roll 'em into the red snow!"

"They knocked the mountain over the durned door," General Dagnabbet reminded him.

"Bah, but that's not to stop us from gettin' out!" Thump replied. "I'll dig it meself. Or me boys, aye, me boys! We'll run 'em in one after another, head down and helmet spike leading, and drill a tunnel to Keeper's Dale afore the hour's through. Ye just give me the nod, me king!"

The way he said "me king!" took Bruenor's breath away, so reminiscent was it of Bruenor's old friend Pwent, and full of the same passion and loyalty. Looking at Bungalow Thump only reinforced to Bruenor that he had taken the correct course in not challenging Connerad for Mithral Hall's throne. Connerad had built something here, as fine as Bruenor's time in the hall.

Bruenor couldn't help but smile. That had been his fondest hope when he'd turned his kingdom over to Banak Brawnanvil that century before. This was the constancy of dwarven culture that so aligned with the sense of order and discipline that had kept their kingdoms so strong through the centuries. In dwarven culture, no one was irreplaceable, and so the fall of a king, no matter how beloved, did not incite fears for the future. The replacement had been properly selected and groomed.

That thought led Bruenor to look to Connerad's right, to General Dagnabbet, and to wonder if, should Connerad fall in the war, Mithral Hall might be crowning her first queen. And aye, Bruenor thought with an approving nod—though Dagnabbet, who noticed it, could only respond with a curious expression—that would prove to be a fine choice!

"If they've gone to Silverymoon, the sooner we're out, the better," King Connerad remarked.

"Aye," Bruenor agreed. "Out and around to take the bridge."

"So we allow them to assault Silverymoon while we try to free Citadel Felbarr?" Drizzt asked.

Every dwarf in the room nodded emphatically. When Bruenor ended, though, he realized that the instinctual reaction told him a lot about the state of the alliance known as Luruar.

Or perhaps he should think of it as the *former* alliance.

"Ye never go in through the gate," Bruenor said to Drizzt and Catti-brie as they crawled along the newly constructed tunnel. "Farmers're always watchin' the gate! Plumpest mushrooms're off to the side." He gave an exaggerated wink, clearly enjoying King Connerad's decision to break out of Mithral Hall.

"Aye, ye send the little one to the gate, but not through, to keep the farmer's attention, don't ye know, ye silly drow?" Catti-brie added in her best Bruenor imitation—and that brought a smile to the faces of all three.

When Connerad made his choice, he'd turned to Bruenor for help, and why wouldn't he? No dwarf in the Silver Marches had a better battle reputation than Bruenor Battlehammer, and it was one honestly earned.

"If we're goin' out, then get out fast," Bruenor advised. "But raid the garden and stay away from the gate!"

That last analogy provided the humor in the small—and new—tunnel that day. By "raiding the garden," Bruenor referred to a game all young dwarves played, a cat-and-mouse tradition with the farmers of Mithral

Hall, or of Icewind Dale, or anywhere else dwarves of Clan Battlehammer had called home. The thought was to create a subtle diversion, in this case by setting dwarves near the Keeper's Dale exit from Mithral Hall, with hammers and picks enough to make a bit of noise, a bit of a stir, outside the halls.

But nothing so compelling or loud as to suggest any immediate breakout. Indeed, other clansdwarves were also creeping out of higher tunnels to the avalanche pack, poking and prodding and freeing boulders to tumble down over the door, in an effort to give any scouts or magical eyes the orcs might have left in place the impression that the avalanche was doing its job and keeping the exit sealed.

In the meantime, the real garden raiders had dug another way out, one that would put them up on the ridge where the giants had been. The orcs were still camped on the other two main exits, the northern and eastern doors, but if Connerad could get a strong enough force out quietly on the northern edge of Keeper's Dale, they could swing around and clobber the force in the north. With that wide door cleared, Mithral Hall could overwhelm the orc force by the Surbrin in short order, before orc reinforcements could begin to arrive.

It was a desperate plan, to be sure, with so many orc armies marching around, but not one of the advisors to King Connerad had argued against it.

The three companions came into a wide round chamber, a natural cave that had been found along the route, and was now full of busy dwarves. There was a side passage off to their right, curling back into the mountain, but the new tunnel was being dug directly across the way, directly across a frozen underground pond.

As the trio neared the closest bank, Drizzt looked at the new dig, trying to sort out the somewhat confusing details as the dwarves skated back and forth across the ice, many carrying buckets, others hauling bundles of great shields all strapped together. Also, the tunnel being dug now was not level, not even gently sloping, but rose at a fairly steep angle, perhaps thirty or forty degrees. The drow looked to Catti-brie, who seemed as perplexed as he, and shrugged.

"Ye don't raid the garden without a fast flight," Bruenor, who was not surprised and indeed had helped organize all of this, told them with a wink. He led them across the lake slowly, pointing out the double tunnel being built. One side was being dug simply, natural stone and ground chopped into stairs, while the other, cut on the other side of a small ridge, was simply a slope, and one the dwarves were smoothing out carefully, even sliding sections of flat rock into place to cover jagged expanses.

"A hunnerd and fifty feet more to the ridge north o' Keeper's Dale," Bruenor explained. "Tunnel's more than halfway there and we're findin' easier ground now."

A crash turned them all around to see a gang of dwarves entering the chamber from the side tunnel, pulling a wagon loaded with firewood and coal and piles of heavy blankets.

"O'er there!" Bruenor ordered, pointing to the corner back where he and the other two had entered, a small area mostly secluded by large stalagmites. "And ye got the curving beams?"

"Aye, King Bruenor!" one shouted back, her smile so wide that it almost took in her ears. She clapped her hands and shouted, "Whee!" and all the dwarves around her began to laugh.

"Should we even ask?" Drizzt said to Bruenor.

"Nah!" replied the dwarf, who was clearly quite elated at getting out into the fight. "Ye're not wantin' to know!"

Off to the side of the trio, an excited young dwarf went running up to King Connerad, prompting the three to silence so they could hear the news.

"We're to the snow," the youngster announced to the king. "And she's not thick about our hole. We're out, me king!"

Connerad looked over at Bruenor and nodded. They had already agreed that Drizzt would be among the first out of the hole so that he could scout around.

Catti-brie turned to the drow and began spellcasting. A few moments later, a profound warmth spread throughout Drizzt's body.

"To protect you from the winter winds," she said.

Drizzt merely smiled and kissed her lightly on the cheek. He had survived scores of winters in Icewind Dale, out on the mountainside or open tundra around Ten Towns, and surely was no stranger to the winter winds. He gave her a wink, though, for surely he appreciated the gesture.

With Bruenor and Catti-brie beside him, Drizzt moved to the up-sloping tunnel, where Bungalow Thump and several others of the famed Gutbuster Brigade waited.

"Ye go out right behind meself, elf," the ferocious dwarf said. Bungalow moved to the tunnel stair and took a great shield off the stack.

"And don't ye forget to get yerself a shield," he called back to Drizzt.

"I fight with two weapons," Drizzt replied, moving up.

Bungalow laughed at him. "Take a shield," he said. "Ye'll put it down when ye get out, but we're needin' 'em up there."

Drizzt did as he was asked, and off they went, up the long stairway. When they reached the top, Bungalow Thump looked back, grinned, then plowed right through into the open air atop the ridgeline framing the northern end of Keeper's Dale.

The wind howled in their ears, and it was a cold one indeed, late in the afternoon, with the meager sun already touching the western horizon. But other than the blowing snow, nothing stirred around them. Despite the whiteness of the snow and the fact that they had been underground for months, they did not need to squint. The sky above remained dark, still in the grasp of the foul drow magic. Bungalow tossed his shield to the snow, which was not deep in this windblown place on the far side of the tunnel exit, and nodded for Drizzt to stack his atop it.

Drizzt complied, still not quite understanding, and before he had even put the shield down, he was crowded by the other Gutbusters, rushing from the tunnel and eager to be rid of their great shields.

"Now don't ye be worryin' 'bout taking back yer own if it's time to get back in," Bungalow Thump explained. "Ye just grab the top one of the pile and take yer ride! Ha!"

Drizzt looked from the shield pile, and already it was considerable, to the tunnel exit just as Catti-brie came out, Bruenor close behind, and Athrogate close behind him, and all three carrying shields.

"You cannot mean . . ." Drizzt replied to Bungalow Thump, and the dwarf howled and bounded away.

"What?" Catti-brie asked, coming over to place her shield on the stack.

Drizzt looked past her to note that some of the dwarves now coming out carried buckets of water, which they carefully poured back into the tunnel, along the smooth side and not the stairs.

The Gutbusters were already forming a wide defensive perimeter around the exit, but there was no sign of any enemies. Even out from the sheltering mountainside, the snow was not too deep, though visibility was fairly low from the constant swirls of blowing snow and the lack of normal daylight.

Bruenor tapped Drizzt on the arm and pointed up to a rocky ridge in the northeast. "Light's gettin' low, elf, and weren't much to start with in this darkened land. Ye think ye can get up there?"

Drizzt nodded.

"Ye'll see the orc camp up by the north door from there," Bruenor explained. "I'm wantin' to be hittin' them soon as the dark's settled deep. We'll get around the mountain and to the Surbrin by midmorning if the weather holds."

"Might be enemies hiding in the cracks around the rocks," Catti-brie pointed out.

Drizzt nodded and smiled at her. "Bring your boys to the base," he instructed Bruenor. Then he trotted off toward the ridge, through the growing throng of Battlehammers exiting the tunnel and stretching in the open air for the first time in many tendays.

As soon as he passed beyond the widening Gutbuster perimeter, he paused, and when he started off once more, Guenhwyvar now beside him, he heard the muted claps and cheers and even gasps from the dwarves behind them. Only a few of them had seen the magnificent panther, of course, and even those who had known the cat before, other than the handful who had been in the lower tunnel when Drizzt and his companions had first come into Mithral Hall, hadn't seen her in decades.

Guenhwyvar led the way to the rocky outcropping, bounding along the icy stones with surefooted ease. Propelled by his magical ankle bracelets and graced with exceptional agility even for one of his dexterous race, Drizzt, too, went up gracefully and swiftly. With the hunting panther leading the way, he was confident that no monsters would spring out at him from concealed cubbyholes.

Stone-to-stone, he leaped, and still the dwarves gathered below, a sizable crowd now and with more still pouring out of Mithral Hall. From Drizzt's high vantage, they seemed more a teeming and amorphous mass than individual figures. The drow had to slow as he got higher. Snow remained thick around the stones and with ice settled firmly beneath it. He glanced back just before he crested the ridge. Several hundred dwarves were out now, their perimeter widening. Looking past them into Keeper's Dale, off to the west farther along the rim, or even up north to the wide passes, Drizzt could see no sign of enemies, other than the tracks left by the giants and their departing war machines.

The fact that those tracks went north, however, did set off an alarm, or at least a series of concerning questions. If the besieging giants had gone off to reinforce the main Many-Arrows army, their ultimate direction would be either south to Silverymoon or Everlund, or east to the Surbrin Bridge and the road to Citadel Felbarr.

Why were they going north? The fastest and easiest trail to the south would have taken them straight west around Keeper's Dale, and if the Surbrin Bridge was their goal, they should have passed just north of this very ridge Drizzt now stood upon.

Those questions drove him upward even faster, his eagerness bringing him over the ridge and in view of the northern door.

Where the orc forces remained encamped.

Exactly as they had hoped, Drizzt thought with a nod, but he glanced again back to the north where the snow had been cleaved by the wheels of huge war machines. Had the giants abandoned the orcs, he wondered? He thought back to the time of King Obould. That same alliance had been tenuous indeed.

With that in mind, he focused more intently on the orc camp, and immediately began to see the troubling signs that this was not as it seemed. The orcs milled around their cookfires and bonfires, seemingly going about their late-day routine—at a casual glance.

But they all had their weapons, Drizzt noted, even heavy halberds and greataxes, and many had their swords in hand, empty scabbards hanging on their belts.

The dwarves wouldn't ambush them.

Drizzt spun, and called the panther to his side.

"Guen, down as fast as you can, and right back into Mithral Hall!" he instructed the cat, who gave a low growl and leaped away.

Drizzt started down at full speed, but the panther flew a dozen of his strides with each powerful leap. She hit one snow-capped rock, and the whole thing began to tip, and for a moment, Drizzt held his breath.

But Guenhwyvar was gone before the stone could roll around upon her, flying through the air to a snowy expanse, then riding a miniature avalanche all the way to the ground.

Bruenor, Catti-brie, and the other dwarves noted the cat's run long before that last snowy slide. They saw Drizzt, too, far above and rushing down.

72

"He's seen somethin'," Athrogate remarked.

"Aye, and wanting us to be on the move," Bruenor replied.

"A charge or a retreat?" Catti-brie asked.

Just to the east of them at the base of the rocky outcropping, Guenhwyvar came rolling down in a cloud of snow. The black ball of snarling feline came out of that frozen tangle at full speed, rushing for the friends.

"We're to know soon," Bruenor remarked. He braced himself, expecting the cat to run him over and sit on him—as had happened so many times in his previous life!

But Guenhwyvar didn't slow, didn't acknowledge the trio at all as she sped by, other than a quick snarl in their direction. She raced off for the tunnel back into Mithral Hall—the dwarves there scattered as she neared—and went straight back into the hole.

"Retreat," Catti-brie mouthed, realizing the signal. "We've been lured!"

"Connerad!" Bruenor yelled, and started running for the young king, waving his arms, though Connerad had surely noted the panther's run as well.

Catti-brie's attention went back to the rocky ridge and Drizzt, still picking his way down with all speed. "What did you see, my love?" she whispered under her breath, her eye roving back up to the crest of the mountain spur, as if she expected a horde of giants to come bounding into sight at any moment.

When nothing appeared, she continued her upward movement, her gaze climbing the mountainside, looking for monsters, looking for some hint.

And there she saw the white dragon, above the high top of Fourthpeak and dropping from on high, and the sight took her breath away.

Beside her, Bruenor heard that gasp and followed the shocked woman's gaze. "Elf!" he screamed, running for the ridge and banging his axe on his shield. "Elf! Dragon!"

The wind had kicked up, moaning about the stones, and Drizzt was still far away, so even when Catti-brie joined in the shouting, Bruenor and she doubted he could hear them. But he did notice the dragon, and the wyrm had surely taken notice of him.

Drizzt veered to a high stone, the dragon closing, and now Bruenor and Catti-brie noted a drow riding the wyrm. Out Drizzt leaped, just an instant before the dragon leveled out, huge wings battling its own momentum, and cut fast to the side. It soared past the rock as Drizzt fell far below.

The ranger hit the snow hard and fell back into it, riding down a small avalanche into another jag of stone.

"Crossbows! Shoot the damned thing!" Athrogate roared, the dragon already turning and coming back in at Drizzt.

But other cries from the north sounded as well. An army of orcs and giants had appeared, coming around a second rocky spur and charging at the dwarves with all speed.

"To the hall, girl!" Bruenor ordered Catti-brie, but he cut the thought short as he turned, to find Catti-brie standing calm, her eyes closed, beginning the chant of a spell.

"To the hall, all of us!" King Connerad corrected, running with his entourage to join Bruenor. "We're not fightin' a horde o' orcs and giants with that beast flying about!"

Connerad grabbed Bruenor by the shoulder, but Bruenor wouldn't budge and wouldn't look away. Up above, Drizzt came back into sight, scrambling upon a high rock, Taulmaril now in hand as he leveled toward the incoming dragon.

The beast flew fast along the mountainside, weaving back and forth—not so much out of fear for the bow as trying to protect its rider.

A streak of silver flew past it, then a second. A third scored a stinging hit on the dragon's shoulder, but the beast didn't slow.

Up on the rock, Drizzt moved to the end as if to leap again, and Bruenor cried out in warning. The dragon swerved outward from the mountain spur, and probably would have caught him in its mouth if he'd followed that course.

Drizzt's leap was a feint, though, and he reversed suddenly and leaped back the other way, deeper into the rocks.

But the dragon was ready for that, too, and its serpentine neck rolled back at the rocks, and from its open maw came a thick blast of freezing breath, chasing Drizzt back, right behind him, following him down, and surely catching him just beyond Bruenor's view.

"Elf!" the dwarf howled—and Connerad and Dagnabbet joined in.

The dragon swooped past the point, wings wide and turning as it tried to slow.

A fireball caught it there, in midair, some fifty feet or so past where Drizzt had disappeared. The beast came through the flames awkwardly with its wings tucking defensively, and turning and rocking, too close to the stones. On its back, the drow crouched low, a translucent shield defensively up over his head.

"Oh, good shot, girl!" Connerad yelled as the dragon clipped the stones and began to tumble, rolling past, finally kicking out, but dropping down below the ridge and into Keeper's Dale.

"To the hall!" Connerad demanded, and he started that way, dragging a reluctant Bruenor.

Over by the tunnel, the dwarves were already in retreat, methodically. They went to the stacks of shields in a line, taking one and diving atop it into the smooth, iced side of the tunnel, riding it back into the tunnels.

A fight was on, though, up in the north, as the leading lines of orcs met with the Gutbusters, and it wasn't one Bruenor intended to miss.

Bruenor shoved Connerad hard toward the tunnel. The younger dwarf caught his balance and swung back, surprised and snarling.

"Ye're the king!" Bruenor yelled at him. "Get yerself in."

"Aye, and yerself's Bruenor," Dagnabbet said, grabbing at the red-bearded dwarf, who tugged away from her. "Get yerself in!"

"Aye, I'm Bruenor, with no throne under me bum, and know that I'm seein' me place," Bruenor explained.

He charged off to the north, Catti-brie and Athrogate right behind.

Only Athrogate ran full out to join in the fighting, though, as Catti-brie and Bruenor continued to stare up the ridge for some sign of their friend, hoping against hope.

Arauthator veered back and forth as he approached the drow, those stinging lightning arrows reaching out far too quickly for the wyrm's liking.

Tiago, his magnificent shield in front of him easily blocking any of the shots, cared less. Much less. This was Drizzt standing on that rock.

Drizzt the Heretic.

Drizzt the Embarrassment.

Drizzt the Trophy.

Out went the rogue drow, as if to leap away down the rock face, and Arauthator veered out. But back went Drizzt, diving into the stones.

The dragon couldn't turn his bulk or slow, but he could, and did, swivel his head, and Tiago lifted his sword in victory. From his perch, he could see the dragon's killing breath catching up to the rogue drow in the rocky crevice.

And then the drow pulled back and curled inward. Arauthator howled in protest as a fireball erupted immediately in front of them.

A tremendous blast seared and expanded as the pair crashed right through. Tiago got as small as he could behind his shield, but still the flames caught him and bit at him.

The dragon rolled, and Tiago nearly fell free.

The dragon clipped the rocky outcropping, dislodging stones and throwing snow, and one of Tiago's legs came free in the awkward impact. Finally Arauthator managed to right himself enough to push off from the cliff, but in a tumble and roll, right over, spinning down over the lip of the gorge.

Somehow Tiago held his seat, but at the price of his sword, which went flying free into the blowing snow, tumbling into the wide canyon known as Keeper's Dale.

Tiago shouted, but it was more a growl than any meaningful word as the drow struggled to hold on, as the dragon, too, plummeted into the vale. At the last moment, Arauthator managed to right himself and collect his wits enough to spread his wings, but still, down they went, skidding and crashing into the deep snow in the bowl of Keeper's Dale.

Tiago lay in the snow, his legs aching, and one, he was sure, was broken. His skin stung from those flames—he could hardly believe the power of that fireball.

When he located Arauthator in the dying light, he expected that the dragon shared his feelings. Smoke wafted from the wyrm's horned head and even in the last moments of daylight, meager as it was, Arauthator's face seemed to glow, radiating heat.

The dragon just growled, long and low, and Tiago half expected the thing to eat him.

"My sword," he said, grimacing as he struggled to sit up. "We must find it."

"Your sword, drow?" Arauthator roared at him. "An army up above—and I will find and eat that wizard!—and you fret for a sword?"

"Vidrinath!" Tiago argued. "Not just a sword! An artifact of the new age, crafted by Gol'fanin in the Forge of Gauntlgrym!"

The dragon's growl seemed more a purr suddenly. "Do tell," the beast prompted.

"You cannot have it," Tiago said flatly. "You would invite the wrath of all of Menzoberranzan! I must find my . . ." He tried to stand, but a wave of agony burned up his leg, and he nearly swooned.

"I will find your sword, drow," the dragon promised. "And you will reward me handsomely for it, and for killing that rogue drow!"

Tiago settled back, suddenly contented. Yes, of course the dragon would find it. Could such a treasure remain hidden from a dragon as mighty as Arauthator?

And yes, they were in no hurry. Drizzt was surely dead, frozen in a tumble of rocks far from any of his friends. They could go up and cut him out at their leisure, likely. The orcs and giants would chase the dwarves back into their hole.

The drow packed his aching leg in snow. His wife would fix it. Perhaps there was a benefit of being married to a high priestess after all, even if that priestess was the wretched Saribel Xorlarrin.

He saw the crevice and leaped for it. He had to get inside, and around a bend—something, anything, to get out of the path of the dragon's killing breath.

But he couldn't make it. He knew that halfway through his leap from the rock.

He did get into the crevice, part of the way, at least, but there was no depth to it, and no turn that would move him away from the cloud of frost that caught him there and filled the area.

Drizzt instinctively curled his cloak around him, but warm though it was, he knew in his mind that it could not protect him from such a lethal weapon as the breath of an ancient white dragon.

And he felt those cold tendrils now, reaching for him, licking at him.

Reflexively, he curled and held his breath, and a great lament washed over him with the thought that he would never see his friends again, that he would never hold Catti-brie again.

He felt himself tightening to the stone as the frosty dragon breath settled over him, cocooning him, icing him in place. The press was great, the ice against his face and hands—exposed skin caught in the blast.

But it didn't hurt. And though he felt the chill, it was not a deathly thing, not a cold that went to his bones and settled there, stealing his very life-force.

No, far from it. Indeed, the weight of the press was more uncomfortable than the chill of the ice. The ice wasn't biting at him at all. He thought of his sword, Icingdeath, but that was a blade to protect from flames, not from cold.

Not understanding, but having more pressing needs at that moment, Drizzt braced himself against the stone and pushed out with all his strength. He heard the ice crackling all around him, but the press remained. Again and again, he pushed against the frozen tomb, cracking it, weakening it, bit by bit. Finally it came free of the rock with a great swooshing sound.

Drizzt staggered and nearly toppled as some fell away, but a large chunk remained stuck fast, frozen to his forest-green cloak. Still he felt no cold bite as he pushed the flecks from his bare arms and hand and face and neck, and still he could not comprehend how he had so completely ignored the killing breath of the dragon.

And then it hit him, as he recalled his last moments in the cave below the tunnel, when Catti-brie had come up to him and cast an enchantment upon him to protect him from winter's bite.

"Good spell, my wife," Drizzt muttered through teeth that were not chattering.

He worked more quickly then, reminding himself that a white dragon and a drow rider—was it Tiago?—might be right outside.

But so too were his friends, out there with the dragon and the deadly drow. With a low growl, Drizzt tore fully free of the wall and spun, whipping his cloak around so that it cracked into the stone, freeing it of some of the heavy ice.

Out to the rock went Drizzt, Taulmaril in hand, ready to strike again at the dragon and its Baenre rider.

But the wyrm was not to be seen.

Drizzt spotted Catti-brie and Bruenor below, and how their faces lit up as they waved to their dear friend. They ran off to the north, motioning for Drizzt to join them.

And Drizzt did, with his bow in hand. From this high vantage, he could strike behind the front ranks, where battle had been joined. From this high perch, the giants would be easy targets indeed.

And from this high perch, he could watch for the return of the dragon.

VENGEANCE OF THE IRON DWARF

Goblins and orcs spun up and out to the side like water flying from the sharp prow of a fast-moving ship, as Athrogate and his spinning morningstars plowed into the line. With abandon, with fury, with the strength of a giant—and a pair of magical weapons as powerful as anything on the field—the black-bearded dwarf howled with glee, accepting hits and dealing devastating blows in return.

To the other dwarves, ferocious in their own right, this one seemed completely unafraid, even welcoming of death, and so it was true.

Athrogate, once of Felbarr, too long a wanderer, cursed and unable to die, didn't care. This seemed to him his time and his place, and as soon as he got through the fodder goblinkin—and he had already turned this end of the line—he intended on making straight for the handful of frost giants behind them.

They'd kill him to death, he figured.

But he didn't care. The rest of the boys would get back into Mithral Hall, and his name would be sung by the skalds—and when King Emerus learned the truth of Athrogate, who had been banished from Felbarr, Athrogate would have his proper revenge.

He flinched as he sent one broken goblin flying off to the side. A shot of lightning, it seemed, crackled just above him. In the distance he saw a giant lurch, then again, and then another, as a line of lightning arrows flew in at them.

Athrogate managed a moment to glance back, to see Drizzt up on high, that killing bow in hand.

"Bwahaha!" he roared, suddenly figuring that he'd not only be a hero but live to brag about it, too.

"Turn the damned line!" he heard Bruenor's voice above the shouts and clatter of battle. "Bend her in! To the hall, boys, to the hall!"

"Bwahaha!" Athrogate roared all the louder. "Bend yer bow, drow, and to the hall! I'll send 'em flyin' with me balls!"

"Hold!" came Bruenor's roar behind him, aimed right for him, and Athrogate skidded to a stop.

"Save some for meself, ye dolt!" Bruenor cried, sliding up beside him and cracking his axe against his shield to emphasize the point.

"Bwahaha!" Athrogate roared.

Bruenor pulled him to the left and away from the rocky outcropping. More arrows stabbed in at the giants, and now their attention was fully on the drow and that nasty bow, boulder after boulder spinning out at the ridge.

Bruenor chopped down an orc and shield-rushed a second, driving it back, and, more importantly, driving himself ahead, Athrogate beside him.

Right behind them, tickling their behinds, came a wall of fire from Catti-brie, sealing the eastern flank of the battle line. And out of that wall of fire stepped a huge elemental beast from the fiery plane, rushing straight out at the behemoths, with goblins and orcs fleeing in terror before it.

Side-by-side, the two dwarves plowed through the ranks, sweeping the line and freeing up dwarves with every step.

"To the hall!" Bruenor yelled repeatedly, instructing those dwarves freed from battle to run straight out, and those still tight against the goblins to fight a retreating action.

So they collapsed around the tunnel entrance, dwarves scooping shields and sliding back down the slope. Out in the east, the giants stumbled away, arrows biting at them, the fire elemental biting at them, and now with Guenhwyvar biting at them, too.

"Ye go in, King Bruenor, and get yer girl with ye!" Athrogate offered. "I'll hold the last o' the dogs!"

"Nah," Bruenor replied. "Got me a better idea." And he lifted his cracked silver horn to his lips and blew a cracking note. "The Pwent'll hold 'em!"

"Come on, girl!" Bruenor called to Catti-brie as the time neared for he and Athrogate to get inside.

Catti-brie nodded and launched one last fireball at a mob of orcs who looked as if they might be regrouping for another charge. She rushed for the tunnel, glancing back at Drizzt, as was Bruenor.

Drizzt waved at them to continue, and smiled confidently.

Catti-brie picked up a great shield and set it down at the tunnel lip, falling atop it. Somehow this seemed to her far scarier than staying out there to battle the orcs, or even the giants, or even the damned dragon. But she felt Bruenor's hand on her back and heard Athrogate's laugh, and it wasn't her choice as the red-bearded dwarf shoved her into the tunnel for a wild and bouncing ride down the steep decline.

She figured out what those curving beams had been for as she neared the bottom and the torchlight—the dwarves had turned this slide into a jump.

She heard herself screaming as she felt herself flying. She hit the water with a great splash, the cold liquid grabbing at her.

But so too were dwarven hands, catching her around the shoulders and hauling her out, then unceremoniously launching her in a slide across the ice around the hole they'd chopped to the far bank where other dwarves—clerics with heavy blankets—waited, with a large fire burning in the corner behind them.

Catti-brie managed to glance back when she heard Bruenor's howl, and saw the dwarf high in the air, arms flapping like the wings of a broken bird. Right behind him came Athrogate, morningstars spinning.

Dwarves hauled them out and sent them skidding across the ice.

"Close the damned tunnel!" went the shouts.

"Not yet!" Bruenor, Athrogate, and Catti-brie all yelled together, and sure enough, a moment later came the last shield, one carrying a dark elf, skidding down the ramp, catching the curve of the jump, and flying gracefully above the pond.

"Take a bath, elf!" Bruenor howled.

But Drizzt didn't. The shield splashed into the water, and Drizzt gracefully rolled upright in his descent before coming down atop it, stepping and leaping so quickly that he barely got his boots wet before settling down on the solid ice.

"Durned elf," a drenched Bruenor grumbled.

"Bwahaha!" howled the equally-dripping Athrogate.

"Curse the gods, I had him!" Tiago fumed. He was back in Nesmé. Saribel tended his broken leg, with Tos'un and Doum'wielle nearby.

"You got your sword back," Saribel replied dryly, her tone making it quite clear that she was less than thrilled with Tiago.

"Arauthator is quite angry," said Ravel, coming into the room.

Saribel glared at Tiago.

"Would it have not better served us all, and Matron Mother Quenthel most of all, if you had come to us with your plan to lure the dwarves out of their hole?" Tos'un dared to ask.

"You knew," Tiago replied. "I made no secret . . ."

"You did not say when it would transpire," Tos'un interrupted, apparently feeling quite brave.

Tiago noticed then that his wife, the high priestess of House Baenre, nodded approvingly at the upstart Armgo noble.

This interrogation had been practiced.

"Arauthator will return to his lair in the Spine of the World, into the month of Hammer, at least," Ravel announced.

"Drizzt Do'Urden is dead," Tiago growled.

"You returned to the spot," Tos'un argued. "He was not there!"

"Cut out of the dragon's ice by the retreating dwarves."

"The orcs saw Drizzt retreat into Mithral Hall."

"They are orcs! They know nothing," Tiago insisted, hoping beyond reason.

"Enough," Saribel quietly ordered them all. "It was a good attempt, and the prize would have been great indeed," she said to her husband. "But yes, you should have allowed all of us to partake in the attempt at defeating the rogue Do'Urden. You put your personal pride above the good of Menzoberranzan."

Tiago could hardly believe what he was hearing from these companions. He was Tiago Baenre, grandson of mighty Dantrag, favored great-nephew of Matron Mother Quenthel Baenre. They were . . . what? Castoff Xorlarrins, a long-forgotten Armgo, and a half-breed not worthy to even be in this room.

He pulled himself to a sitting position and glared at all of them in turn. "Who leads this expedition?" he asked.

"Matron Mother Quenthel," Saribel answered without the slightest hesitation.

"She is not here," said Tiago. "Nor is Gromph, nor any other matron mother, nor any ranking Xorlarrin."

"You are the weapons master of House Do'Urden," Ravel reminded him. "I am the House wizard. We are of equal rank."

"I am Baenre and our House is in Menzoberranzan, created by the great Matron Mother Baenre," Tiago reminded.

"As I am Baenre, Husband," said Saribel. "And high priestess of House Do'Urden, second only to Matron Mother Darthiir herself." She paused and snickered, and reiterated, "Matron Mother Darthiir," with a dismissive chortle.

Tiago stared at her hard, wondering how greatly Matron Mother Quenthel would punish him when she discovered that he had disemboweled the witch named Saribel.

"Are you claiming leadership over the drow in the Silver Marches?" Tiago asked incredulously, a feeling he was clearly not trying to hide.

"I am," Saribel said without hesitation, and she looked to Ravel and Tos'un, and both, to Tiago's utter amazement, nodded in agreement.

Tiago started to argue, but Saribel cut him short.

"We are not long for the surface," she explained. "Almost all of our kin are in the tunnels about the dwarven citadels now, or guarding the underground ways to the city called Silverymoon, sealing our enemies in place. We will starve the dwarves this winter to force them out into open battle, but you and I will not likely see that fight, Husband, for Matron Mother Darthiir calls, and House Do'Urden awaits."

"You cannot be serious," Tiago argued. "Drizzt is in there, in Mithral Hall. They will come out. He—"

"You said he was dead," Saribel reminded. "So when we return to Menzoberranzan, claim yourself as the killer of the rogue Do'Urden."

And pray that he never shows himself again, Tiago thought but did not say, for such a humiliation as that would finish his ambitions in Menzoberranzan.

"Rest, Husband," said Saribel, and she rose and started away, the others collecting in her wake, except for Ravel, who remained behind.

"I had him," Tiago said when he was alone with his wizard friend.

"Had you returned with his head, it might have gone better for you," said Ravel.

"What do you mean? What do you know?" Tiago demanded. "And pray tell me where Saribel has found such courage!"

"Your answers are all one and the same," said Ravel. "When I went to Arauthator after your return, Gromph Baenre was waiting, and he was not amused."

Tiago sucked in his breath.

"And he grew less amused as the dragon revealed its own great displeasure," said Ravel. "It is a tenuous alliance we hold with the two white dragons, my friend, and one clearly very important to Gromph. And it quickly became quite clear to me that Drizzt Do'Urden was not, is not, important to Arauthator or to Gromph."

"So Saribel acts with the imprimatur of the archmage."

"And of the matron mother."

"It makes no sense," Tiago said, shaking his head. "Drizzt Do'Urden is in there. The greatest prize of all is within our reach. Why would they not see that?"

"The greatest prize to you," said Ravel.

"Why are we House Do'Urden?"

"There was a vacancy on the Ruling Council the matron mother wished to fill with a Baenre-dominated House. It was a brilliant move, you must admit. With House Xorlarrin moving out, there seemed to be a struggle impending between Baenre and Barrison Del'Armgo. But now Matron Mother Quenthel dominates the Ruling Council too completely for any to connive against her."

"But why Do'Urden?" Tiago pressed.

"An empty Hou—"

"A *cursed* House," Tiago interrupted. "And one resurrected now for one reason only."

"To humiliate the avowed enemy of Lolth."

"And why not kill him?"

Ravel shrugged and shook his head. "They will, likely," he answered. "But in the matron mother's own time. Matron Mother Quenthel is being very conservative and cautious. She remembers the fate of her mother, whose head was cleaved in half by King Bruenor. We have attacked seven major strongholds, Tiago, not even including this worthless town you now claim as duke. Seven major strongholds. War with Silverymoon alone would bring great struggle to Menzoberranzan, if the claims of that city's wizardly powers are not exaggerated."

Tiago shook his head, having none of it.

"Seven," Ravel repeated, and he recited them slowly for emphasis, "Citadel Adbar, Citadel Felbarr, Mithral Hall, Sundabar, Silverymoon, Everlund, and the elves of the Glimmerwood. The orcs, the giants, and the dragons—particularly the dragons—make this possible."

He ended there and shrugged again, then started away with his unspoken conclusion hanging in Tiago's thoughts.

Tiago had risked Arauthator for his personal desire to kill Drizzt. Gromph and the matron mother had gone to great lengths to enlist the dragons, so said the whispers.

Tiago flung a pillow across the room and crossed his arms over his chest, sneering.

And plotting.

Drizzt was in that dwarven hole, and despite his claims, Tiago did not believe for a moment that the rogue drow was dead.

"But he will be," Tiago whispered. "And I will carry his head into Menzoberranzan."

Winter settled deep around the Silver Marches, and hammers rang in the dwarven halls. But so too did bellies rumble, particularly in Citadel Felbarr, and more particularly in Citadel Adbar, whose lifeblood was trade and whose trade had been halted.

Winter settled deep around the vast orc encampments, but with the granaries of Hartusk Keep at their disposal, the hearty orcs were not dismayed.

Beleaguered Silverymoon welcomed the respite, her vast legion of wizards and priests more than able to feed the populace. In the south, the mighty city of Everlund crouched, hushed, knowing that doom was not far, knowing that the snows would recede and the orc horde would come on.

The snows piled, the cold wind blew strong that year, as 1484 turned to 1485 in the Winter of the Iron Dwarf.

CHAPTER 4

GROWLING BELLIES

DRIZZT TURNED A CORNER AND SPRINTED AHEAD, A HORDE OF ANGRY enemies close behind. He turned back and let fly an arrow, silencing one loud-mouthed orc. But then he had to dive down to the side, roll right back to his feet and turn another corner as a volley of spears and large rocks flew out at him.

A sharp corner, and Drizzt found himself face-to-belly with a huge ogre. Without hesitating, the drow leaned backward, all the while his feet propelling him forward. He saw the ogre's club descending, chasing, but he was the quicker, stabbing straight up into the ogre's groin.

How the brute hopped, and when it landed, Drizzt was behind it, launching into a circuit, scimitars slashing the back of the brute's thigh one after another.

On Drizzt ran, and he couldn't help but smile when he heard the commotion as his pursuers turned the corner, and no doubt stumbled right into the howling ogre.

One more turn in the corridor had the drow in his last run, the metal wall in front of him, set with a metal grate in the direct center. Never slowing, he sheathed his blades and pulled out Taulmaril, nocked an arrow, and let fly. The magical arrow struck a bar of the metal grate, sparks flying everywhere, briefly illuminating the wall.

Drizzt heard the metal screeching as it slid aside, and as he neared, he heard the dwarves calling out. A torch came up behind the hole in the wall, the center place where the grate had been, lighting the way for Drizzt to dive through, hardly slowing.

As soon as he rolled out of the way, the dwarf brigade slid a ballista in place, a strange, thick spear set to throw.

"Go!" he told them, knowing the monsters to be close behind.

Off went the spear, whipping down the hall and crashing into the nearest enemies. The hollow missile collapsed in on itself, spraying hot pitch all around.

Howls echoed down the hall, and how the dwarves laughed and patted one another on the back as they slammed and hammered a solid plate back into the wider metal wall that sealed the corridor.

"The next plate's ready in the fourth southern chamber," one yellow-bearded fellow said to Drizzt. "If ye're meanin' to go right back."

"Enough for today," Drizzt replied. He had been forced to call upon Guenhwyvar out there in the Upperdark. "Tomorrow, perhaps."

The yellow-bearded dwarf tilted his head and stared curiously at the drow. "Eh, elf?" he asked. "No sign, then?"

Drizzt could only shrug. After being chased back into Mithral Hall from the rim of Keeper's Dale, the dwarves had turned their attention back to the lower tunnels. At Bruenor's request, and Connerad's bidding, they had developed a system of opening up their barriers, just a bit and just for a few moments, so that Drizzt could go out and scout around the tunnels.

They were more than halfway through the month of Hammer now, the first month of 1485, and Drizzt had been out several times.

He had found no sign of Wulfgar and Regis, no sign of anything except that the monsters were here, orcs and ogres and goblins and drow, and their noose, if today was any indication, was tightening around Mithral Hall.

Bruenor and Connerad had been discussing the possibility of trying to break out into the tunnels, perhaps to come back to the surface just beyond the Surbrin in the east, then turn back and break the siege from without.

From what Drizzt had seen of the countless camps and the ordered garrisons, that was just what the enemy wanted.

They weren't going to break out through the Upperdark without heavy losses.

And if Wulfgar and Regis were still down there, they weren't getting anywhere near Mithral Hall.

That thought proved most unsettling to the drow, for given the abundance of dark elves he had noted in the tunnels, it was clear to him that if Wulfgar and Regis were anywhere near this region in the Underdark, they were either dead or imprisoned.

He put his face in his hands and breathed a deep and steadying sigh, trying to hold out hope for his friends, but also preparing himself for the very real possibility that he would never see them again, alive or dead, and that he, Catti-brie, and Bruenor would never learn of their fate.

A line of dwarves moved through the large iron door and into the reinforced vault Citadel Adbar used as a larder, bending low against the tug of heavy ropes as they towed a trio of large carts.

"Four hunnerd pounds in each," remarked Nigel Thunderstorm, of the Felbarr Thunderstorms, a family known for its culinary skills. Nigel had come to Adbar some fifty years before, accepting the invitation of King Harbromm to serve as his personal chef. It was supposed to be a temporary position, with Nigel expected to return to Felbarr when his Ma, Nigella, retired. But in Adbar he had found a home, and a wife, and now, two children besides.

His life had been busy and good, his reputation another high mark for the Thunderstorms, whose family tree boasted chefs and brewers in many dwarven communities around Faerûn. And now, with the winter weighing heavily on the besieged citadel, King Harnoth leaned on Nigel even more, affording him the responsibilities of rationing. Any mistakes Nigel made would cost dwarves their lives, given the state of the pantries.

He directed his fellows around the larder, choosing ingredients to pad the meager portions. "Lots o' spice," he kept muttering, for a strong taste could help mitigate the lack of volume.

The band had just begun to load their sacks when the first dwarf cried out in shock and pain. All eyes went to him, staring at him as he staggered around, then looking past him to a most unwelcomed site: a dark elf holding a hand crossbow.

"To arms! Guards!" The cries went up, and the dwarves didn't wait for reinforcements to arrive through the tunnel, but charged ahead, wielding spoons and ladles and anything else they could find to chase this intruder away.

Nigel Thunderstorm hopped about trying to make sense of it all. A drow in his larders! How? The tunnels were sealed. His thoughts were still spinning when battle was joined, and a dozen more dark elves appeared, stepping from invisibility, firing off their poisoned bolts and drawing swords to meet the dwarven charge.

A lightning bolt brightened the cavern, rebounding off several stalag-mite beams. Three dwarves went down beneath it, jolting on the floor in uncontrollable spasms.

The drow were running then, but not really retreating, it seemed to Nigel. More likely, they were staying away from the ferocious dwarves, reloading as they went and launching hand crossbow bolts back at their pursuers.

"Formations!" Nigel screamed. The notion came to him that the dark elves were using the dwarves' aggressiveness against them, were splitting them up to catch them in a side battle with favorable odds. "Tighten it up, I say!" Nigel went on, calling out specific names to bring back wayward dwarves too eager in their pursuit.

Drums and horns and growing torchlight from the tunnel brought hope. Aye, the legion had arrived, and the drow would be slaughtered. Still, Nigel couldn't believe they were in here. How had they gotten past the guards, and why in this place?

The sound of sudden and desperate coughing turned him to the right-hand wall of the larder, and there he found some answers. A magical green cloud had come roiling up, sending his dwarves staggering away, many vomiting, some crawling, all gasping.

But Nigel looked past those unfortunate fellows, and to the great bins stacked by the wall, full of grains, and now, full too with some noxious and poisonous cloud.

Across the way came a similar unwelcome sound, and a second cloud appeared around the salted meats and fungi.

"Ah, ye dogs," Nigel muttered, shaking his hairy head in disbelief. There was no fighting to be heard in the larder, then, and Nigel could spot no dark elves—nor could any other dwarves, given the way they were moving about and looking around in confusion.

"Ah, got 'em!" cried a dwarf at the far end of the hall, and two forma-tions went running that way, Nigel in close pursuit. They saw the caller come staggering back, a pair of hand crossbow darts in his chubby face, and with his chest torn open by the slash of a drow blade.

Beyond him, the dwarves saw the retreating dark elves, along a tunnel that had not been there before. A magical tunnel, a passwall spell, and the dwarves could only look on helplessly as the wall reformed, sealing them off from the drow.

Behind them, the coughing and gasping and spitting continued, and the noxious clouds roiled around the largest piles of stores.

The clouds ruined a good portion of Citadel Adbar's food supply.

Drizzt spotted Catti-brie walking along a wide corridor in the upper section of Mithral Hall. He started to call out to her, but paused, noting her dress.

She wore her basic tan breeches, but Drizzt hardly noticed. Her light purple blouse was of the finest material, with colors shifting so that even from this distance, even in this somewhat dim torchlight, the shirt made her beautiful eyes seem all the bluer.

The untucked shirt reached below her waist, to midthigh, but its sleeves barely reached the woman's elbows, and were tied off there, leaving her forearms—and her two distinctive spellscars, one the symbol of Mystra, the other a unicorn's head in homage to Mielikki—clear to see. The curiosity of that gave Drizzt pause, for it was the first time Drizzt had seen the woman publicly baring her forearms and those spellscars.

Something else, though, had him even more off balance, and it took him a long while to put his finger on it.

The shirt, this shirt, he realized—and lost his breath. He hadn't seen this particular garment in a century. It had belonged to the gnome called Jack, or Jaculi, a most wicked little trickster, trained by illithids and in league with Clan Karuck, a band of marauding half-ogres. Drizzt had put an end to Jack the Gnome and had claimed the robes—that very shirt—as properly-gotten loot. Not dirt, not grime, not spilled blood could stain the fabulous, clearly magical garment, nor could the ravages of time affect it, apparently. Catti-brie had been buried in that shirt a century before.

Under stones in the cairn in Mithral Hall, covering the decomposing body . . .

The realization rattled Drizzt to his very heart. She was wearing the shirt she had been buried in.

She had visited her own grave!

He tried to call out to her, but swallowed hard, unable to get the words past the lump in his throat. He started running instead, and caught up to her, his hands trembling as he grasped her shoulders, and his dumbstruck expression revealing all the fears and doubts.

Catti-brie tugged him close, her composure collapsing now that she had found someone to hug.

"You went there," Drizzt whispered to her.

"I had to."

"How did you . . . why did you . . . the stones . . ." Drizzt stammered.

"Athrogate helped me," Catti-brie explained.

"I was here," said Drizzt, pushing her back to arms' length. "Bruenor was here. We would have accompanied . . ."

Catti-brie shook her head solemnly, denying the notion outright. "I could not have borne your own tears mixing with mine," she explained. "Athrogate was unbothered. He did not know the Catti-brie who was, and hardly knows the Catti-brie who is. He found the whole trip to the graveyard perfectly amusing. Worthy of a song, even."

"That was likely the most trying part of the trip," Drizzt said lightheartedly.

But Catti-brie didn't agree, as much as she clearly wanted to. She tried to say no, but no sound came forth, and her eyes welled up, thick with tears.

Drizzt pulled her close for another hug. He couldn't imagine what it must have been like for the woman, to go to her own grave, to see her own rotted corpse, to take the burial shirt from it, even! How could she have summoned the strength to do such a thing? Why had she done such a thing?

This time it was Catti-brie who broke the clench, pulling back from Drizzt, sniffling hard to clear teary mucus, and blowing out a hard breath to steady herself.

"Why?" Drizzt asked.

"To make it real," she replied. "To make it more than an exercise of thought."

"Why the shirt?"

"Because it's mine, a part of Catti-brie, given to her, to me, by my husband. And it is magical and powerful, beyond its ability to remain clean of all dirt and stains."

"What do you know?"

"I studied at the Ivy Mansion. And when I was there, I happened upon some magical texts about such robes as this . . . well, a blouse for me, but a robe to Jack the Gnome. Like the ring you gave to me, it is more than it seems. Most of its powers are subtle, particularly when it is worn by a fledgling wizard, as I was before the advent of the Spellplague. But now I understand."

Drizzt looked at her curiously. "Are you saying you went to the grave to retrieve the shir . . . robe?"

"Partly," she admitted, but unconvincingly. It was clear to Drizzt that her primary goal in opening that cairn was to find a tangible reality to the supernatural experiences that had befallen her.

"It is a tool in our fight, and I'd be a sorry Battlehammer if I shied from something helpful out of weak feelings! Wearing it, I am armored from sword and from spell, particularly from spells. Wearing it, my own spells resound more powerfully—perhaps this blouse, this Robe of the Archmagi, will make my fireball take down the giant right before the giant cuts down my husband. Surely that is a risk that was worth the cost."

"The cost?"

The words made Catti-brie wince. Yes, there had indeed been a cost to the woman for visiting that grave and reclaiming the fabulous garment of Jack the Gnome.

Her lips moved as she tried to elaborate, but Drizzt didn't let her go there again, instead pulling her close for another hug, one that ended the discussion, one that would, hopefully, allow Catti-brie to put the cairn, her grave, behind her now, once and for all.

***

King Emerus Warcrown lost his breath in the icy wind when he went out through the secret door on the western face of the Rauvin Mountains, that thirtieth day of the month of Hammer in the Year of the Iron Dwarf's Vengeance. He bent low and drove into the raging blizzard, and what a storm it was! It had only begun a couple of hours before, but already the blowing snow reached to the dwarf's knees.

He plowed through, leading his army. The snow was not a deterrent to them. The desperate dwarves of Felbarr had been waiting for a storm such as this to cover their exit through the new tunnel they had dug, through the new wide door leading them into the Cold Vale.

The sun had not yet risen, and even when it did, they knew that the darkness would not substantially lighten, but under the weight of this storm and under the magical clouds of the darkened sky, they hoped to escape.

They knew their way, due west, for this exit location had been chosen for that very reason: it would lead them straight to the main orc encampment.

Whispering to hold tight to their formation, for to be separated here was surely to be lost and killed by the fury of the storm, the bulk of Felbarr's garrison, all but that minimal number of dwarves needed to secure the lower tunnels, scarred the new-fallen, and new-falling, snow with their determined march.

Just a short while later, perhaps no more than a hundred yards from the mountain exit—though it was no longer visible to the dwarves—they saw the first lights of campfires.

"Make yer growls come from yer mouths now, boys—enough from the bellies, I say!" King Emerus addressed his charges, moving with determination among the ranks. "Remember them ye got in the halls, too many mouths and not enough food! Ye think on that and stand straighter, me boys—and me girls!" he added playfully as he moved past Fist and Fury, the Fellhammer sisters, who were eager as always for the coming fight.

"Less'll die out here than in the halls if we're sittin' and waitin'," Emerus reminded them. "And better to die in battle than in bed, I say!"

He raised his voice as he finished, and motioned for that to be echoed up and down the formation.

"Now, me boys!" Emerus yelled. "A hunnerd steps to our enemies, and let them know the steel o' Felbarr!"

And off they went, into a full charge, howling back at the howling wind, every step kicking snow that was caught in the raging storm and twisted around them.

In that howl, in that storm, in that darkness, came to the orcs a louder roar and a deeper and more solid darkness, as the Felbarr legions hit the orc camp in full charge, running over sentries huddling low in their furs, sentries barely noting the approach of a dwarf army in this terrible blizzard. Some managed to scream out in warning, most managed only to yelp in surprise, before the dwarven wall plowed them under.

Axes took out tent poles, swords poked through the fabric, heavy boots stomped anything that moved. Orcs and goblins died by the dozen, by the score, by the hundreds, before any organized defense rose up against the boys of Felbarr, and even then, the dwarven momentum was too great, the bloodlust too entrenched.

In the east beyond the Rauvins, the sky brightened with dawn, and King Emerus knew hope when he looked at the blood-soaked ground around him, snow piling on bodies, almost all of them goblinkin.

But very quickly, Emerus's hope turned to dismay, for their great victory, their great slaughter, had barely touched the depth of this encampment, and now in front of them, the goblinkin tightened their ranks, and behind them, the frost giants lifted their boulders.

"Fight on!" Emerus cried, and Ragged Dain and Parson Glaive cried beside him, and all the dwarves of Felbarr roared and doubled their charge.

Only now it was a battle and no longer a slaughter, a pitched battle, where the shield lines disintegrated into a wild brawl in short order.

Caring not at all for their orc allies, the giants flung their huge rocks into the melee with impunity. They couldn't see their specific targets in the wild storm, of course—King Emerus could hardly make out goblin from orc from dwarf, and more than once held his breath as his mighty sword swept ahead, hoping that it was no ally at the end of the blade.

It would be forever after known as the Battle of Midwinter, on a field in the Cold Vale not two miles from the pond where King Bromm of Adbar had fallen, in the midst of the greatest storm of that brutal season. Three thousand goblinkin, mostly orcs, died that day in the piling snow, and a score of giants fell beside them.

But it wasn't enough.

Wise old King Emerus understood it immediately in the first wild volleys of the pitched battle, some halfway through the orc encampment. The wind and the snow, the orcs and the goblins, and those awful giants—who did not shy from any wintry weather—halted the charge and the momentum, and not the power of Emerus's finest, seven of the ten dwarven legions of Citadel Felbarr, nearly three thousand battle-hardened dwarves, could drive them away.

"Press on, me king!" Ragged Dain implored the old dwarf. "We'll take 'em to the land o' the dead!"

"And ourselves," Emerus replied under his breath. Still, despite the clear disaster unfolding here, despite his every instinct telling him that they could not win, King Emerus almost . . . almost . . . rallied his charges and pressed into the thicker wall. Behind them loomed the other dwarves of Felbarr, hungry in their dark holes, trapped above and below. This was their chance, their break. They had to get out, get to the Glimmerwood, perhaps, and find some way to turn either west to Mithral Hall or north to battered Adbar.

But they could not. Like the boys of Mithral Hall a month earlier, the dwarves of Felbarr found nothing in front of them but certain doom.

And nothing behind them but starvation . . . except . . .

Except they were not alone, King Emerus reminded himself. This was not the only chance, the last desperate stand. Mithral Hall remained, and Adbar too, and perhaps from the south would come relief from Everlund and Silverymoon.

His doubts of that had led him here, and still they lingered, but in the face of this utter defeat, he wisely cast aside those doubts.

"Turn 'em home," he told Ragged Dain and Parson Glaive.

"Me king?" Ragged Dain asked in surprise, but Parson Glaive was nodding.

The battle lines rolled back to the east, back to the foothills and the new gate, the second Runegate, that the dwarves of Felbarr had dug, and the clerics of Felbarr had enchanted.

They got back in, staggering, stumbling, most bleeding from many wounds, and the last group to leave the battlefield was the entourage of King Emerus himself, Ragged Dain and Parson Glaive beside him, and with Fist and Fury scoring the last kills of the day, the sisters taking down a pair of orcs that foolishly chased Emerus to the gate.

In rolled the dwarves, rambling along their tunnels, and the orcs and giants saw the open doors in front of them and eagerly pursued.

They did not understand the power of dwarven Runegates.

Barely five running strides in, Emerus and his band only a few steps ahead of them, the first of the magical glyphs exploded, fire and lightning filling the entryway, laying low orc and giant alike.

Stubbornly, another monstrous force pressed on, stepping over the bodies of their fallen kin, and ultimately invoking the last of the magical glyphs, the ones designed to swing shut those heavy stone doors—and as they closed, squashing bodies and pressing back giants with ease, a huge iron locking bar fell into place behind them, sealing the tunnel from the storm—and the storm of monsters—without.

And sealing in twoscore surprised orcs.

King Emerus led the sudden turn, and his sword struck the first blow in the final slaughter of the day.

CHAPTER 5

MADNESS

ADNESS.

He had no notion of the passage of time, no idea where they were, no thought any longer of where they might be going, and hardly a care for any of it!

"I can see nothing," he whispered harshly to his halfling companion—at least he hoped he was whispering to his halfling companion. He couldn't see his own hand if he'd held it up to his face, let alone Regis.

"We've no choice," Regis whispered back, much more quietly. "They are behind us—we cannot turn back. The only way is ahead, through the orc patrol."

"I'm as likely to hit you as one of them," Wulfgar warned.

Regis's sigh was not one of disagreement. He took Wulfgar's hand and put it atop his head—a head that was no longer adorned with the fabulous beret. "Just keep your swings higher than that," the halfling quipped.

But Wulfgar wasn't laughing. They had come to the end of the line, he believed, and, indeed, almost hoped. When they'd ventured out to the east of Mithral Hall, they'd been forced lower, and now into regions where the illuminating lichen was sparse and the darkness near total. Even Regis, possessed of superior lowlight vision, could barely navigate the tunnels. For poor Wulfgar, there was only eternal night.

"No," he decided. "I'll swing every which way. How many did you say? Five?"

"At least. Perhaps six or seven."

"I go alone," Wulfgar said.

"They'll kill you!"

"The way will be clear for you, I promise," said Wulfgar.

"No—" Regis started to argue, but Wulfgar cut him short.

"I'm only slowing you down," the barbarian said. "I can see nothing. How many times have I cracked my thick skull on these unyielding stones already? Better that you go on alone."

"You're talking foolishness," the halfling said with a growl.

"Foolishness would be for both of us to die out of a misplaced sense of valor."

"Friendship, not valor," Regis corrected. "And never misplaced."

Wulfgar thought it over for a few moments, then conceded the point. "Aye, my friend, and I would argue as you do now if our places were reversed. But they are not. You can find your way out of here, particularly with this hat you have so mastered, and with your understanding of our enemies' ways and language. You can escape, but I cannot."

"We don't know that."

"And you have reason to escape," said Wulfgar. "How many times have you told me of beautiful Donnola? Find your way out. Find your way back to her. Tell her of me."

"Of course," said Regis. "I will introduce—"

"Wulfgar is a fine name for a halfling child, I think," the barbarian interrupted.

Despite himself, Regis couldn't help but chuckle at that, but if Wulfgar thought him convinced, the notion was dispelled a moment later.

"We are the Companions of the Hall," Regis insisted. "We fight as one, and die as one, if that is what the fates decide."

"The fates?" Wulfgar said with a laugh. "The fickle fates granted me this second life—it is all borrowed time, and now I repay that debt. Fear not, my friend, for I am not afraid. Surely not! I go where I should already be, where my wife and children reside.

"And," Wulfgar said, putting on the beret Regis had just given to him, "you do not know that they will win. Where is your faith in your friend?"

He gurgled as he finished, as his features and body altered from that of a large human to an ogrillon.

"Lead me as far as you safely can," Wulfgar bade the halfling, and he extended his hand, which Regis took in his own.

They started slowly along the tunnel. There were no side tunnels or forks, but still the going was very slow, Wulfgar's every blind step hesitant. They neared a bend in the corridor, and a smell assaulted them.

The orc patrol was just up ahead, in a wider stretch of corridor.

"*Gareke,*" Regis whispered to his friend.

"What?"

"*Gareke,* the orc word for torch," Regis explained. "Call for it when you come upon them."

"*Gareke?*"

"You'll have a better chance than if you're simply flailing in the darkness," whispered Regis, his voice going very quiet. He dropped Wulfgar's hand then. "Stay low. Perhaps a hundred steps ahead, but there are rocky overhangs."

"I smell them," Wulfgar assured him, and he started off, bending low as Regis had advised, and keeping the head of Aegis-fang out in front of himself.

A few moments later, he heard shuffling, faintly but distinctly, from ahead.

"*Gareke?*" he called to the orcs.

They called back to him, a line of gibberish he couldn't begin to decipher.

"*Gareke,*" he said again, more forcefully, and he kept moving, faster now.

More gibberish assailed him, and something—an arrow, he thought—skipped off the wall beside him.

Wulfgar lowered his voice to ominous, rumbling tones, and demanded, "*Gareke!*"

He heard muttering up ahead, growing louder. He brushed his head on a low overhang and winced, the painful memories of too many such collisions still clear in his thoughts.

He could see nothing, but sensed that he had come through some entrance, like an archway framing a room. It felt airier suddenly, as if he had moved into a wide—and hopefully higher-ceilinged—area. An orc yapped at him from just a couple of strides ahead, and there were others all around him, he sensed, and for a moment, he thought to take up his warhammer and begin his frenzied assault.

But instead, he said once more, "*Gareke!*"

There came some mumbling, and Wulfgar expected a spear to drive into him at any moment. He was relieved indeed when instead he heard the scrape of steel on flint, and a quick shower of sparks briefly illuminated the area—enough for Wulfgar to see the half-dozen orcs before and to either side of him, those nearest with spears leveled for him.

The sparks spit into the darkness again, and Wulfgar clenched his warhammer tighter. His magical disguise wasn't likely very good, and the revealing light of the torch would surely give him away.

But he'd get the first hit.

The torch flared to life.

Wulfgar was wrong—he didn't strike first.

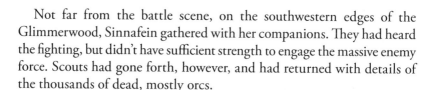

Not far from the battle scene, on the southwestern edges of the Glimmerwood, Sinnafein gathered with her companions. They had heard the fighting, but didn't have sufficient strength to engage the massive enemy force. Scouts had gone forth, however, and had returned with details of the thousands of dead, mostly orcs.

"They tried to break out against great odds," Sinnafein remarked to Myriel when the young elf female had returned from the blasted area around the Runegate.

"Many dwarves among the bodies," Myriel replied solemnly. "It was a costly attempt, my lady."

"A desperate attempt," Sinnafein corrected. "They need to break the siege."

"They are safe in their citadel," replied Myriel. "We have no reports of the orcs even trying to break into Felbarr, or of any massing of forces that could attempt such a thing."

"Aboveground," said Sinnafein. "We do not know what is happening below the surface. All we know is that King Emerus came forth with most of his legions, and against an enemy force that still greatly outnumbered his own. That he would do such a thing in midwinter, indeed in a blizzard . . ."

"The blizzard was tactical cover," another younger elf, Domgarten, put in. "It would seem that Felbarr used the storm as cover to gain surprise on the orcs. And it worked, judging by the destruction at the eastern end of the orc encampment."

"And what would King Emerus have gained if his plan had worked and he had chased the orcs away from this exit?" the Lady of the Moonwood asked.

"He would have broken the siege," answered Myriel.

"Temporarily, only," said Sinnafein. "There are many more orcs, a much larger gathering, at Felbarr's more common gates not far to the south of here, and another sizable force across the Surbrin, besieging Mithral Hall."

The other two elves looked to each other for an answer.

"Perhaps he meant to go to Mithral Hall and enable a greater breakout there," Myriel offered at length.

"In that blizzard?" Sinnafein asked doubtfully. "By the time they reached the river through the piling snow, word of their breakout would have spread to all the orc forces. And the dwarves would then be fighting with fingers blackened by the cold."

"Then why?" asked Myriel.

"For the orcs' food," Domgarten said suddenly, the revelation coming to him. He looked at Sinnafein and nodded as if it was all coming clear to him. "They came out not to break the siege, but to raid the orc encampment. They came out for supplies!"

"They are hungry," Sinnafein agreed. "They are desperate."

"First Mithral Hall and now Felbarr," Myriel lamented. "It would seem as if our dwarf neighbors are no better off than any other kingdoms of Luruar."

"What can we do, Lady?" Domgarten asked.

"The dwarves will try again," Sinnafein replied. "It would seem as if they have no choice in the matter. We cannot help them in their holes, but perhaps we can soften their enemies should they come out again."

She turned to her two trusted scouts. "Go and find as many as you can collect and bring them to me in this place. Perhaps we near the time when we of the Moonwood stop simply surviving and begin taking some actions that will help restore the lands to proper form."

The two nodded, bowed, and ran off, leaving Sinnafein alone. She went quickly to a nearby tree and moved up its branches as gracefully as a squirrel, coming to sit on a limb some thirty feet up from the ground, which afforded her a grand view of the Rauvins—and of the orc encampment between the forest and the mountains.

She considered the plight of her people, and how they were no doubt much better off than their human and dwarf neighbors. The elves of the Moonwood had no real home, unless the whole of the Glimmerwood could count as such. Their mobility was their freedom. The orcs could not catch them in an underground citadel or a walled city. Could not catch them and could not count them, and could never quite be sure of how many might come against any raiding parties they sent into the forest at any given time.

Even if Silverymoon fell, and all three dwarven citadels beside her, Sinnafein's clan would survive. Right in the heart of a new and vast orc kingdom, they could survive.

But it was not a life Sinnafein desired. She had many friends in Silverymoon—indeed, many of her people had close kin in that city, which was heavily flavored by elven traditions and architecture. And even among the dwarves, Sinnafein counted many friends. Mithral Hall had once been very closely allied to the Moonwood—Drizzt Do'Urden, friend to King Bruenor, had fought beside Innovindil and Tarathiel, two leaders of the elf clan and two of Sinnafein's dearest friends. Their heroics, battling the original king Obould, were not forgotten by Sinnafein or her people.

Nor were the efforts of Clan Battlehammer and King Bruenor. Many in the region blamed Bruenor now for signing the treaty that had allowed the Kingdom of Many-Arrows to gain a hold on the land, but Sinnafein was not among that group.

Nay, she remembered that long-ago time, and had not forgotten the pressures that had forced Bruenor's decision, as, apparently, so many of the human kings of the region had done. To her, it all seemed a convenient rewriting of history to assign blame, that Sundabar and Silverymoon and all the others needn't take any of the blame upon themselves.

Sinnafein's clan was guilty of the same, she supposed.

But Sinnafein knew better, and she understood that the kingdoms of Luruar would now stand together, or surely they would all fall. The prospects of living forevermore under the shadow of Dark Arrow Keep did not sit well with the elf.

Not at all.

Wulfgar squinted against the sudden torchlight, and the sting of the flame served as a reminder to him of how long it had been—tendays!—since he'd seen any substantial light.

He was ready to attack, or thought he was, but the light shocked and slowed him. He would not be the first to strike, but he did note, in the first moment of the light, that orcs had moved around him on both flanks. He had to act quickly, or he would find spears thrusting in at him from too many angles to block.

But the orc behind him and to the left gasped and went tumbling back in front of him, slamming into the next in line. And then the orc behind him to the right similarly gurgled, and it too went tumbling.

The other orcs roared in protest and lifted their spears.

Wulfgar, still barely able to see, raised Aegis-fang defensively.

The orcs let fly, but they weren't aiming for him, he realized as the missile flew past him and back the way he had come.

Regis!

He heard his halfling friend cry out, then heard the click of a hand crossbow, and the orc directly in front of Wulfgar shrieked in pain and stumbled backward. The two on the floor struggled against unyielding garrotes. The remaining three howled and started their charge.

Out to the left went Aegis-fang, stabbing like a spear, the mithral head of the warhammer connecting on the side of the orc's face and driving it hard into the wall.

Wulfgar jabbed the weapon's handle out in front of the leading orc on that side, bracing the butt of the weapon against the wall and halting the orc's progress. Wulfgar leaped in against the brute, pressing it into the wall and turning the angle of his warhammer.

He drove out to his left, the hammer's head cracking under the jaw of the last of the orcs, and the brute went flying back.

Around went Wulfgar in a sudden spin, and he let fly the warhammer as he came around, the weapon spinning into that same orc and driving it away. Still turning, Wulfgar fell against the orc he had pinned into the wall.

He felt a sting in his belly, the bite of a knife.

He grabbed the orc by the front of its tunic and spun, hoisting the creature and hurling it across the corridor to slam into the wall.

Wulfgar's hand went reflexively to his belly, and came back covered in blood.

He looked to the two orcs choking on the floor, hideous leering specters over their shoulders, tugging the garrotes. One went still; the other was soon to follow.

He glanced at the first orc he had struck, dazed and down on one knee.

He called Aegis-fang back to his hand and finished the beast with a heavy chop. Turning, he saw the sudden charge of another orc, the beast's spear leveled for Wulfgar's belly.

Off flew Aegis-fang, the hammer exploding into the chest of the orc—the same orc Regis had shot in the face. The stubborn fool came on groggily, with a dart in its cheek, and then flew back into the darkness.

Wulfgar heard Regis whimper behind him, and the sound spurred the barbarian on in rage. He turned and kicked out with all his strength, driving his foot into the throat of the slumping orc he had thrown into the wall. At his call, Aegis-fang returned, but he didn't put it to use again. Instead he turned and rushed to his friend.

Regis was standing, bent over slightly at the waist, so that the butt of the spear that was embedded in his chest was set upon the ground. He said not a word as Wulfgar approached, but gave Wulfgar a look that expressed remorse, as if he was sorry he had failed his friend.

"We have to move," Wulfgar said. The barbarian grabbed the spear shaft gently, but even that slight touch had Regis trembling in pain. Inspecting the wound, Wulfgar knew that he could not extract it; surely he'd take half of Regis's lung with it if he tried.

He set Aegis-fang on the ground and grasped the staff in both hands. "No choice, my friend," he said to Regis. "Brace, I beg."

Regis tensed up and clenched his teeth. The knuckles on Wulfgar's left hand, the hand gripping the shaft right by the entry point, whitened as the mighty Wulfgar locked his grip. The muscles in Wulfgar's neck and along his arms corded then as he began his determined press. His hands were barely five finger breadths apart, giving him little room to bend the shaft, and it seemed impossible that a man could break the thick wood with only that small gap between his hands.

But Wulfgar had made his reputation in both lifetimes on doing things that seemed impossible for a mortal man.

His muscles corded more distinctly. He sucked in his breath.

"Prepare!" he warned his little friend through clenched teeth, and Regis began to make a sound that seemed half whimper and half determined growl.

Wulfgar, too, growled, and sucked in his breath again, and with a sudden jerk, he twisted his right hand down with tremendous force while keeping his bracing left hand level. The spear snapped, Regis swooned, and Wulfgar caught him before he hit the floor. For a moment, he thought the halfling might be dead, so still did Regis lie in his arms.

It wasn't until the halfling snored that Wulfgar was sure he was alive.

"What?" Wulfgar asked quietly as soon as the absurd notion hit him.

At around that same time, another missile soared in from the darkness behind them, not the second but the third missile to strike Regis in that fight, Wulfgar realized when the small hand crossbow dart hit the halfling's shoulder.

Wulfgar staggered backward, rising to his full height. He threw Regis over his left shoulder, grabbed up Aegis-fang in his right hand, and hurled it down the hallway at the dark elves he knew to be there.

He spun around and fled, pausing only to gather up the torch in his free hand as he passed it. He hated the idea of carrying such a beacon, but without it he could not hope to press on. He kept his arm locked around the bouncing Regis, holding him in place, but freed up his hand to transfer the torch so he could recall his warhammer with his right hand. As soon as Aegis-fang appeared, Wulfgar wheeled and sent it spinning off into the darkness behind him yet again, and then again, over and over, scrambling as fast as he could and trying to hold back the drow.

To his relief, the corridor split a short distance later, then spider-webbed into a myriad of side tunnels. Better still, these walls were lined with some quartz or mica or some other shiny mineral, and the torchlight bounced every which way.

There was no method to the barbarian's chosen course. He did not slow long enough to consider one. He just went on, turning at almost every junction, determined to not allow enough of a tunnel behind him for one of those sleeping darts to reach out and take him down.

Regis was just beginning to stir when Wulfgar plodded on softer ground, on some light-colored powdery soil that he did not know.

"Welcome back," he whispered to the halfling, and was about to add the suggestion that Regis stay very quiet when the ground gave out beneath him. Then they were sliding, not tumbling, riding the powdery soil down to a lower level. The torch sparkled off a million reflective surfaces. They were in a vast cavern, columned with stalagmites and stalactites—but only for a moment.

He rolled over as he slid and had to abandon both the torch and Regis or risk rolling right atop the halfling, perhaps driving the spearhead in deeper. He came to a stop against the side of a stalagmite, Regis sliding into him with a groan and the torch disappearing under a sandpile on the floor.

Then there was only blackness, and no sound except the whimpering of Regis beside him. Gradually Wulfgar's eyes adjusted enough for him to make out general shapes. There were illuminating plants in here, though sparse in number.

He couldn't make out Regis on the ground, so he gingerly felt around to gauge the halfling's position before gently lifting him once more. He could see the shadows of the stalagmites and stalactites, though, just barely, and so he went on. They had fallen a long way, but not long enough, not with dark elves on their trail.

Wulfgar plodded through, ankle deep in the soft sand. Gradually his eyes grew more accustomed and gradually the ground firmed up once more, and Wulfgar gained speed and confidence.

He knew he was nearing the edge of the cavern, knew that a tunnel lay ahead, and one with enough illumination for him to continue along, it seemed.

But not enough illumination to reveal to Wulfgar that the lip of the tunnel entrance was about a hands' breadth too low for him to run under it while standing upright.

He felt the hot explosion as his forehead smashed into the stone. He felt his legs running out in front of him, felt himself falling backward. He even heard Regis cry out in surprise and fear.

Somewhere, Wulfgar was conscious of all of that, but he was falling, falling, far, far away.

CHAPTER 6

WHEN HAMMER FALLS

Ye goin' out today?" Bruenor asked Drizzt one morning late in the month of Hammer.

Drizzt shook his head.

"No more," Catti-brie answered from behind him as she walked up to join the two.

"Our enemies have tightened their grip on the tunnels about the lower levels," Drizzt explained. "Unless you know another way for me to get out into the Underdark, we'll not be leaving Mithral Hall anytime soon."

"Might be that we could get out to the surface," Bruenor offered.

"Like last time?" Catti-brie sarcastically answered.

"Nah," said the dwarf. "Just the four of us, yerselfs and me and Athrogate. Out quiet in the night."

"To do what?" Catti-brie asked.

"I've been thinking the same," Drizzt unexpectedly put in, and Catti-brie turned her surprised expression to him. "But alone. Just me. Perhaps I can find ways to sting our enemy and make their wintertime siege even more unpleasant."

"I was thinkin' more that we might get to Felbarr or Adbar," Bruenor explained. "Ain't heared a thing from 'em since we last met in Emerus's hall. No doubt but that they're farin' worse than us 'specially me brothers in Adbar. They been living their winters on trade, so says Connerad, but now there's none to be had."

"Unless they opened the way to Felbarr," Drizzt offered.

"Ye don't believe that, elf."

Drizzt couldn't disagree.

"There's no point in going out," Catti-brie offered. "Not now. The snows are blowing deep. The wind will freeze your bones—"

"The snow will provide cover for me, and you can protect me from the cold," Drizzt replied.

"And the dragon?" the woman answered.

"We canno' just sit here, girl!" Bruenor roared suddenly. "Three dwarven armies stuck in their holes while the cities fall and them orcs tighten their fist about us! We canno' have it, no. I need to know o' me brothers. Connerad needs to know what's what in Felbarr and Adbar. How's he to plan blind?"

"I can get there," Catti-brie said. "To Felbarr at least, where I've been only recently."

The other two looked at her curiously.

"Drow elf ranger can't cross the tunnels, but yerself can?" Bruenor asked doubtfully.

"With spells," Catti-brie explained. "Clairvoyance and clairaudience. I can send my eyes and ears to King Emerus's Court . . . I think."

"Well why didn't ye say so afore now?" Bruenor demanded.

"I'm not very good at such divination magic," the woman admitted. She remembered her days in Lady Avelyere's Coven in the floating Netherese city called Shade Enclave. So many of the sisters there studied the divination spells diligently. They thrived on information. But Catti-brie had little interest in that school of magic. Ever had she preferred invocation, throwing fireballs and shaking the ground with thunderous bolts of lightning.

"Can ye do it or can't ye?"

"I can try, but I'm never certain of what I see."

"If yer eyes're there, ye're seein' what ye're seein'," said Bruenor.

"It doesn't work like that," Catti-brie replied. "Divination magic is . . . interpretive, bits and pieces of information, some true, some inferred, some wrongly perceived. It is an art form, and one I did not learn as I should have."

She looked from Drizzt to Bruenor and nodded. "But I will try."

"Can't be askin' for more, me girl," said Bruenor. He moved over and put his hand on Catti-brie's shoulder, but turned to regard Drizzt with a wink. "And see what ye might see up above while ye're at yer spellcasting. Might be that me and th'elf can find us some fun outside the hall, eh?"

Tears in his eyes, Regis gently piled the last stone on the tomb he had built for Wulfgar. The halfling's shoulder ached and blood still streamed from the wound. He knew that he didn't have much longer before he succumbed, but at the same time, he had no idea what to do.

He had gone back the way they'd come, into the large sandy chamber, and had found no promising outlets—indeed, everything seemed to lead back to where they had been, where the orcs and dark elves had been.

The other way, down this side tunnel where Wulfgar had cracked his skull, the corridor dived, and the air grew thick with moisture. Around a bend and down a chute, Regis had been led by the sound of water, dripping like a heartbeat, occasionally splashing. He hadn't gone farther, figuring that anything lurking in Underdark ponds wasn't something he would wish to engage.

But now he had to go there, he told himself, and he had to do so decisively and straight away. He was running out of time.

He assumed the form of a goblin shaman once more and started off, hugging a wall in the slick corridor. He heard the water again, dripping, the cadence too fast for a normal heartbeat, but too slow for his own at that moment.

Around the next bend, the halfling found himself in more complete darkness, and before his sensitive eyes could fully adjust, he inadvertently dipped his foot in the water.

Running water. It was an underground river, not a pond.

Regis knelt on the bank and spent a long while allowing his vision to acclimate. Gradually he could make out the flowing water—a wide and yawning river. There was some lichen on the opposite bank, revealing a wall that marked the end of this cavern. He dipped his hand in the flow. It was not strong. Slowly, crouching all the way, he made his way to the end of the cavern to the right, where the water exited, and left to where it entered. To move beyond this place in either direction meant going into the river, likely even under the water.

Regis glanced back the way he'd come, back in the direction of Wulfgar.

He couldn't go back, and he couldn't stay here.

He put his hand in the water again. It was chilly, but not too cold.

"By the gods," the halfling whispered. He removed most of his gear and his clothing, tucking all of it into his magical belt pouch's extra-dimensional space.

He pulled his dagger back out almost immediately, but looked at it forlornly. The snake-blades had not yet reformed. Back in went the dagger and out came the rapier, which he tucked under his belt, opposite the pouch.

He was taking too long, the pain in his shoulder reminded him. With a last glance back, Regis steeled himself and went into the water, finding it to be about waist deep. He started downstream, but quickly reversed, thinking that if the current increased, he would not be able to return to this place.

To the left he went, soon coming to the small chamber's wall.

He shuddered. He knew what he had to do.

Half swimming, half crawling in utter blackness, he moved only his right hand forward, keeping his left pinched in tight against the wound. He couldn't see the blood staining the water around him, but he knew it was there, and knew too that marine predators could often smell blood.

It was almost too much for the poor halfling. At one point, he tried to stand up, but found there was no room between the water and the ceiling.

He continued along stubbornly, and still the ceiling pressed in on him, not enough room to stand, not even enough for him to turn around and catch a breath.

Was there even a point to this, he wondered, for surely he had already gone far beyond the distance that anyone without genasi blood could possibly cover?

He was out of options. He was surely doomed.

But then Regis saw a flicker of light up ahead, just a reflection of a reflection, and nothing substantial. It was gone even as he consciously registered it.

Lichen, perhaps?

The halfling drove ahead against the meager current with all the strength he could muster. Then he saw more lights, flickering and dancing as they entered the moving liquid.

He pressed ahead, and now even his deep-diver lungs were beginning to ache for air. The lights were all around him, and he barely resisted the urge to spring up when he realized they were torches.

Slowly he moved upward. Goblins? Orcs? Drow?

He peeked out and his heart lifted. These were not his monstrous enemies but men and women, humans and elves, and even some dwarves— a large encampment.

Regis stood and whimpered, and some nearby men spotted him.

Their eyes went wide, but no wider than the halfling's smile.

Regis's smile disappeared when a wall of spears came flying at him.

Catti-brie splashed her hand in the water, shattering its stillness, her frustration mounting. She had created the scrying pool perfectly, and yet her spells would show her nothing more than her own reflection.

She heard Lady Avelyere's voice in her head, scolding her for her stubborn focus on explosions and battle, when information and knowledge were the key to true success.

With a sigh, the woman walked from the scrying pool, pushed through the curtain, and fell into a comfortable chair in front of the burning hearth.

So many thoughts swirled in her mind. She knew that Drizzt and Bruenor would indeed go out into the blizzards, and yet, she couldn't even glance up there magically to guide them or forewarn them.

She felt helpless. She felt useless.

What had she done wrong? She felt the divination magic still burning within her, and yet she could not see the halls of Citadel Adbar, or peer through the whiteness of winter above, or glance into the throne room of Felbarr, which she knew quite well.

She visualized it again in her mind's eye, remembering her last visit there. She thought of Emerus and Ragged Dain and Parson Glaive.

She stared into the hearth, into the flames. Without even realizing it, she clenched her hand on the powerful ring Drizzt had given her.

A subtle peace washed over her, a feeling that the fire in the hearth, that all fires, were one, reaching back from the Prime Material Plane to the Elemental Plane of Fire. All connected . . .

The image of Felbarr's throne room appeared to her, but distantly, hazily, behind the flames of the hearth.

Catti-brie sucked in her breath and leaned closer, staring and listening. She was there, in the flames of the fire burning in King Emerus's hearth. She could see the old dwarf king and his advisors.

"We're to lose him, I fear," she heard Emerus say.

"He's young and reckless, that one," agreed another—it sounded to Catti-brie like Parson Glaive, but she couldn't really see him and didn't know him well enough to be certain.

"Young and heartbroken for the loss o' his twin, ye mean," said Ragged Dain, sitting beside Emerus.

"And desperate," King Emerus agreed. "Adbar's feeling the hunger more'n ourselves, and all in Felbarr've bellies grumblin'. Can't hold. Not for them and not for us."

"Hammer's just fallen," Ragged Dain lamented with a shake of his head. "And Alturiak's just begun. We've not got the food . . ."

"We'll get out," King Emerus said determinedly, but Catti-brie felt a quiver in the back of his voice, and in that tremor, in that lament, the image of a battle flashed in the diviner's mind, a fight in a blizzard, Felbarr dwarves against a huge force of orcs and giants and in the midst of a terrible storm.

Was it a memory? A premonition?

The confusion threw Catti-brie from the scene, and she could not recreate it. She put aside her anger—wasn't this always the way with divination spells, so full of half-truths and symbols and so divorced from time and space?—and stubbornly held to the remaining bits of magic. She saw a torch, then, and through a torch's flame, along some dwarven halls.

Was it Felbarr still? Adbar? Perhaps even the lower reaches of Mithral Hall?

Dwarves, shivering and gaunt, their expressions sullen, stalked about as the image of the Undercity widened in Catti-brie's vision. It was not Mithral Hall, and it didn't look much like Felbarr, either, for it seemed to be partially, at least, aboveground.

"Adbar," she decided.

She heard the whimpers behind the doors and windows. She felt the anger, the helplessness, the frustration, the hunger.

Most pointedly, the hunger.

The city was starving. She saw piles of dwarf bodies, the old and the young, in the town square.

That pile of corpses turned insubstantial in front of her, disappearing, but the sense of them remained.

She spied a pair of dwarves walking, staggering and bowed, weak with hunger.

Catti-brie fell back in her chair and let her spell fly from her. The magic was dissipating anyway, she told herself, though she knew the truth: she couldn't bear to witness any more of this.

She sat there for a long while—the feeling of time passing was lost to her—digesting all that she had seen, trying to make sense of it, to separate the images in time, memories from premonitions, and both from the present.

She heard the room's door open and felt Drizzt's presence as he entered.

"We have to find a way out," she said before he got to her.

Confusion and fear followed Regis to the bottom of the river. He scrambled about, trying to find some rock or something that would shield him, then turned back for the lower-ceilinged area, the tight tunnel, where their spears could not reach him.

But why had they attacked him? It made no sense.

A spear stabbed into the river bottom immediately in front of him, turning him around in a hurry.

What had he done? Why would they attack a naked halfling?

And then he remembered that he wasn't a halfling at all, not in appearance at least.

He tapped his beret, reverting to his natural form. He began screaming the truth before he resurfaced, though all that came out was an undecipherable grunt and a flood of bubbles. He splashed through the surface, arms waving frantically, screaming wildly, "Wait! Wait!"

A flying club was already on the way, though, and it struck him hard and knocked him nearly senseless as he pitched back under the water. He felt himself drifting, then felt a strong hand grab him roughly by the right arm—and up he went, right out of the water to be hoisted roughly and unceremoniously onto the bank.

He fell down hard, half-conscious after the hit to the head, and he nearly swooned. The jolting had moved that dastardly spearhead, sending waves of agony flowing through his little frame.

"Wait . . . wait," he begged.

He heard stirring all around him, heard voices, though they seemed very distant.

One voice rang out above all, silencing the din, and soon after came a second voice, a chanting refrain.

Regis felt the warmth of magical healing washing over him, inviting him back to the realm of the living. Breathing easier, the waves of pain subsiding, the dizziness straightening, great relief overwhelming him, he managed to open his eyes.

He sucked in his breath again, feeling a sword tip at his throat. His gaze rode up the blade, gleaming silver in the torchlight, so near and ready to murder him, until it settled on the swordsman.

Or swords*woman*, actually, he realized as she came into focus, with her long, dark hair, wide, shining brown eyes, and a frame that exuded strength and health.

"You should explain yourself, halfling," she said to him. "Or goblin."

"Halfling," he squeaked.

"Goblin when he first came up," some other man said.

"Disguise," whispered Regis, and he managed to turn one hand up to point at his blue beret. "Magical hat."

"Prove it," said the swordswoman.

Regis slowly moved his hand up and tapped the beret, and became a goblin once more. The woman gasped—they all did, and more than a few growled. Regis quickly pulled the hat from his head and immediately reverted to his natural halfling form.

"My name is Regis," the halfling said quietly. "A friend of King Bru— King Connerad. And of Drizzt Do'Urden."

"Drow friend!" he heard someone say, and heard too, several people spitting.

"No," Regis blurted. "I fought in Nesmé. Fought against the drow, and the orcs, and . . ."

The woman retracted her sword and helped him to sit up, and still he winced, for though the priest had helped him a bit, he still had a spearhead sticking in his shoulder.

"How did you get here?" she asked.

"We went for Mithral Hall, to bring aid to Nesmé," he explained. "We didn't make it. The way to Mithral Hall is blocked. We tried to get to Citadel Felbarr."

"You are a long way from Citadel Felbarr," said the woman.

"I don't know where I am." Regis admitted.

"Well, if you are who you say you are, then know that you are among friends," the woman said, sliding her sword away.

"None I would have expected to find down here."

"We are all who remain of Sundabar," the woman explained. "I am Knight-Captain Aleina Brightlance of Silverymoon, though I served King Firehelm in the siege of Sundabar and was there when the city fell. We fled through the granaries to the Everfire Caverns, and here we are, settled in the dark ways of the Underdark."

"Sundabar fell," Regis mouthed, nodding. "Yes, we heard that. That's why we tried for Mithral Hall. We knew Nesmé could not hold." He paused and looked at the woman curiously. "But that was months ago."

Aleina nodded grimly.

"My friend has healing spells," she said. "Let him tend to your wound."

Regis started to nod, but stopped suddenly and held up his hand, even grabbed the priest, to stop the spell. "My friend . . ." he explained. "He will need your spell more than I."

"Friend?" the priest said. He turned for the river.

"Through the tunnel, downstream," Regis explained. "I concealed him with stones. I must get back to him." He started to rise, but Aleina put her hand on his shoulder.

"You have a friend back beyond the tunnel?" she asked, and she turned to regard the cleric curiously.

"It is a long swim," he confirmed.

"How did you get through?" she asked Regis. "Upstream, even! What other magic have you about yourself, Regis of Nesmé?"

"None!" he blurted. "Well, not much. I am of Aglarond, a town called Delthuntle on the shores of the Sea of Fallen Stars. I made coin as a deep diver—oysters and pearls. This is not so long a swim for me."

Doubtful expressions loomed all around him.

"How many friends are on the other side?" Aleina asked at length.

"Just one. We must hurry, I beg!"

Aleina looked at the priest, then nodded. "How many?"

The priest turned and called off to some others, then a few moments later, reported, "We have five enchantments we can offer at this time."

"You and me, then," Aleina said and she began stripping off her gear. "One for the halfling . . ."

"What enchantment?" Regis asked.

"To breathe under the water," the priest explained.

"I don't need it, but my friend will."

"It is a long swim," Aleina reminded him.

"One I just made, and I was not moving fast."

"Torvache, then," Aleina said, motioning to a large man nearby, and he too began stripping his gear.

"Perhaps you should not go, Knight-Captain," the priest offered. "It could be a trap."

"If it is, you'll be glad to have me beside you," the woman answered. Now wearing only a slight undergarment, she belted on her sword once more.

A short while later, the group entered the river, tied together with a long tether. The priest held a small dagger he had enchanted with magical light. With the current behind them, they were back in the small cavern in a short time, and Regis led the way onto the bank, rushing up the tunnel. The others, with swords and mace in hand, were close behind.

As they neared the tomb Regis had constructed to protect Wulfgar, the halfling's hopes sank. It had been opened, stones tossed aside . . .

"Wulfgar," he breathed, then started to call, but Aleina clapped him on the shoulder and motioned him to silence.

"He was here!" Regis insisted.

"He still is," came a voice from up ahead, and Wulfgar came into the tunnel, mighty Aegis-fang in hand. He came into the light, and Regis grimaced at the sight. The tall man was filthy and covered in dried blood, his wolfskin cloak matted and torn. New blood showed on his forehead where he had cracked it on the stone lintel.

"Unsettling it is to awaken in a grave," he said to his friend. He wasn't looking at Regis, though, but at the others, particularly at the woman.

"I didn't want them to find you," Regis replied.

"Them?" Wulfgar asked, staring still at the woman.

"The drow and the orcs," Regis said, and he turned to Aleina. "Not *them*."

He tried to meet Wulfgar's gaze once more and explained, "Refugees from Sundabar . . ." His voice trailed off as he realized Wulfgar wasn't really paying attention, and was looking past him to Aleina. The halfling considered her as well, and understood his friend's interest. The shapely woman's minimal clothing clung to her every curve. Her brown hair was matted, of course, but that only made the woman's round brown eyes seem all the larger.

Despite her trials in the Underdark these months from Sundabar, Aleina Brightlance exuded health and solidity.

"There will be time for this later. Let us be gone from this place," the woman said, clearly noticing Wulfgar's gaze. She had met it with her own. She motioned to the priest, who moved to Wulfgar and began to cast a spell.

"Water breathing," Regis explained. "You'll need it."

CHAPTER 7

MOVING TARGETS

MORE THAN TWO HUNDRED WERE HERE, COME TO THE CALL OF Sinnafein, and the elf lady looked around the clearing in the center of the Glimmerwood with satisfaction and pride.

When war had come, bringing the hordes roaming the borders of the forest, the elves had abandoned their villages for a defensive posture they had perfected centuries before. They called it *hallaval planeta*, or "wandering warrior," a nomadic lifestyle seeking safety in constant movement about this land they knew so well. They had spent the better part of the year, certainly since Bromm's fall, and even before that to a great extent, operating in small bands, often secluded from others of their race. The borders of the Glimmerwood were littered with the rotting corpses of orcs shot down by elf patrol bands, but in the course of these many months, only a few elves had been wounded, and not one had been killed in battle.

The orcs couldn't kill what they couldn't catch.

And now the orcs weren't pressing in on the Glimmerwood—not even the frost giants ventured too far into the elf-haunted forest. Of all the kingdoms of Luruar, this one, the clan of Moonwood elves, had fared best, even more so than Everlund, whose walls had not yet trembled under the weight of giant-hurled boulders. The elves did not need the trade with any of the cities. The Glimmerwood gave them all they required, and more.

"It is good to see you, my lady Sinnafein," said a tall warrior named Vyncint. "Our lives these days, in small groups . . . we do not know how others fare." He shook his head. "That is the pain of the wandering warrior. You must trust in your friends, though they are lost to you in dangerous times."

"By all accounts, all of the groups have fared well," Sinnafein replied, and Vyncint nodded.

"And now you would end this," he said. "Why?"

"Why indeed?" asked another, a deadly archer named Allafel, brother of Tarathiel who had been killed by the original King Obould a century before. "What do you know?"

"That all of the kingdoms about us are in dire need," she answered. "That Sundabar has fallen, Nesmé, too, and Silverymoon is sorely pressed." She moved out more to the center of the field and its gathering, as she spoke loud enough for all to hear. "I know that the dwarves are caught in their holes, all three citadels, and they grow desperate with hunger. They have tried to break out from Mithral Hall and Felbarr, but were chased back into the holes in short order."

She paused as she came up to grim-faced Allafel. "They came forth from the safety of their fortified citadels against great odds. Indeed, unbeatable odds."

"That speaks to their desperation," Allafel admitted.

"No less is true of Citadel Adbar," Vyncint added. "My fellows and I have haunted that region to the northeast. Many battles have been fought; the dwarves are relentless in their attempts to break the orc siege."

"Relentless and unsuccessful," another elf added.

"You have called us together that we can aid the dwarves," Allafel reasoned, and there was a measure of accusation in his tone, though it was not without sympathy, Sinnafein noted hopefully.

"If we do not, then all that we have known about us as neighbors and allies will likely perish," Sinnafein replied. "Only the orcs will remain."

"Not all of the dwarves have been the best of neighbors, Lady," Allafel reminded, and Sinnafein recalled immediately the incident to which the brother of Tarathiel likely referred, a most unpleasant argument with the dwarves of Adbar who had "come like orcs to fell the trees of the northeastern forest," so the reports had claimed. The dwarves, under duress due to a great demand for weapons from Sundabar, had run short of fuel for their forges, and so they had crept down to the Glimmerwood in the hopes of taking a few wagonloads of lumber.

Allafel and some friends had met them, and had turned them away, but the encounter had not been without some minor bloodshed on both sides.

"Better even at that troubled time than the orcs, surely," Vyncint said before Sinnafein could, and to Sinnafein's relief, Allafel conceded the point with a nod.

"What do you propose, Lady?" another elf called from behind.

"The minions of Many-Arrows are grouped in vast encampments," another reminded her. "We would have to cut the trees of half the Glimmerwood to fashion enough arrows to truly thin their ranks."

"As soon as we sting them hard, they will come against us, of course," Vyncint said.

"With fire," Allafel added.

"Do you believe they will not do exactly that in any case?" asked another, and Sinnafein smiled when she saw Myriel walking up to stand in front of Allafel. "When they are done with the cities in the south, when the dwarves are dead in their holes . . . when Adbar falls and they mean to power her forges. Do you think they will take only a few wagons of our trees then, Master Allafel? They will raze the land without regard, to feed their fiery frenzy."

"It is time to suspend *hallaval planeta*, I believe," Sinnafein said. "It is time to concentrate and coordinate our warriors, to strike hard at the orcs in the hopes that at least one of the dwarven citadels can break the siege, and they, in turn, can join with us to bolster their kin."

"Our numbers are few, our enemies vast," Vyncint reminded. "What can we do?"

Sinnafein had no logical response to the reality of Vyncint's words. He was being honest, and not trying to play a negative role or to challenge her authority, minimal as it was.

She tried to sort her options, to find some way the elves might prove effective, though the smallest of the orc encampments she had seen outnumbered the whole of the Glimmerwood's elven force a hundred to one. A long and uncomfortable silence passed.

"What can we do, Lady?" Allafel prompted.

"We can try," was all that Sinnafein could offer in persuasion to her kin.

To her surprise, though, that was enough.

VENGEANCE OF THE IRON DWARF

"They are cutting," came word a few days later. A band of orcs had come to the forest's edge to take lumber for their campfires. Likely that was happening all the time now, away from this southeastern stretch. By concentrating their forces, the elves had surely left vast swaths of the Glimmerwood open to orc lumbering intrusions.

But now, finally, the monsters had come to the forest within reach.

Off went hundreds of elves, silent as shadows, invisible in their forest domain even in winter with most of the trees bare of leaves. Practiced and coordinated, they broke into smaller bands, and each of those took up positions to form a semicircle around the orcs.

Perhaps threescore of the ugly brutes were at work with their axes, supported by a quartet of frost giants, milling around just beyond the forest's edge, piles of rocks beside them at the ready.

A bird whistled, but it wasn't a bird.

Answers came back, two, three, four, as the elves took up their positions.

Several of the orcs even looked up curiously, perhaps not quite as stupid as the elves believed.

It hardly mattered, though, for with those few whistles, the elven bands had identified their target, and on a five-whistle quick count more than two hundred arrows went off, a near-equal number aiming for each of the frost giants. The behemoths staggered and stumbled under the weight of the blows, with nearly every shot on target, more than fifty elven arrows entering each giant's flesh almost instantly in a great moment of trauma and explosive agony.

And by the time those arrows struck, each of the skilled elves had already set another arrow to a bowstring, and the rain of death began upon the orcs, sweeping outward from close to back.

How they scrambled!

A few took up axes and charged the forest, and fell only a few steps later, riddled with arrows. Most retreated, diving from stump to tree to stump, breaking clear and running, missiles chasing them every step. Farther out, two of the giants still stood, one merely trembling, using every bit of his strength just to avoid tumbling down in darkness, the other stubbornly trying to lift a rock.

Five short whistles later, a stinging swarm of arrows reached out again, and the giants were of concern no longer.

Now the elves focused once more on the fleeing orcs, and one after another, they, too, went tumbling down.

In mere heartbeats, four giants and fifty orcs lay dead or dying around the Glimmerwood's edge, with just a handful running for the orc encampment. A few others might still be about, hiding, but the orders had been explicit, and they were not to draw swords and go out to finish off any of the wounded or those hiding.

And indeed, those orders proved prudent moments later when the orc encampment began to swirl toward the forest like a great black cloud of locusts.

So came the call to scatter, and the elves did, in coordinated fashion, running off into the forest in predetermined groups of five.

The orc wave rolled into the Glimmerwood without resistance.

Many trees went down under orc hatchets then, the frustrated creatures taking out their anger on the living targets that could not flee.

For not an elf did they find.

Some groups of orcs foolishly probed deeper in pursuit, and each in turn was sent running, half of them dying, the others stumbling out to rejoin the main orc force.

"They will be better prepared when next they come to collect their timber," Allafel said to Sinnafein and the rest when at last the orcs broke off and returned to their camps.

"We killed more than threescore, and a handful of giants besides," Vyncint reminded, a measure of satisfaction in his voice.

"They lose that number each day to attrition, and yet their ranks continue to grow," Allafel replied.

"It felt good," Vyncint countered, drawing a smile from Allafel, who certainly would not disagree.

"They will be more prepared, and no doubt the word of our ambush will spread to the orc encampments all around our home," Sinnafein agreed. "To the beasts in the northeast besieging Adbar, and to those camped across the river holding tight about Mithral Hall."

"So what, really, can we do against them?" Allafel asked.

"Truly, Lady," Myriel added.

Sinnafein looked at her young protégé and saw the pain that Myriel had felt in even asking the despairing question, but Sinnafein knew, too, that the question was an honest one.

"Will sixty dead orcs and a few dead giants make a difference if King Emerus tries again to break out from Citadel Felbarr?" Sinnafein asked them all.

"I don't know, but likely not," she admitted before any of the others could answer. "Likely not," she reiterated glumly. "We will find more opportunities to strike at the beasts."

"But we'll not likely prove this effective again," Allafel interrupted.

Sinnafein nodded, conceding the point. "We will find patrols, and we will slaughter them," she told her people. "We will find orc scouts too far out from their allies, and we will kill them. Perhaps this vast horde will be thinned by another two hundred when King Emerus comes forth again. Perhaps only by one hundred. But that is one hundred fewer spears the dwarves will face."

"But will it make any difference?" Vyncint asked.

Sinnafein looked at him, trying to keep a measure of optimism in her expression and her voice. They had just won a great and sudden victory, at least, yet here they were, their mood as dark as the sunless sky above them. "I do not know, and likely not," she admitted again.

"But we must try," said Allafel, nodding at her, and she appreciated his support.

"Though there is nothing more," Sinnafein admitted. "What can we do to truly wound our ugly enemies?"

It was a rhetorical question, of course. They had discussed this at length, but to Sinnafein's surprise, to Allafel's surprise, to the surprise of all the elves, there came an answer, and one from a source more surprising still.

"Aye, and now there's where we might be helpin' ye," said a female dwarf carrying a massive mace over one shoulder. Beside her came a man in simple, loose-fitting brown robes—the garb of a monk, it seemed.

A hundred bows went up and turned upon the intruders, elves whispering excitedly and confusedly as to how these two might possibly have gotten through their sentries unseen.

"Who are you?" demanded Allafel, sword in hand, and those around him, too, had weapons drawn.

"Me name's Amber," said the dwarf. "Amber Gristle O'Maul o' the Adbar O'Mauls. This one's me friend Afafrenfere—if ye canno' say it proper, just sneeze, and he'll answer to that! Ha!"

Other elves—the sentries—came rushing in behind the pair, bows in hand and confused expressions clear to see. They, too, had no idea of how these two might have slipped through the perimeter. They, like the others, did not understand the power of the magical enchantment that had been put on this unlikely pair of companions, or the even more unlikely pair that had put those enchantments in place.

"Now to yer question o' what ye might be doin'," the dwarf went on. "We got a couple more friends near-about that might be offerin' ye a bit o' advice and more than a bit o' aid on that matter," she said, ending with a wide and confident smile and an exaggerated wink.

PART TWO

THE GOD INSIDE YOUR HEART

"I AM NOT A COURAGEOUS GOBLIN. I PREFER TO LIVE, THOUGH OFTENTIMES I wonder what my life is truly worth."

Those words haunt me.

In light of the revelations Catti-brie has offered of my goddess, Mielikki, that all of goblinkin are irredeemably evil and should be rightfully put to the sword, those words haunt me.

For they were spoken to me by a goblin named Nojheim, a fellow of intelligence and wit, surprisingly so to me who had never so deeply and honestly conversed with a goblin before. He claimed cowardice because he would not stand up to the humans who had captured him, beaten him, and enslaved him. He questioned the worth of his life because he was truly that, a slave.

They came for Nojheim, and they caught him, and it is forever my shame that I was not able to help him, for when I next saw him, he had been hanged by the neck by his tormentors. Reeling from the scene, I stumbled back to my bed, and that very night I wrote, "There are events that are forever frozen in one's memory, feelings that exude a more complete aura, a memory so vivid and so lasting. I remember the wind at that horrible moment. The day, thick with low clouds, was unseasonably warm, but the wind, on those occasions it had to gust, carried a chilling bite, coming down from the high mountains and carrying the sting of deep snow with it. That wind was behind me, my long white hair blowing around the side of my face, my cloak pressing tightly against my back as I sat on my mount and stared helplessly at the high cross-pole.

The gusty breeze kept Nojheim's stiff and bloated body turning slightly, the bolt holding the hemp rope creaking in mournful, helpless protest.

"I will see him forever."

And so I do see him still, and whenever I manage to put that terrible memory out of thought, I am reminded of it.

Never more poignantly than now, with war brewing, with Bruenor deriding the Treaty of Garumn's Gorge as his worst error, with Catti-brie, my beloved Catti-brie, insisting that on Mielikki's word, on the sermon of the goddess we both hold dear, those humans in that long ago day, in that long-deserted village along the Surbrin whose name I cannot remember were justified in their actions.

I cannot reconcile it. I simply cannot.

The implications of Catti-brie's claim overwhelm me and loosen the sand beneath my feet, until I am sinking into despair. For when I kill, even in battle, even in righteous defense, I feel that a part of my soul departs with the vanquished foe. I feel as if I am a bit less goodly. I mend my soul by reminding myself of the necessity of my actions, of course, and so I am not locked in the dark wings of guilt in any way.

But what if I carry Mielikki's claims to their logical conclusions? What if I force my way into an orc or goblin settlement that has shown no aggression, no intent to wage war or commit any other crimes? What if I find that nursery as Catti-brie mocked in her dwarven brogue, with the old dwarven cry of "Where's the babies' room?"

Surely then, by the sermon of Mielikki, I am to slaughter the goblin children, infants even. And slaughter the elderly and infirm even if they have committed no crimes or no acts of aggression.

No.

I will not.

Such an act rings in my heart and soul as unjust and cruel. Such an act erases the line between good and evil. Such an act would stain my own conscience, whatever Mielikki's claims!

And that, I believe, is the ultimate downfall of reasoning beings. What pain to the murderer, to the heart and soul of the one who would kill the elderly and infirm orc, or the goblin child? What stain, forevermore, to steal the confidence, the righteousness, the belief in oneself that is so critical for the sensibilities of the warrior?

If I must wage terrible battle, then so be it. If I must kill, then so be it. If I must.

Only if I must!

My clear conscience protects me from a pit too dark to contemplate, and that is a place I hope Bruenor and Catti-brie never enter.

But what does this mean in my servitude to Mielikki, to the concept of a goddess I believed at peace with that which was in my own heart? What does this mean for the unicorn—her steed—that I call from the whistle about my neck? What does this mean for the very return of my friends, the Companions of the Hall? They are beside me once more, we all agree, by the blessing of, and at the suffrage of, Mielikki.

Catti-brie claims the voice of Mielikki with regards to the goblinkin; she is a priestess of Mielikki, with magical powers granted her by the goddess. How could she not speak truly on this matter?

Aye, Catti-brie relayed the truth of what the goddess told her.

That notion pains me most of all. I feel betrayed. I feel discordant, my voice shrill and out of tune with the song of the goddess.

Yet if my heart is not true to the word of Mielikki . . .

Fie these gods! What beings are these who would play so cruelly with the sensibilities of rational, conscientious mortals?

I have racked my brain and scoured my memories for evidence that I am wrong. I have tried to convince myself that the goblin named Nojheim was actually just manipulating me to try to save its skin.

Nojheim was no poor victim of the humans, but a vile and conniving murderer kept alive by their mercy alone.

So it must be.

And so I cannot believe. I simply cannot. I was not, I am not, wrong in my initial understanding about Nojheim. Nor was I wrong about Jessa, a half-orc, a friend, a companion, who traveled for years beside me, Thibbledorf Pwent, and Bruenor Battlehammer himself.

But I must believe that I was wrong, or must accept that Mielikki is. And how can that be?

How can the goddess I hold as the epitome of goodliness be wrong? How can Mielikki's song chip the veneer of truth I hold in my heart?

Are these gods, then, fallible beings looking over us as if we were no more than pieces on a sava board? Am I a pawn?

Then my reason, my conscience, my independent thought and moral judgment must be cast aside, subjugated to the will of a superior being . . .

But no, I cannot do this. Surely not in matters of simple right and wrong. Whatever Mielikki might tell me, I cannot excuse the actions of that slaver Rico and the others who tormented, tortured, and ultimately murdered Nojheim. Whatever Mielikki might tell me, it must hold in accordance with that which I know to be true and right.

It must! This is not arrogance, but the cry that an internal moral compass, the conscience of a reasoning being, cannot be disregarded by edict. I call not for anarchy, I offer nothing in the way of sophistry, but I insist that there must be universal truths about right and wrong.

And one of those truths has to be that the content of character must outweigh the trappings of a mortal coil.

I feel lost. In this, the Winter of the Iron Dwarf, I feel sick and adrift.

As I ask of the dwarves, the humans, indeed even the elves, that they view my actions and not the reputation of my heritage, so I must afford the same courtesy, the same politesse, the same decent deference, to all reasoning beings.

My hands shake now as I read my writings of a century before, for then, with my heart full of Mielikki's grace, so I believed, I revealed little doubt.

"Sunset," I wrote, and I see that descending fiery orb as clearly now as on that fateful day a century and more removed. "Another day surrenders to the night as I perch here on the side of a mountain, not so far from Mithral Hall.

"The mystery of the night has begun, but does Nojheim know now the truth of a greater mystery? I often wonder of those who have gone before me, who have discovered what I cannot until the time of my own death. Is Nojheim better off now than he was as Rico's slave?

"If the afterlife is one of justice, then surely he is.

"I must believe this to be true, yet still it wounds me to know that I inadvertently played a role in the unusual goblin's death, both in capturing him and in going to him later, going to him with hopes that he could not afford to hold. I cannot forget that I walked away from Nojheim, however well-intentioned I might have been. I rode for Silverymoon and left him vulnerable, left him in wrongful pain.

"And so I learn from my mistake.

"Forever after, I will not ignore such injustice. If ever I chance upon one of Nojheim's spirit and Nojheim's peril again, then let his wicked master be wary. Let the lawful powers of the region review my actions and exonerate me if that is what they perceive to be the correct course. If not . . .

"It does not matter. I will follow my heart."

Three lines stand clear to me now in light of the revelations offered by Catti-brie.

"If the afterlife is one of justice, then surely he is," so I told myself, so I believed, and so I must believe. Yet if the afterlife is the domain of Mielikki, then surely Nojheim cannot have found a better place.

"Forever after, I will not ignore such injustice," I vowed, and so I mean to hold true to that vow, for I believe in the content of the sentiment.

Yes, Bruenor, my dear friend. Yes, Catti-brie, my love and my life. Yes, Mielikki, to whom I ascribed the tenets that make me whole.

"It does not matter. I will follow my heart."

—Drizzt Do'Urden

CHAPTER 8

INFLUENTIAL FRIENDS

YOU KNOW THIS INFORMANT WELL ENOUGH, THEN?" SINNAFEIN ASKED her elf companion as they carefully concealed their small sled under an overhang in the riverbank. The river was frozen over, but one could never take such things for granted, and so the pair had half walked, half ridden the sled to the western bank.

"For many years, decades even," answered the other, a beautiful and lithe elf maiden with blue eyes that seemed to glow in the dark of night, so intense was their inner sparkle. Her thick, reddish-blonde hair was tucked under a furred hood that framed her delicate face. Without the hood, her hair would hang to her lower back.

"A drow?"

"A friend, I said," the elf maiden replied. "One who understands the ways of the Underdark."

"But if a drow . . ."

"You press me, Lady. I told you that I have eyes upon our enemies. That is all you need to know."

"So your informant is not connected with this invasion, you assure me?"

"I would do no such thing," answered the other. "He is connected with everything, in one way or another. That is his way. And since these drow that have accompanied the minions of Many-Arrows are from Menzoberranzan, my friend surely has spies among them."

"Perhaps even helping them," Sinnafein said bluntly, and she stopped in her work, letting the other hold the boat, and put her hands on hips.

"You waited until we were out here to make your accusation, Lady Sinnafein? That does not seem so wise to me."

"There are a dozen bows trained on you as we speak," Sinnafein warned.

"Seventeen, by my last count," the other answered, casually going about tying off the sled so that the howling wind did not send it skidding away across the ice. "But still, why come all the way out here when you could have gotten these inquiries out of the way back in your encampment when the dwarf Ambergris first introduced us?"

Sinnafein stared at her hard, but did not otherwise answer.

"Good lady, we would have needed no convoluted plan to catch you, were we working with the drow and the orcs," the light-haired elf said. "We found your clan easily enough, and walked into your encampment without notice. We could have brought an army of drow and orcs and giants beside us, were we working with your enemies, were my informant at all loyal to the matron mothers of the city of Menzoberranzan."

"And to whom is he loyal?"

"To himself, first, foremost, and always," came the answer, accompanied by a laugh. "And to some ranger named Drizzt Do'Urden for some reason I cannot fathom. Whatever his ultimate goal, which is no doubt convoluted and will surely involve him finding some way to turn this war into personal gain, I promise you that this mission of ours is as it seems."

"You promise me," Sinnafein replied. "You? One I do not even know. From a clan I do not know. With a name, Mickey, that I have never heard."

"A nickname," Mickey replied.

"And your real name?"

The other laughed and shrugged. "I go by Mickey."

"You are hardly inspiring confidence," Sinnafein said.

"Because I am weary of the game. Have your archers let fly if that is your wish, though we both know that you'll do no such thing. Turn back now and skate back across the Surbrin again, though we both know that you'll do no such thing. Your options are limited—indeed, they are none. You wish to help the dwarves, but you cannot. You wish to repel the orcs, but you cannot. So sit back in your forest and wait for grim tidings as the cities fall and the citadels become armories for the minions of Many-Arrows. They will take your trees one by one until there are no more trees to take, and no more places for you and your people to hide.

"But then, you know all of this, Lady of the Glimmerwood," Mickey went on. "My old friend led me and my sister, along with that silly dwarf and her monk companion, to you to be of help, and this help we have offered openly and honestly. Take it or do not, but please, bore me no longer with your suspicions and fears."

Sinnafein's expression did little to hide the fact that she was taken off-guard by the straightforwardness of Mickey's response.

"Do you even understand the level of trust we have shown to you by simply revealing ourselves to you?" Mickey asked quietly.

Sinnafein looked at her carefully. The dwarf and monk had come to them first, and had then introduced a select few to the three curious elves, these two sisters and another, who had appeared at first as if he could have been of Sinnafein's own clan, though Sinnafein suspected a disguising magic about him since he would not approach and spoke to them only from the shadows. Later, alone, this old friend of Mickey's, whom Sinnafein suspected to be a drow, had revealed some startling details to Sinnafein. He knew of her, and had known her husband once upon a time. And he had hinted, too, that Tos'un had returned to Menzoberranzan, though he had said nothing directly and had promised Sinnafein that they would discuss the matter further once plans for the elves' entry to the war had been set in place.

"I am going on to Mithral Hall, as we discussed," Mickey declared, and she stepped away from the river toward the southwest, where Fourthpeak towered. "If you do not trust me, then the sled is yours. If you fear that one of your personal rank and title should not be a part of such a dangerous journey, then pray tell one of your archers to replace you on the journey. I care not either way."

Sinnafein stepped right in front of her and looked long and hard into Mickey's eyes, trying to read this strange elf.

Mickey's responding smile proved truly disarming. If Sinnafein had been anything other than an elf, surely the charm would have fully ensnared her. Still, even without that magical enhancement, the lack of any real choice reverberated within Sinnafein, compounded by her continuing guilt.

She and her husband, Tos'un, had started this war, after all. Tos'un had betrayed Sinnafein, wounding her legs and leaving her helpless to die at the blades of the pursuing orcs. But leading that hunting orc band was Lorgru, son of Obould. Lorgru's unexpected mercy in returning Sinnafein to her people had given rise and momentum to the hateful words of this terrible warlord, Hartusk.

With that truth hanging above her, Sinnafein found that she could not refuse this opportunity.

She motioned to the distant archers to stand down and started off with Mickey to the southwest.

They passed many signs of orcs, and saw great encampments on distant ridges. Sinnafein shook her head repeatedly.

"We cannot get there," she told Mickey as the wind began to pick up around them.

Mickey laughed at her. "They are only orcs," she replied.

Her carefree attitude struck the elf curiously, as did Mickey's unwillingness to move from shadow to shadow. She was walking to the north door of Mithral Hall, a straight-line course with nothing but the blowing snow to obscure her, and it seemed to Sinnafein as if her companion would not have veered even if their path took them through the heart of a vast enemy encampment.

Somehow no enemies spotted them or walked up in front of them in the blowing snow, and the pair came to a ridgeline, looking down at a small dell, framed on the north by a rising wall of stone, and on the south by the foothills of Fourthpeak. Also to the south stood some worked columns, and Sinnafein knew them to mark the entry corridor to Mithral Hall's northern door. A grouping of tents sat in front of those columns, half-buried in the drifting snow.

Mickey did pause then, and crouched, staring off toward the camp. Several huddled forms milled about, including one considerably larger than any orc.

"We will move down straight for the nearest column," Mickey explained. "Once we get there, if the way beyond is clear, you run for the doors. Do not wait for me. They'll not let you in, but when I join in, I have a spell that will walk us through."

"We'll be seen before we reach that column," Sinnafein said, and Mickey nodded.

"There are likely dozens of orcs in that encampment," Sinnafein warned, and Mickey nodded.

"And giants, perhaps?"

"Likely," said Mickey.

Sinnafein drew out her sword, but Mickey shook her head. "When we reach the column, you go to the doors."

"I am not some unskilled and coddled noblewoman," Sinnafein protested.

"I never said you were. When we reach the column, you go to the doors."

"Leaving you alone to face the swarm of enemies?"

Mickey started walking off toward the column, and a frustrated Sinnafein shook her head and sighed. It occurred to her then that the strange elf didn't even have a weapon about her, with no sword belt over her furred coat, and none under it as far as Sinnafein could recall.

The Lady of the Glimmerwood sighed again and rushed out, hurrying to catch up with Mickey, who was walking easily, straight for the column, a course that would take her near to the tents. And she was making no effort at all to conceal herself.

Sinnafein drew her sword as she came up beside Mickey.

"Oh, put that silly thing away," the other elf told her.

They neared the column. They heard the whoop of an orc sentry behind them.

"To the doors with you, and quickly," Mickey said, and she grabbed Sinnafein by the arm and with supernatural strength sent the Lady of the Glimmerwood stumbling and skidding toward the doors. "And pray do knock!"

By the time she collected herself and halted the momentum, Sinnafein was nearer the door than the column. She looked back at the clicking and clapping sound and noted some spears flying out of the haze of the blowing snow. She winced and fell back, for just by the missiles that had flown past Mickey's position, Sinnafein realized that the elf had been beset by a barrage of deadly rain indeed.

She wanted to call out, but she stumbled to the great stone doors instead. She drew out her own weapon, but only to use the metal pommel to pound on the doors—and how meager did the sound seem against the unrelenting howl of the winter wind.

Behind her, Sinnafein heard a scream, then another, then a cacophony, a communal howling of, apparently, agony and terror. She noted some tumult but couldn't make it out, and the screaming continued.

And Sinnafein continued pounding on the door, and now she, too, was screaming, calling for the dwarves to let her in.

She kept looking back, though, and she started and nearly jumped from the ground when a distinct form came into sight, that of Mickey casually walking toward her.

And a larger form—indeed, a gigantic humanoid form—rushed up behind Mickey.

"Giant!" Sinnafein cried, and started for the behemoth, and winced and screamed when she saw the frost giant's huge hammer come swinging down for the top of Mickey's head.

Up shot Mickey's hand to intercept the hammer, and Sinnafein winced. The giant put all of its tremendous weight behind the blow, slamming the weapon down as if trying to drive the elf maiden into the ground like a tent stake. Sinnafein sucked in her breath, certain she was about to see Mickey crushed in front of her.

But the hammer stopped, caught by the lithe elf's hand and held right there, hovering inches above her head. Faster than Sinnafein could follow, Mickey pivoted and rushed forward to snap off punches, one, two, straight into the giant's knees. Each blow sounded like a huge tree limb breaking, and Sinnafein gasped again when one kneecap shattered and the other leg bent backward under the tremendous weight of the blow.

The frost giant pitched forward, tumbling onto Mickey, burying her where she resolutely stood.

But no, like the hammer in front of the behemoth, Mickey caught the brute, and Sinnafein could only stare wide-eyed and slack-jawed as this elf named Mickey, who was not even Sinnafein's size, twirled the behemoth above her head and launched it back the way it had come, spinning through the air to crash into one of the columns at the entryway.

Still holding the giant's huge warhammer, Mickey approached. "Have they not answered your call?" she asked.

Sinnafein just stared at her, and backed off a step.

"No matter," Mickey assured her, and began to cast a spell. A moment later, with a swirl of commotion beginning again behind them as the larger encampment of orcs and giants learned of the battle, Mickey opened a dimensional door and bade Sinnafein to lead the way in.

"Don't ask," Mickey added when Sinnafein just stood there gaping at her. She took Sinnafein by the shoulder and guided her into the dwarven complex. When the pair stepped through, they were assaulted again, this time by surprised dwarven sentries.

Fortunately, those bearded warriors recognized the two as elves and not orcs before any serious blows could fall.

"Pray tell your King Connerad that emissaries of the Glimmerwood have come to help you escape your"—Mickey paused and sniffed—"smelly hole, good dwarves."

Noting the wide-eyed dwarves looking past her and her companion, Mickey turned and glanced back to see a horde of orcs charging for her dimensional door. At the moment, a barrage of spears led the way.

Mickey dismissed the magical portal with a snap of her fingers, and she and the others heard the rain of missiles tapping against the unyielding northern gates of Mithral Hall.

"They are stubborn beasts, aren't they?" Mickey asked. She turned back to find a brigade of dwarven warriors, weapons bared, staring at her and her elf companion with expressions a long way short of confident.

"And Drizzt Do'Urden," Mickey said to them. "He is here, of course. Tell him that friends of his have arrived to help him in his cause."

"Ye think we're walking the two o' ye to the court of our king?" one dwarf asked.

"Just relay my messages," Mickey instructed him. "Let your king and the others decide if we are to be admitted or not."

"Aye, but for now ye drop yer weapons!" the dwarf demanded.

"I have no weapons," Mickey answered as Sinnafein willingly surrendered her sword and a long dagger she kept holstered inside her boot.

The dwarves all looked at Mickey incredulously, which confused her until Sinnafein explained, "The warhammer."

Mickey seemed, and indeed was, genuinely shocked to realize that yes, she was still holding a giant's warhammer, one taller than she, and heavier, though she was holding it aloft with one delicate hand.

***

"Oh, but be sure that ye'll tell us all we're wantin' to know," Winko Battleblade said in a cruel warning, and the tough dwarf shoved his prisoner facedown to the stone floor, then kicked the ugly orc for good measure.

"Aye, and wouldn't ye be better just spittin' it out now and saving us the trouble o' hearin' yer screams?" asked Winko's cousin Rollo, a young warrior barely into his twenties and barely finished his training. "For if ye do, might be that I'll kill ye quick!"

The orc, which had been captured in the tunnels just outside of Mithral Hall, squirmed and covered its face.

"Take its fingernails, then its fingers," said Rollo.

"Take me time, most of all," Winko agreed with a wicked laugh, and all those around knew that the tough dwarf could surely back up his ferocious demeanor with action. Some of the dwarves shifted uncomfortably, but none spoke out.

There came a commotion then, however, and a dwarf up in front of the patrol band gave a yelp and fell to the side.

A huge black panther padded past the startled and frightened dwarf. Guenhwyvar came right up to the main group of dwarves and sniffed carefully at the orc, who cringed and curled even tighter in terror.

"Bah," Winko Battleblade grumbled, fully expecting what was coming next as Drizzt Do'Urden appeared from around the bend in the corridor.

"Ye're just in time for the fun," Winko said, his tone less than inviting. "But the fun's me own, don't ye doubt."

"Fun?" Drizzt asked, moving into the group and noting the captured orc.

"Aye, we're taking its fingers . . . slowly," young Rollo said with a grin—a grin that disappeared quickly under the weight of the ranger's responding scowl.

"Do tell," Drizzt prompted, his voice even, yet thick with warning.

"We caught the rat out in the tunnels," explained another, a grizzled old veteran that Drizzt recognized from many years before, though he could not remember the fellow's name.

"Aye, and now he's goin' to tell us what other rats are out in the tunnels," said Winko. "One finger at a time."

He reached down for the whimpering orc, but Drizzt interrupted him, grabbing Winko by the forearm. The dwarf roughly pulled away and fell back a step, staring threateningly at Drizzt.

"Here now, ye keep yer drow hands to yerself, Mister Drizzt Do'Urden," he said with open contempt.

"And you keep your own off of this prisoner," Drizzt replied. As the dwarf started to argue, Guenhwyvar interjected a timely growl.

"Hey now, we caught the dog," Rollo complained.

"Ain't much changed, 'ave ye?" asked the grizzled old veteran. "Aye, but I remember yerself, Drizzt Do'Urden, when ye come here them forty years ago and hunted down Battlehammer dwarfs and elfs alike what would fight back against them Many-Arrows orcs. And now yer House's come a'callin', don't ye know, and here ye are, protecting orc scum yet again. Ye been thinkin' on this war a long time, ain't ye?"

"Here, but what're ye sayin'?" an incredulous Winko asked the older dwarf. He nodded as he asked, though, clearly sorting out the veteran dwarf's nefarious implications—that this war had been part of Drizzt's plan all along.

Many sets of eyes, narrow and scrutinizing and threatening, fell over Drizzt then.

"Battlehammers don't torture," the drow said resolutely. "Clan Battlehammer is above that."

"It's an orc!" Winko said, and he kicked the sniveling prisoner.

"I care not!" Drizzt yelled at him. "And not again!" he warned, pointing down at Winko's boot.

"Or what, drow?" Rollo demanded, coming forward—until Guenhwyvar's roar sent him skipping backward.

"I speak for King Bruenor on this," Drizzt stated.

"Bruenor ain't king!"

"Bruenor was king, for many years, or have you forgotten?" Drizzt demanded.

"Aye, and take care yer words, Winko Battleblade," said the old veteran. "I got no hackles for this one, be sure, but I'll be defendin' me king Bruenor from yer mouth, don't ye doubt!"

"You cannot torture a prisoner," Drizzt said. "This is not who you are, or who we are. Cage him in the dungeon, but treat him well—for your own sake!"

"Are ye threatening me then?"

"For your own sake, from the judgments of your own heart," Drizzt calmly explained. "You do not want to carry the echoes of a prisoner's screams for the rest of your days. I beg you, good dwarf, do not throw away that which elevates Clan Battlehammer. Do not throw away the righteousness that gives strength to our weapon arms."

Winko stared at him for a long while, clearly at a loss.

"More o' them dog orcs out there threatening the hall!" Rollo yelled for him. "Ye're thinkin' we're to sit back and let 'em come? Do ye care at all, ye damned drow?"

138

"I've two friends out there in the tunnels beyond Mithral Hall, perhaps captured, likely dead," Drizzt retorted, and he moved very near the upstart young Rollo, towering over him. "Two dear friends."

"So take yer cuts on the orc and get it to squeal!" Rollo argued.

"No!" Drizzt shouted back in his face. "No!" He stepped back then, and calmed, his shoulders slumping a bit. "No. That is not the way. That cannot ever be the way."

"Yerself ain't no Battlehammer," Winko said.

"Might not be, but I am," came a voice behind, and Drizzt turned and the others looked past him to see Bruenor striding down the corridor. "Not a king no more, eh, Winko? But still a Battlehammer by blood and by deed. Any here thinkin' to argue that?"

The dwarves respectfully bowed their heads at Bruenor's approach, and Winko even greeted him as King Bruenor.

"They mean to . . ." Drizzt started to say.

"I heared ye, elf," Bruenor interrupted.

"I cannot allow it," said Drizzt.

"Nor can I," said Bruenor. "Go, boys," he told the dwarves. "Bring yer prisoner to a sturdy cage, but don't ye beat him. We're Battlehammers, and Battlehammers don't be doing that! And feed him."

"We ain't got enough food for ourselfs!" Winko argued, and others groaned and nodded their agreement.

"Then don't be bringing back anymore o' them alive!" Bruenor shouted in his face.

There followed some staring and a bit of grumbling, but Winko and the others gathered up the orc as ordered, and moved off down the tunnel.

"It is unlikely that the orc can tell us anything we don't already know about the forces arrayed against us," Drizzt told Bruenor when they were alone.

"The beast might have some word on me boy and Rumblebelly."

"I've likely gained a bit of the orc's trust already," said Drizzt. "I will talk with him, repeatedly."

"We can't be takin' prisoners, elf," Bruenor said. "Winko weren't lyin'."

"I know, but we cannot be torturing prisoners either, Bruenor, even if they are orcs or goblins. Are we to cast aside all that makes us confident in our own righteousness? Are we to lose our very hearts?"

Bruenor didn't respond, his expression showing nothing of where he stood on that particular issue.

"I'll speak with the orc prisoner for as long as it takes," Drizzt promised.

Bruenor nodded. "Lot o' the boys got some doubts about ye, elf," Bruenor admitted a moment later, and Drizzt nodded, unable to disagree. "What Tomnoddy Two-shoes said about forty years ago . . ."

Drizzt sighed. "When I returned here in the time of King Obould VI, in the last days of King Banak, I did join in the hunt for rogue dwarves and elves," Drizzt admitted, "at the request of King Banak. His son, King Connerad, though he wasn't king then, did not argue the matter with his father. They were lawbreakers, crossing into Many-Arrows land and murdering orcs in the dark of night. King Banak feared an all-out war if he could not control the growing anger among the folk of Mithral Hall. Lord Hralien of the Glimmerwood elves—"

"The Moonwood, we called it then," Bruenor remarked, and Drizzt nodded.

"Hralien and his people were sterner still with those they caught. But still . . ." Drizzt paused and shook his head.

"Didn't feel much good, eh?"

"There is sometimes a strange moral cleanliness to ugly battles," Drizzt admitted. "Have you ever known me to hesitate with the blade when the fighting has begun?"

"Aye, but when ye got yerself a prisoner," Bruenor admitted. "Nothing's clean about it. Ugly business. Ugly orcs."

"But we do not torture them," said Drizzt. "We cannot throw away our very hearts."

Bruenor stared at him, seemingly caught somewhere in between, but had no answer.

"They've dragons," King Connerad said to his elf guests, including the good Lady Sinnafein, whom Connerad knew well. "Had one waitin' for us last time we breaked out." He indicated Catti-brie, who sat at one end of the small table. "Weren't for that one there, I'm doubting that many o' me boys would've made it back into the halls."

Sinnafein turned to the woman. "The whispers coming forth from Adbar spoke of your return, my old friend," she said. "It is a magical world and a strange time, and so I allowed myself to believe the rumors of the meeting in Citadel Felbarr, with King Bruenor and Catti-brie returned to the Silver Marches, alive and young once more."

"Aye, but now that ye're seein' her . . ." said Bungalow Thump, sitting to the left of King Connerad on the side of the table to Catti-brie's right, with Sinnafein and Mickey across from them.

"It is beyond my sensibilities," Sinnafein admitted. "Beyond my sensibilities, and that is something one would rarely hear spoken by the Lady of the Glimmerwood. To have at this dark time two of the great heroes of old of the Silver Marches returned to us . . . Surely the gods have blessed us that we might defeat this darkening."

Beside her, the strange elf called Mickey chortled, mocking the somber and serious mood and the nods of the others seated around the table, and drawing all eyes to her.

"Heroes," she said in explanation. "What are humans and dwarves in the face of a dragon? Arauthator, the Old White Death, mocks your pretentious god-talk."

"Is it customary for yer minions to mock ye so?" asked General Dagnabbet, who was seated on Connerad's right, giving voice to the thoughts on all of their minds.

"Minion?" Mickey said with a laugh.

"My companion is not of the Glimmerwood," Sinnafein started to explain, but Mickey cut her short.

"I am here as a favor to a friend of your drow companion, Drizzt Do'Urden," she explained.

"Do tell."

"In time," Mickey replied. "When Drizzt is here. And where is he?"

"He was in the lower tunnels," King Connerad answered. "He's there all the time, fightin' orcs."

"Aye, and probably mad at bein' called away," said Bungalow Thump. "So here's hopin' ye got something to say what's worth hearin'."

"Do you think listening to a plan to get out of your hole is worth hearing, good dwarf?" Mickey asked teasingly, and all three dwarves came forward in their seats anxiously.

Mickey grinned and chuckled, and just then the door banged open and in strode Bruenor Battlehammer, flanked by Drizzt Do'Urden and Athrogate. Drizzt went right to Sinnafein, who rose up to wrap him in a tight hug.

"My old friend, it is so good to see you in these dark times," Sinnafein whispered.

"We'll lift the darkness," Drizzt promised.

Sinnafein pulled back and offered her hand to Bruenor. "Good king," she said. "The Glimmerwood shares the elation of Mithral Hall at your return!"

"Aye, Lady, and know that I'm a bit gladder to be breathin' than dead!" Bruenor said with a grin, and he took her hand in a hearty shake. "Work to do! Aye, and killin' orcs—the best work to be found."

Drizzt took the seat next to Catti-brie, with Bruenor and Athrogate pulling up chairs on the opposite side of the table from them.

"They come to tell us how to break out o' here," King Connerad explained.

"You need to come forth," Sinnafein said as the newcomers turned her way. "The other citadels are in desperate times and need your help."

"We tried, Lady," King Connerad said.

"This time you will have help," Sinnafein promised. "You come forth, through the north door."

"Bad door for breaking out," Bruenor remarked. "Narrow exit, uphill run."

"Aye, and with a big camp sittin' right there waitin'," General Dagnabbet added.

"My people will hit that camp, and hard," Sinnafein assured them.

"There's a thousand orcs there, might be close to two," said Bungalow Thump. "And a horde o' giants beside 'em!"

"Aye, and with a dragon up on the hill, if like last time," said Bruenor. "Not to doubt ye, Lady, and not to turn aside yer offer, but yer folks're too thin to cut through that band . . ."

"You'll get out," Mickey interrupted with certainty. "And with little loss. The orcs will regroup and come back against you, but you will simply turn around and go back in. Some of you. One legion, with Bruenor, Drizzt, and you, Catti-brie, will break free with us and flee to the northeast, across the Surbrin and into the Glimmerwood."

"You make it sound so easy," Drizzt remarked. "We got out last time, and routed the immediate forces, but they were waiting. We could not have run far."

"This time will be different," Mickey promised. "The plan will work. Sinnafein's people will get you across the river to safety."

"And the dragon?"

"Let me worry about the dragon," said Mickey, and that brought nothing more than doubting stares.

"We are confident that we can get you out," Sinnafein said.

"Aye, that I see, but I'll be needin' more than yer good hopes, Lady," said King Connerad. "As I told ye, we almost didn't get back into the hall last time!"

"Dismiss that one," Mickey said to Connerad, and she indicated General Dagnabbet. "And that one," she said, pointing to Bungalow Thump.

The dwarves huffed and puffed at that indignity, but Mickey casually turned to the strange dwarf who had come in with Bruenor and Drizzt. "And you are?"

"Name's Athrogate," he answered.

Mickey nodded and smiled knowingly. "You may stay."

"Yerself's settin' the meeting, are ye?" King Connerad asked skeptically, and beside him, both Bungalow Thump and General Dagnabbet crossed their arms over their chests defiantly.

"If you would hear the next words I have to say, then they will leave," Mickey calmly explained. "And all of your guards as well. And I will have your word—all of you who remain—that what I tell you will be held in the strictest confidence."

King Connerad started to argue.

"There is no debate to be found here, good king," Mickey interrupted. "You do as I ask, or I have nothing more to say."

"And ye leave us in the halls?" Connerad asked.

"No," Sinnafein and Mickey answered together.

"What I have to offer in private is assurance," Mickey told him. "The plan remains intact whether you hear it or not, though I suspect that you will plan more accordingly, and come forth with more confidence, if you hear what I have to say."

The surprised and confused onlookers all looked to Sinnafein then for an explanation, but she could only shake her head and shrug.

"Take the guards, all o' them," King Connerad told his two dear friends.

Bungalow Thump nearly choked on that order, but General Dagnabbet rose immediately and bade him to go with her. The disciplined soldier knew her duty, and would not allow pride to interfere.

As soon as they were gone, Mickey turned to Drizzt. "I am here on behalf of one who knows you well," she said.

"Bwahaha!" Athrogate howled, and that surely clued Drizzt in as to whom Mickey might be referring.

"What's she sayin', elf?" Bruenor demanded. "Who's—" He stopped short when Drizzt put a hard glance over him, then guided Bruenor's gaze to Athrogate.

"No," Bruenor said with a groan. "Canno' be."

"Bwahaha!" Athrogate roared.

"Him again, and why's meself not surprised?" Bruenor replied. "Always is his hand in the jar."

"None can know that," Mickey said. "Menzoberranzan is here in support of Many-Arrows, and our friend will not compromise his position, as you can well understand."

Drizzt looked at her curiously when he noted the way she had said "our friend," pointedly not speaking the name of the drow he suspected.

"Of course," Drizzt replied. He looked to King Connerad. "It is an amazing risk he takes."

"Jar—" Bruenor started to say, but Drizzt cut him short with an upraised hand and a sharp look.

"Pray speak yer words," King Connerad declared.

"Nay, pray do not," Mickey ordered.

"Bruenor?" asked Connerad.

"Bah, but ye got to be trustin' us on this one, me friend."

"They speak of one who would be sorely compromised," Catti-brie explained.

"A drow from Menzoberranzan," Sinnafein put in, casting a judgmental glare at Mickey.

"Sometimes of Menzoberranzan," Drizzt agreed.

"Aye, and all the time he's for himself, don't ye doubt," said Bruenor. "But I'd rather have that one on me side than fightin' aside me enemies."

Drizzt nodded.

"Our friend asked me for help, along with my sister, and so we agreed," said Mickey. "We came to the Glimmerwood with two of your former associates, Amber and Afafrenfere. And with the help of Sinnafein and her people, we learned of all that has transpired and so laid our plans."

"Good plans," Sinnafein added. "You come out hard and with all you can spare, indeed with all you have, and we will help you rout the orcs camped in front of your northern gate."

"Another ten thousand in the east," King Connerad reminded her. "And half that in Keeper's Dale again, from what me boys're tellin' me."

"And so you'll turn about with most of your forces, as we said," Mickey replied. "You will be safely back behind Mithral Hall's great gates before the orc reinforcements arrive. But you," she added, turning to Bruenor, "will take with you Mithral Hall's greatest legion—and your powerful friends, I hope—and come with us to waiting boats."

"Boats?" Connerad asked. "River's frozen!"

"We'll not go until the water runs free," Sinnafein explained, "near the end of the month of Ches, likely. If we tried now and were seen, the orcs would chase us across and dog our every step and so our gains would be short-lived."

"We will be across the Surbrin and melted into the Glimmerwood before the orcs arrive," Mickey added. "And if we are clever, and if we are quick, the minions of Warlord Hartusk will not even know the truth of it—that a legion of dwarves had broken free of their hole, ready to go and free Adbar and Felbarr, who are in dire need."

"And if we're all comin' out and their dragon drops upon us, what then?" King Connerad asked.

"It will not," said Mickey.

"But if it does?"

"If Arauthator is about, we will deal with him, I assure you," said Mickey.

"Yerself assures me?" Connerad echoed incredulously. "Against a dragon? How can ye make such a claim, lass?"

Mickey smiled, wickedly it seemed, and turned to Drizzt as she answered, "Because we have our friend."

All eyes followed her gaze to the drow ranger, who stared at Mickey for a long while, then began to nod his agreement.

They had Jarlaxle.

CHAPTER 9

BY THE GODS

Shontiq A'Lavallier leaned against the stone wall of the tunnel entrance, trying to keep his focus on the sentry task at hand, but his mind constantly drifted back to the city of Q'Xorlarrin. So many possibilities teased the shadows in front of the drow wizard, both with the openings available to him in the fledgling city and with the opportunities that were opening up for practitioners of his craft, given the encroachments of Lolth into the Weave.

But first they had to be done with this increasingly tedious surface war, Shontiq kept reminding himself. It had started promisingly enough with some truly enjoyable battles. Shontiq had been at the side of Ravel, noble son of House Xorlarrin—though he now used the surname of Do'Urden—weaving the lightning web that had engulfed the front line of Knights in Silver when they counterattacked across the Redrun. And how deliciously effective and lethal that lightning had been on the riders in midstream.

And then Sundabar, and truly there had been no previous experience in Shontiq's eventful life to match the thrill of watching the fall of Sundabar. He had been among the lead wizards in the last assault that had toppled the city, crawling through the tunnels to the substructure of the guard tower. Shontiq couldn't suppress a grin as he recalled again the image of the lightning net climbing up the stones of that tower, the foolish humans leaping from the tower's top.

Glorious.

But now the siege had stalled, and this thing called "winter" seemed quite boring to the impatient drow. There were no seasons in the Underdark, but up here, all was buried under a blanket of uncomfortable snow. This season was almost over, the orcs had assured Shontiq and the others, and the slaughter could soon resume.

But it had been a long few months, and longer still because Shontiq had been assigned to this region, the tunnels north of the city called Silverymoon. By all accounts, this city would likely serve as the next conquest, but for these months, the region had offered nothing but boredom, unlike the Upperdark regions around the three dwarven citadels, where skirmishes were common as the desperate bearded folk tried to break free.

Here, though, there was nothing. The folk of Silverymoon seemed content to remain within their walls, and given the reputed number of wizards among their ranks, including their leader whose nickname was Thunderspell, they were no doubt weathering the winter, indeed all of the siege, with little discomfort. Shontiq believed that they should be applying more pressure to the city, with magical and war-machine bombardment day and night. He had said as much to Ravel, and it seemed to him from the Xorlarrin's response that Ravel did not disagree.

But Ravel had warned him to stand down. Tiago had turned his sights to the dwarves again—to Mithral Hall, for some reason Ravel would not disclose.

Shontiq could not let the matter drop, however. Not in his mind, at least. Not with the incessant boredom closing in all around him. He was now in the second rank of advance scouts, with only one fellow drow, a lovely maiden named Sahvin Sel'rue, between him and the open tunnels of the Underdark.

Many times did Shontiq fantasize about running out among those dark ways to find the encampments near to one of the dwarven citadels, to again use his magical repertoire to summon forth ice storms, to freeze the blood of his enemies and hear their dying screams, instead of the mundane tasks he was assigned in this eventless region.

The drow heaved another resigned sigh. He knew that he should be fanning out to the east of Sahvin Sel'Rue's quadrant, but really, what was the point of such an exercise? Silverymoon was behind them, with the only notable route blocked by a large encampment of orcs and ogres. If the folk of the city came forth into the tunnels, they'd be tied up long enough with the monstrous fodder for Shontiq and the other dark elves to be long on their way to link up with Ravel's band in the northwest.

He felt his magical wards dissipating and thought that he should renew them.

But to what end? Every day he came down to this area, protected from fire, protected from ice, protected from arrows, and with his array of magical wands at the ready on his belt. Every day, for hours and hours. Occasionally he might talk Sahvin into some playful recreation, at least, but the witch was in a most foul mood this day and had gone off to her haunts without even responding to his advances.

Strangely, Shontiq hadn't even protested, because in truth, he hadn't even cared.

Perhaps the many tendays down here had turned even that former pleasure into tedium.

So he stood there alone and he thought of Q'Xorlarrin. He'd be a good soldier here in this glorious campaign, and then he'd return home to make the most of his opportunities—and there would be some, he was certain, because some of the other drow wizards would surely fall in the fighting in this campaign, and particularly since Ravel would be going to serve in this ridiculous House Do'Urden in Menzoberranzan.

There would be room for ascension.

The wizard waggled his fingers and produced a ball of fire, hovering above his open palm. He stared at the dancing flames, marveling at their interplay. Perhaps he could bring forth a sprite from the elemental plane of fire, a pet of sorts to dance around and amuse him.

He wondered what such a fiend might sound like when he dropped an ice storm upon it.

"Yes," he muttered quietly, staring into the flames as if looking for such a creature there in the palm of his hand.

His attention was diverted then by movement down the corridor. He turned his head to look at it, thinking to dismiss the ball of fire, but before he even began that dispelling, he recognized that it was Sahvin approaching up the long corridor.

Shontiq nodded in greeting, thinking the female was waving at him.

But then he realized she was warning him, telling him to flee.

Shontiq started to throw his ball of flame to the side, but again his attention was grabbed by the movement down the hall, as Sahvin Sel'rue sprinted toward him. And behind her there were lights—torches! Sahvin shook her hands at him, shook her head at him, and then the woman dived down suddenly into a forward roll, just as a spinning missile swept over her tumbling form.

It went through Shontiq's mind that he should have renewed his magical wards.

Then the warhammer went through Shontiq's mind, quite literally, and his every thought blew away in an instant.

The conjured magical flame tumbled as the wizard dropped, landing right beside him, licking at his arm and robe, but he didn't feel it.

Sahvin Sel'rue ran past him then, and had no time to pause and see if he was still alive, or to pat out the flames now growing on the sleeve of Shontiq's fine robes. Glancing at the thick head of the warhammer embedded in the brains of her companion, she saw little point in going to Shontiq anyway, except perhaps to retrieve the weapon.

Her eyes did flash as she considered that possibility, for surely it seemed a wondrous weapon, despite the gore splattered about it.

She just kept going. She had no choice. A powerful force of humans and elves licked at her heels, led by a Knight in Silver, a raging barbarian who seemed as big and formidable as a frost giant, and a clever little halfling who had already put one hand crossbow dart into Sahvin's backside.

She could feel the poisoned tip burning there, but she didn't dare slow to remove it.

Around a corner and up a natural chimney, and she'd be back among the orcs, and she could warn them and organize them, and filter through their ranks . . . and run away if they were overrun.

The main orc encampment, in a large cavern, had been designed perfectly to fit the information presented to the forty dark elves advising this group.

They knew, for example, that the people of Silverymoon had no underground route to get around their location to the tunnels north of them. The drow had scouted this region of the Upperdark extensively.

They knew, as well, that the folk of Silverymoon could not come forth from their walled city aboveground without being spied by the many eyes they had upon the place.

And they knew, of course, that the other underground citadels of the region, the three dwarven fortresses, could not come forth to the aid of Silverymoon, aboveground or in the Underdark, without them knowing it long in advance.

They did know, as well, that a small force from Sundabar had escaped into the Underdark through the subterranean granaries and the Everfire Caverns below those. But this was a fleeing mob, after all, full of old women and children, of peasants and farmers and nothing more, and within a tenday or so after the fall of Sundabar, this mob had been put out of mind. Perhaps the refugees had found their way to Everlund, or had escaped out to the east. More likely, most were dead in the Underdark, killed by falls or starvation or displacer beasts or umber hulks or any of the hundreds of deadly pitfalls and monstrous enemies to be found there.

And so when the siege of Silverymoon had been solidified for the winter pause, this cavern had been perfectly designed, with defensive walls and high watch points, with ballistae even, aiming to the tunnels entering the southern rim of the cavern, the tunnels coming from Silverymoon.

Everything was aiming to the south, every barricade, every weapon nest, every scout position.

A general sense of confusion and dread emanated from the words of the returning drow scout, therefore, when Sahvin crawled into the northern rim of the cavern encampment warning of a powerful enemy force close behind.

More than a score of dark elves were in that camp, along with two hundred battle-hardened, well-armed, and well-armored orcs; scores of ogres; and a brigade of giants. Had they reformed their lines and turned their weapons around, the approaching force of refugees would have had no chance of breaking through them, let alone of defeating them.

But there were thousands coming, Sahvin had assured them. From her perspective, judging by the sheer number of torches and the discipline, speed, and confidence of the march, the leading band of powerful warriors—including a commander of the Knights in Silver—there could be little doubt that this was a coordinated squeeze. Silverymoon or one of her allies—perhaps a new force from outside the Silver Marches—was cutting off the main retreat lines and falling upon this encampment with all of her weight.

The dark elves barely broached the possibility of standing their ground and fighting, and instead, in full, fled through the lower tunnels into the deeper Underdark.

Giants jostled ogres, ogres thumped orcs, and orcs shoved and punched one another in the confusion that ensued. Where to go? Where to turn?

"Formations!" one orc leader cried, but no one knew what that even meant in this oddly-shaped cavern with tunnels coming in from all sides, from above, and from below.

One band of orcs moved to a wide northeastern tunnel, though to scout or to flee the others did not know. Nor did it matter, for such a barrage of arrows met them as they exited the room that those few surviving the surprising onslaught staggered right back in.

Toward that tunnel ran a powerful square of ogres and giants, shoving a wall of orcs in front of them, and with scores of orcs trailing in their wake.

But from a side tunnel in the east came the first enemies, led by Sundabar warriors and a Knight in Silver, and by a giant of a man and a halfling beside him.

And they were led by a devastating volley of spears and by a warhammer thrown so powerfully that it dropped an ogre dead where it stood.

Orcs charged at the enemy, but more orcs broke the other way, running for the western exits.

The square of ogres and giants took a different route. Hearing the commotion of thousands, it seemed, they charged down the tunnel from which the arrows had come. If an unfortunate orc being pushed in front of the defensive shield array tripped and fell, it was crushed to death in short order by ogre feet and giant boots. Down they went, thinking to burrow into the back ranks of this approaching army.

They crossed an area of broken stones and found many spikes among those rocks, cleverly set as caltrops. Monsters roared and the square's integrity shuddered. Ogres stumbled aside, grabbing at broken feet.

Another barrage of arrows reached forth from the darkness, raining and stinging.

But the monsters rolled on eagerly, ready for the kill.

Rolled on and on, and found a room where a hundred small candles burned—small candles they had thought the torches of an army far back along the straight corridor!

They were chasing ghosts, they came to realize finally, when they were far from the encampment, far from the orcs and few ogres they had left behind . . .

Far from the actual fighting.

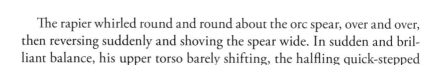

The rapier whirled round and round about the orc spear, over and over, then reversing suddenly and shoving the spear wide. In sudden and brilliant balance, his upper torso barely shifting, the halfling quick-stepped forward and thrust once and again, and the orc fell away with blood spurting from two holes in its chest.

Regis used the momentary pause to quickly cock and load his hand crossbow, and he sent a dart into the ear of an orc across the way, one charging into battle farther down the line. The beast stutter-stepped and grabbed at its ear, howling in pain rather than bloodlust now.

Then it staggered and pitched forward, and the sword of a Sundabar swordsman cut it down.

"Well fought and well shot, little one!" came a voice from the other way, and Regis turned to salute Aleina Brightlance, rapier coming up to his forehead, then diving out in front of him to turn aside the swipe of an orc's sword.

That orc pressed on, thinking its momentum would carry it to the kill, and indeed, it disengaged the weapon and pressed it forward at the apparently vulnerable target.

But up came a three-bladed dagger, intercepting the sword in a deft hooking motion, followed by a twist that nearly broke the blade and turned the orc's arm out wide.

That gave Aleina the perfect opening. She drove her opponent back with a slash and thrust, but turned the thrust to the side in time to slide her sword through the chest of Regis's enemy.

That orc tumbled between them and Regis rushed behind it, intercepting the orc coming back in at Aleina, his rapier taking it in the shoulder, then the neck.

The creature staggered, Regis retreated, and Aleina lopped off its head.

"Aha!" she cried. "Four kills! What will your giant friend think of that?"

Her boast was cut short as a heavy missile soared in at the pair from the side beyond Aleina. They both yelped and fell away, stumbling back into formation. Before their brains could unscramble from the surprise—was it a giant-thrown boulder?—the duo recognized the missile as an orc, and one quite dead, from the weird way it lay there, all twisted and broken. Glancing back from where it had come, they quickly discerned the source.

"I doubt he'd be impressed," Regis replied dryly. The source of the recently living missile was Wulfgar, standing amidst a pile of broken orc and ogre bodies, his hammer chopping out in front of him with heavy, brutal strikes.

"By the gods," Aleina Brightlance muttered.

"Tempus, I believe," Regis answered, and they both shuddered as Aegis-fang came down hard on the ogre's head, exploding the misshapen noggin into a shower of blood and gore.

"That marks ten at least," Regis remarked, following Aleina forward to find more foes. "And four of them ogres, by my count."

"I can count," Aleina grumbled.

Regis grinned and couldn't resist. "And that does not include the ones he killed before we ever reached this chamber."

Aleina cast a sidelong glare at him, but it was one filled with the heat of a good-natured rivalry and no true scorn.

"Your friend will claim a higher total than I," she admitted when the horns blew behind them, indicating that the force out in the tunnel, leading the giants on a wild and fruitless chase, was coming in fast.

"To the south!" Aleina called to her charges. "Sweep clear the tunnels to Silverymoon!"

Aleina moved past Regis to lead the pivot. They had never entertained any idea of a pitched battle in this cavern. Their force was more mirage than reality. They had hit fast and hard, and indeed, it could be called nothing short of a rout, with scores of monsters dead, and the survivors running. But this was the delicate part, Aleina and the others knew. If those enemies still remaining in the cavern realized the ploy and the intent to flee, they might come on again, and that battle might well give enough time for the giants and ogres to return.

Indeed, soon after she had started to the south, drawing the forward line around, Aleina noted a distant orc up on a natural pedestal of stone, calling for its charges to turn and fight.

But that orc was hit, suddenly and brutally, and went flying away.

Aleina turned her gaze back to the north to see Wulfgar's wicked grin.

"By the gods," she muttered once more, under her breath.

Regis awakened propped in a chair in a small room. The chamber was bare save for a single chair and a heavy, ironbound door just a couple of feet in front of the seated halfling. Not sure how he'd gotten to this place, the halfling instinctively leaned forward and reached for the door, only to find his right wrist shackled, chained to a peg set in the floor behind the chair.

Regis studied the tight metal bracelet, seeking a locking mechanism. But there was none to be found, just a smooth metallic ring—it looked like mithral—too tight for him to even think about slipping his hand out.

A magical shackle, but how?

His thoughts immediately went to the dark elves, and he found it hard to breathe. He shook his head, trying not to get ahead of himself, telling himself to recount the events. He remembered the planning for the assault—he had led the way on that. The initial charge was clear to him, as was entering the cavern beside Aleina Brightlance.

They had routed the orc force, and pressed through into the tunnels Aleina had assured them would take them to Silverymoon. Indeed, Regis had some recollection of the calls of the advance runners, indicating that the defenders of Silverymoon were in sight.

He looked at the shackle again, at the material and the simple, elegant design, and ran the fingers of his other hand over it gently, searching for a lock, though he was certain of a magical seal. He hoped again that this wasn't a drow shackle, and held that thought and his breath as the door to his room opened.

Regis breathed an audible sigh of relief when a man, a human, entered the room. Tall and broad-shouldered, and certainly an imposing figure, Regis found it hard to place the man's age. He had a thick head of hair with a bit of yellow in it, though it was mostly gray. His white beard was long and neatly tapered, and his dark eyes, ringed by fine lines, bespoke the wisdom of age.

"I trust you are not harmed," he said in a deep and resonant voice and an accent that, like his fine clothing, spoke of culture and sophistication.

That realization gave Regis pause. He looked at the man more carefully and thought perhaps he recognized him.

"Confused, perhaps, but not harmed," he answered.

"Good, then perhaps I can help clear up your confusion," the man said. He waggled his fingers and cast a quick spell. A chair appeared directly in front of Regis. The tall man spun it around and sat straddling it, leaning his elbow on its straight back. With his free hand, he reached into a pocket and pulled forth Regis's hat of disguise, which he hung on the corner of the chair's back.

"Let us begin with your lying," he said.

"M-my what?" Regis stammered, staring at the hat. "Where am I? Is this Silverymoon?"

"Yes, and you were invited in," came the reply.

"To be shackled?"

"After you lied."

"I . . . I . . ." Regis fought for an answer, but really had no idea what was going on. He remembered more now, but it was still hazy.

"I came in with Knight-Commander Ale—"

"Aleina Brightlance, yes," the man interrupted. "And with the refugees of Sundabar, though you were not one of those."

"No, but we found . . ."

"I know your tale, little one. I am well acquainted with Aleina and have spoken with her at length."

"Then you know I am no enemy of Silverymoon."

"I know that you lied to me," the man answered. "We had priests watching with spells enacted when you and your large companion were questioned. Your friend, Wulfgar, spoke truly, but as for you, Mister Parrafin . . ."

"My name . . ." Regis breathed.

"Spider Parrafin, so you said, but that was not the truth."

"It is a half-truth."

"Do tell."

"Spider Parrafin is the name of my . . . of my second life. I was reborn—it is a crazy tale, I fear. My name really is Parrafin, and the name I gave myself when my father would not . . ." He paused and huffed. There was so much to tell.

"Spider," he said. "They called me Spider because I could climb walls so well. So I kept the name, and so, yes, my name is Spider Parrafin."

"The priests claimed that to be a lie, and I am inclined to believe them."

"Because in my heart, I do not hold to that identity," Regis admitted. "And so to the perceptions of the priests with their spells, it would seem as if I was lying."

"Pray continue," the tall man said when Regis paused.

"My true name is Regi—" the halfling started to explain, but he stopped and stared harder at the man, recognition clicking into place. "I know you," he said.

"Regih?" the man echoed.

"You were an advisor to Lady Alustriel," Regis said. "But that was a century and more ago. Nay, wait, you were the High Mage of Silverymoon!"

"That is no secret."

"Do you not know me?" the halfling asked, but then caught himself. "No, of course you do not. My real name is Regis, and it is a name that you know, or knew."

The wizard held his hands out, clearly at a loss.

"I was friend to Bruenor Battlehammer, once Steward of Mithral Hall," Regis said. "Friend to Drizzt Do'Urden."

"A fanciful tale," the man replied in a tone that sounded less than convinced. "And your friend . . ." He stopped there, his face twisting with confusion, and he mouthed, "Wulfgar?" He stared back at the halfling, then shook his head, a perplexed look upon his face.

Regis grinned. "It is true," he said. "Fetch your priests and cast the spells, I pray. And you are Taern Hornblade, yes? The wizard they call Thunderspell?"

The man was hardly listening, as he was clearly trying to wrap his thoughts around this startling information—though surely not as startling to one of Taern's wizardly skills, or one of his age, for even with the time spent in the magical forest of Iruladoon and even with the years after his rebirth, Regis wasn't nearly as old as this human.

"What does it mean?" asked a woman's voice, and Aleina entered the room.

"If it is true, then it would mean that these two you found in the Underdark are older than anyone in Silverymoon who is not an elf and is not . . . me," the high mage replied.

"It means more than that," Regis added.

"Go and fetch the one called Wulfgar," Taern bade Aleina. "They have a tale to tell, and it is one we should hear."

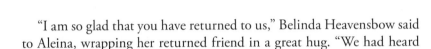

"I am so glad that you have returned to us," Belinda Heavensbow said to Aleina, wrapping her returned friend in a great hug. "We had heard that you survived the Redrun to get to Sundabar, but feared you dead in that catastrophe."

"I surely would have been, but for the blessings of the gods," Aleina replied.

"The last one into the keep, no doubt," Belinda said, and she rubbed Aleina's arms and smoothed Aleina's thick brown hair, plainly needing that tangible proof that her dearest friend had returned to her. They were the same age, less than a year from thirty, born within a week of each other, and to parents who had been close friends. They had joined the Knights in Silver together, and had served together for several years, until Belinda had resigned to help out her ailing father in his archery shop in Silverymoon's trade district.

Aleina nodded solemnly. "Never will I forget that image," she whispered. "Sundabar in flames, her wall fully breached, and with that foul drow elf flying around on a dragon, presenting King Firehelm's severed head as his garish trophy." She paused and swallowed hard, wincing against the pain of the memory.

"You must tell me all when you are ready," Belinda bade her.

Aleina stared at her friend and nodded, recognizing the source of the curiosity. Belinda was a fierce warrior, and had climbed ahead of Aleina, even, in the Knights in Silver, before she had returned to her father's side. While Aleina had gone on to become a knight-commander, she had never once believed that Belinda would not have done the same if circumstance hadn't intervened. But it was not to be, and so over the last few years, Belinda had lived vicariously through Aleina's exploits, always asking for tales of battles and skirmishes, and even prompting detailed stories regarding the more mundane aspects of Aleina's duties, like arresting brawlers in a bar fight in Silverymoon.

"I've much to tell," Aleina admitted.

"Four months in the Underdark!"

"That is the least of the tales," Aleina assured her. "Four months of hiding and little more."

As if on cue to give life to her words, Aleina noticed movement beyond the open front of Belinda's shop, and looked out to see a familiar figure seated on the porch of the tailor shop across the street. Winter had not let go its grip yet, and the day was cool, but Wulfgar hardly seemed bothered by it as he threaded a needle. He pulled off his wolfskin cloak and then his torn shirt as well, and sat there barebacked as he mended the garments.

"Oh, I'm sure you'll find a bit of those Underdark months to talk about," Belinda teased and stepped beside Aleina to get a better view of the huge barbarian, with his chiseled chest and muscular arms.

"Do you know who that is?" Aleina asked.

"There are rumors echoing about the streets."

"More than rumors. That is Wulfgar reborn, hero of old, who reclaimed Mithral Hall in the first days of King Bruenor Battlehammer's return to the Silver Marches. And that warhammer leaning against the rail is Aegis-fang."

"Truly?"

"Truly."

"An impressive man, even without the history," Belinda purred.

Aleina couldn't disagree, particularly since she had actually witnessed that one in battle. "Twenty kills in the fight that brought us from the tunnels alone," she told her friend, "including a dark elf and four ogres. Twenty kills by himself."

"He is barely more than a boy."

"In this life," Aleina reminded. "He was a century old when first he died in the frozen north of Icewind Dale. And now he lives again and has grown anew into a young man."

"Into quite a young man," Belinda said with a giggle.

"It is all too confusing," Aleina admitted. "I wonder, would he kiss with the calm and wisdom of an older man, or with the hungry eagerness of one barely more than a boy?"

"A most vital question, and one surely in need of a proper investigation," said Belinda. Her eyes sparkled, and a mischievous grin erupted on her face as she considered the question. "Perhaps a bit of both."

Aleina started to respond, but lost herself in the view of Wulfgar, who was standing then and working hard to wipe some of the blood from the winter wolf cloak. She couldn't contain her smile, and her brown eyes, too, sparkled with mischief.

"A pleasing thought, I agree," Belinda remarked.

Aleina didn't answer, and didn't care that she was wearing her thoughts openly.

"Perhaps I will tell you the answer when I find out," Belinda teased, and as Aleina reflexively turned to glower, her friend danced away, laughing, back to her work deeper inside the shop.

Aleina thought to go and help Belinda, but she paused and turned back, her eyes drawn back to the magnificent form of mighty Wulfgar, hero of legend reborn.

Hardly aware of the motion, Aleina licked her lips.

CHAPTER 10

TRUSTING A MOST UNUSUAL DROW

Drizzt and Catti-brie hurried along the halls of upper Mithral Hall, rushing to the summons of King Connerad. The dwarf "eyes"—scouts in watchposts higher on the mountain—had brought word just a tenday before that the Surbrin was starting to clear of ice, so this sudden call was not unexpected.

The third month of Ches would turn to Tarsakh in just over a tenday, and winter was finally letting go its grip upon the land.

As they approached King Connerad's war room, they heard Athrogate bellowing out some ribald song about beards and drapes and rugs, and then heard a responding laugh, dwarf and female, that rang familiar to Drizzt. He smiled and nodded at Catti-brie.

"Ambergris?" she asked, and he nodded again.

The dwarf guards moved aside as the couple approached, though one—Drizzt remembered him as Rollo, the young warrior beside Winko in their unfortunate encounter—shot a glare at Drizzt as he passed.

Inside the room, they spotted Bruenor sitting beside Connerad, with General Dagnabbet and Bungalow Thump huddled near. All four turned to regard them, and all four wore grim expressions. Not so grim were Amber and Athrogate, though, standing off to the side, laughing heartily and exchanging bawdy rhymes.

"We're to go, elf," Bruenor said.

"Tomorrow," Bungalow Thump added. "Soon as the second sunrise is in full west and low o' the darkening."

Drizzt nodded, but it took him a moment to digest that strange explanation of the time of day. The brightest hours on the surface were mid-morning and late afternoon, the spans when the sun was under one rim or the other of the blackened sky but not below the horizon. That second short period of relative light had come to be called the second sunrise, even though, by that point in the day, the sun was actually lowering.

"North door," Connerad explained as the pair walked up, and the dwarf king shook his head skeptically.

"I would expect faces beaming with eagerness," said Catti-brie, "but what I find is dour and grim."

Even as she finished, Athrogate erupted in side-splitting laughter, and Amber began to giggle so ridiculously that she could hardly finish her song of two couples, a dwarf and his firbolg bride, and his sister and her firbolg husband, brother of her sister-in-law.

"So the dwarf's got a sister who's smilin' so wide," she chanted, catching her wits when she saw that the other six were now looking her way. "And his own wife's not knowin' when her husband's inside."

Athrogate howled and slapped his knee.

"Enough!" ordered Connerad, and he turned his glare fast to Bungalow Thump, who had also begun, to chuckle.

"And yerself?" he asked. Dagnabbet couldn't resist a bit of a laugh.

"Funny to think on it," Bruenor said dryly.

Connerad sighed. "Pray be gone, the two o' ye," he said to Athrogate and Amber. "Go and play the night away. We'll be fightin' tomorrow, eh?"

The two started out of the room with Athrogate muttering, "Probably not much fightin' for us coming out if I'm knowin' me old friend."

"I cannot but agree with the wild dwarf," Drizzt explained to the others when Athrogate and Amber exited the room. "And true enough, from my own experience."

"Orcs've built a powerful force up there after them elfs came in," Connerad said. "Sure but there's a hunnerd big new tents north o' the gates." He nodded to the side, where his engineers had constructed a scale model of the entire region in great detail. Connerad led the others over there and nodded to Bruenor, who stepped up.

"North door," he said, pointing it out on the model. "Lots o' orcs here, just outside it. And a huge force o' orcs and giants here," he explained, moving his hand to the north of that position.

"The main force about Mithral Hall," General Dagnabbet said.

"Aye, and there's a good run for them to Keeper's Dale, to the Surbrin Bridge, and shortest to the north gate, all downhill," Bruenor added, pointing it out on the map, moving his hand along the model mountain passes to each location.

The orcs had grown wiser, Drizzt realized, nodding. Or more likely, the dark elves guiding them had shown them a better setup to support and hold the siege. Now they had nominal, though still sizable, forces at all three of Mithral Halls gates, but with a reserve ready to roll in for support in short order, and in shortest order of all, as Bruenor had pointed out, to the north gates.

"We'll have most o' the orcs about Mithral Hall on us afore the last of our boys've cleared our gates," Bruenor finished.

"Amber came in alone?" Drizzt asked.

"Hole opened in the north gates," Bungalow Thump explained. "Just a hole, and out fell the girl. And then, afore me boys could even get a look, poof, the hole's gone, and the door's thick and solid again."

Drizzt nodded. He had seen such a portable hole put to use before, and by the same most unusual drow he was certain was now directing this escape.

"No change of plan?" Catti-brie asked. "North gate, she said?"

"Said them elfs're ready, and with a trick or two planned for them orcs and giants," said King Connerad.

Drizzt looked to Bruenor and shrugged. "You have seen that one at play before," he reminded the dwarf.

"Aye," Bruenor agreed. "But think on it, elf. Yer friend's got himself in trouble many the times with them matrons in Menzoberranzan. Now's his chance, eh?"

Drizzt stared at him curiously, but Catti-brie caught on and looked at Drizzt with sudden alarm.

"What?" Connerad and Dagnabbet said in unison.

"Might be a good way for yer friend to get in the good graces o' them snake-whippin' witches," Bruenor elaborated.

Drizzt pondered the possibility of Bruenor's suspicions for just a moment. It made sense, he had to admit. Surely any drow could be offering quite a prize to Matron Mother Quenthel and the others by tricking the dwarves into opening their doors—and perhaps a bigger prize still for delivering Drizzt Do'Urden to them.

"No," he said, shaking his head and growing more confident with every movement. "He would not betray me, would not betray us, and certainly would not betray Athrogate. Not like this."

"He's been known to play games within games," Catti-brie said.

"But this would be no game," Drizzt replied. "If what you fear came to pass, then many dwarves would fall—indeed, Mithral Hall itself would fall. There would be no turning back. His stone would be cast forevermore, and that is something he is never wont to do."

"Cast against yerself," said Bruenor.

"Aye, and he would not do that. Not with such irredeemable finality. He would not do that to Zaknafein, who was once his friend."

Catti-brie and Bruenor exchanged looks at the mention of Drizzt's father. They shrugged in unison.

"Second sunrise, then," Bruenor told Connerad and the other two, and none of them looked particularly confident.

"Ye're sure it's no trap, are ye?" Connerad asked. "Because that's what I'm hearin', but sure not what I'm seein' in yer face."

"Aye," said Bruenor. "No trap. A most unusual one's this fellow. But he's more than a bit o' honor about him, even though I'm not for understanding it all."

"Nor would Lady Sinnafein betray us," Drizzt said.

Connerad turned to Dagnabbet and Bungalow Thump in turn, then back to his three guests. "Second sunrise," he agreed, "and may Clangeddin sit his hairy bum atop o' them orcs!"

A volley of arrows rained into the encampment, centered on the massive tents of the frost giants. The arrows were more of a nuisance than a danger to the behemoths, since there was no concentrated fire in those first volleys. Orcs ducked for cover, goblins ran around screaming and trying to form some sort of shield walls, but the giants came out strong, rocks in hand, ready to pay back the hated elves for the deaths of their kin across the river in the Cold Vale.

As predicted by Sinnafein, the giants had altered their tactics, and when they charged the tree line they believed held by the elf archers, they did so in close ranks, and with a leading barrage of hurled boulders.

But the elf archers were long gone, fleeing even as their third volley of arrows went up into the air. The two persons remaining in the stand of pines thought the boulders no more than a nuisance, less so than the arrows had been to the giants.

In charged the giants in tight groups, massive clubs lifted and ready to bat elves from the trees, or fall upon the lithe folk and crush them flat.

But as they neared, several of those trees bent outward suddenly, pushed to their breaking point, and from the two openings came gigantic, horned coppery heads.

The giants skidded across the snowy ground, falling all over each other to be away.

But not fast enough. Tazmikella and Ilnezhara spat forth their acidic breath, melting the closest behemoths, burning and biting at all behind.

There were more than two hundred giants in that vast encampment, and had they thrown the whole of their power at the dragons in coordinated fashion, they surely would have overwhelmed the wyrms in short order.

But not like this. Not caught by surprise. Not in the sudden reversal and shock of seeing the enemies with dragons of their own—and though only two had shown themselves, who knew how many more might be lurking nearby?

The giants, wisely, were more concerned with fleeing than fighting, and they turned as determinedly as they had charged, stumbling and staggering to get away.

Trees bent and snapped as the dragons came forth, bursting from the line in all their terrible splendor. They leaped up into the air and breathed again on the giants, this time enveloping the groups in clouds of thick gas. The dragon sisters quickly turned and swept back behind the pines, disappearing from sight, their role done.

Those giants they had hit with the second breath weapon were not burned. Their skin was not melting from biting acid. And they continued to run, but more slowly, much more slowly.

And now the elves returned, and the magically-slowed behemoths made wonderful targets. Group commanders selected targets methodically, and the arrow volleys that reached out came like a swarm of stinging bees.

One giant dropped, a second stumbled and fell bloody to the snow.

Far in the back among the tents, not many of the orcs and goblins had even seen the dragons, but they recognized the rout in front of them, and if two hundred giants could be so easily and completely turned around, fleeing in abject terror, then what chance did they have?

And so the rout was on in full, with the main encampment of Many-Arrows that besieged Mithral Hall splintering in confusion and terror.

At that moment, down the sloping ground to the south, the north gates of the dwarven citadel banged open, and out came Clan Battlehammer in all its glory, led by a furious drow ranger, a monstrous black panther, a Chosen of Mielikki, and the legendary King Bruenor Battlehammer himself.

Winko Battleblade and his cousin Rollo came out of the north gate side by side, banging their swords on their shields and hungry for battle. It had been a miserable winter in Mithral Hall, short on rations and constantly prodded by orcs and ogres, goblins and giants, and darker things still, and now it was past time to pay back the ugly dogs.

There was one other who might need a lesson, they both knew, as did their friends around them, and so they kept their eyes on the drow Do'Urden as they rushed along the snowy incline leading from the doors. Drizzt had helped pave the way for the filthy orcs of Many-Arrows to launch this war. Drizzt had forced the Treaty of Garumn's Gorge upon Bruenor, as Winko's telling went, in a clever ploy to allow the orcs to gain a foothold here in the Silver Marches, right on Mithral Hall's doorstep.

After all, was it a coincidence that the dark elves leading the legions of Many-Arrows bore the surname of Do'Urden?

One misstep by Drizzt here and Winko's gang of twenty were going to fall over him and pummel him into a pile of mush.

So they watched Drizzt now as the battle was joined, orcs rushing from their encampment to meet the breakout. Curiously, Drizzt and his two companions, the dwarf and woman claiming to be Bruenor and Catti-brie, broke to the right, away from the main group. The drow led the splinter group, or rather, his bow did, with a stream of mightily-enchanted arrows swarming into the gathering of orcs and ogres at that flank.

Just the three of them—no, four, Winko and the others realized when the giant panther appeared, leaping upon an ogre and bearing it to the ground beneath raking claws—splintering from the main force of General Dagnabbet to engage an entire flank of monsters . . . What game could this be?

"He's to reveal himself as the traitor he be, or I'm a bearded gnome!" Winko cried to his fellows, pointedly using the same phrase that King Bruenor had made famous a century and more before. With the main fight right in front of them fast turning to a rout by Dagnabbet's mighty force, the fiery Winko led his band off toward the right flank—not to reinforce Drizzt and the others, but to kill them when they turned back upon Mithral Hall and showed their true allegiance to the invaders.

Rollo followed that up with a call of "Huzzah," but his voice trailed away. At that moment, Drizzt hit the orc line in full stride, scimitars in hand.

Rollo's mouth stayed open, as did the hanging jaws of all Winko's band. Drizzt leaped and twirled, wide-held blades slicing orc faces. He dived to the ground and came up fast, and came up stabbing, and more orcs fell away.

Now the young dwarf who claimed to be Bruenor reincarnated joined the fray, his axe strokes launching orcs two at a time as they tried to press in. Drizzt flashed back in front of Bruenor, clearing a thin swath of ground in front of the dwarf, and as soon as the drow had passed, Bruenor charged in his wake, shield-shouldering one orc to the ground, splitting the head of a second with his axe.

In the span of a few heartbeats, it seemed, several orcs and an ogre lay dead.

The woman cried out, and Bruenor turned and retreated straight for her. The panther launched itself into a mighty leap that carried her over the ducking orcs. After dispatching yet another of the ugly brutes, Drizzt ran faster than Winko and the others could begin to believe. The speeding drow leaped just as Catti-brie's tremendous fireball went off behind him, right in the midst of the pursuing monsters.

That moment, that image, became frozen into the minds of the onlooking dwarves: the drow high in the air, his dark form silhouetted by a brilliant explosion of roiling orange flames, his hands moving to sheath his scimitars even as he flew as if propelled by the blast. He landed on his feet, but threw himself forward and to the ground, tucking into a roll and turning as he went to come back to one knee facing the orcs, and somehow, impossibly, with his magical bow back in hand.

The fireball was still breaking apart when the first lightning arrow shot off into the diminishing conflagration, taking a smoking ogre right in the chest and sending it spinning to the ground.

Fires burned on tents, fires burned on orcs, fires burned on ogres, some still standing, many on the ground in the half-melted snow.

And one greater, living fire remained, and it, too, took to the battle, striding into the midst of a trio of coughing, smoking ogres. Already badly wounded by the fireball, the brutes had no chance against the wizard's fire elemental, and as the first fell under the weight of a heavy, flaming punch, the other two tried to stagger away.

But the panther came back in full charge, the dwarf howling his battle cries, and the drow letting fly an arrow with every step, close behind.

"Cousin," a subdued Rollo whispered, "you're a bearded gnome."

By the time Drizzt, Catti-brie, Bruenor, and Guenhwyvar rejoined the main dwarven battle group, the rout of the orc encampment was well in place, with few monsters still fighting.

"Ah, but here they come," Bungalow Thump warned the companions when they roared in beside his Gutbusters. "Get ye ready for we're in it now!"

His words seemed perfectly on target. They had charged out well aware that this encampment was nothing more than a stop-gap force, set to slow down any attempted breakout until the main force could arrive. And now, it seemed, that main force was indeed on its way, for up ahead, the mountain slopes were dark with swarms of orcs and goblins, with charging ogres and giants, rolling down in fury, it seemed, to overrun the dwarves.

"Brace!" came King Connerad's call, echoed up and down by the undercommanders. "Shield wall!"

Drizzt looked to the dwarf king, who was not far away, and saw his doubts clearly on his face. "He will call for a retreat into the hall," the drow said to Bruenor.

"Nah!" Bungalow Thump protested, but Bruenor couldn't help but nod. The force charging down at them seemed truly overwhelming.

Unseen by the dwarves and their allies holding position in front of the gate, one man outran all the others, easily outpacing even the lithe elves and the dragon sisters, who were now back in elf form, in the wet spring snow. Afafrenfere felt as if his body was but a shell, an image created to give shape to his life-force, which was without weight. With huge, swift strides, he bounded after the retreating monsters, and whenever he came upon a straggler, he was swift to the attack.

Out lashed his hand or his foot, always properly aimed, always with the strength of a giant behind it, and always singularly lethal. Afafrenfere wasn't striking with a corporeal punch, kick, or knee, or even headbutt, but rather with his very life energy, concentrated like a deadly spear.

Again, his physical form merely gave shape to the blow, following the flow of his inner strength into the unenlightened target.

He knew that Grandmaster Kane was guiding him now, shaping his energy and throwing it forth. He welcomed the intrusion, basked in the lesson.

Carry no doubts, the voice in his head told him as he bore down on a giant—one that had noticed him and was turning to meet the charge.

Afafrenfere felt as if he was flying when he launched into a running leap. Over the swinging club of the monster he flew, over the giant's shoulder, and as he passed, he felt his hand shaking suddenly, tiny quivers moving in a blur. He slapped the giant across the face, not hard, but solidly, and Afafrenfere felt strangely weary, as if he'd just run the breadth of Faerûn.

He flew down past the behemoth, turning as he dived into a graceful roll that set him upright and on his way as if he had never missed a step, and by the second stride, he felt his strength returning anew.

Trust was all he heard when he instinctively and silently questioned what had just occurred.

Afafrenfere had no more time to consider the incident, or even that the giant was now giving chase. A group of orcs had stopped in front of him, turning for a fight, weapons bared and ready.

And without a thought, Afafrenfere willingly leaped into their midst, scattering them with his unexpectedly bold assault. They were back soon, though, in a circle around him, a dozen enemies closing in methodically.

Closer, closer, close enough to prod at him with their weapons.

He leaped straight up into the air and spun. Around he went, lashing out with his foot, with his hand, and again, blocking each and every stab or slash with his hardened shin, or simply the delicate turn of a well-placed hand.

He turned a second circuit and a third, and the orcs fell away, one kicked in the face, a second swept over its own spear, a third taking a fast triple punch in the face as the monk finally touched down.

And up he went again, right away, just as high and spinning once more. Too fast for his enemies, too quick to the strike or the block.

When he landed that second time, only a handful remained. Out lashed Afafrenfere's side kick, shattering an orc's kneecap. Around went the monk with a full circle kick, driving that wounded orc into the next in line, and as those two tangled, a third tripped up and dived in at the monk.

Out went Afafrenfere's open palm, square in the face of the bending, over-balanced orc, using its momentum against it and shattering its neck bone.

Without even thinking of the movement, Afafrenfere backflipped right over the trio of orcs coming in behind him with leveled spears. He landed behind them instead, squarely and ready, his stabbing fingers diving into one's kidney, shattering a second's spine, and as the third turned, so did the monk, his rising circle kick snapping the spear shaft and driving through and up under the creature's chin.

It flew away, leaving Afafrenfere gaping in disbelief at the power that coursed through his body.

He could hardly register what had just occurred, and only the closing giant snapped him from his trance.

What do I do? he silently asked. He was no match for a frost giant.

But his answer came as the energy coalesced inside of him, gathering into a tangible ball. His body trembled, his eyes rolled up to show the whites, his arms reached forward, shaking.

And he felt this energy thrown from his corporeal form, thrown into the charging giant, and there, it lashed like lightning.

Afafrenfere staggered back a step and stared incredulously as the giant skidded to a halt, shaking and trembling, slightly at first, but gaining momentum with each passing heartbeat.

Soon spasms rocked its body, bouncing it around. The behemoth held its feet for a few more heartbeats, though its massive sword went flying away.

Then to the ground it went, to its back, where it jerked and thrashed violently, ending with a sudden scream, arms reaching to the sky, mouth wide, and as if that scream took with it the last of the giant's energy, the behemoth simply fell limp.

Before he even went to it, Afafrenfere knew that it was dead.

From a slap.

From a trembling hand, Grandmaster Kane's quivering palm.

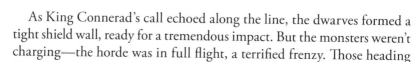

As King Connerad's call echoed along the line, the dwarves formed a tight shield wall, ready for a tremendous impact. But the monsters weren't charging—the horde was in full flight, a terrified frenzy. Those heading directly for Mithral Hall seemed suddenly to realize their error and veered left and right, scattering to the side trails—even the giants.

"What?" Bungalow Thump demanded, clearly dismayed. "Catch 'em, boys, and kill 'em to death!"

Off went Thump and his brigade, hollering and giving chase—until General Dagnabbet ordered them back.

"Close ranks!" she called. "They're baiting us to split asunder!"

More than one Gutbuster grumbled in protest, but these were Battlehammer dwarves, loyal and obedient.

Despite the monstrous flight, the fighting surely wasn't finished, and the sounds of battle erupted once more just north of the gates of Mithral Hall. Catti-brie threw more devastating fireballs and brought forth a second elemental. Drizzt sent lines of magical arrows burning into monstrous flesh. Bungalow Thump got his wish and launched his furious Gutbuster Brigade headlong into the midst of a swarm of orcs.

And Bruenor and Connerad fought side by side, two great kings of Mithral Hall joined in common cause.

Despite the fact that most of the supposed orc reinforcements had run away left and right, the battle wavered on the edge of disaster for a short while, until a barrage of arrows swarmed down from the hills, thinning the orc press. On came the elves of the Glimmerwood in tight ranks, three hundred strong, three hundred longbows working as one, sweeping aside the nearest monsters as they patiently made their way to the dwarves.

"Well met again, King Connerad," Sinnafein said to him when the allies had united, the battle all but over with only a few pockets of resistance remaining.

"Aye, and all for yer hugs," said another woman, and the group noted the approach of Ambergris and Athrogate, both with weapons covered in the blood of their enemies set on their shoulders. "But be quick about it, eh?"

Drizzt could hardly contain his smile when yet another walked up, a man who seemed to be carrying no weapons at all, yet who, Drizzt was certain, had played a large role in the victory.

"Well met again," Drizzt said to Afafrenfere, who bowed respectfully.

The monk started to reply, but Ambergris cut him short. "Time for that later, eh?" she reminded him.

"Indeed," said Sinnafein. "Have you properly divided your forces?" she asked King Connerad.

"Bruenor's leaving with yerself," the young King of Mithral Hall answered. "And them that's going with him know their place."

"Then we must be away at once, to the boats on the Surbrin's banks and across the river into the cover of the Glimmerwood," Sinnafein answered.

"Aye," Connerad agreed. He looked to Bruenor. "How I wish I might be going with ye, me king."

"Yer place is in the hall," Bruenor replied.

"Would Bruenor've said the same for himself when he'd been king?"

"No," Drizzt answered before Bruenor could.

Connerad nodded and smiled. "Aye, but Bruenor didn't have Bruenor to go and lead his army," he said. "I'm knowin' me place in this, for the good o' Clan Battlehammer, and I'm knowin' Bruenor's place is out there." He nodded his chin to the east.

"And I'm knowing that we'll be together again afore summer's on in full," Bruenor replied, and the two shared a solid handshake.

Then Bruenor and his companions, along with Bungalow Thump and the Gutbusters, and three hundred of General Dagnabbet's finest soldiers, went off with Sinnafein and the elves. King Connerad and General Dagnabbet watched them go, while the remaining dwarves around them raided the orc encampment of all its worthwhile supplies, returning to Mithral Hall with arms full of much-needed food.

The orcs and their monstrous allies were back to the battlefield in short order, a huge force prepared now for the surprises that had befallen them that late afternoon. They chased the last of Connerad's forces back into Mithral Hall, then argued and grumbled that the dwarves had found a way to resupply, and that the wretched elves had helped them.

And the angry forces of Many-Arrows had no idea that the elves had not been alone in their retreat back across the Surbrin.

CHAPTER 11

THE POSSESSED

GROMPH GAVE A LITTLE CHUCKLE, ONE THAT SURELY DID NOTHING TO bolster Tiago's hopes.

"The orcs are fracturing," the archmage said.

"But that is not true," Tiago protested, a bit too vehemently, he realized when Gromph scowled.

No one ever wanted to look into one of Gromph Baenre's scowls.

"Hartusk is gathering his forces in Hartusk Keep . . ."

"In Sundabar, you mean," Gromph quickly corrected, and in a tone that would brook no dissent. He had already made it quite clear to Tiago that he fully expected the powers of Luruar to retake the blasted city before the next winter.

"The warlord gathers his forces, all of them, and Arauthator and his son are soon to return, by your own account," Tiago reiterated.

"The wizards of Silverymoon will fight them to the end," Gromph replied. "Arauthator has already said that he wants no part of that powerful city."

"Then we will bypass it," Tiago said, and he turned to Ravel for some support.

"Everlund's defenses are surely more conventional and less rooted in the arcane arts," the wizard son of Matron Mother Zeerith Xorlarrin agreed.

"Moving Hartusk farther from Dark Arrow Keep and from Sundabar," said Gromph with a chortle.

"It will be a quick and brutal assault," Tiago insisted. "We will cripple Everlund, though not likely topple her, and then turn fast to strengthen our gains—"

" 'Our'?"

"Hartusk's," Tiago quickly corrected. "With Everlund wounded, Silverymoon will sue for peace."

"You have forgotten three dwarven citadels and the forces of the Glimmerwood," said Gromph.

He could not have been more wrong. The place that never left Tiago's thoughts was one of those dwarven citadels, Mithral Hall, where Drizzt Do'Urden had taken refuge.

"Felbarr is fully sealed, Adbar in disarray by all accounts, and the folk of Mithral Hall have tried to break out—twice—and were put back in their filthy hole both times by the forces still arrayed about the three gates," said Tiago. "The elves are a nuisance and little more. I would take Arauthator and his son over their lands and send the elves in full flight—those few who survived!"

Gromph seemed to be mulling that proposal over, at least.

"Please, Archmage," Tiago pleaded. "We can inflict more pain and use that to secure the gains for Warlord Hartusk. He and his giant allies will keep the kingdoms of Luruar engaged for years to come. If we are taken from Hartusk's side now, with Everlund and Silverymoon intact, the collapse will be swift for Hartusk and our enemies, I fear, will fast turn their eyes to Menzoberranzan and Q'Xorlarrin."

The anxious tremor in his voice could not be missed, he realized, and so he was betraying his true designs. But it could not be helped, and Tiago could not turn away, not with Drizzt Do'Urden so near!

Gromph began to chuckle again, but this time it seemed more with true amusement. "Tarsakh is upon us," he said, referring to the fourth month of 1485, which had just dawned. "You and your cohorts have until the dusk of Eleasis. Fifteen tendays, and then I will come for you and will hear no arguments."

"Matron Mother Quenthel will agree to this?" Ravel dared to ask, for Gromph had made it clear that he had returned to them this day under orders to bring the drow home.

"The drow of Menzoberranzan, excluding the nobles of House Do'Urden, return to Menzoberranzan with me this day," Gromph explained. "The soldiers of Q'Xorlarrin are Matron Mother Zeerith's to recall, should she so choose."

Ravel nodded eagerly, Tiago noted, for his wizard friend had already told him that Matron Mother Zeerith did not agree with Matron Mother Quenthel's desire to so abruptly end this war. There were gains to be made here, Zeerith believed, and so, likely, Ravel and his friends would have some dark elf support here, at least.

"Thank you, Archmage," Tiago said with a deep and respectful bow.

Gromph looked at him one last time, chuckled again, and disappeared with a snap of his fingers.

"Are we truly alone?" Tiago asked Ravel, who was already casting a spell of divination.

Ravel nodded.

"Fifteen tendays," said Tiago. "Mithral Hall will come forth within that time, surely, and Drizzt Do'Urden will be mine."

"Your thoughts of the rogue possess you like a canker worm, my friend," said Ravel. "We were never here to hunt for Drizzt, as has been made clear to you repeatedly."

"We are House Do'Urden! Deny not the connection."

"To humiliate him," Ravel argued. "To foul his name."

"You speak like a priestess," said Tiago. "Like your sniveling sister, my wife. When I enter Menzoberranzan with the head of Drizzt Do'Urden, none will deny the glory, and all will give praise to Lolth that her betrayer has fallen."

"Praise to Tiago, you mean."

"Well-earned," Tiago replied, and he looked out the window of his makeshift palace in the ruins of Nesmé and smiled wickedly.

***

Doum'wielle sat on the edge of her bed in a candlelit room, staring across at Khazid'hea. The sword was in its sheath, leaning against the wall, but it was in her head as well, calling to her.

Their games are not beyond you, Little Doe, the sword whispered in her mind, for it knew that she was considering Tiago and Ravel and the others, and their constant maneuvers to gain advantage.

Or power. Tiago had taken her to gain power over her, and over her father, and she knew, too, that was hardly the farthest Tiago would go to get what he wanted. Perhaps he would think it advantageous to murder Tos'un, and if so, then surely her father was doomed. Or perhaps he would enslave her, and use that to control Tos'un, a noble of a rival House, to his advantage.

She couldn't deny the possibility.

We will kill him . . . the sentient sword began to whisper, but she blocked it out. That sword was as arrogant as any wizard or warrior Doum'wielle had ever known, other than perhaps Tiago himself, and it probably believed its ridiculous whispers.

Doum'wielle knew well enough that if she battled Tiago Baenre, he would cut her into little pieces with hardly an effort.

And that could well happen, and could well happen very soon, before they returned to Menzoberranzan.

Even if not, the young woman had to rub her face nervously, for what life awaited her in the dark corners of the drow city? She had only been there a short while, and that in a privileged position, treated as a noble of Barrison Del'Armgo, even.

But she had seen the sidelong glances, the hateful stares, the disgusted glances aimed her way. They called the matron mother of House Do'Urden, this elf named Dahlia, Matron Mother Darthiir. *Darthiir*—that was their word for the surface elves, and it was spoken with more contempt than *iblith*, the drow word for living offal. In the minds of the dark elves, Dahlia, a surface elf, was filthier than garbage.

Which was why Matron Mother Quenthel had elevated Dahlia to sit at the Ruling Council. By putting Matron Mother Darthiir in command of House Do'Urden, by giving Dahlia a seat at the spider-shaped table, Quenthel Baenre had thumbed her nose openly at Doum'wielle's great-aunt Mez'Barris Armgo, and at all her other rivals. Matron Mother Quenthel had brazenly put forth the worst insult she could find to the sensibilities of the drow, daring them to defy her.

When they could not, when they could offer little protest against the worst insult possible—a surface elf, no less!—Matron Mother Quenthel's hold on the city had grown much tighter.

Half of Doum'wielle's blood was made up of that same surface elf heritage, that same worst insult, and Doum'wielle had been raised among the darthiir.

Khazid'hea called to her again, but Doum'wielle ignored it. The sword couldn't really grab at her from this distance any longer. She had no thoughts of abandoning it, though, and figured it might be the only thing that kept her alive in the trials she was certain to face in short order.

How had it come to this?

How had she gone from being a princess of the Glimmerwood to being the plaything of a dark elf noble who served House Do'Urden beside her father and her?

And Tierflin, her brother—her *murdered* brother! Why . . . how . . . ?

Doum'wielle dropped her face into her hands and fought back sobs.

The door to her room banged open, and Tos'un rushed into the room. She turned to him, expecting him to leap upon her, but he veered suddenly and went to the sword instead, swiftly drawing it from its scabbard.

Then he came on, and the look on his face warned her that he was going to kill her.

She fell back, but Tos'un stopped short and flipped the sword to hand it forth to her, pommel down.

"Take it," he told her.

She paused.

"Take it!"

Doum'wielle grabbed up Khazid'hea, and the sword flooded her with calming thoughts.

"Little Doe," Tos'un said. "Oh, my Little Doe. Fear not and regret not, I pray you. What is done is behind us and cannot be undone. The road before us is one of danger, I agree, but also one of promise!"

Doum'wielle wanted to shout out the reminder of what the drow had done to her, but she bit it back, and indeed, before she could formulate any other retort, she was already beginning to understand her father's reasoning.

"Your resolve is your only armor," Tos'un explained. "Any doubts will be seen as weakness, or worse, as regret. And if you regret the past, if our hosts get any hint at all that you might revert to the foul ways of *darthiir*, your end will not be pleasant. And understand, my daughter, that in such an instance, I will stand beside them."

He stared at her with hard eyes, then turned on his heel and left the room, leaving a dumbfounded Doum'wielle staring at her deadly sword.

How had Tos'un known her doubts? She hadn't spoken a word . . .

The thread of thought dissipated in a vision of power and glory: her parade as a returning hero to Menzoberranzan; her private audience with the matron mother herself. Perhaps she would be the one to help mend the ties between the elven peoples, surface and drow.

She was half-drow, and so they would accept her, and those whispers of "*darthiir*" would not land on her, but on the hopeless and helpless Dahlia.

No, she would be Little Doe, who used the cursed surface blood in her veins as a means to further aid her newfound family, as she had done in diverting the dwarves of Adbar into the Cold Vale to be slaughtered by Hartusk and the great Old White Death.

She stared at the sword and smiled.

She imagined Tierflin's blood bubbling up around her hands, warm and sticky.

It was not an unpleasant feeling.

He sat cross-legged, feet up tight beneath him, his hands on his bent knees, palms upward. His back was straight and tall, stretched to its limits, but it was a posture achieved with an effortless grace. Brother Afafrenfere was well-practiced in this art of meditation and so his consciousness was far, far away, floating free in the clarity of nothingness. He was at rest and he was at peace, absorbing mere existence, letting his life energy flow freely, letting the outside world in.

He didn't guide the thoughts that began to come to him as he moved to deeper levels of universal consciousness. He didn't fight the flittering images, memories, and notions, didn't deny them. There was only truth here in this deep meditative trance.

He felt again the movements of his body, techniques and attack routines far beyond his experience. Grandmaster Kane had taken him to that easeful place, had controlled his twists and strikes and blocks with a fluidity and precision Afafrenfere had never imagined possible. He knew that the great monks of the Order of the Yellow Rose were tremendous warriors, able to defeat fully armed and armored heroes with their bare hands and no more armor than a simple woolen robe, but never had he imagined the speed and grace and anticipation he had known in that brief and ferocious battle.

His life-force had seemed a tangible thing to him then, like a line of glowing energy within him, one he could clearly visualize, one that, in the end, he could actually grab.

As he had done under the tutelage of Grandmaster Kane, or rather, under the spell of the possessing spirit of the great man. Kane had borrowed from Afafrenfere's life energy, had focused it and shaped it like a missile, and that simple slap, just a tap, had sent the energy into the enemy, vibrating, growing, fusing with the monster's own life-force and corrupting it to Afafrenfere's—to Kane's—will.

He had killed a frost giant with a touch and a command.

The mere thought of the power nearly sent Afafrenfere careening from his meditation, but he held his place, his stillness, and his nothingness.

In this exercise, too, he was being aided by the spirit he had allowed to accompany him on this journey. In this meditation, perhaps the most personal of experiences, Afafrenfere knew that Kane was with him.

For a moment, that repulsed him. His physical form shuddered, and he nearly broke the trance in sudden revulsion, trying only to get away.

But he felt the calming influence of the ancient Grandmaster of Flowers, the greatest man of his order, a monk who had transcended the physical to become a being of the higher planes.

Even here, yes, he realized. Even in his meditative trance. He was deeper into it than he had ever achieved before because Kane was showing him how to receive, how to sink, how to let that which was in his heart be guided not at all by that which was in his muddled mind.

And so he was at peace again.

And he felt the movements and the quivering palm.

He was training without moving, mentally creating muscle memory through simple but profound insight.

The possibilities of the world, of this existence, seemed vaster and wider and more intriguing. Every day promised knowledge.

Brother Afafrenfere was truly at peace.

She spent most of her waking moments plotting, as was required of every matron mother, particularly the Matron Mother of Menzoberranzan.

Every strand of her web had to be precise and carefully nurtured—and carefully watched. The insect uncaught would surely try to break those strands, and the fall of one strand could lead to catastrophe.

She had pushed them all very hard. She had strengthened her alliances, bought off potential rivals, and then pressed hard with her demands on the Ruling Council and particularly with the rejuvenation of House Do'Urden.

She had made enemies and cowed them; that was the drow way. But such actions required vigilance.

Quenthel sat in her private chambers, surrounded by beautiful slaves who would not move unless she told them to move. Her thoughts turned inward, exploring the memories of Yvonnel the Eternal that had been imparted to her by the illithid Methil. From Yvonnel, Quenthel learned to better spin that web. From Yvonnel, Quenthel understood the length she could go to cow Mez'Barris Armgo, among others, and the diligence she would need to prevent that one and her cohorts from finding their way around her spidery designs.

She couldn't suppress her smile—so rare a sight, that!—when she let Yvonnel's memories take her back to the Time of Troubles, when House Oblodra had used the chaos among the gods to press their advantage. Their psionic powers had worked without interruption, while every other House in the city, most especially Baenre, had been crippled by the absence of the Spider Queen.

But Yvonnel had played that time out beautifully, and so House Oblodra was no more.

It would not be difficult for Quenthel to replicate Yvonnel's successes. All she needed was care. All she needed to do was spin the web precisely and hold her guard over the precious strands of intrigue.

And now Quenthel could succeed where Yvonnel had failed—in fact, she had already done so. She had wreaked havoc on the Silver Marches with few drow soldiers lost. She had dishonored the rogue Do'Urden by inciting the wrath of the folk of Luruar against the mere mention of his name.

The war had gone as planned.

Was there now more that Matron Mother Quenthel might gain from this surface incursion?

The air in front of her comfortable chair shimmered, signaling an arrival, and Quenthel sat up straighter and neatly crossed her hands on her lap.

Gromph stepped out of his teleport spell to stand right in front of her.

"You granted Tiago his permission?" Matron Mother Quenthel asked.

"Fifteen tendays, as we agreed."

Quenthel nodded.

"All of Menzoberranzan's drow have been recalled, as you commanded," Gromph said. "Only Tiago and the other nobles of House Do'Urden remain, along with the two hundred that Matron Mother Zeerith Xorlarrin supplied for the effort. Whether they remain or not—"

"They will," Matron Mother Quenthel interrupted.

Gromph looked at her curiously, and skeptically.

"Zeerith cannot resist," Quenthel explained. "She knows her place as a satellite of House Baenre—her city survives at our suffrage alone. But in this war, she has been granted a measure of independence, which she covets above all. She will not turn from the Silver Marches until she is sure there is no more to be gained."

"There is no more to be gained now," said Gromph. "Not without risking the wrath of great surface nations. Will Cormyr come to the aid of Everlund if that city is pressed too greatly? Will Silverymoon lash back with magical fury to overwhelm the Many-Arrows legions? And how long will the stupid orcs keep the dwarves in their holes?"

"That is not our concern, Archmage. Q'Xorlarrin is not Menzoberranzan, should the powers of the World Above seek vengeance beyond the borders of the Silver Marches."

"But House Do'Urden is our concern, and her nobles remain."

"Including two of Matron Mother Zeerith's children, and descendants of House Barrison Del'Armgo."

"And a Baenre—"

"No!"

Gromph backed away a step, clearly taken aback, and the predictable reaction brought a wicked smile to the face of Matron Mother Quenthel. Tiago had been one of Quenthel's favorites after all. Would she so readily disown him as a rogue?

"Every drow from Menzoberranzan who went to the Silver Marches marched under the banner of a single House," Quenthel explained. "A rogue House, plotting independently through a scheme that was put in place by the advance spy of House Do'Urden."

"Drizzt," Gromph said.

Quenthel nodded.

"And if Tiago confronts Drizzt?" Gromph asked. "You understand that is why he begged to remain."

"Of course."

"And if he gets his wish and finds Drizzt Do'Urden?"

"There are two possibilities."

"Do tell."

"If Tiago kills Drizzt, the peoples of the Silver Marches, the kingdoms of Luruar, will be indebted to House Baenre for ridding them of their scourge, will they not?"

Gromph's incredulous scowl showed Quenthel that he did not agree.

"If Drizzt is victorious," Quenthel pressed on, her voice rising with her sudden certainty, "then we will claim great losses at the hands of a common enemy."

Gromph's incredulity faded then, replaced by a smile that soon became a chuckle.

"Do not mock me, Archmage," Quenthel warned.

"It will not work," Gromph said bluntly.

Quenthel sucked in her breath, verily trembling with anger that she would be so boldly challenged as she spun one of the strands of her web.

"It was Tiago who flew about the Cold Vale on the great dragon, holding aloft the head of dwarf king Bromm," Gromph reminded. "It was Tiago who took the head of King Firehelm of Sundabar, and took that, too, on his dragon parade."

Quenthel began to twitch, trying to reconcile these truths against her plans.

"Duke Tiago, he called himself," Gromph went on. "Duke Tiago of Nesmé, and hundreds died under his months of tyranny. He is no hero to the people of Luruar, Matron Mother. His name is more hated than that of Drizzt, I am sure."

"His name," Quenthel mused.

"Tiago Baenre," said Gromph.

"Nay," Quenthel corrected, and her sly grin returned. "Tiago Do'Urden."

"Perhaps I should have brought him back," said Gromph.

"No," Quenthel replied, her mind spinning as she tried to adjust her thinking to where this might all lead. "What more can they do in the Silver Marches, in your estimation?"

"Everlund is vulnerable," Gromph admitted. "Beyond that, I do not know. They have dragons, after all, and a host of frost giants."

"Will they keep the dwarves in their holes?"

Gromph shrugged. "Without the forces of Menzoberranzan guarding the tunnels, and with the spring melt on in full, and the fighting on the surface soon to resume, it is likely that the dwarves will find their way out. Whether they come forth or not to the aid of the other kingdoms of Luruar, I cannot say. There is bitter animosity now, from all I can glean."

The matron mother nodded and became more at ease. "Fifteen tendays," she said, "and we will have our answers. Let it play out."

"There are many possible outcomes," Gromph warned.

"There is chaos, you mean," Quenthel corrected, speaking the word with reverence.

"Chaos is joy," Gromph recited, one of the litanies of the Spider Queen. "But should we not prepare to control the end of this chaotic time?"

"As our dear dead mother would do?" Quenthel asked sarcastically, and she tapped her forehead to remind him of the gift Methil had given her.

Gromph conceded that with a nod.

"Watch closely, but from afar," Quenthel ordered.

"To guide the chaos?"

"Ultimately," said Matron Mother Quenthel, who sounded very much like her mother in that decisive moment.

CHAPTER 12

WHERE ARE THE DAMNED DRAGONS?

THE GOBLIN SHAMAN WISELY DUCKED AWAY INTO THE COMPANY OF others of its kind at the sight of the great Tiago.

The drow was in a foul mood this day, storming around the camp of the Many-Arrows minions besieging the city of Silverymoon. He had drawn the orc leaders together around a large fire and made no secret of his displeasure as he dressed them down.

The goblin wasn't well versed in the orc language, but his skills had improved enough—and it really wasn't that much different from the goblin tongue anyway—so that he could make out the gist of the dark elf's rant.

They hadn't pressured Silverymoon enough, apparently. The city was too intact. The defenders should be reeling, short on food and without morale.

It sounded rather silly to the goblin shaman, who knew well that the wizards and priests within the magical city had easily enough fed the citizenry with conjured food and drink.

This drow was flailing in anger, nothing more.

After the tirade died down, however, Tiago selected a few of the orc leaders and herded them into a tent, setting many guards, giants mostly, to keep the perimeter wide.

The goblin shaman milled around with the horde, easing his way to a cubby behind some stacked crates. He took a deep breath, trying to still his nerves. He didn't like dealing with drow in this manner. He could fool the orcs and goblins and surely the ogres easily enough, and evoke no more than a curious glance from a giant, but a dark elf might see right through him.

But so be it, he silently told himself, and he fished the small potion vial from his belt and imbibed it.

He waited a moment for the effects to take place, then moved out as silently as he could, cutting as direct a course for the command tent as possible. He might be heard, but he wouldn't be seen. The potion was one of invisibility.

He veered from the tent flap and the two wary giant guards, and instead made his way to the side. He pressed his ear against the skin, hoping he might catch the conversation within, but to no avail. He had to go in, and so he did, easing himself under the tent flap. Good luck was with him, and he slipped in near some casks and crates at the side of the wide tent. He quickly eased behind them, all the while fearing that a drow noble might detect his presence, invisible or not.

He quieted his breathing and listened.

And learned.

Tiago's entourage left the encampment soon after, and, his invisibility long worn away, so did the goblin shaman, abandoning his watch post to run off in the dark of night to a particular copse of trees—and a particular stump of a felled tree within.

He glanced around, making sure he wasn't seen, then reached carefully into a crack in the trunk, releasing a cleverly hidden lever. The flat top of the trunk popped free on one side and the goblin lifted the secret trapdoor back on its hinges and quickly scrambled onto the ladder within, closing and sealing the trunk behind him.

Down he went to a small anteroom, where he stood with his arms extended unthreateningly, well aware that several crossbows and a side-slinger catapult or two were aimed his way. He tapped his beret and was Regis once more.

"Well met, little rat," said Gunner Grapeshot, the artillery dwarf commander in charge of this secret tunnel and trapdoor the industrious folk of Silverymoon had dug. "What d'ye know?"

"Lots," Regis replied, hustling by. "Lots for Lord Hornblade and the knight-commanders!"

Gunner Grapeshot clapped him on the shoulder as he sped past.

—————————— ᘉᖆ ——————————

"Where are the damned dragons?" Tiago roared at Ravel. They were back in Hartusk Keep—the ruins of Sundabar—and the drow warrior was not in a good mood.

"Arauthator said he would return in the Melting," the Xorlarrin wizard replied. "That time is upon us. Patience, my friend . . ."

"Patience?" Tiago interrupted with incredulity and animosity. "The Baenre and Barrison Del'Armgo soldiers are gone. You tell me to have patience while the matron mother has none, clearly."

"Beware your words, Husband," said Saribel, entering the room.

"We were winning," Tiago replied in low and even tones.

"We still are," Ravel replied. "The dwarves are in their holes, Silverymoon is locked, Sundabar and Nesmé have fallen, and Warlord Hartusk's army only swells with new monsters eager to drink in the blood of our enemies."

"The dwarves . . ." Tiago spat. "Do you think we'll keep them in their holes when they realize that few drow support the orcs in the tunnels?"

"What does it matter?" Saribel asked sharply, drawing Tiago's narrow-eyed glance. Most would wilt in the face of that dangerous look, but Saribel stood taller. "Fifteen tendays and the hourglass sand is already falling fast. We will strike again, beautifully and powerfully, and leave the mark of House Do'Urden burned forever upon the memories of those survivors in the Silver Marches. And then we will be gone, back home, to House Do'Urden in Menzoberranzan, to revel in the glory of victory."

Ravel nodded with her every word, but Tiago seemed less than convinced.

"So hungry for glory," Saribel berated him with her wicked grin unrelenting, "and too foolish to know that greater glory awaits us in our homeland. We are the instruments of the matron mother, idiot husband. We will carry House Do'Urden forward, step by step, until we and great Baenre surround Matron Mother Del'Armgo on the Ruling Council."

"Third House?" Tiago asked, his voice full of doubt, for indeed, those Houses between Barrison Del'Armgo and Do'Urden were quite capable and powerful. Tiago ran the list silently in his thoughts, trying to sort out which House might be a likely target for House Do'Urden's attempted climb. Despite trying to keep his thoughts private, he found himself shaking his head. Every House above Do'Urden was formidable, and none were without powerful allies. For all her bravado, for all she had already done to assert her dominance, Tiago couldn't see Matron Mother Quenthel taking so great a risk as to go to war beside Do'Urden against any of the other noble Houses.

Perhaps the matron mother would allow the Houses Melarn and Vandree to finally destroy House Fey-Branche, now that the matron mother had extracted Minolin Fey to serve in House Baenre.

Perhaps soon after, Baenre and her allies would turn upon the Melarni and their Vandree allies, eliminating those two Houses, too, from the Ruling Council. By the time the blood dried, the Fifth, Sixth, and Seventh Houses of Menzoberranzan might well be no more, allowing the fast ascent of Matron Mother Quenthel's pet House of Do'Urden.

"Soon after," Tiago whispered with a derisive snort. He had experienced enough of Menzoberranzan's politics to know that such maneuvers would take years, decades even, and all of that with Matron Mother Mez'Barris Armgo wearing her dangerous scowl.

He shook his head. He could see none of it, not anytime soon. Matron Mother Quenthel had already extended herself to the limits of tolerance, between usurping the Eighth House with her Do'Urden creation and granting a ninth seat on the Ruling Council to her sister Sos'Umptu. All of Menzoberranzan, and even the Q'Xorlarrin soldiers serving here in the Silver Marches, whispered at the brash moves by Matron Mother Quenthel. Only the threat of House wars and a web of powerful allies were keeping the city from exploding into an all-out civil war. The threat of war could often be a greater shackle than the war itself.

And even if Saribel's hopes began to materialize and House Do'Urden began her ascent up the rungs of the Ruling Council, what did that matter to Tiago? He was a Baenre, by blood and birthright, and that House would ever rule supreme in Menzoberranzan, and surely over House Do'Urden, which was no more than a shadow cast by the matron mother for her own advantage.

"But of course you have other plans, do you not, Husband?" Saribel accused with a wicked grin. "It is not about Menzoberranzan for you, is it? Or about the glory of House Baenre or House Do'Urden, or about the structure and security of Q'Xorlarrin."

"Why would I care for Q'Xorlarrin?" he asked dismissively.

"It is my Hou—"

"Was," Tiago pointedly interrupted.

Saribel conceded the point with a nod, but that knowing, wicked grin never left her face. "This is all," she said, lifting her arms to take in the environment around her, "about Tiago to you. It is personal, intensely so. It is about the glory of Tiago, and of those gains you can make here to further your personal power in Menzoberranzan."

"Are you any different, Matron Mother Do'Urden?" Tiago asked, sarcastically throwing Saribel's own ambitions to rule House Do'Urden back in her face.

"No," she admitted. "But I see the gains of this war already achieved. Few drow have fallen, though many enemies are dead, and Warlord Hartusk is entrenched enough to cause havoc and misery to Luruar for decades to come. And all in the name of Do'Urden. We have already won, Husband."

"Almost," said Tiago.

"Fifteen tendays," Ravel said from the side. "One hundred and fifty days to coax the rogue from the dwarven hole and kill him."

"And so I shall," Tiago vowed.

The room's door banged open and in strode Warlord Hartusk with determined, powerful strides.

"Where are the dragons?" the brutish orc demanded.

"A question I just asked," said Tiago.

"The Melting has begun," Hartusk growled, using the nickname of the fourth month. "It is time, but we need the dragons."

"We have thousands of soldiers," said Ravel. "Tens of thousands! We can press Silverymoon and assail Everlund even without . . ."

Hartusk's growl, so full of anger and threat, cut him short. "The dwarves came out," he said.

"Which dwarves?" Tiago and Ravel asked together, both clearly surprised and intrigued.

"Mithral Hall," Hartusk explained. "They burst from their door, then ran back in before my armies could swarm over them. But they stole supplies, many supplies, and so they are safe in their hole once more. I need dragons to keep them in, and to dig, aye to dig into their halls, that orc spears will find dwarven hearts."

Tiago smiled knowingly and nodded.

"Everlund," Warlord Hartusk demanded, and Tiago smiled all the wider, pleased that the orc leader was perceptive enough to understand that Tiago doubted their intended course. If the dwarves were breaking out behind them, prodding farther to the south would be foolhardy.

"Arauthator said he would return, and so he shall," Saribel put in.

Warlord Hartusk stared at her for a few moments, then snapped his glare onto Tiago. With a growl and a great harrumph, the brutish orc strode from the room, slamming the door behind him.

"He doesn't even know yet," Tiago remarked, referring to the recall of the Menzoberranyr, with fully three out of every four dark elves—perhaps more—who had come in support of the war leaving for the deeper Underdark.

"This should prove to be fun," Ravel said dryly.

"He is an orc," Saribel put in, "easily distracted, easily pleased."

"You intend to sleep with him?" Tiago asked, drawing a scowl from Saribel.

She turned to her brother instead and asked, "Well?"

Tiago, too, turned to Ravel, but his expression was one of honest curiosity.

"Lorgru didn't have the time to gather them," Ravel answered his sister.

"So you have them?"

"They are in the crypt in Dark Arrow Keep."

"Then go and get them," Saribel demanded.

Ravel heaved a sigh and looked over at Tiago with great lament. "The sword and armor of the first King Obould," he explained. "Gifts for Warlord Hartusk."

"Where did you get such an idea?" Tiago demanded, and Ravel held his hand out to Saribel.

Tiago's incredulous gaze fell over her.

"While you plot and connive for the lust of the rogue Do'Urden and the sake of your own glory, I am thinking of the wider view, Husband," she said.

"Hartusk usurped Lorgru," Tiago reminded. "You are likely to incite a civil war among the orcs!"

But Saribel was merely shaking her head. "Putting that fiery greatsword in the hands of Warlord Hartusk will remind all of the time of Obould," she said. "And so we begin again the whispers that this was all ordained, a plot by Lolth and Gromph executed by King Obould the First and a drow spy named Drizzt Do'Urden to secure a foothold in the Silver Marches for just this day. It was Tos'un Armgo's idea. He remembers well the days of the first King Obould."

Tiago stared at her for some time, impressed and a bit afraid. In the end, he could only mutter once more, "Where are the damned dragons?"

"Regis heard Duke Tiago with his own ears," Knight-Commander Aleina Brightlance reminded the sitting Lord of Silverymoon. Beside her, Regis shifted nervously from foot to foot, very aware of the withering gaze of the great Taern Hornblade, the battle-mage they called Thunderspell.

"You ask me to weaken my garrison with the hordes of orcs and giants encamped around Silverymoon on the word of a halfling I barely know?" Lord Hornblade replied. "A halfling *you* hardly know?"

"So once more you doubt my story?" Regis asked. "And the tale of Wulfgar? I thought we had settled this, Lord Hornblade. Have not your priests . . ."

He paused when Hornblade held up his hands in defeat. "Yes, yes," he said. "You are Regis of Icewind Dale, once steward of Mithral Hall. Your claim has been verified."

"But you just said—"

"And friend to Drizzt Do'Urden," Hornblade went on. "Drizzt Do'Urden of House Do'Urden of Menzoberranzan, who have come to the surface to prod forth the legions of Many-Arrows. To bring misery to my door."

"You cannot believe that," Regis quietly mouthed.

"Duke Tiago Do'Urden of Nesmé has executed hundreds," Lord Hornblade said. "He led the fight that killed King Bromm of Citadel Adbar. He cut off the head of King Firehelm in Sundabar and flew about the city on his pet dragon with the trophy. Aleina saw it herself! Did you not, Knight-Commander?"

"I saw Tiago," Aleina carefully answered.

"Tiago *Do'Urden*," said Hornblade.

"Tiago *Baenre*," Regis corrected. "Of House Baenre, First House of Menzoberranzan."

"He calls himself Do'Urden."

"I do not know why," Regis admitted. "But whatever it may be, Drizzt is not a part of it. Wulfgar and I were separated from him and King

Bruenor in the upper tunnels of the Underdark, trying to get to Mithral Hall. Drizzt has nothing to do with the aggression of Many-Arrows, Lord Hornblade, unless it is to put an end to that aggression by the blade."

"Was it a Do'Urden felled by Wulfgar's throw of Aegis-fang when my troupe made our last run to Silverymoon?" Aleina added. "For that drow was surely killed by the blow."

Lord Hornblade's expression and uplifted hands bade them both to relent.

"If you are wrong about this, Silverymoon will be in desperate straits," Hornblade said.

"We are not asking for a large force," Aleina said. "And we will need only enough wizards to keep us from the searching eyes of the orcs."

"And the drow and the dragons," Hornblade corrected. "You will need powerful magic to deceive the eye of a dragon."

Aleina bowed her head, conceding the point.

"They are rallying their forces at Sundabar, determined to sweep southeast of Silverymoon and strike at Everlund," Hornblade said quietly, repeating the report Aleina had delivered. He rubbed his hand deliberately over his cheeks and beard, staring hard at the duo.

"It is a wise move for them," he decided. "Everlund will be no easy battle, surely, but the city has not the magical firepower Silverymoon can deliver, and it is that magic that keeps the dragons warily high when they pass over our walls."

"It is a fool's errand," Regis argued. Aleina gasped, and Hornblade arched one eyebrow. "They stretch their line past powerful enemies. This is our opportunity. Give us resources, I beg, Lord Hornblade. We will peck at their lines and cripple them before they can begin their march. We will choose the battles and the fields upon which they are fought, and so the orcs will lose and lose again. And should they choose to come against you, it will be with a depleted and dispirited force."

"Well-argued, I admit," Hornblade said. He looked to Aleina. "And you are determined to lead this force? I had hoped to promote you to the leadership of the Knights in Silver and the defense of the city, and now you tell me that you will not even remain in Silverymoon?"

The woman could not suppress her obvious intrigue at the intriguing prospect the Lord of Silverymoon had just dangled in front of her. But she shook her head.

"It is a good plan," she decided. "Our enemies cannot overrun Silverymoon, nor can they get into the dwarven citadels. Their thirst for blood has driven them to err. This beast, Hartusk, needs a conquest, but his lust exposes his flanks. I will be the tip of the sword that stabs relentlessly into those flanks."

"A cavalry group," said Lord Hornblade. "Fifty riders, including the three illusionists you'll need to keep you safely hidden, a pair of skilled battle-mages, and four priests specializing in the healing arts."

"Fifty warriors plus the nine," Aleina bargained. "Plus the ten, I say, adding a third battle-mage. And an extra horse, a large one, and as fine a pony as can be found."

Lord Hornblade stared at her and grinned. "Forty-eight warriors, counting yourself, plus the horse and pony for your new friends, and—"

"The ten," Aleina said, matching his grin.

"And if I may," Regis said after a long pause, and both looked to him with surprise. "Credits for me at the apothecary? I am an alchemist of no small skill, and carry all the tools necessary to ply my trade." He tapped his magical pouch.

Lord Hornblade could only chuckle. "Perhaps I should surrender and simply ride with you," he said, and though it started as a joke, by the time he finished the sentence, he and Aleina were looking into each other's eyes quite seriously.

CHAPTER 13

THE HAUNTED KING

Brother Afafrenfere walked so lightly on the mud and meager snowpack that remained northeast of the Glimmerwood that he left no tracks. Nor did he make a whisper of sound, gliding like a shadow through the trees.

He came upon a pair of orc sentries, simply walked right up to them. When they noticed him, it was already too late.

Afafrenfere's right elbow went into the throat of one, turning its scream into a gurgle. Up swept his left hand at the same time, lifting the other orc's spear harmlessly high and wide. The monk turned fast, right palm sweeping out and up, catching the orc in the chin and nose and lifting its face to the sky. Afafrenfere stepped into that blow with his right foot, placing it between the orc's feet and putting his shoulder beside the orc's. Out went his right hand again—or still, since it was the same movement—not to hit the orc this time, but to flash past the beast's head.

Now the monk turned again as he pulled back, right hand catching the orc's hair and driving it forward to stumble and trip over the monk's strongly planted foot. It pitched forward, Afafrenfere helping it along, driving its face right into the trunk of a thick oak with a sickening crunch.

The first orc was on the ground by then, on its knees, grabbing at its throat and gasping for air.

Afafrenfere's circle kick snapped its neck.

The monk moved along, now carrying the orc's spear, which he had deftly taken as the brute had dived into the tree trunk.

Being human in the dark of night, he might have seemed at a disadvantage surrounded by orcs with their lowlight vision. But it was not so. The monk's senses were perfectly attuned to his task, every rustle, every movement registering so clearly and distinctly, every smell wafting to him—and he knew when those scents revealed an orc.

He lifted the spear beside his right ear and leveled it. He closed his eyes. He didn't need them—indeed, they would likely distract him. He smelled the orc ahead and sensed it in ways he didn't even understand, whether it was a formerly imperceptible sound or some sixth sense screaming at him to beware.

He waited, letting the signals and sounds come to him.

A slight rustle and he turned the spear tip out just a bit.

He didn't throw the spear at the orc, at least not in his thoughts. He saw the spear as an extension of the target, as if it belonged there all along and he was just allowing it to return to its rightful place.

The orc sentry tumbled out of the brush up ahead, the spear through it, back to front. It struggled and whimpered, but Afafrenfere passed it as he continued on his way and stomped a heavy foot upon its throat, ending its misery.

The monk glanced up at the mountain peak to his right, judging his distance from it and the one to his left, and picturing in his mind where the dragon Ilnezhara had told him to go. Reflexively, he reached into his belt pouch, running his fingers over the small, smooth stone she had given him. He could feel the pulsing magic within the stone.

Look deeper, a voice inside Afafrenfere's head implored him.

He clutched the stone more tightly, brought it from his pouch and up to his heart. He closed his eyes and let himself fall within the smoothness of the stone, deeper and deeper.

He saw the dragon eye looking back at him, felt the approval, and knew that Ilnezhara had "watched" him kill the orcs.

Afafrenfere replaced the stone in his pouch and went on his way.

Silent.

Deadly.

Bruenor shook his head. "Should've been Felbarr," he whispered. "Ain't likin' this, elf."

"Hartusk is mustering his forces about Sundabar, too near to Citadel Felbarr," Sinnafein explained. "Were we caught in a pitched battle there, the orcs would likely reinforce, and with greater numbers than we could possibly defeat."

"Y'ever been to Citadel Adbar?" Bruenor asked her. "Ah, but she's a fortress to see! She's got rings of defense pits, walls and bridges crisscrossin' all about. If them orcs're using the outer rings as their own now, we'll not get near the place."

"But we shall," Sinnafein replied. "For the Haunted King is about. And now the beasts of Many-Arrows have had enough of his raids and have laid a trap at last."

"The Haunted King?" Catti-brie asked.

"King o' Adbar," explained Amber. "Ain't been right in the head since his brother got himself killed."

"These foothills are thick with orcs," Drizzt said, and as he did, he looked up to the northeast, where several campfires could be seen on the southern slope of a low mountain trail. He pointed it out to Bruenor and Catti-brie, who nodded.

"More than we can defeat, likely," Sinnafein admitted. "But with their eyes turned northward all, looking toward Adbar. My archers are in the low forests—"

"As is me monk," said Amber with a grin. "And a bit farther, I'm guessin'."

"—blinding the sentries," Sinnafein finished.

"Forevermore," Amber explained.

Drizzt's hand reflexively went to Taulmaril. He wanted to be out there hunting, but they had arrived too late for that.

Reports came filtering back to the group soon after, elves sketching topographical maps of the area and indicating the location and strength of the orc positions. The most troubling report came from Myriel when she at last returned, long after midnight, to describe a position of scores of frost giants.

Bruenor cast an uneasy look at Sinnafein at that revelation. "Felbarr . . ." he muttered. "We should've gone to King Emerus."

"They were not here just a few days ago," the elf replied. "We had no reports of any giants about at all. Nor should they have passed this way as they went in answer to Hartusk's muster."

"Might be that them orcs're wantin' to put down the Haunted King afore they begin their march south," Amber reasoned. "He's been stinging 'em, so 'tis said, and might that he's stinged 'em too many times."

Sinnafein looked around, clearly unsure.

"We come this far," Bruenor put in. "Ain't for lettin' a few giants stop us now, are we? I bringed Bungalow Thump and his Gutbuster boys along just for the party, and the party's all the better with giant knees needing to be crushed."

The world made no sense to him any longer. All had been well. Even after the death of his father, who had lived a long and prosperous and battle-filled and glory-filled life. Harnoth and Bromm had been pained when putting the stones on old King Harbromm's cairn, of course, for what loyal and loving son would not? But there was a sense of rightness about that passing, a feeling that this was the inevitability of life, and the proper passing of the torch, generation to generation.

Now, though, the world made no sense to Harnoth. Bromm had been taken from him so quickly, so unexpectedly.

They were supposed to grow old together, raising their own broods and passing the torch as they each went to join their Da in the Halls of Moradin. They were supposed to share decades together in battle and in leadership, leaning on each other, propping each other through the trials of ruling mighty Citadel Adbar, the Armory of Luruar.

It wasn't supposed to be like this. But Bromm was gone, and Harnoth could do nothing about it. He should have been there beside his brother, he thought every night since the tragedy in the Cold Vale.

He should have been there to save Bromm, or to die beside him. But he wasn't, and all the "should haves" and "might have beens" meant nothing.

Nothing.

Because Bromm was dead and gone, and he wasn't coming back.

And the world made no sense to Harnoth, the sole king of Citadel Adbar, and made even less sense to him when the hordes had come to surround his proud fortress, and the dark elves had come to hide in the shadows of the tunnels, killing his kin.

And he could do nothing.

He could not bring back his brother.

He could not make sense of the world.

So King Harnoth—the Haunted King, they now whispered—could discern only one acceptable course: he would fight.

Even through the deep of winter, he went out, oftentimes alone, but sometimes, as with this expedition, surrounded by his fiercest and most fiercely loyal fellows, hunting the vermin who had slain his brother.

Oretheo Spikes was there beside him this time, and when he looked upon his dear friend, it occurred to Harnoth that the Wilddwarf battlerager was becoming as haunted as he. Perhaps it was the lack of food. Rations were meager indeed in Citadel Adbar, and many had succumbed. Oretheo's eyes were as hollow as Harnoth's own.

But it might not be the short rations, too. Oretheo had been there for the Battle of the Cold Vale—indeed, he was the only dwarf to return to Adbar from that slaughter—and he had seen King Bromm's cruel death, had seen Warlord Hartusk with Bromm's severed head in hand.

King Harnoth glanced back at the exit channel that had led them from Citadel Adbar, and his mind's eye went farther, back to the fortress itself.

To the pile of dwarf bodies, stacked in the mausoleum as neatly as firewood, awaiting the coffin masons.

He looked back to the exit channel and thought back to Citadel Adbar, and thought, too, that today would be a good day to die.

"Here," Mickey said, pointing to the detailed map of the region southwest of Citadel Adbar. She indicated a long valley between two mountain spurs.

Sinnafein glanced at the other leaders, particularly at Bruenor, who shook his head doubtfully.

"They got giants," the dwarf explained. "Giants to put up in them hills on both sides, to rain stones upon hairy heads."

"It will be seen to," Mickey replied. "This is the place."

"I ain't thinkin' it is," said Bruenor.

"Then your brothers of Adbar will die there without you," Mickey answered.

Bruenor and his friends, Sinnafein too, fixed the copper-haired elf with angry stares.

"This is the place," was all that Mickey would say to those doubting looks, ending any further arguments. "Be quick."

"I'll take the lead," Drizzt offered, but Mickey's sister appeared then, shaking her head pointedly at the drow.

"The monk is in position?" Mickey asked.

"Awaiting King Harnoth, and Drizzt," replied the other, who called herself Lady Z.

"Awaiting th' elf?" Bruenor asked.

"Come, drow," Lady Z bade Drizzt. "We have a most important task for you."

Drizzt looked to his friends, mostly to Catti-brie, who wore her suspicions clearly on her face.

Mickey walked over and took Drizzt by the hand and pulled him off to the side. He instinctively tried to resist, but quickly realized that he might as well be trying to hold back an avalanche. It was easier to follow her.

"Go with my sister," Mickey explained to him privately. "She will send you to Afafrenfere's side, and he will guide you to King Harnoth."

Drizzt stared at her skeptically, not catching on.

"Ilnezhara—Lady Z—will explain in more detail."

The drow's expression did not change. "My friends and allies are here."

"This goes beyond them," Mickey explained. "It is our mutual friend's idea, one to gauge the reputation of Drizzt Do'Urden more clearly among the folk of the Silver Marches, and one, perhaps, to begin repairing that reputation."

She let go of Drizzt's hand and motioned him toward Ilnezhara, but the drow still hesitated.

"Our friend is long-sighted and clever," Mickey reminded him. "Perhaps as much so as any of the lesser beings I have ever known."

"Lesser beings?" Drizzt echoed, thinking that a rather curious, and rather telling, way of putting it. He thought of some of Jarlaxle's previous associates and wondered if he might again be dealing with a mind flayer.

"Go, or do not," Mickey said a bit more sharply. "But be quick in any case because the monk cannot wait for much longer."

Drizzt nodded before he crossed over to Catti-brie, gave her a kiss for luck, and promised that he would see her soon. "Watch over her," he said to Bruenor and Athrogate, "and you watch over them," he added to Catti-brie.

He sprinted off to catch up to Ilnezhara, who was moving off.

"What's that about, then?" Bruenor demanded when Mickey walked back over to join them.

"It is about positioning the pieces on the sava board for a quicker kill," she replied, and turned to Sinnafein. "You know the place, and the way?"

The elf nodded.

"Be quick!" Mickey said sharply, and with that, the strange elf turned and leaped away, and what a leap it was, lifting her high and far to disappear into a copse of trees some thirty strides away.

"By Moradin's hairy bum," Bruenor muttered.

"She threw a giant," Sinnafein dryly reminded them, and off they went.

In tight ranks, the war band followed, some three hundred Clan Moonwood elves supported by Bruenor's two hundred shield dwarves, half of them Gutbusters. With speed and discipline they churned up the field, arrows set to bowstrings, heavy hammers, axes, and swords drawn and ready.

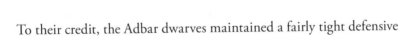

To their credit, the Adbar dwarves maintained a fairly tight defensive formation. But they were in full flight, running from a rain of giant boulders that had wounded several and left three dead.

Their deaths were on him, King Harnoth knew. He shouldn't have come out this far with his twoscore loyal minions.

They had been baited, bit by bit, over the last two tendays. Harnoth had come out, sometimes with a small group, other times, like this day, with a powerful force, but the orcs had been falling back. Each day King Harnoth had to go a bit farther from Adbar's defensive channels to find enemies to slaughter.

This day, too far, perhaps. They had rounded a mountain spur to discover a line of giants behind and above them, and the heavy rain of huge stones had driven the dwarves farther still.

"We can make Twin Pine Valley and run back to the north," Oretheo Spikes told the young king.

"We're not for knowin' what's in Twin Pine," Harnoth replied. He settled his gaze firmly on the Wilddwarf leader. Oretheo Spikes had not come out often. His duties had kept him securing the lower levels of Citadel Adbar, but since few drow had been seen about those tunnels of late, he had joined his king.

"Well, I'm knowin' what's behind, and it canno' be worse than what's ahead," Oretheo Spikes replied, and Harnoth had to shrug and nod his agreement.

On they ranged, sending scouts out to the left and right flanks, and word soon came back that they were being shadowed by large orc contingents.

They were in for a brutal fight this day, King Harnoth knew. Too brutal. He thought of his brother, and fully expected that he'd be seeing Bromm again very soon.

Likely this very day.

He had known all along that it would eventually come to this, where the orcs had seen enough of his excursions and so had set him up for the big fall.

He'd kill ten or more before he fell, he vowed to himself, and he was more than willing, and more than ready, to go to Dwarfhome and the table of Moradin.

Ah, but for the others!

That thought nagged at him and haunted him, particularly since Oretheo Spikes was along this day. Oretheo, the dwarf Harnoth would choose as his successor. The young dwarf king could accept his own fate—indeed, would welcome it—but to think that he was going to take forty others with him wounded him profoundly. Taking his chosen successor with him wounded Harnoth even more.

And for what? What had Citadel Adbar gained with these excursions, with these exercises in angry vengeance?

Or perhaps they would make Twin Pines Valley and so run back to the north and freedom.

"Double-time!" Harnoth ordered his minions. "We can outrun a few ugly orcs!"

But no sooner had he issued the command than the line ahead of him skidded to an abrupt halt, dwarves in the front ranks locking shields, those in the second ranks leveling spears and crossbows.

"Square!" King Harnoth and Oretheo Spikes both ordered at the same time, and the dwarves hustled to a tighter defensive position.

"I am no enemy!" came a call, and Harnoth took some hope as those dwarves in the front seemed to relax just a bit, a few standing taller. The young king pushed his way through the ranks to come up between a pair of shield dwarves.

"Nor am I," said a second voice, and Harnoth's eyes widened when he saw the speaker: a dark elf moving up beside a human.

"I am a friend to Mithral Hall, a friend to Adbar, once a friend to King Harbromm," the drow said. "My name is known to you, and that name is Drizzt Do'Urden."

Dwarves bristled, and the spears leveled once more, and more than one stubby finger squeezed a bit tighter on a crossbow trigger.

"We seek King Harnoth," said the human beside Drizzt. "Please be quick, for your position is tenuous indeed, with enemies all about."

"Adbar names no drow as friend!" King Harnoth cried. "And trusts no drow!"

"Then let me prove my fealty," Drizzt replied. He came forward, hands empty and up high. The human followed him with a similar posture.

They walked right to the shield line.

"You are Harnoth, King of Adbar?" Drizzt asked.

"No, he ain't!" came a rough and grumbling voice from the side, and a stocky fellow in ridged armor shouldered Harnoth aside. "Yer meanin' to speak to Adbar, ye speak to me, drow!"

"Well met again, Oretheo Spikes," Drizzt said.

King Harnoth and all the other dwarves looked to the Wilddwarf for an explanation.

"We met at King Emerus's table," the drow explained, pointedly looking at King Harnoth. "Introduced by King Bruenor, who has returned to aid in the war with Many-Arrows."

"So I been told," said Harnoth, and he shouldered past the shield dwarves to stand immediately in front of the drow.

"And so it is true," said Drizzt. "Now, pray be quick. I have been sent to lead you to Sourpuss Gap." He pointed to the southeast, to a valley between two peaks not far away.

"Giants on Horngar's Horn," King Harnoth said, shaking his head, and indicating the mountain on the northeastern side of the indicated valley.

"That is the only way," the man beside Drizzt told him. "Every other trail is thick with orcs. They will slow you and catch you with forces far beyond your own."

" 'Ere now, ye watch how ye're speaking to me king," said Oretheo Spikes, but Harnoth held his hand up to keep the Wilddwarf back and silent.

"All the region is thick with orcs, and even now their noose tightens about you," Drizzt explained. "I am Drizzt, friend of Bruenor, as your shield dwarf Oretheo Spikes can confirm. I beg that you trust in me now, and quickly, for we are running out of time."

"I knowed what ye said ye was," was all Oretheo Spikes would offer.

"We're runnin' our own way," King Harnoth started to say, but Drizzt cut him short.

"If you stay, you will perish. They are too many, and they were waiting for you. You'll not make the valley in the north, if that is your plan, for surely that's the way the orcs expected your retreat."

"Retreat?" Oretheo Spikes roared. "Bah, tactical flank!"

"They were waiting for you, King Harnoth," Drizzt said. "Surely you knew this would happen soon enough."

"Waiting because a drow elf told 'em we was coming?" asked a suspicious Oretheo Spikes.

"Possibly," Drizzt replied, deflecting the accusation. "Though my friend and I have seen no other drow about."

"Was speakin'—"

"Enough, good Oretheo!" Drizzt snapped at him. "I've no time, nor do you. Sourpuss Gap, with all speed, or know that none of you will return to Citadel Adbar this day." He looked to the human, and they shared a nod, and both ran off to the southeast.

"We will clear the trail!" the human called back.

The forty dwarves bristled around Harnoth—he could feel their eyes upon him, seeking guidance.

"That was the one at Emerus's table?" he asked Oretheo Spikes.

"Aye, him with the one claimin' to be King Bruenor."

"And was it?"

"I be thinkin' aye."

"Sourpuss Gap, then," King Harnoth decided, and he sent his dwarves on a run. He looked to the east, though, as they rounded the mountain.

They would be coming dangerously close once more to the ridgeline full of giant stone-throwers.

But still they ran, and with all speed, down the trails through stands of pine and boulder tumbles. They made the entrance to Sourpuss Gap easily enough, and there found Drizzt and the human waiting for them, and there found, too, a legion of orcs coming the other way.

"Ah, but ye traitorous dog!" Oretheo Spikes started to say to Drizzt—started, but didn't finish, for in the middle of his rant, the drow put up a bow and let fly a lightning arrow down into the gap, blowing down a pair of orcs with that single shot.

"Form here!" the human ordered. "Tight square!"

King Harnoth wasn't sure of what he should do. He noted a peculiar smoke beside the drow, and fell back yelping in surprise as that smoke became a corporeal form, a giant black panther who leaped away immediately toward the advancing orc line.

"More behind!" came a cry from the rear of the dwarven formation.

"Those are yours," Drizzt told King Harnoth. "Strengthen the back of the square!"

A giant boulder crashed down through some nearby trees, snapping branches. A second followed, this time missing the copse and bouncing down nearer to the dwarven position.

"Ah, ye dog, what'd'ye do to me and me boys?" King Harnoth yelled at Drizzt.

On came the orcs, a huge force, roaring up the pass. On came those from behind, who had pursued the dwarves all this way. Over on the ridgeline of Horngar's Horn, several boulders went flying into the dark sky.

"We're fully catched, me king!" Oretheo Spikes cried.

Boulders crashed all around, only good fortune keeping any from flattening a dwarf or two.

With a growl, King Harnoth pushed out through his shield dwarves, moving for Drizzt with his weapon in hand.

The drow just kept up a stream of arrows at the charging orc force, though, and just before Harnoth reached him, a cry rose up from several dwarves, indicating the giants' position. Harnoth glanced that way and understood their confusion, for up on the ridge of Horngar's Horn, something was going on.

Something powerful.

Trees shuddered and shook as if in a hurricane. No boulders came forth, though many giant roars and shrieks—of pain and terror, they seemed—surely did.

"Just kill the damned orcs!" King Harnoth cried, shaking his head. He had no idea what might be happening, and had no time to sit and figure it out.

"The orcs from the rear!" Drizzt ordered him. "Focus on those behind." He turned to the human and said, "Afafrenfere, go!"

The man leaped away, rushing around the dwarven defensive square to help greet the pursuing orc force.

"More in front!" King Harnoth yelled to Drizzt, and indeed, that seemed quite true. The charging horde looked like it would overrun Harnoth's position.

But orcs in the front ranks began to falter and stumble suddenly, tumbling down to the ground and slowing the charge. It took Harnoth a few blinking moments to realize that those front ranks were under a barrage of arrows, unrelenting and deadly. And then came cries from unseen orcs far back in the ranks, and Harnoth realized that battle had been joined in full with this group coming out of Sourpuss Gap, that the ambushers had, in turn, been ambushed.

A massive fireball erupted in the midst of the orc line, and from it stepped a giant made of fire, swatting and burning all the monsters nearby.

"King Bruenor has arrived," Drizzt whispered to him. "With friends. Pray hold the line, King Harnoth."

Breathless, King Harnoth scrambled back through his square and urged his dwarves on, and they did indeed hold the line, focusing all their power on the pursuing orc force. No more boulders came at them from the ridge on Horngar's Horn, nor did any of the orcs coming out of Sourpuss Gap even reach their position.

Through it all, Drizzt calmly stood there, guarding the back of Harnoth's turned square, Taulmaril the Heartseeker in hand, a line of devastating arrows reaching out to destroy any who ventured too near.

And the elven rain continued as well, with Sinnafein's hundreds of archers showering the orcs with death. Somewhere out among that group, Guenhwyvar roared, and Drizzt nodded, confident that another foul orc had met its death. He heard a sour note from a cracked silver horn, and knew that the spirit of Thibbledorf Pwent, too, had joined the fray.

"Elven rain and dwarven mud," Oretheo Spikes said, coming up to Drizzt as the battle neared its end.

Drizzt looked at the Wilddwarf and couldn't help but smile, grimly, for Oretheo Spikes was covered in mud and blood, some of the latter likely his own.

"Sorry for doubtin' ye, elf," the Wilddwarf said. "But suren it's been a long and tough winter, eh?"

"Indeed," said Drizzt. "But the spring will be brighter."

Oretheo Spikes clapped him on the shoulder and turned back, but remained as King Harnoth came up to join them.

Tears streaked the young dwarf's face, and he looked to Drizzt, unable to speak, but clearly nodding his approval. Few orcs remained, and the force approaching from Sourpuss Gap was one of allies, led by a red-bearded dwarf with a one-horned helm, banging a many-notched axe upon a shield set with the foaming mug standard of Clan Battlehammer.

"We thought ye might be needin' a bit o' help," Bruenor said to Harnoth, and the two shared a great hug.

"Aye, and more's to come," said a black-bearded dwarf standing behind the former King of Mithral Hall. He spun a pair of glassteel morningstars. "And more to murder. To put things a'right and back in their order!"

Before Athrogate could offer his signature belly laugh to punctuate his bad rhyme, Amber Gristle O'Maul of the Adbar O'Mauls gave one for him.

Bruenor looked Harnoth in the eye. "We'll break yer siege, then on to Felbarr," he explained. "Our friend Emerus is sure to be waitin'!"

"I'm owin' yer friend an apology," Harnoth replied, and he glanced over at Drizzt, who stood with a young, auburn-haired woman in a most remarkable blouse and with blue tendrils of some magic Harnoth did not understand curling around her bare forearms. "For suren was I doubtin' him."

"He knows," Bruenor assured the young king. "Ye need not say it. That one, he knows better'n any."

CHAPTER 14

STINGING GNATS

RIZZT WALKED INTO A CLEARING ON A HIGH BLUFF OUTSIDE OF CITADEL Adbar two days later. Below him, some battles continued, but the victory was essentially complete. After the rout of the giants on Horngar's Horn and the orc legions they were supporting, the three armies—Sinnafein's elves, Bruenor's dwarves, and the might of Citadel Adbar itself—had wasted no time putting the other pockets of orc enemies to the sword.

And always there remained this fourth force, all but unseen, whispered about in hushed tones by the elves and dwarves, and often revealed by the screams of terror of their enemies.

Now, it was clear, Citadel Adbar was free, and while Drizzt had come to the call of a secret ally—one whose identity he strongly suspected—Bruenor, Sinnafein, Catti-brie, and Oretheo Spikes were plotting the road to Citadel Felbarr.

"So at last you will reveal the truth to me," Drizzt said when he walked into the clearing to join Mickey and Lady Z, beautiful elves both, who waited for him there.

"Which truth?" Mickey asked. "There are many truths. Some concern you, and some do not."

"Start with those that concern me."

"End with them as well," said Lady Z, who Drizzt thought the more haughty and less friendly of the two.

"Start with Jarlaxle then," said Drizzt.

"The less you speak that name aloud, my old friend, the happier I will be," said another voice, and out of the trees—not across the way, but those right behind Drizzt, those Drizzt had just passed—came the drow mercenary. He walked up beside Drizzt and bowed gracefully, brushing his huge hat on the ground. "Well met, again."

"And it would seem that I am in your debt once more," said Drizzt, offering a respectful bow of his own.

"I do what I do for my own sake as much as yours, so the only debt I hold over you is one of friendship," Jarlaxle graciously replied. Lady Z rolled her eyes—and those eyes seemed strange to Drizzt at that moment, as if she had let down a bit of her disguise, enough for him to see a hint of a draconic undertone.

His thoughts of mind flayers vanished, and Drizzt felt his knees go weak as he realized the truth of these rather remarkable sisters. He thought of the giants on Horngar's Horn, and of the frenzied flight of the main encampment of enemies north of Mithral Hall. He knew what beasts could invoke such terror—and knew, too, that his enemies were employing just such beasts in their war.

"Have you figured it . . . *them*, out yet?" Jarlaxle asked, and like Drizzt, he turned his gaze to the strange sisters.

Drizzt continued to stare at Lady Z, and the "elf" responded with a wicked smile, and flared her now clearly reptilian eyes. Drizzt swallowed hard, uncomfortable and unsure. He heard Bruenor's warnings about Jarlaxle's possible motives ringing in his thoughts once more, and it took him a long time indeed to tear his gaze from the elf who was not an elf and look back at the mercenary.

"I have hints, nothing more," he said.

"He knows what we are," Lady Z told Jarlaxle.

"Ah, but does he know why we are here?" her sister asked.

"I'll not deny that," Drizzt said to Jarlaxle, though he was staring once more at Lady Z, unable to tear his gaze from her. She knew it, too, he could tell, and was enjoying it immensely.

"Which?" the ever-cryptic mercenary asked.

"Dragons," Drizzt answered.

"Well played!" Jarlaxle congratulated. "I give you Tazmikella and Ilnezhara, sisters as they claim, but hardly contained within the pretty elf trappings they have chosen."

"What is your game, Jarlaxle?" Drizzt asked.

"I have come to support friends."

"You have gone to war with Menzoberranzan? With Matron Mother Quenthel, or whomever it is that now rules that wretched place?"

"I would not go that far."

"Are these the same dragons Tiago calls his own, then?" Drizzt asked, and he regretted it as soon as the words left his mouth. Both of the women scowled fiercely at him, and nearly overwhelmed him with projected thoughts of them melting him where he stood and eating him after.

"The orc warlord Hartusk has gained the assistance of a couple of whites," Jarlaxle explained. "Our allies here are not white dragons, not chromatic dragons at all, and I think you owe them an apology for even insinuating as much."

Drizzt stared at them hard, but didn't offer anything in the way of an apology. "Am I to believe that the orcs commandeered the help of dragons all by themselves?"

"I believe that Matron Mother Quenthel, and Gromph, likely played a role."

"I am not well-versed in dragonkind," Drizzt admitted. "These two before me are not chromatic, you say?"

"We are metallic," Tazmikella answered, coming forward. She stopped short of Drizzt, smiled rather wickedly, then took his breath away as she reverted to her natural form, a gigantic copper dragon nearly filling the lea in front of him.

"Copper," Jarlaxle said dryly, and he chuckled a bit, clearly enjoying the discomfort that marked Drizzt's unavoidable backstepping. "Exciting ladies, trust me."

"Why would they . . . ?" Drizzt started to ask.

"We have our own reasons, and they remain one of those secrets that do not concern you, Drizzt Do'Urden," Ilnezhara answered for Jarlaxle.

"They have come with you, and they . . . they wage war on the orcs and giants who are allied with Menzoberranzan," Drizzt managed to stammer, trying very hard to get his legs back under him. He had met a couple of dragons before, and never had it been a pleasant experience.

"Which is why I must insist on your ability to keep a secret," said Jarlaxle.

Drizzt turned on him sternly. "Why do you wish Menzoberranzan to lose?"

208

"Lose?" Jarlaxle replied with feigned incredulity. "Menzoberranzan has no real stake in any of this, of course. They're just causing trouble. From my perspective, the Silver Marches are much more profitable to me if they're held by the kingdoms of Luruar, not if Many-Arrows darkens the area and ruins the trade."

Drizzt listened to every word and believed none of it. There was something more at play here, but he also knew enough about Jarlaxle to realize that the truth of his involvement surely went much deeper than his offered reasoning, and into convoluted twists and turns that would make the most ferocious of Lolth's chaotic disciples shake her head in disbelief.

"I want the orcs to lose," Jarlaxle added, his voice full of certainty and sincerity. "Menzoberranzan has all but abandoned them now, their games complete in this region. This is not a difficult choice for me, though again, your secrecy is much appreciated."

Drizzt looked at him, looked him straight in the eye, silently conveying that he would expect an answer to his question at some other time.

"Now, there is much afoot with the Melting on in full," Jarlaxle said. "My friends here have agreed to show us, if you are willing." He pointed to the side of the lea, where now sat a pair of leather contraptions and the straps that made up saddles for dragons.

"Are you ready for a rare thrill, my friend?" Jarlaxle asked, when Drizzt did not respond.

"To ride a dragon?" Drizzt replied, his voice barely a whisper.

"There are several ways to ride a dragon," Jarlaxle said, and Ilnezhara giggled—rather lewdly, Drizzt thought, and he let the thought go at that.

"And they are all thrilling," Jarlaxle finished. "Come, let us go and see the lay of the land, that we might better plot the destruction of our common enemies."

Catti-brie sat alone that night in front of the bonfire burning in the dwarven encampment along one of Citadel Adbar's defensive channels. There was no need for secrecy now. The entire garrison of Adbar had come forth, save those few brigades securing the lower tunnels. And Adbar was the largest of the dwarven enclaves in the North, housing nearly twenty thousand dwarves, and with a garrison that included among its ranks nearly half that number of battle veterans. The force of five hundred that had rescued King Harnoth's battle group and opened the way for Citadel Adbar to shatter the siege now numbered almost nine thousand.

The elves were out and about—any approaching enemy force large enough to threaten the power assembled here would be spotted long before they neared the camp.

Catti-brie, too, turned her eyes outward. She cast a divination spell, eager to explore this new power she had come to understand in the long months trapped in Mithral Hall.

She peered into the flames—too intently at first, she realized when nothing came to her. She sat back and forced herself to calm down, to suppress her eagerness, and so allow herself to be more passive and more receptive. She even reached forth and put her hand into the flames, feeling their tickling dance, her ruby ring glowing with power and energy as it protected her flesh. And that magical band, in the dance of the flames, brought Catti-brie's thoughts more fully into the living fire, and through the flames to the Elemental Plane of Fire.

She saw through the flames and into another fire.

She saw orcs. Thousands of orcs. Tens of thousands of orcs. They danced along ruined walls, and drummed on the stretched skins of some unfortunate victims. They punched each other as they passed in their wild dancing. Males threw females to the ground and leaped atop them, and the same was true in reverse. And the song played in her head, a discordant cacophony of whoops and hollers and snarls and hisses punctuated by the occasional scream, usually caught somewhere between ecstasy and agony.

Catti-brie felt as if she were playing voyeur to a strange orgy of unbridled bloodlust, manifesting itself in an orgy of unbridled lust.

But she couldn't turn away. It was simply too overwhelming, too powerful, too . . . vile. They ripped each other's skin. They bit each other savagely, drawing blood. And they drank that blood, even licked it from one another. And they rubbed it all over their half-naked, and often fully naked, bodies.

It took Catti-brie a long while to get past the immediacy of the powerful images to recognize that this was Sundabar she was viewing.

Broken, despoiled, violated Sundabar.

And she saw thousands of campfires around the place, and through her ruby ring sensed thousands more. The woman lost her breath at the realization of the sheer size of Many-Arrows' forces.

"Hundreds of thousands," she whispered. But what was she seeing? Was it the past, the fall of the proud city? The present, where the orcs were known to be mustering?

Or was this the future of Luruar?

It was all too confusing, but again, the woman did not concentrate on it too deeply, and rather, let the fires guide her.

She found herself gazing through the hearth of a quiet room, where three dwarves slumped in chairs, their expressions full of misery and despair. Citadel Felbarr, she realized, though she did not recognize these particular dwarves.

But she knew it was Felbarr, and she could feel the desperation.

And so she went, from fire to fire, around the lands, to orc camps and ogre clusters, to destroyed Nesmé and crouched Silverymoon.

She fell back, startled, at the sudden sight of a magical fireball or some other explosion, with roiling flames lifting up into the air and curling under to form a cap and stalk like some tall mushroom.

Orc forms silhouetted by the brilliance of the blast rushed around frantically, and a line of riders—human riders!—crested the hilltop the orcs had taken as a camp, weapons shining in the firelight.

And then in the magical light as the area lit up Catti-brie recognized the uniform of the Knights in Silver, the famed Silverymoon garrison. She soon found the leader of the band, turning her mount and yelling orders, and though Catti-brie couldn't see much of the fighting from the angle afforded her by the flames, she knew that the orcs were being routed.

Despite her receptive determination, or perhaps because of it, the woman leaned forward intently. An orc came at the Knight in Silver, and the woman dispatched the creature with a quick parry and thrust.

An ogre appeared at the side of Catti-brie's line of vision, and she wanted to call out a warning to the Knight in Silver, but she couldn't.

Something flashed past the knight and the ogre flew away. Even as Catti-brie tried to sort it out, she fell back and cried out in shock.

Wulfgar.

The diviner laughed and wept, tears streaming down her face, as the realization hit with overwhelming force and speed.

Wulfgar!

And a pony rushed past him, the rider firing a hand crossbow off one way and throwing a ceramic ball the other way, then drawing a three-bladed dagger and a fabulous rapier as he too rushed happily and eagerly into battle.

They were alive.

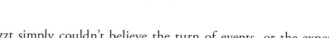

Drizzt simply couldn't believe the turn of events, or the experience that had been offered him. The air was cold, but it hardly bothered him, given the thrill of the ride and the view—oh the view!—Tazmikella was affording him. The Silver Marches rolled out below him as the dragon soared on high. Dark silhouettes of mountains and a million points of firelight assailed his sensibilities, threatening to overwhelm him with the sheer scale and grandeur of it all.

Flashes in the south caught his attention, and caught Tazmikella's as well, apparently—and her sister's, carrying Jarlaxle beside them. The dragons veered and swooped lower, following the line of the Surbrin below and speeding across the lands.

They passed the great bridge east of Mithral Hall, keeping high over the campfires of the besieging orc force. Drizzt could see them clearly, four separate encampments, with one by the Surbrin, one to the west in Keeper's Dale, and two up north, with the largest by far being the north-ernmost. The orcs had returned to the same strategy they had employed when Drizzt and the others had broken out.

The drow noted it carefully, measuring the size of the bands as he sorted various strategies for overrunning the fools.

That scene was left far behind in short order as the dragons rolled across the miles, the wind so strong that it blew tears from Drizzt's lavender eyes.

Up again went Tazmikella, slowing now as she approached the region where they had seen the flashes. Far in the distance, Drizzt noted a great concentration of fires and magical lights. It was Silverymoon, with the orc siege force holding the fields around it, and those fields nearest the city's wall magically lit to aid the sentries. For a moment, the drow figured that Jarlaxle and his dragon friends must be taking him to that place—a city where he had once known great friendship and special allies—but Tazmikella banked suddenly, soaring out to the west.

On a bare hilltop, a battle raged. From this great height, Drizzt couldn't make out many of the particulars, but it became clear to him that a force of riders was routing and scattering an orc encampment.

He smiled and nodded. "Are we going to help?" he asked his mount, having to shout to hear his own voice above the wind. Reflexively, Drizzt reached for Taulmaril, and thought it would be a fine thing indeed to rain lightning arrows upon the orcs from this most extraordinary mount.

"They do not need us," the dragon answered, and her great voice was not at all thin in the wind. "Nor do we wish to reveal ourselves too soon to our enemies. Let their dragons be located and engaged before we are known."

"A closer look?" Drizzt asked. He couldn't resist the pull of that battle, or the idea that someone down there possibly needed him. "Quickly?"

In response, the dragon dived suddenly and even tucked her leathery wings, gaining speed in free fall. She spread wide those wings and leveled out so gracefully and powerfully that Drizzt felt as if his stomach was still falling, and he could hardly hold himself upright in the saddle against the tremendous press of changing momentum.

By the time he had straightened himself and secured his seat, the battle was already behind him. He glanced back for a fleeting moment, and noted an orc looking back at him in confusion.

And noted . . .

"Turn back!" he yelled at Tazmikella.

"No," came her calm and unequivocal response, and now the battle was far, far behind them indeed.

Drizzt looked back anyway. He had to. And though he could see nothing more than the distant flames by then, that last image burned in his thoughts.

Wulfgar.

PART THREE

THE KING OF DWARVEN KINGS

Brother Afafrenfere was sitting on a large stone—reclining actually, and looking up at the blackened sky, where the stars should have been, though alas, there are no stars to be found in the Silver Marches at this dark time. He was not startled by my presence, for surely he knew that the stone he carried was a beacon to the dragon Ilnezhara, and so allowed her to use her magic to teleport me in beside him.

I greeted him, and he gave a slight nod, but he just kept staring up into the darkness. And he did so with an expression I surely recognized, for it is one I have often worn myself.

"What troubles you, brother?" I asked.

He didn't look over, didn't sit up.

"I have found a power I do not quite understand," he finally admitted.

He went on to explain to me that he had not come to the Silver Marches, to this war, alone—and that, not even counting Amber, Jarlaxle, and the dragon sisters. He tapped a gemstone set in a band around his forehead and told me that it was a magical phylactery, now holding the disembodied spirit of a great monk named Kane, a legendary Grandmaster of Flowers of Afafrenfere's Order of the

Yellow Rose. With that phylactery, Kane had made the trip beside Afafrenfere, indeed, even within the thoughts of Afafrenfere.

"To guide me and to teach me, and so he has and so he is."

Then Afafrenfere did sit up, and detailed for me his feats of battle, where swarms of goblins would disappear in front of his jabbing and spinning limbs, where he could strike and be on his way before his opponent could begin to counter, where he had killed a giant with a slap of his hand, then using that connection as a conduit so that he could fashion his own life energy as a missile and use it to break the life energy of the giant.

I didn't quite understand the technique, but the man's awe at his accomplishments spoke volumes to me. They reminded me of my own realizations that I had attained the highest levels of skill in the drow academy of Melee-Magthere, that I had somehow learned to be as fine a warrior as Zaknafein, my father.

I was more surprised than Zaknafein on that day so long ago when I finally defeated him in our sparring matches. I had planned the victory down to every block and every step, to every twist and angle, but still, when I at last realized the enormity of what I had accomplished, I had spent some long hours indeed simply staring and pondering.

And so I thought I understood what Afafrenfere was feeling, but soon I discovered that his dilemma was not merely surprise at his own prowess. No, he summed it up in one word, spoken humbly and with a clear tremor in his soft voice: "Responsibility."

There is an emotional weight that accompanies the expectations of others. When desperate people look to you for help, and you know that if you cannot help them, no one else can . . .

Responsibility.

"We will guide the dwarves well in this battle day," I remember saying to Afafrenfere, and remember, too, that he was shaking his head with dismissal even as the words left my mouth. Not because he doubted our mission this day—indeed, he was actually more confident in it than I—but because Afafrenfere was talking in grander terms.

He was talking about the man he had been, and now, with this growth, about the man he felt he now needed to be.

Afafrenfere's situation was complicated by the sudden infusion of power, I expect. Grandmaster Kane was training him, intimately, and so he was rising to a skill level he had never before imagined, and the shock of that had awakened within him a realization that he was part of something bigger than himself, and responsible for things beyond his personal needs.

I hadn't ever really thought of my own situation in those terms, not specifically, and not with any confusion, but only because my very nature from the earliest days of self-reflection aligned me with those same beliefs and expectations for myself that Afafrenfere was apparently now experiencing as a sudden and confusing epiphany.

I hadn't the time to sit and discuss it with him any longer, of course, for we were off immediately to find King Harnoth and his fighting band, that we could guide them to their place in the upcoming maelstrom.

But I couldn't help but grin as I made my way through the pine-covered slope beside the monk from the Monastery of the Yellow Rose. He was now learning the same epiphany I had long hoped to see within Artemis Entreri.

I could see the trepidation on Brother Afafrenfere's face, but I knew that it would soon enough fade, to be replaced by a sense of true contentment. He was given something, a blessing, that most people could never experience. Through the help of Grandmaster Kane, he was given a glimpse of his potential, and so he knew that potential to be true and attainable.

So many people never see that—they may quietly hope for it, or imagine it in their private moments, but they will never believe in it, in themselves, to go out and reach for it. Fear of failure, of judgment, of being mocked, even, will keep them curled in a bubble of security, averting risks by keeping their hands close to their vests.

So many people live small, afraid to try to do great things, conditioned from childhood to find their place in the order of things, the proverbial "pecking order," and simply stay there, curled and small, their arms in close.

Wanting to reach, but afraid to grab—it is the comfort of familiarity, of a niche carved within the expectations and judgment of others.

"Know your place" is a common refrain, and so many other similarly destructive "truisms" chase us throughout our lives, particularly in those early years, exactly when we're trying to determine that very place. Voices of doubt and warning, often spoken as advice, but always limiting, always designed to keep our arms in close, that we will not reach.

Because when we reach, when we seek that place we have only seen in our imagination, we threaten the order of things, and threaten most especially the place of those who have found a better roost.

And when we dare to reach, and when we excel, and when we gain from our reaching a level of power or wealth or privilege, then too comes the weight of that which Brother Afafrenfere was contemplating when I encountered him on the other end of Ilnezhara's teleport spell: responsibility.

For now Brother Afafrenfere understood that he could accomplish much more than he had ever dreamed possible, and so now his heart demanded of him a measure of responsibility.

That weight, so clear in his eyes when I came upon him, reminded me that Brother Afafrenfere was a good man.

—Drizzt Do'Urden

CHAPTER 15

FIELD OF BLOOD AND FIRE

HE WAS THE POINT MAN, FOR NONE COULD TRAVERSE THESE TUNNELS with Drizzt's skill and stealth. He found his memories and put himself back to those first days when he had left Menzoberranzan. He had entertained no notions that he would survive back then, a young drow in the place called the Night Below, the most deadly environment on Toril.

But he had survived.

He had become the Hunter, all of his senses tuned to common cause and instant reaction. He had found his way, and he had survived, and more than that, he had thrived.

And so he was now the Hunter, moving through the tunnels with not a sound, prepared to be aware of any enemies long before they might mark his presence.

He reserved his greatest caution for fellow drow—they had been thick around these tunnels not long ago. But no more, it seemed. Jarlaxle's claim that Menzoberranzan had all but abandoned the orc cause rang true to him then, and brought him hope.

All he found were orcs and ogres, half-breeds of both races, and other goblinkin.

Still, he kept his bow shouldered and his scimitars sheathed. It was not his place to engage these enemies, even if the situation presented an easy kill.

Behind him came the sisters, in elf form, the second line in this procession exiting Citadel Adbar.

Whenever Drizzt happened upon an enemy position, he faded back and there waited with Bruenor and the others while Tazmikella and Ilnezhara routed the monsters.

None would escape.

And the scout, the Hunter, would begin anew, traversing the southern tunnels in front of the band, marking the way so the dragon sisters could clear it.

The thousand dwarf soldiers came behind, securing the gains, setting waypoints and defensive positions. Sinnafein and her elves had remained on the surface, in the region around Citadel Adbar, ready to strike hard at any orcs who might come on the scene. The elves would scatter them and chase them away so that they could not besiege Adbar once more.

King Harnoth had remained in Citadel Adbar at the urging of King Bruenor and Oretheo Spikes. The Haunted King was in no state of mind to make this journey. All the leaders of Adbar had come to see Harnoth as a figurehead only, and they hoped and prayed to the dwarf gods that the son of Harbromm and brother of Bromm would regain his balance and his sensibilities as the war began to turn to their favor. To that end, Harnoth had his own journey in front of him, along with the bulk of Adbar's forces and the elves, and with enough commanders surrounding him to help him along his way.

"We're more than halfway to Felbarr," Oretheo Spikes, who led the eight hundred of Citadel Adbar in the Underdark expedition, explained to Bruenor and Drizzt on one occasion when the dragon sisters were off routing a nest of ogres. Oretheo knew this dark trail better than any, and indeed had led the last expedition that had gone to the court of King Emerus and then returned to Citadel Adbar. "And it's more a straight run now."

"Then likely the tunnels will remain nearly empty of enemies for the next few days, before we come again into an orc nest," said Drizzt. The fighting—or rather, the slaughter at the claws of the dragon sisters—had been heavy immediately beyond Adbar's tunnels. The enemy positions had thinned greatly in the last few days as they moved out away from the dwarven fortress, as the dwarves had, of course, expected.

Citadel Adbar had been ringed underground by the minions of Many-Arrows, and so too, they believed, would Citadel Felbarr be encircled.

"Aye, and so ye tell yer two elf girls this, elf," Oretheo Spikes said—and Bruenor was nodding with every word, clearly knowing where this was heading, "when we're inside smellin' distance o' Felbarr, the fun ain't all for themselves. Me and me boys're planning to smash a few orc heads. We got a winter o' pain waiting to be paid back, don't ye doubt!"

All around the fiery Wilddwarf, the huzzahs and heigh-ho's went up, Bruenor among those cheering. Drizzt looked at Catti-brie, and neither of them could resist joining in. They were ready for a fight.

More than ready.

"The Battle of Hilltop," Ravel said to an animated and agitated Warlord Hartusk a few days after Aleina Brightlance and her raiders had smashed the orc position north of Silverymoon. The drow wizard was echoing the words of the orc courier who had come in with the news.

Hartusk rose from his throne and paced around Ravel and the courier, eyeing the drow dangerously with every step.

"Be at ease, Warlord," Saribel said from the side. She, like Ravel, could see the orc's murderous intent.

"They sting us like gnats, and we do not slap at them!" Hartusk said with a low growl.

"Tiago has gone for Arauthator," Ravel reminded him.

"The month of Mirtul is half over. We should be on the march!" said Hartusk. He rose up tall and took a deep breath, expanding his powerful chest. He wore now the fabulous armor of King Obould, the greatsword strapped diagonally across his back, its decorated pommel and hilt showing over his right shoulder.

He was an imposing beast, Ravel had to admit.

"How many?" Hartusk asked, and for a moment, it was hard to tell which of the two, Ravel or the orc courier, he was addressing. Gradually the seething warlord shifted his gaze over the orc.

"Fifty dead . . ." the poor trembling orc meekly replied.

"Not ours!" Hartusk yelled at him. "How many attacked our camp in this fight?"

"The Battle of Hilltop," the orc clarified.

That, of course, was the name their enemies had put upon the rout on the bald hillock north of Silverymoon, a name that made it sound like an honorable battle instead of a slaughter in the dark of night against an undefended position.

It was a name that didn't sit well with Warlord Hartusk.

The sword swept off his back in the blink of a surprised eye, the blade igniting as it came free of its sheath. The burly orc never slowed in his movement, one fluid lift and twist and downward stroke that cut the orc courier in half, shoulder to hip.

That same mighty sword, the sword of King Obould, had similarly halved Tarathiel of the elves before the horrified eyes of Drizzt and Innovindil a century before.

"I wait no longer!" Hartusk roared, and the orcs in the chamber began to whoop and holler and leap around.

"Too long we have sat and waited. The Melting is over and Everlund awaits. We march this day!"

The orcs cheered and leaped and danced. Ravel looked to Saribel with concern. They had discussed this very possibility with Tiago before Ravel teleported him to the Spine of the World in his quest to speak with, and hopefully retrieve, Arauthator. The power of Menzoberranzan was gone now. The contingent from Q'Xorlarrin numbered far too few to exact much influence here. Warlord Hartusk was beyond their control. For all they might coerce and deceive the dimwitted and brutish Hartusk, in the end, his word would rule the day.

"Gather my commanders!" he ordered the orcs in the room. "To the courtyard!"

He swept from the hall, the orcs rushing in his wake.

"What are we to do?" Saribel asked her brother.

Ravel shrugged as if it hardly mattered. "We sack Everlund, I expect."

"Tiago and the dragons have not returned!"

Ravel moved to the room's outer door, the one that went to the very balcony where Tiago had cut off the head of King Firehelm of Sundabar. "Have you looked outside?" he asked Saribel, waving his hand to invite her over to join him in the view—the view of thousands and thousands of campfires stretching to the horizon all around the ruined city now known as Hartusk Keep.

"A hundred thousand?" he asked. Then he answered his own question with a snort and a remark, "Closer to two hundred thousand, I would guess.

"And the giants remain, by the hundreds. And thousands of ogres. Do you think Everlund will stand against this? Eight soldiers for every man, woman, and child in the city. Hartusk will run it over."

"He stretches his line," Saribel argued. "Silverymoon . . ."

"Why do we care?" came Ravel's blunt reminder. He stepped over and draped his arm over Saribel's shoulder. She bristled and even growled—for what male should dare do such a thing uninvited?—but calmed quickly as Ravel added, "My dear sister, high priestess and soon-to-be Matron Mother of House Do'Urden, let us enjoy the spoils of Everlund. We will find treasures to soothe Arauthator, and by extension Archmage Gromph and the matron mother. We will take slaves, many slaves, to serve House Do'Urden. I will set up a portal to walk them to our soldiers in Menzoberranzan."

"The journey from Everlund will be more difficult than the one to the city."

"Undoubtedly," Ravel agreed. "Is that our problem?"

Saribel calmed considerably then, nodding as she looked out over the vast encampment of Many-Arrows' soldiers.

She shook her head again, dismissing her fears, and throwing aside, too, the escape route Ravel had just hinted at. For with this force, it seemed impossible to Saribel that Warlord Hartusk would lose. Everlund would surely fall, and even if the raiders from Silverymoon continued to disrupt the orc supply lines, Hartusk would sweep back to the north with soldiers to spare. Perhaps Silverymoon would survive, for to go against her walls was surely folly.

But surely any who came out of that magically-enhanced fortress would be crushed.

Below the door, the sounds of cheering rose once more, as Warlord Hartusk came forth from the keep in all his splendor and began his call for the march to battle.

Soon the very stones of the keep trembled under the roar of orc voices and the stamp of orc feet.

Saribel's eyes lifted higher, to the north, past the Rauvins to the Spine of the World. For all of Ravel's assurances and all of the sheer power arrayed in front of her, she wished then that she might see Tiago flying toward her astride the white wyrm, Arauthator, and with Aurbangras close behind.

They had been assured that their flanks would be completely secured, and so the dwarven wedge formation plowed into the orc position at full charge. Bruenor and Oretheo Spikes led the way initially, but one burp from Bruenor's cracked silver horn brought an ally into the fight up ahead of them. Indeed, Thibbledorf Pwent floated through the orc lines as a gray mist, then materialized in their midst, whirling and striking with wild-eyed frenzy.

"Cavern left!" Bruenor cried right before his line met the orc shield wall, and on that command, the back half of the left line of the wedge broke away into a second wedge, forming fast and charging off into a side chamber.

The place was full of orc archers, hoping to snipe at the back ranks of the dwarves after the initial collision.

It was a fine defensive strategy, except that Drizzt had scouted the region well indeed, and had reconnoitered that second chamber. And so the dwarves had practiced a new twist to their basic wedge formation, adding a second, flying wedge.

Worse for the orc archers, this breakaway formation was made up of a hundred dwarves, every one of them a member of Mithral Hall's famed Gutbuster Brigade, with Bungalow Thump leading them in.

Bruenor had a hundred of his boys from Mithral Hall around him, but still he felt strange in this particular assault, exposed even.

Drizzt was not with him, nor Catti-brie or Wulfgar or even Regis.

He locked shields with Oretheo Spikes and ducked low, bracing his shoulder as the first wave of orcs counterattacked, rushing in and slamming hard. But the disciplined wedge split and scattered those orc ranks, the monsters breaking on it like water creased by a ship's prow. And on came the Wilddwarf berserkers, charging up to the second rank of dwarves, including one immediately behind Bruenor, who set their hands low and helped the Wilddwarves in their frenzied leap, hoisting them over the front line of shield dwarves to spring into the midst of the orc ranks.

As soon as the catapulted dwarves cleared them, Bruenor and Oretheo decoupled their shields and fiercely charged ahead. They were the point of the wedge, driving hard with their fellows pressing them forward, and with the back ranks of orcs now fighting furiously against Wilddwarves and the specter of Thibbledorf Pwent.

There were as many orcs in those twin caverns as dwarves, but the battle precision of the dwarves sorely outmatched the brutes. Whenever the orcs created a breach, the practiced dwarves built a secure shield wall, but whenever the dwarves created a breach, those orcs caught suddenly in the open turned and fled.

These exchanges occurred over and over, and each time the dwarves gained ground.

Bruenor's axe dripped blood, as did his broken nose. He had caught the edge of Oretheo's turning shield when one orc leaped into his partner. His boots slipped on the blood covering the floor, the blood of orcs and dwarves, these two mortal enemies come together in quarters too close.

The lines wavered both ways. Dwarves fell and tried to crawl behind their brethren, who shielded up and leaped forward to put their wounded fellow behind the barricades. Orcs fell, but kept crawling forward, biting at the legs of the hated dwarves.

"Ah, ye dog!" Bruenor roared, slamming one orc in the face with his shield then stepping back as he turned suddenly, his axe whipping across to open the orc's chest, shoulder to shoulder. The spray of blood flew back in Bruenor's face, but he didn't even notice it. He was falling then, to a different state of mind.

He heard the whispers of Dumathoin.

He felt the pride of Moradin.

His muscles bulged with the strength of Clangeddin.

He felt as if he was in that throne again, in Gauntlgrym, the power of his gods infusing him beyond the boundaries of this mortal coil.

Despite protocol, he leaped out ahead of Oretheo Spikes, and swept his magnificent many-notched axe across, and two orcs went flying. Another soared back the other way on Bruenor's immediate and powerful backhand.

"Bruenor, no!" Oretheo Spikes tried to call, but the words disintegrated as they left his mouth, as he realized the sudden power of his shield partner. Oretheo Spikes leaped to his left, linking with the next dwarf in line, closing the gap left by Bruenor's charge.

And none tried to call Bruenor back—indeed, they all cheered now and fought even more ferociously, taking Bruenor's lead, as orc after orc went flying away, chopped nearly in half, sometimes fully in half, by the powerful strokes of Bruenor Battlehammer.

The orcs noticed the red-bearded dwarf, too, and at the center of their line where the wedge pressed forward behind the wild-eyed Bruenor, they began to falter, falling all over each other to get away from this possessed Wilddwarf.

Finally the orcs got an ogre up in front of Bruenor. The monstrous beast used its height and reach to strike down over Bruenor's shield, its club cracking hard on the dwarf's back. Behind Bruenor, other dwarves cried out.

But if Bruenor had even felt the blow, he didn't show it. Instead he used the opening of the overbalanced ogre to his advantage. He turned his shield aside and slipped sidelong, his axe sweeping across to strike the brute inside its right knee, bending and then cracking the shattering leg. Bruenor flipped the axe and swept it back, catching the inside of the left knee and shattering that leg, too.

He tore the axe free and flipped it again as back went his arm, chopping in hard against the ogre's left side. And around went the dwarf, a full backward circuit so that he came around with his axe leading right into the ogre's right side.

The beast was sinking, sinking, and Bruenor's next strike took it on the side of the chest, and his next circling backhand nearly took its right arm off at the shoulder.

Bruenor hopped, straightening up suddenly, and he leaped high and lifted his axe higher, now gripping it in both hands.

Down it came, splitting the ogre's head in half. The dwarf bulled forward, slamming his shield into the dead ogre's chest, sending it flying over backward. And on Bruenor went with a great leap that landed him on the ogre's chest. There he held his axe out wide to his right, his shield out wide to his left, and threw back his head to issue a wild war cry.

That was enough for the orcs. The wedge formation would have broken them eventually, but they clearly wanted nothing more of the exploits of Bruenor Battlehammer.

On came the dwarves with howls of victory, running the monsters down, though many orcs managed to scramble out the back side of the cavern.

"Finish the cavern to the left!" Bruenor yelled to those dwarves on that side of the chamber—though from the sounds, the Gutbusters were surely routing the archers.

"The rest of yerselves with me, boys!" Bruenor howled, and started forward in pursuit.

He stopped even as he took the first strides, though, hearing battle in the tunnels up ahead. Orcs clogged up the retreat there, with many trying to get back the other way, back into the cavern to fight the dwarves.

A familiar silver-streaking magical arrow brought a smile to Bruenor's face, one that only widened when he heard the roars of some familiar dwarven voices, voices he had heard often in the days of his second childhood.

Drizzt had gotten to Felbarr, and now Felbarr had come forth.

Only a very short while later, standing ankle deep in blood, Bruenor Battlehammer and King Emerus Warcrown shared a great hug.

Citadel Felbarr was free.

"Look at them," Undercommander Preston Berbellows remarked to his companions on the ridge north of the valley where the slaughter had commenced. His derision was hard to miss, surely, and was not missed by one of those he did not realize was nearby.

"Indeed, do," said Aleina Brightlance, riding up beside the man, who shifted uncomfortably in his saddle at her appearance. She looked at him curiously, even shaking her head in disbelief. They had just won a great victory, taking hardly a wound in waylaying a large and heavily-guarded Many-Arrows caravan.

She understood the undercommander's attitude, though, despite her head shaking. Preston had called for a direct attack on the caravan when they spotted it rolling down the Surbrin Vale. But Aleina, on the counsel of those two of whom he now spoke, had overruled him. They had, instead, carefully prepared the battlefield in this place, setting traps and dominating the best ground in the vale.

She couldn't suppress a grin as she noted some movement below, knowing now from so many recent experiences what was about to occur.

"All of you," she went on. "Look at them, these two vagabonds brought to me in the Underdark by the grace of good fortune."

She paused there and guided their stares down into the vale just in time to see Regis and his pony go darting across in front of an ogre, the halfling poking his rapier into the brute's face to make it extra angry. The ogre spun, trying to catch up to and squish the halfling.

It didn't even see the huge man, Wulfgar, who had quietly walked his horse up the other way as Regis was distracting the ogre, and was now standing tall in the saddle.

It still didn't see Wulfgar, but it did note the swinging head of his marvelous warhammer. The ogre's head snapped back under the tremendous weight of the blow. It straightened, just long enough to get smacked a second time, and down it went in a heap.

"We fight for common cause," Aleina declared, her commanding tone aiming the remark squarely at the derision of Preston Berbellows. "For Silverymoon, for Everlund, for Sundabar and the hopes of rebuilding."

Those around her began to cheer, except for Preston, who stared at her, angry and embarrassed.

"For Mithral Hall!" Aleina shouted. "For Adbar and Felbarr and for the Moonwood elves!"

The cheering heightened, but Aleina struck a more somber tone then, when she added, "For the memory of dead Nesmé."

Cheering faces became grim faces, and many nods agreed with the woman.

"Ride now, left and right," she ordered them. "The enemy caravan is broken and all are fleeing. Let a few escape, but just a few."

Preston Berbellows took up his reins and began to turn his horse, but Aleina grabbed him by the forearm, ordering him to stay.

"Let them tell their ugly kin that the road is not secure, that the Knights in Silver have not forgotten the Redrun, and that their victory is not as complete as they have come to believe."

As the soldiers in her command began their charge, Aleina shouted after them, "They will pay for every inch of ground!"

She turned to Preston, her face stern.

"Yes, Commander?" he asked innocently.

"Rivalries can be a good thing," she said. "Do you agree?"

"Commander?"

"I wagered with that one, Wulfgar, over there, who might kill the most enemies as we made our way to Silverymoon," Aleina explained. "Truly, the competition drove me harder, though I came to know very quickly that I could not pace him and that warhammer he carries."

Preston didn't blink, and tried hard—too hard—to put on an expression to show that he didn't really care.

"So a rivalry can foster a positive competition," she went on. "Or it can be destructive. You are a fine rider, a fine knight, and mighty with your sword. Do you think you can match him?"

"Commander, I . . ."

"Challenge him," Aleina said. "When we leave this place, go to Wulfgar and tell him that you will kill more of our enemies than he in our next battle."

Preston Berbellows straightened in his seat and, despite himself, swallowed hard. He knew there was no way he could compete with the mighty barbarian named Wulfgar.

"Challenge Regis, then," she said with a laugh.

Preston stuttered a protest. "The little one? He has too many tricks . . . his bombs and those infernal crossbow darts . . ."

"Then just admit it and leave it at that!" Aleina scolded. "Your jealousy tears at the fabric of trust that binds our band, and I'll not have it!"

"Yes, Commander," Preston said, trying again unconvincingly to sound contrite.

"Yes, Undercommander," she said. "And so gather a trusted companion and ride south to Silverymoon to report our progress. And there you will remain, in loyal service to Lord Hornblade."

"Commander! Aleina, I . . ." Preston shook his head, clearly at a loss. These two had served together for a long time. At one point, there had even been whispers of a secret courtship, though that had not been the case.

"I'll not have it," Aleina said again, quietly and evenly. "Go now."

Preston heaved a great sigh and turned his horse away, trotting, then galloping from sight.

Aleina understood it all too clearly. Those rumors had not been discouraged by Preston Berbellows, and though Aleina had never thought of him as anything more than a comrade and friend, she understood the source of the conflict.

She looked down into the vale again to see Wulfgar and Regis riding easily, side by side, talking of the battle, no doubt, and with much laughter between them.

Yes, she understood. Preston saw it, and so did others, written so clearly on her face when she looked upon Wulfgar. The thought made her shrug and giggle, and admit to herself that she felt like a youngster again, just barely a woman, unburdened by the cynicism of years, and light in the hope of romance.

She kicked her horse into a trot along the ridgeline, heading down to intercept Regis and Wulfgar. Those two had laid out the plans for the ambush, down to the smallest detail, like painting the shafts of the arrows so that they would flicker more menacingly in the meager daylight as they rained death upon the caravan drivers and guards.

She caught up to the pair when they were still within the vale. They had stopped and dismounted, and now the halfling was painting something on the side of a large stone set into the ridge. He stepped back and swept his arm out, presenting it to Knight-Commander Aleina.

The Battle of Silver Arrows
18 Mirtul, 1485 DR

"Our greatest victory yet," Aleina said.

"We should go and celebrate," Wulfgar replied, and from his tone and expression when she turned to him, Aleina understood his intentions. And her heart surely fluttered.

Regis caught the implications too, apparently. He sighed and said, "I have to go brew some potions," then moved straight for his pony and started away, leaving the two alone.

Aleina didn't have to ask what Wulfgar had in mind, and even if it was not what she believed, she figured she could lead him there anyway.

CHAPTER 16

THE PUPPET MASTER

OF ALL THE INSANE THINGS YOU HAVE DONE OVER THE CENTURIES, THIS one is by far . . ." Kimmuriel had to stop there, at a loss for words—and surely that was an almost unique event.

Jarlaxle was quite pleased with that, as he clearly revealed with his grin.

"You brought dragons here?" Kimmuriel asked. "Dragons to battle the whites Gromph and Matron Mother Quenthel enlisted in our cause?"

"Does Gromph know that?"

"No."

"Better to keep it that way," said Jarlaxle. "If he knows of it, he will likely have to take action or face the wrath of Quenthel."

Kimmuriel's usually impassioned face screwed up as he tried to decipher that logical mess. "You think the archmage would quietly approve," he reasoned at length, "but that he would not be able to support you because of the ramifications he would suffer in Menzoberranzan."

"You underestimate Gromph Baenre," Jarlaxle replied. "He knows that I am here . . ."

"I told you as much!"

"And that I have brought the dragons and so do battle against the minions of Many-Arrows," Jarlaxle went on. "He knows, but he cannot let anyone else know that he knows. Surely you understand the value of such logical and believable deniability. It is the way of life in Menzoberranzan, is it not?"

Kimmuriel half turned away and stared off into the distance, no doubt recalibrating his thoughts around that remarkable revelation.

"Tiago and his cohorts remain because of Gromph's advice to the matron mother," Jarlaxle remarked, just to get it out there and bring it to the forefront of Kimmuriel's calculations.

"No," Kimmuriel corrected. "They are part of Matron Mother Quenthel's too-clever web. But Gromph did not argue against her, from what I've gathered in my time with him."

"Your time in his thoughts, you mean."

Kimmuriel bowed to concede the point. The main reason Kimmuriel was training Gromph in psionics, after all, was because that gave him and Jarlaxle, the co-leaders of Bregan D'aerthe, intimate access into the goings-on in Menzoberranzan through the eyes of the city's archmage. As Kimmuriel trained Gromph, so too did he read the archmage's mind.

"And you believe that Archmage Gromph does not, or would not, disapprove of your actions here?" Kimmuriel asked.

Jarlaxle shrugged. "I am not dead."

"I have not sensed any of this in my time with him."

"Did you know to look for it?"

"It is a startling claim, I admit."

"You'll not find the direct proof, in any event," Jarlaxle told him. "Even in Gromph's mind. Understand, my cerebral friend, that when you enter there in your training sessions, still you see only what Gromph wants you to see. He is not practiced in the art of psionics as are you, of course, but he is a drow of tremendous intelligence, will, and arcane skill. He'll not ever reveal to you anything that would get him in the bad graces of Quenthel or the Spider Queen.

"But here I am," Jarlaxle finished. "Alive and well. And Gromph surely knows more than you expected and yet, he has not destroyed me and has not come for me, to drag me back to the whip of Matron Mother Quenthel Baenre."

"To what end? For him?" Kimmuriel asked.

"I doubt he's thought it out that far," Jarlaxle replied. "But certainly he is angry. Lady Lolth has struck out for Mystra's arcane domain, for the Weave itself, from which Gromph derives his powers. And in that realm of the arcane, his powers are greater than any other in Menzoberranzan, perhaps likely even greater than any other of our race. And yet, despite that, Gromph understands that he remains a male."

"The female children of the noble Houses will flood Sorcere in its next class," Kimmuriel admitted.

"Of course they will. For the grace of Lady Lolth, yes? A grace, a station, reserved for them." Jarlaxle gave a little knowing laugh. "My dear brother Gromph will not be the Patron Father of Menzoberranzan, after all, will he?"

Kimmuriel could only sigh. Emotions were such destructive things.

"So what are Tiago's ambitions, then?" Jarlaxle asked. "What greater glory does he seek?"

"You know the answer."

"Drizzt Do'Urden," said Jarlaxle, and he huffed and shook his head. "What is it about this one that makes so many feel the need to challenge him? For Artemis Entreri, it was a reflection in a mirror he could not bear to view. But for Tiago?"

"A quick means to an end," said Kimmuriel. "The head of Drizzt will gain him instant recognition and status. He is not a patient sort."

"He is as impulsive and quick to devour the meal as a human," Jarlaxle agreed.

"He travels with Warlord Hartusk, but his eye is ever northward," Kimmuriel explained, "waiting for Mithral Hall to break out."

"Drizzt is not in Mithral Hall."

"He does not know that."

Jarlaxle rubbed a hand over his face, a sparkle coming into his red eyes.

"What are you thinking?" Kimmuriel asked.

"Strange of you to ask such a question."

Kimmuriel responded with a sour look—for they both understood the power of Jarlaxle's eye patch. Indeed, Kimmuriel would rarely ask such a question as he had just posed, and instead just peer into someone's thoughts. He couldn't do that with Jarlaxle, to his ultimate frustration.

"I am thinking that perhaps we should give Tiago what he wants," Jarlaxle admitted. "Before he and his idiot army can cause too much more damage."

"He will be recalled in the later part of Eleasis, just over three months from now," Kimmuriel explained. "So said Gromph and the matron mother."

"Then we must be quick," Jarlaxle replied. "It takes a bit of time to shape the course of a region as large and diverse as the Silver Marches, after all."

Jarlaxle shuddered uncomfortably, as he always did when stepping out of one of Kimmuriel's unconventional teleport spells. He had always been intrigued by these strange alterations, distinct from the Weave and powered by thought, for it seemed to him as if the psionicist could simply bend time and space his way for this one instant he needed to usher Jarlaxle through.

Perhaps he could find some way to learn this trick, Jarlaxle mused—as he did every single time he stepped through one of Kimmuriel's . . . distortions. He couldn't quite bring himself to call this bending of space a gate—

Jarlaxle shook his head, even slapped himself on the cheek, to focus his thoughts. The campfire was not far in front of him, and surely there were many sentries about.

He crept up toward the light.

"Do you intend to leave a trail of little Wulfgars all across Faerûn?" he heard Regis scolding the barbarian. The drow mercenary smiled and thought to head right in, but then Wulfgar's reply gave him pause.

"I intend to enjoy this second life," Wulfgar answered.

"Then fall in love!" Regis suggested.

"I am."

"At every stop?" Regis asked.

"I hope so."

Jarlaxle's smile widened, thinking he had found a man after his own heart. He wanted to stay back then and let Wulfgar expound upon the joys of hedonism, but he reminded himself that sentries were likely near and that he was, after all, a dark elf not named Drizzt Do'Urden.

"Ah, Wulfgar, I have some sisters I should introduce to you!" he said cheerily, stepping into the firelight—and Regis and Wulfgar were to their feet in the blink of an eye, weapons in hand, though Regis's weapon was actually a turkey leg.

"Jarlaxle?" they both stammered together.

"Well met, my old friends!"

"Never that," said Wulfgar.

"My new friends, then, and glad you will be for the company. I come with news of Drizzt and the others."

"How did you find us?" asked Regis, and Jarlaxle did not miss the nervous glance the halfling tossed Wulfgar's way. Yes, this band of raiders had gone to great lengths to hide their whereabouts from prying eyes and prying spells—there were magical wards all around the encampment.

But they did not understand the subtle power of psionics, and psionics was not magic, nor was it a physical sense. Their wards could hide them from orcs, from most drow, from dragons even, but not from Kimmuriel.

"Drizzt, Catti-brie, Bruenor, and Athrogate made their way safely into Mithral Hall, but they are not there now," the drow explained. "Citadel Adbar is free, and so, now, is Citadel Felbarr, through underground routes at least."

The halfling and the barbarian exchanged dumbfounded stares.

"It is time for you to rejoin them, I expect," the drow went on. "King Connerad begs your presence—soon. He will break free of Mithral Hall through the eastern door in front of the Surbrin. There he will find allies, and better will it be if your raiders are among those allies."

"You come with this message from King Connerad?" Wulfgar asked skeptically.

Jarlaxle bowed.

"The time is upon you," he said. "And what a relief it will be to Silverymoon and to Everlund when word spreads southward that the three dwarven armies have joined in the fight!"

He dipped another bow, never taking his eyes off the faces of the two startled heroes.

"I found you," he reminded them. "And your band is but fifty strong. If I wanted to have you killed, a simple note of your location to Warlord Hartusk would have you overrun in short order."

Regis shrugged first, but Wulfgar couldn't argue the point.

"You can thank me by keeping my name out of your discussions," the drow told them, and with that, Jarlaxle felt the tug of Kimmuriel's thoughts and stepped backward, simply fading from the view of Regis and Wulfgar, stepping miles away across time and space bent by Kimmuriel.

Now Jarlaxle had to go and convince King Connerad that his, and his garrison's, presence were requested at Mithral Hall's eastern gate.

"King Harnoth's already crossed the Surbrin in the north," Bruenor told Emerus as they gathered at council. They were not in King Emerus's normal audience hall, however, having moved far to the northwest of the main area of Citadel Felbarr, where dwarf tunnelers were digging their escape behind enemy lines and into the Glimmerwood.

"He should be rolling straight into Dark Arrow Keep then," King Emerus declared, and beside him, both Parson Glaive and Ragged Dain nodded their heads in agreement.

"Bah, but we had to convince him not to!" said Oretheo Spikes.

"One step at a time, me friend," Bruenor explained. "The upper ways o' the Underdark're cleared and lets us get us all out o' here and into the forest. We break the siege at Mithral Hall—"

"But ye're meaning to leave the siege in force about Felbarr?" Ragged Dain interrupted.

"Felbarr's free from below, Mithral Hall's to be free above," Bruenor replied.

"The orcs won't know whether to reinforce the tunnels or the surface camps," Drizzt explained. "Our greatest advantage is coordination of our forces. We pick the battlefields."

"Aye, and their stinking corpses litter them," Bruenor added.

"By every report and all that we saw in coming here, they've few drow left in support," added Catti-brie. "Without that directing and guiding force, we will have them running every way but the correct one."

"So we go into the Glimmerwood, then across the river to join in the fight for Mithral Hall?" King Emerus asked.

"Aye, the eastern fight, by the bridge, where Connerad'll come roarin' out," said Bruenor.

"Some of you will go to Connerad," Drizzt corrected. "Most, actually, but a few may be called to rendezvous with King Harnoth and join the fight north of Mithral Hall."

"That'll be yerself, elf," said Bruenor, and Drizzt nodded. That much had already been arranged. Drizzt could move quickly and stealthily, after all, and coordinating the movements of the armies would be the key to victory.

"Without reinforcements from the north, the bridge can be won," Drizzt explained. "And those orcs in Keeper's Dale, far to the west, will have no way to join the fight in time."

"We can go and crush them after," said Ragged Dain.

"Aye, or might be that we then come back across the river and pay a visit to the ugly dogs surrounding Felbarr," Bruenor said. "We'll know.

We got better eyes and better heads than the orcs, don't ye doubt. They'll not ever find us where they expect us, and'll always be seeing us where they ain't wantin' us!"

"We got eyes? What eyes?" King Emerus demanded.

"Same eyes what got me and me boys out o' Mithral Hall," Bruenor replied. "Same eyes what bringed me boys with the elfs to Adbar, to save Harnoth and break that siege. Same eyes that bringed me and me boys and Oretheo and his boys to yerself."

"Warlord Hartusk looks south to Silverymoon and Everlund," Drizzt put in. "He does not even know of the return of Bruenor Battlehammer, or that Mithral Hall has a brigade of Gutbusters running free. Or that Adbar is free and has made her way to Felbarr. He is oblivious to the cracks behind as he walks out farther upon that branch."

"Branch? Bah, I mean to chop the whole damned tree down!" Bruenor declared, and he pounded his fist on the table.

He and King Emerus eyed each other intently for a few heartbeats, then Emerus nodded his agreement.

They came forth the very next day: Bruenor and Bungalow Thump and the boys of Mithral Hall, Oretheo Spikes and the eight hundred of Citadel Adbar, and King Emerus and two thousand of Citadel Felbarr's best.

They found the boats at the Surbrin, as had been arranged with the Moonwood elves, and the legions of Felbarr and Adbar silently drifted across to the bank north of the Surbrin Bridge and the eastern door of Mithral Hall.

The orc force just south of their position was considerable, they realized, and the campfires in the northwest spoke of a second force many times that size.

Even worse, and unexpectedly, another enemy force had come into the region, here on the eastern side of the Surbrin, down in the south bear to the bridge.

"Got to take and hold that bridge," Bruenor muttered, already formulating a plan.

"Harnoth and the boys of Adbar better not be late," King Emerus solemnly said to Bruenor, his eyes still gazing to the northwest and the swarms of campfires.

"Aye," Bruenor could only agree, for if that force in the north joined the battle at the bridge, Connerad's forces and this battle group would be overwhelmed in short order.

Bruenor turned to Drizzt as he finished, and the drow nodded. Drizzt kissed Catti-brie, promised to see her soon, and ran off into the night to rendezvous with Afafrenfere to help counsel and guide King Harnoth's march, as had been arranged.

Drizzt

"Do you ever tire of this?" Tazmikella asked Jarlaxle that same night, she and her sister having immediately left the dwarven force when they had first come out into the Glimmerwood. Tazmikella had gone to find Jarlaxle, and Ilnezhara went off in search of another principal for the upcoming events. Tazmikella was in her elf form now, reclining comfortably under the dark sky.

"Dear lady, I live for this," replied the drow, who had just returned from Mithral Hall.

"You have informed the four allied groups of the breakout. When will you tell the enemy?"

"When will your sister return?" came the somewhat flippant response.

"She is here," Ilnezhara answered before Tazmikella could. Also in the guise of an elf, she walked up to join the pair.

"That was quick," Jarlaxle dryly replied.

"I had not far to search," replied Ilnezhara. She looked to her sister. "Arauthator and his son have returned. They flew along the line of the Surbrin this very night, then turned southwest to the ruins of Sundabar."

Both of the sisters looked to Jarlaxle then.

"I believe it is your move," said Tazmikella, with a wry smile. "It is time to betray the dwarves."

CHAPTER 17

WAITING FOR THE WHITES

DRIZZT HAD TO SUMMON ANDAHAR AND RIDE THE UNICORN HARD TO keep up with the running Afafrenfere. With his magical anklets, he had been able to pace the monk on foot for a short distance, but he had tired and Brother Afafrenfere showed no signs of wearying.

They covered many miles that night, leaving the campfire lights of the vast orc encampment north of Mithral Hall, and the Frost Hills that housed the dwarven complex, far behind. Nearly a third of the way to Dark Arrow Keep, they found the large dwarven force of thousands marching under the command of King Harnoth and his generals, and with Sinnafein's elves patrolling all around.

Still outside that perimeter, Afafrenfere stopped and crouched. Drizzt dismounted to move beside him.

"Dismiss your mount," the monk bade him. "You'll need the unicorn no longer."

"Perhaps I will ride scout for King Harnoth."

"The scouts are in place all around us," Afafrenfere explained. "The elves of the Moonwood know we are here."

Drizzt nodded, but still hesitated as he tried to figure out where best he would fit in with this group. Was he going to join the fight at Harnoth's side, or ride back to stand beside Bruenor and Catti-brie? Would he be better served astride Andahar in either scenario, riding the length of the dwarven battle line, Taulmaril in hand?

That was for another day, he realized, and he bade Andahar to be gone.

"Jarlaxle has determined that you will be with me when the fighting starts," Afafrenfere told him, as if reading his mind.

Drizzt eyed the monk curiously.

"With me and the sisters," the monk explained.

"I worked with Tazmikella in the journey to Citadel Felbarr," Drizzt replied. "She walked as an elf through tight tunnels. Now that we are upon the surface once more, I had thought that she and her sister would likely take wing."

"They will."

Drizzt's expression grew more intrigued and more tentative all at once.

"We have saddles," Afafrenfere explained.

"Ah, but that's a dizzyin' thing," Athrogate sputtered when he walked through Kimmuriel's time-space distortion beside Jarlaxle. He stopped and blinked, confused for a moment to see that it wasn't Jarlaxle standing beside him, but Beniago.

"Put these on," the drow said to him, handing him some shackles.

"Eh?"

"For any orc or ogre sentries we might encounter until we get to Tiago."

"I thought meself was wearin' the mask," said Athrogate, catching on that it was indeed Jarlaxle beside him, though with the magic of Jarlaxle's wondrous mask, the drow looked exactly like Beniago.

"I'll not reveal myself to Tiago," Jarlaxle replied. "Nay, not to that favored child of House Baenre. This is Bregan D'aerthe coming to inform him, not Jarlaxle."

"And if he catches on? Who's first to die, yerself or meself?"

"Tiago," Jarlaxle assured him, and he started away. In front of them, a vast army crawled, lumbering across the miles, heading south from the ruins of Sundabar to the Moon Pass through the Nether Mountains.

Warlord Hartusk was reaching farther, just as Jarlaxle had hoped.

Before long, orc sentries had surrounded the pair, along with a particularly nasty-looking ogre.

"A prisoner!" more than one cried with glee when they spotted Athrogate. The ogre even moved toward the shackled dwarf.

"Back away. The dwarf is not your concern," Jarlaxle ordered them. "I warn you only once." He met the dwarf's gaze and silently begged for patience. If the ogre reached for Athrogate, the dwarf would shed the phony shackles and put his glassteel morningstars, Whacker and Cracker, against either side of its misshapen head.

"Bring me to Tiago immediately," Jarlaxle ordered. "I have dire news!"

The orcs seemed to hardly hear him, the ogre not at all, so entranced were they by the presence of a hated dwarf. The ogre leaned in closer and reached . . .

A glob of green goo slammed the brute in the face, sending it reeling backward into a tree. There, the viscous material grabbed at the tree as well, pinning the ogre, its head fully engulfed. It clawed at the goo desperately, but futilely.

The orcs grew agitated, hopping around, brandishing weapons, and all looking at Jarlaxle and the wand that had somehow appeared in his hand.

The drow casually pulled out a large feather, as if it had magically appeared behind his ear, and threw it to the ground. A moment later, that feather became a gigantic bird, thick-legged, thick-bodied, and with a beak as long as a tall man's forearm. It ran for the struggling ogre and drove its beak against the brute's trapped head, stunning it. Up came a three-clawed foot, disemboweling the helpless ogre with one devastating slash.

And the bird pecked and bit at the spilling entrails, the thrashing, dying ogre helpless to dissuade it from its gory feast.

"I told you to take me to Tiago immediately," Jarlaxle said to the orcs.

A short while later, Jarlaxle and Athrogate walked into a tent where Tiago, Saribel, Ravel, and some other drow, undoubtedly also of Q'Xorlarrin, had settled after the day's hard march.

"Beniago?" Tiago asked, clearly perplexed.

"Take off those shackles," Jarlaxle instructed Athrogate, and the dwarf shook himself free of the bonds.

"Do you know my associate, Athrogate?" he asked the others. "A fine spy for Bregan D'aerthe these last decades."

"What is the meaning of this?" Saribel demanded, as usual, impressing Jarlaxle with her quick wit and lightning mental reflexes.

"You march for Everlund?" Jarlaxle, still disguised as Beniago, asked.

"What are you doing here?" Tiago demanded. He glanced around; Jarlaxle noted that all of the drow were on edge.

"Are you here by order of Menzoberranzan?" Saribel demanded.

"I am here with news," Jarlaxle calmly replied. "You can listen or not, as you choose.

"High Priestess, pray enact a divination spell," Jarlaxle said to Saribel, "that you will know the veracity of my claim."

When Saribel was done casting her enchantment, Jarlaxle began. "This is Athrogate, a long-time associate of Bregan D'aerthe, and one, as you can see, particularly suited to spying on the enemies of Hartusk in this particular conflict. He went to Nesmé at my bidding, and to Mithral Hall from there, with my blessing."

He noted that Tiago seemed to perk up quite a bit at the mention of Mithral Hall.

"You did this on orders from Menzoberranzan?" Tiago asked.

"From Matron Mother Quenthel?" Saribel added, and it wasn't hard to notice her glare at her husband as she named the matron mother specifically.

"Bregan D'aerthe is free to use its own discretion here on the World Above," Jarlaxle reminded them. "I thought it prudent to learn of the dwarves, and so I sent Athrogate."

"And now you are here," said Tiago. "Why?"

Jarlaxle turned to his dwarf associate and held forth his hand, bidding Athrogate to explain.

"They're coming out," the dwarf told them, as he had been instructed. "Morning after tomorrow. King Connerad and his boys're bursting from Mithral Hall, don't ye doubt, through the east door to take the bridge over the Surbrin."

"The d-day after to-morrow?" Tiago stammered. "You know this?"

"He just told you," Jarlaxle intervened. He didn't want Athrogate to say any more. The dwarf's words had been carefully orchestrated, and Jarlaxle's own improvisations carefully added, for Saribel's spell would surely show no lies in anything they had said, but saying more risked losing all.

"You are certain?" Tiago asked Jarlaxle.

"I am always certain, cousin," said the double agent, who, like Beniago, really was the distant cousin of Tiago Baenre. "That is why I am alive."

Tiago rubbed his face and paced around excitedly. "I knew we were premature in our march to Everlund!"

"Because the dwarves would come forth?" Saribel was quick to scold. "They are inconsequential, and why should we care? Let them battle Many-Arrows to the death of both—it matters not."

Tiago fixed her with a hard stare, Jarlaxle noticed.

"You keep playing as if we can win, or as if there is anything to win," Saribel continued. "This has been made clear to you, Husband."

Jarlaxle thought it perfectly delicious that hot-humored Tiago did not draw his sword. He chewed his lip, but he didn't even lash out verbally against Saribel Xorlarrin—because she was Saribel Do'Urden now, but more importantly, she was also High Priestess Saribel Baenre.

"There is something to be won here," Tiago said, his tone decidedly more threatening suddenly. He was talking about Drizzt, Jarlaxle knew, and apparently Tiago's bloodlust for that one exceeded any good judgment he might have had regarding Saribel—and likely regarding anything at all.

"Come with me," Tiago ordered Jarlaxle, and he started for the tent flap.

"With you?" Jarlaxle replied.

"To Warlord Hartusk. He must be informed of this development."

Again he started for the tent flap, but stopped once more when Jarlaxle laughed.

"This is your fight, Tiago, and for all the seasons I've grown and learned, I cannot begin to figure out why you want it," Jarlaxle said. "You have been chasing this rogue for two decades, and to what good end?"

"The end is in sight, at the Surbrin Bridge on the day after tomorrow."

"Whose end?" Jarlaxle quipped. Tiago stared at him threateningly, and for a moment, Jarlaxle thought the impetuous young fool might move against him.

"I advise you as others have warned you," Jarlaxle calmly explained. "You have made great gains here in the Silver Marches, for your Matron Mother Zeerith's fledgling city and for your own fledgling House in Menzoberranzan. Matron Mother Quenthel is pleased by her expedition here, with such minimal loss and with her fist tightening over all who might dare oppose her. You risk much in going after this rogue."

"Matron Mother Quenthel herself granted us these one hundred and fifty days, Beniago of Bregan D'aerthe," Saribel intervened, surprisingly. "She did not tell us how we must use them. What would make a Houseless male think that his words would carry more weight than the blessings of the matron mother?"

Jarlaxle considered that for a few moments. He had tried to dissuade Tiago from going after Drizzt, even though he was glad that Tiago was likely going after Drizzt—for now, after all, Jarlaxle could honestly pass any interrogation the matron mother might put his way in days to come.

"As you will, Priestess," he said with a bow. "And as you will, Cousin Tiago." And he bowed again. "I had information I thought pertinent, and so I have done my duty and delivered it to you. And now I, and my spy here, will leave you to your choices."

He bowed once more, and Athrogate laughed as they felt time and space bending once more. Kimmuriel, watching the proceedings through Athrogate's thoughts, had recalled them far, far away.

Kimmuriel was shaking his head when Jarlaxle and Athrogate walked through that warp to return to his side.

"Exactly as I told you it would transpire," Jarlaxle said to the psionicist's doubting expression.

"So you believe," said Kimmuriel.

"Do you doubt that Tiago will go after Drizzt, and surely astride Arauthator? You heard Saribel—even she is too eager for the prestige the head of Drizzt might bring to warn Tiago away."

"And if Hartusk pivots his force at this news?" Kimmuriel asked.

"They cannot get to the Surbrin Bridge in time."

"That will be of fine comfort to the dwarves when they are faced with a hundred thousand orcs."

Jarlaxle's expression soured. "I liked you better when you didn't understand sarcasm," he remarked.

"I always understood it. It just took me some time to recognize that it might be necessary when communicating with inferior minds."

Athrogate began to laugh, but stopped with a puzzled expression, then scratched his head.

"Hartusk will not turn," said Jarlaxle. He removed his magical mask and became Jarlaxle in appearance once more. "Everlund is the bigger prize and the bigger threat. Now that winter is over, the city will find allies soon enough, and so will become forevermore lost to Hartusk. He is a fool, prideful and war-hungry enough to believe that he can sack the city, then move back on the dwarves. And in truth, there are more orcs and other monstrous allies remaining behind Hartusk in the Upper Surbrin Vale than all the dwarves of all the citadels combined."

"But Tiago will turn from Everlund?"

"Tiago has a dragon," Jarlaxle answered. "He believes that he will be at both fights, of course."

"And you think him wrong."

Jarlaxle shrugged and considered the dragon sisters. Ancient and huge, Arauthator was no minor wyrm, after all. And though his son was nowhere near that venerable state, Aurbangras too was quite powerful. Tazmikella and Ilnezhara were formidable indeed, but in a fair fight, Jarlaxle would be hard-pressed to wager on them against the whites, or even against the Old White Death alone.

Jarlaxle never fought fair.

"Is there an end game in your plans?" Kimmuriel asked, a simple question on the surface, but one that nagged at Jarlaxle.

"Of course," he said with a smile, his red eyes twinkling, though only one was visible now as he adjusted the eye patch that kept Kimmuriel out of his thoughts.

The eye patch that kept Kimmuriel from recognizing Jarlaxle's confidence as a complete lie.

"He bade me to wish you well, and to tell you both to be safe," Afafrenfere said to Bruenor and Catti-brie in private, after the monk had spoken with Bruenor, King Emerus, and Oretheo Spikes to lay out the final disposition of the coming battle.

The monk had arrived in the late afternoon of the day before the dwarves would spring their attack on the orc encampment around the Surbrin Bridge. Bruenor and Catti-brie, of course, had been quite concerned to find Afafrenfere coming in alone without Drizzt by his side.

"Was thinkin' th' elf'd be here fighting aside me," Bruenor replied.

"Drizzt has a larger role to play," the monk replied.

"Eh?"

"What do you know?" Catti-brie demanded, and the monk grinned. "Brother, I find no humor in your cryptic references," Catti-brie sternly scolded him. "Drizzt is my husband—I am returned to this world for him and no other."

"Aye, and same's for me!" said Bruenor, and he ended with a harrumph that became a confused frown. "Excepting, o' course, that he ain't me husband," he clarified.

"He would be here if he did not understand the importance of his role," said the monk.

"And pray tell, what is that role?"

Afafrenfere looked up, drawing their eyes to the darkened sky. "You will see him when the battle begins in full," he explained, and gestured skyward.

"Eh?" Bruenor asked again.

"That is all I can say," the monk replied with a bow. "Look to the sky when the wyrms scream. You will understand."

"The wyrms?" the dwarf and Catti-brie said together, but Afafrenfere merely bowed and started away—and at such a speed that he was far out of their range before either of the two could figure out what to ask him next.

The monk didn't slow as he left the secret dwarven encampment far behind. He rolled across the miles with ease, tirelessly, until he knew that he was again in the region where King Harnoth and the elves had quietly camped. Off to the east, down by the Surbrin, he found Drizzt and the sisters, still in the form of elves.

"Jarlaxle has not returned?" he asked.

"We know our role in the battle," Ilnezhara answered.

"And our role?" Afafrenfere asked, indicating Drizzt as well.

"Hold on?" Tazmikella quipped sarcastically.

"This is beyond you, and beyond Jarlaxle," Ilnezhara said. "He has made his play with the drow Tiago at our insistence. Now he will fade from the battlefield as we do what we must."

"What are you talking about?" Drizzt asked the sisters, but he was looking, too, at Afafrenfere as he spoke.

"Our enemy's dragons will likely join the battle," Afafrenfere explained.

"We are hoping as much," Ilnezhara said.

Drizzt rocked back on his heels and digested that. Evidently, the plan was for him to be riding a dragon when that dragon went into battle with another dragon.

"Catti-brie," he whispered at length. "We should have brought her."

He started to explain, but lost his voice as the two elves in front of him stripped off their garments and suddenly transformed, becoming a pair of graceful and lethal copper dragons. Afafrenfere was already approaching with his saddle, Drizzt noted, the other saddle sitting hooked to a tree branch behind him.

"The battle is still hours away," the drow protested.

"We will go to a better vantage," Afafrenfere explained.

"He is a stubborn fool!" Tiago fumed.

"Did you expect anything different?" Saribel answered. They had gone to Warlord Hartusk to inform him of the possible breakout from Mithral Hall, and to ask him to turn around to crush the dwarves.

Warlord Hartusk hadn't seemed impressed by the suggestion.

"Everlund is before him, the jewel of his conquests," Saribel reminded. "Our front ranks are but a few days from the city."

"And our rear guard but a hard day's ride from the Surbrin Bridge," Tiago shot back. He paused for a few moments, playing it out in his thoughts. "Get your brother," he ordered.

Saribel looked at him as if he had slapped her.

"I beg of you," Tiago pleaded. "Gather Ravel and the others."

"All of this for Drizzt Do'Urden? You intend to take the white dragons from Warlord Hartusk in this, his moment of glory?"

"We will be back to his side, the dwarves crushed, long before he comes in sight of Everlund."

"The dwarves crushed and Drizzt's head in your bag, you mean."

"Yes."

"Husband . . ." Saribel said with a resigned sigh.

"Your brother," Tiago insisted again. "Gather as many of the soldiers of Q'Xorlarrin as you can, and through the spells of Ravel and his fellows, return to the north, I beg. Steal as many orcs as you can, and with your spells and worg mounts, travel fast for the Surbrin Bridge. Let us be done with this, my wife, for the glory of House Do'Urden, and the gain of Q'Xorlarrin."

"For the glory and gain of Tiago, you mean."

"It is all one and the same, is it not? Matron Mother Quenthel left us here, without Menzoberranzan's forces. Are we expected to be no more than handmaidens to an orc warlord?"

It was a strong point, Tiago thought, when he noted Saribel's slight and likely inadvertent nod.

"Or are we to behave as drow?" Tiago pressed. "As servants of Lady Lolth? Intelligence and initiative win the day, my wife, and win the trophy."

"I am quite certain that if you bring pain to Gromph's white dragon friends, he will turn you into a skitter-newt," she warned him, but that was the last of her protests, and she sent her handmaidens scrambling to find Ravel.

A short while later, his saddle secured and he secured to it, Drizzt held his breath as Tazmikella leaped into the dark sky. She flew back to the east, Ilnezhara in front of her, gaining height and speed.

The wind stole the tears from Drizzt's eyes and sent his white hair and forest-green cloak flying out behind him. He held on tightly, amazed all over again by the acceleration and the steep climb. The air grew colder as the ground diminished below them.

Higher they went, the darkened sky looming above them. Drizzt held his breath as Tazmikella entered the roiling blackness, and for a moment, the drow was fully blinded, as if a darker night had fallen upon him.

And then he saw the stars as Tazmikella came through the other side of the drow enchantment.

The stars!

The mere sight of them relaxed Drizzt. It was notably colder up here, and his teeth chattered a bit, but it wasn't too uncomfortable, not even enough to draw his attention from the starlit sky.

The notion came to him that he owed it to the Silver Marches, to the dwarves who had trusted him and taken him in, to the folk of Silverymoon, which had been as his second home for decades, and indeed, to all the folk of the region, to rid them of this atrocity. This spell, this abomination, stole the sunlight and the starlight. With the blessings of Lolth, the dark elves had brought a bit of the Underdark to the surface world.

It could not stand.

He would not let it stand.

Drizzt understood that, though he had no idea what he might possibly do against the spell of blackness that had come to the North.

And yet, he would somehow remove it. And now there was only serenity, only a peaceful and calm glide on the high winds. His dragon mount was silent as she effortlessly soared through the night, and that silence reminded Drizzt of the whispers that dragon flight was as much magic as the mechanics of a giant bird. Surely Tazmikella's soundless glide seemed magical to him, as did the flight of Ilnezhara beside him.

He looked to Afafrenfere and noted the monk's expression, and understood that Afafrenfere was as entranced as he by the spectacle of dragon flight, or perhaps by the simple beauty of the normal night.

It didn't matter. It was quiet and calm, and ultimately serene. Drizzt recalled his many nights on Bruenor's Climb in Icewind Dale, when the stars seemed to reach down all around him, to lift him up into their eternal bosom. He felt that way again, like he was part of the night sky, part of the vast heavens, part of something immeasurably larger than himself.

And so he sat back and relaxed and simply enjoyed the sensation.

He was disappointed when Tazmikella dived back down through the Darkening, then set down on a high plateau a short while later, on a mountain just north of Mithral Hall, and with both of the northern orc encampments in sight. The smaller one near Mithral Hall's north door was to Drizzt's right, while the much larger one to his left filled the Upper Surbrin Vale.

"Here, we wait," Tazmikella explained, returning to her elf form after Drizzt dismounted. "My sister and the monk will set their watch over there," she added, pointing to the east, to another peak nearer the Surbrin. "When Arauthator and his son arrive, we will know."

"And then?"

"And then, Drizzt Do'Urden, you will come to understand that you are a little thing after all."

She moved closer then and reached up to gently stroke Drizzt's hair, eyeing him with a suggestive smile.

He recoiled and Tazmikella stepped back, her face a mask of confusion.

"My wife would not approve."

"But would you?" she asked, her voice the purr of a predatory cat. "If not for her, Drizzt Do'Urden?"

Drizzt swallowed hard. It was hard to deny the dragon's beauty in this form. He reminded himself that it was an illusion, that she was a dragon.

Finally, he took a deep breath and shook his head. "I am not . . ." he stuttered, trying to find the words, and not really happy about the prospect of rejecting a dragon. "I mean . . . this is not the way that I . . ."

Tazmikella's laughter stopped him. "Jarlaxle told me as much about you," she said, and Drizzt couldn't tell if she was complimenting him or mocking him.

"Such a pity," the dragon said, and she moved to the lip of the plateau and sat down, bare on the stone, staring out to the orc camps and beyond.

Drizzt moved beside her—not too close—and sat down, and Tazmikella nodded her approval.

"You will enjoy tomorrow," she promised, and that was the last thing either said that night as they sat there under the abomination of the Darkening, waiting for the whites.

CHAPTER 18

PRELUDE

"WORG RIDERS," REGIS REMARKED TO ALEINA AND WULFGAR, ASTRIDE their horses beside his pony. The troupe was up on a mountain pass in the Frost Hills, overlooking the juncture where the Rauvin joined the mighty Surbrin. A few miles to the north of their position loomed the Surbrin Bridge, out from Mithral Hall's eastern door.

"Some," Aleina agreed, shaking her head and looking quite grim.

"What do you know?" Wulfgar prompted.

"Drow," she replied. "As many drow as orcs. Some saddled on worgs, others riding summoned spectral mounts. It is a small troupe, but no doubt formidable with so many dark elf magic-users in its ranks."

"Funny thing about wizards," Regis remarked, "if they are ready for you, you will die horribly. If they are not ready for you, they will die horribly." He narrowed a sly eye to each of his companions in turn, a mischievous grin on his face.

"They ride in anticipation of the fight, no doubt," said Aleina. "Which means that Hartusk is aware of this breakout attempt your . . . friend, relayed to you. A trap?"

"No," Wulfgar said with confidence. "And we do not know that these riders are aware of Mithral Hall coming forth. Where is Hartusk and his tens of thousands, were that the case?"

"Too far," Aleina replied. "And so he sends these swift riders instead."

"Then it is still the time to fight," said Regis. "For Mithral Hall and for us." He pointed down to the rivers, noting the spot where the enemy riders would likely cross the Rauvin, where there were the ruins of an old bridge that now seemed more of a scattering of stones than an actual structure. However, nowhere else around it were any bridges or fords evident. The worg riders would likely pick their way across right where Regis had indicated, that they could then ride hard the few miles to the orc encampments around the Surbrin Bridge. "We can get to the crossing in front of them and fight them there, and there is where they will be most vulnerable."

He looked to Wulfgar, who nodded, and to Aleina, who seemed less than convinced.

"If their eyes are truly for Mithral Hall, then we will have complete surprise," the halfling reminded them.

"And if not?"

"Then we will fight them and wound them," Wulfgar put in. "And kill many of the drow. And if we cannot win, if we are to die, we do so knowing that we have divided our enemies and so have given our allies more time to break free."

Aleina looked at him, the two locking stares for a long while. The knight-commander nodded grimly, her determined expression revealing clearly that she fully expected to die this day.

But so be it.

North of the main encampment besieging Mithral Hall, the orc scouts that noted the movement of a huge dwarven force had three problems.

First, unbeknownst to them, a pair of copper dragons, whose eyes were keener than those of an eagle, circled overhead, watching for them.

Second, those dragons carried riders, and could deposit them in position to intercept couriers in short order.

And third, those riders were Afafrenfere and Drizzt Do'Urden.

Or was he Drizzt Do'Urden? For those who knew him best would know him as the Hunter then, moving silently across the open tundra, a whisper of wind, a flicker of shadow. Tazmikella had put him down far from a pair of running orcs—far enough so that she wouldn't be noted by any of the Many-Arrows minions in the area. With his magical anklets, Drizzt had little trouble gaining on them.

As he drew near and finally had them in sight, the ranger saw that they were not two any longer, but four, for another scouting pair had joined up with them.

"Good," the drow muttered. Better to have them all in one place.

He eased Taulmaril over his shoulder and set an arrow as he ran. He let fly once, then again, as he neared, and then there were two once more.

Drizzt dropped the bow, drew his blades, and came in with a forward roll, coming up to his feet in a slight crouch right in front of the two orcs, who immediately stabbed at him with their swords.

The ranger flipped his hands, blades down, and out the scimitars went, left and right, in a double backhanded parry that drove both swords out wide. He held the block longer on the left with Twinkle, allowing the orc in front of him on the right to disengage, and so it did, spinning its sword up higher for a downward chop.

The expected defense would have called for the drow ranger to flip his right-hand blade, Icingdeath, back up for a second parry.

But the Hunter didn't play by conventional expectations.

Instead, with brilliant speed and precision, the Hunter pressed with Twinkle, out to the left, and snapped that scimitar up and across to block—not as effective a block as he could have attained with Icingdeath, of course, but one that left him in a position clearly confusing to his enemies. For now his right hand was free, and was underneath the defenses of the orc whose sword Twinkle had just stopped.

Out snapped the deadly drow's right hand, underneath the block, and the orc recoiled and the drow launched Twinkle back the other way as the orc on his left pressed in. He could have moved forward and right, pacing the retreating orc and so driving Icingdeath home for a killing blow, but he retracted that blade even as Twinkle moved across for a backhanded, downward block, and had Icingdeath again stabbing forward, this time to the left, over the block, forcing the second orc back.

Again the drow retracted without a kill, because he understood the lack of balance in his scrambling opponents. He crossed his arms in front of him, Twinkle pointing diagonally out and up from his right shoulder, Icingdeath pointing diagonally down from his left hip, and he sprang from the crouch straight for the confused orcs. Twinkle swept down and across, Icingdeath swept up and across, and the scimitars scored identical wounds, hip to ribs, on the orcs, though from opposite directions.

The Hunter immediately pulled the blades in close and rushed between the pair, quicker than they could follow. As his arms swung in to his sides, he tossed the blades, which crossed in the air in front of him, and he caught them in opposite hands, and now with his thumbs away from the crosspieces.

He stopped abruptly and pushed his arms down and back, stabbing both blades out behind him into the futilely-turning orcs.

And around spun the Hunter, to find his enemies twisted and bleeding and stumbling.

The openings were clear.

The scimitars were swift.

The orcs were dead.

The ogre slowed, seeing the running approach of the smaller figure. Afafrenfere was close indeed before the behemoth recognized him as an enemy, and indeed, was up in the air, spinning head over heels.

The ogre reflexively dropped its club and lifted its hands to catch the puny human, and it did grab Afafrenfere, one hand clamping on each hip, as he came over and laid out straight on his back. Any watching ally of Brother Afafrenfere would surely have sucked in his breath at that dangerous moment, and certainly the ogre believed that it had just caught a meal out of midair, like a hunting cat catching a bird.

Except that this particular bird was more an eagle than a wren.

The monk drove out his feet at that moment, double-kicking the brute in the face with head-snapping force. Before the ogre could throw him aside, the monk retracted and snap-kicked again, one straightened foot after the other, his toes jabbing into the unfortunate ogre's eyes.

The brute let go with one hand to slap at its torn eye, and it tried to let go with the other hand as well, except that the monk wouldn't let it. Afafrenfere clamped on tightly to that hand as he contorted his body and threw it into a spin, using the stunned ogre's distraction to his great advantage. With ferocious momentum, Afafrenfere looped and looped around, twisting the arm, turning the ogre's shoulder forward and down.

The ogre stumbled.

The monk dropped to the ground, but did not let go with either hand, and instead bent the ogre's hand at the wrist, pressing it palm up behind the brute's back, then leaping up and driving the hand in front of him, somehow finding the leverage to send the ogre into a forward flop to land facedown on the ground.

The brute roared and shook its head vigorously to clear the confusion. As it opened its pained eyes and looked up, it was just in time to see the bottoms of the feet of the murderous monk as Afafrenfere descended from his high leap.

Jarl Fimmel Orelson looked up curiously at the rocky mountain walls, noting the unusual rumbling. He was the leader of Shining White, the leader, in fact, of all the clans of frost giants that had come to join in the War of the Silver Marches. He and many of his giants had gone no farther south than this encampment, the western bank of the Surbrin beside the thick stone-and-mithral bridge the dwarves had constructed across that waterway.

Many giants had died at Sundabar, and a few of Jarl Orelson's closest friends had been killed in the battle of Nesmé. Now, with the apparent retreat of the bulk of the dark elves, Jarl Orelson had taken command of Many-Arrows' besieging forces, with direct control over this one surrounding Mithral Hall. Hartusk had protested of course, the warlord's bloodshot eyes firmly set on Everlund, but after the last disaster where the dwarves had punched out in the north and sacked an encampment, Jarl Fimmel Orelson would hear none of it.

"What is it, Jarl?" asked Finguld Boomer Felloki, one of the most notable frost giant warriors.

Fimmel Orelson looked at his old friend and noted the weariness in Finguld's eyes. They had won many victories, particularly early on in the campaign. They had slaughtered the Knights in Silver at the Crossing of the Redrun, had obliterated the town of Nesmé, had destroyed King Bromm of Adbar and his dwarven legions in the Battle of the Cold Vale, had twice put Mithral Hall's dwarves, and once Citadel Felbarr's dwarves, back in their holes. But it had been a long winter, and the most recent reports had not been nearly as promising.

That second battle with the dwarves of Mithral Hall had left many giants dead—an entire clan had subsequently decided to return to the Spine of the World. Farther south, Silverymoon had held strong against the siege. There were reports of troubles in the Underdark, with the dwarves coming forth—and even one report that Adbar and Felbarr had been joined again through the upper tunnels.

And worst of all had come the hints from the northeast, from the region around Citadel Adbar, where the siege had been broken and an entire legion of frost giants killed.

Jarl Fimmel Orelson hadn't confirmed those whispers of tragedy from Adbar, but he suspected that something, at least, had happened up there, and that things had not gone so well for his fellow frost giants.

And now he heard the mountain rumbling, and he didn't know what to make of it.

That was because he didn't know of a similar event a century before, when the dwarves, besieged by King Obould, had burst out through the eastern wall of this very mountain, Fourthpeak. Nor did he know that the mine tracks they had constructed way back then, to allow for the sudden and violent breakout, were still in place, and that the wall they had later constructed over the impromptu exit was not nearly as solid as it appeared—for it appeared as the natural stone of the mountain, and the orcs didn't even know that it was not.

And he didn't know that the rumbling he now heard was a train of heavily-laden mining carts, rolling swiftly down the tracks, speeding to a collision with a wall that was designed not to stop them.

The last time the dwarves had broken out of this place, the mining carts had been full of dwarves, bold warriors ready to bounce down the side of a mountain to lead the charge.

Not this time.

The stones exploded, and the carts came flying through, high up on the mountain wall. Flying, and falling, and now scattering their cargo of flaming kegs of burning oil.

The orcs and ogres, giants and goblins scrambled under that rain of fiery death, of burning kegs tumbling from on high and splattering on the ground, throwing their flaming debris far and wide. Truly, the unexpected spectacle inflicted far more fear than actual damage on the besieging army. The carts could not be guided in their flight, and they mostly piled around or on top of one another, and their thrown cargo, too, could only cover a fairly small area, nothing the size of this encampment.

For the monsters, though, the surprise was complete, and terrifying, and that was what King Connerad was obviously playing for in leading with the attention-grabbing, horrifying spectacle of the flaming mining carts. He didn't plan to lose the surprise, either.

From up in the hole of the mountainside came the fire of dwarven artillery, side-slinger catapults and ballistae launching their payloads all the way to the Surbrin Bridge, demanding the attention of the monstrous force.

And while they had that attention, while they had Jarl Fimmel Orelson roaring orders to counter the breakout on the mountainside, King Connerad and General Dagnabbet and the whole of Mithral Hall's remaining force came forth, the eastern doors banging open, a wedge-shaped shield wall rushing out.

Jarl Fimmel Orelson was still running around, ordering his minions to respond to the crossbows and catapults with a barrage of boulders, when he heard the commotion in the northeast at the eastern doors. When he heard the orcs, who were closest to that portal, screaming for support.

The frost giant grabbed Finguld by the vest and yanked him around. "Get help to that door!" he ordered, and he shoved the giant away. He lifted his horn then and turned to the east, toward the encampment on the other side of the Surbrin Bridge, and blew three clear notes, calling the orcs camped across the river to arms.

Then he looked around, surveying the area and the damage, measuring the continuing barrage spewing forth from the broken mountainside, and estimating the volley his giants might return. Jarl Orelson was a seasoned veteran, and he nodded grimly. His forces would hold the dwarves in place long enough, he was confident, and the main force would roll down upon them from around the mountains in the north in short order.

Many dwarves would die here, he silently vowed, and he looked back to the broken mountainside once more and smiled, thinking that their desperation would cost King Connerad dearly. In breaking out, they had opened the way for Jarl Fimmel Orelson to break in.

All around the frost giant leader, orcs screamed and goblins burned and dwarves rained death from on high. By the doors, the orc ranks were already breaking and falling back—fleeing in full retreat, actually, and surely they meant to run across the bridge and far away.

But Jarl Fimmel Orelson would stop them, and would turn back the tide of the ambush in short order. He would fight the dwarves to a standstill, as he had reinforcements close at hand and they could not.

"Come quickly!" Wulfgar bade his halfling friend, splashing the last few feet from the cold water. The Silverymoon raiders had crossed the Surbrin and rushed to the Rauvin's rocky ford. Led by Regis, they had gone around setting their traps. But now the worg-riding enemies were in sight, and approaching fast. Aleina and the others had already retreated to the small wood not far from either river, and Wulfgar could see the knight-commander at the tree line, waving to him, bidding him to hurry.

"Almost done," replied Regis, who was still on a rock in the river, easing a ceramic ball under its raised edge.

"Now!" Wulfgar ordered. "We are out of time!"

"Go, go!" Regis said to him. The halfling looked back over his shoulder and noted the enemy approach—they could hear the worgs in the charge growling now. "Go, or they will see you."

"I'll not leave you to die!" Wulfgar argued.

"I do not intend to die!" Regis snapped back, and he held up a potion vial, one Wulfgar recognized as an elixir of speed. "Now go!" When Wulfgar hesitated, the halfling looked at him plaintively. "Trust me," he said quietly.

Wulfgar nodded and sprinted away, and Regis went back to his work.

The barbarian tried not to look back too often in the short sprint, reminding himself repeatedly to trust in Regis. Aleina was waiting for him at the tree line, handing him the reins of his mount as he entered. He leaped astride beside the knight-commander and looked back, nodding, to see Regis at last running from the riverbank, his little legs pumping furiously under the influence of the potion, covering the ground with his speeding strides.

The worg riders were still some way back, and Wulfgar continued to nod, thinking his friend would surely make it.

But then he saw something else, and he stopped nodding, his eyes widening and his jaw dropping.

And the riders around him pulled hard on their reins, forcing their suddenly-nervous horses into a short backstep, shrinking back under the canopy.

Above the approaching worg riders came two great white forms, shining brilliantly even in the dim light of the Darkening, speeding fast for the river.

And there was Regis, running out in the open!

Wulfgar started to call out, but Aleina grabbed him, and surely he understood that he could not betray their position. He looked around frantically, the dragons coming fast, the halfling apparently oblivious . . .

Wulfgar rolled from the side of his mount, hit the ground in a spin, and hurled Aegis-fang long and far, spinning it past the approaching halfling. Clearly startled, Regis stopped and ducked, and reflexively turned to watch the hammer as it flew past. In that turn, he saw the wyrms, and before he ever turned back, the halfling was flat on the ground, trying to make himself very, very small.

Aleina, Wulfgar, and all the others faded back farther into the shadows of the trees, and then those trees began to shake wildly in the windy wake of the speeding dragons, the air crackling, the wind rushing like a tornado with their passing. Despite the best efforts of their skilled riders, the horses shrieked in terror, and more than one of the raiders fell to the ground, trembling.

But the dragons apparently did not notice. They were already long gone, flying fast to the north.

Wulfgar looked back to Regis, who to his credit was already up and running for the trees once more, but the barbarian could not keep his gaze there. He rushed to the side, to a small clearing, to view the departing wyrms. He had noted their passengers in their passing: a pair of dark elf warriors.

"What do we do?" he heard Aleina ask at length, and from her tone, Wulfgar realized that she had likely asked him that question many times by the time he had noted it.

"Lady, we should flee this place," one of the other riders replied.

"Nay, we've come for a fight, and we've found one!" another argued, and so it went, back and forth.

Time was running short. The worg riders were nearing the river's southern bank even then, and Regis came to the tree line, unseen by their enemies.

Aleina Brightlance took it all in, but seemed at a loss, and surely Wulfgar understood. The enemy force was here, the moment of their fight had come to them, but if those dragons had noted them and meant to turn around . . .

"Hold and wait for it," came the unexpected voice of Regis as he scrambled up on his pony. He had been lying in the open with a pair of white dragons soaring right over him, yet he, above all, seemed perfectly composed and ready for the fight. And Wulfgar couldn't help but smile when he looked upon the gallant little one.

"When do we charge?" Aleina asked, deferring to Regis, who had prepped the battlefield.

"Oh, you will know, good lady," Regis replied slyly, and he even tossed Aleina a knowing wink as he patted the pouch of holding he had belted on his hip. He looked to the river and nodded. "We'll all know."

And with that, Regis began handing out potions—to make his allies stronger, to make them faster, to protect them from fire, to protect them from cold, to imbue the drinker with a veteran's understanding, to heal wounds. He emptied his pouch of holding at that time, every potion he had brewed over the last tendays that might be of use, because he looked at the approaching enemy, and thought of the enemy that had just flown past.

The group worked diligently and methodically, time running out, to get the best enhancements to the person who would benefit the most. The archers who would remain in the rear were protected from cold, in case the dragons returned with their frosty breath, where the archers would be the likely target. Strength and speed to the front ranks, that they could hit hard and wound their superior enemy quickly, for the sake of their allies in the north even if they were overrun here.

Regis kept a couple for himself, including only a single potion of healing. He had enough tricks he might play, with his hand crossbow and his strange dagger and his hat of disguise, and he did not need potions the way some others did.

He might be clever enough to survive, he tried to tell himself.

But there were drow.

He was full of resignation, full of steel, but full, too, of doubt.

They glided up nearer the Darkening, Tazmikella and Ilnezhara soaring around with hardly a flap of their wings, and with remarkable calm and silence.

Drizzt glanced over at the other dragon, at her rider, Afafrenfere, sitting serenely, and apparently reveling in the wind. He seemed to be looking inside, finding this flight a catalyst for his meditation.

Drizzt nodded. He understood the feeling. He wanted nothing more than for the dragons to climb through the roiling darkness so he could see the sky once more. But of course he could not have that. They were up here for a reason, and despite the dragon's insistence that he and Afafrenfere should simply hold their place and worry about nothing at that time, Drizzt found himself peering down to the distant ground, far, far below.

They were over the orc encampment, the large northern one that housed the main army besieging Mithral Hall.

To the north, not so far now, a second army waited.

Drizzt's eyes, though, were continually drawn to the south, along the snaking Surbrin River. He heard the distant explosions, he saw the fires burning around the eastern base of Fourthpeak. He noted the dark masses, orc armies and dwarven armies, rolling together. As of this point, it didn't seem like Bruenor and the secret army had joined in the battle, but it would not be long, Drizzt understood.

Catti-brie was down there, ready to go to battle. And Drizzt would not be beside her.

"Trust in her," he whispered to himself, though the words were lost in the wind.

Tazmikella banked and swooped sidelong into a turning dive. Beside them, Ilnezhara followed suit, though she veered out suddenly to the south and began to climb again almost immediately.

Was she going to the fight at the bridge, Drizzt wondered? The thought nagged at him—he should be the one to go there, not the monk.

"They turn." He heard Tazmikella, the dragon's voice tugging him from his private contemplations.

The drow leaned over and tried to get a view beneath, and could indeed see the orc encampment, much closer now, stirring and elongating toward the southeast, along the pass that would take them east of the mountain, with a straight run to the Surbrin Bridge.

"Tell them," Tazmikella ordered.

Drizzt brought up Taulmaril and aimed the bow to the north. He hesitated and shifted, though, and let fly his silver-streaking magical arrow to the distant east instead.

The flare flew and arced toward the Surbrin, cutting through the dark sky.

It informed King Harnoth and his thousands that their trial had begun.

Drizzt reached for another arrow, smiling grimly, thinking that Tazmikella would swoop down upon the monstrous army, affording him some wonderful shots. Giants, he thought. He would focus his deadly rain on the giants.

But Tazmikella was not diving any longer but climbing, lifting up once more into the magical darkness of the sky.

"Are we not engaging?" Drizzt yelled to her.

"Wait for my sister's return," came the reply.

Drizzt looked to the south, but Ilnezhara was long out of sight. He glanced down, shaking his head. He thought the dragons were supposed to ensure the rout here.

"She is nowhere near!" he protested.

"If you are so eager, I could roll about until you fall from the saddle," the dragon replied. "Perhaps you will crash upon a giant and help Harnoth's cause."

"I . . . what is this about?" he demanded.

"It is about something for which you are inconsequential," Tazmikella answered. "And about something for which you would be wise to remain quiet."

There was something in her tone, a deep unease, that gave Drizzt pause. He wanted to ask her. He looked again to the south, where Ilnezhara still was not to be seen.

She hadn't gone to the battle at the Surbrin Bridge, he understood then.

"Perhaps when he has his trophy, we can return to Menzoberranzan," Ravel said to Saribel, as they moved north among the rear ranks of the raider force. "I am eager to see what gains we might make for House Do'Urden when word of our grand victory spreads wide. And no doubt Matron Mother Quenthel will be eager to spread that word!"

He looked to Saribel for some response, some sign that she agreed with him, but she remained impassive, sitting atop her floating light blue disc, followed by other priestesses of House Xorlarrin and Saribel's own handmaidens in appropriate ranks behind her.

"We will find great glory," said a voice at the side, and Matron Mother Zeerith's two children glanced over and cast a sour look at Doum'wielle Armgo, riding a wretched-looking horse. She was the only one of the drow contingent riding a living creature, and not a fine one at that, while the handful of priestesses glided on their discs and Ravel and the other ten Xorlarrins, associates of his in the days before he became the archmage of House Do'Urden, all sat astride summoned spectral mounts of light that resembled the Underdark lizards they rode in the deep tunnels.

They hadn't expected to be on this particular road this day. They had been traveling with Warlord Hartusk's vast army as it made its sprawling way to the south and the great city of Everlund. Word from Bregan D'aerthe had abruptly turned back Tiago and his companions, though, and they had enlisted fourscore orc worg riders to ride with them for Mithral Hall's eastern gate and the Surbrin Bridge.

"What do you know of glory, child?" Saribel asked Doum'wielle in the most condescending manner she could manage.

High Priestess . . . High Priestess . . . a voice in Doum'wielle's mind warned, her sentient sword reminding her of her place. Doum'wielle was glad of that, for never had she felt so naked and alone.

"Killing Drizzt Do'Urden will bring us great glory," she remarked, but quietly.

Saribel laughed at her, a horrible, mocking cackle.

"Us?" Ravel asked with a smirk.

"You will know no glory, child of the *darthiir*," Saribel chided. "Your veins run thick with the blood of the betrayers."

"Not as much so as the blood of our matron mother," Doum'wielle responded without hesitation, and clearly without thinking it through.

The Xorlarrin siblings scowled back at her with hateful, even murderous, expressions. Doum'wielle recognized her mistake immediately, and understood, too, at that moment, that if she had expected Matron Mother Dahlia or anyone else in Menzoberranzan to protect her, she was sadly mistaken.

Without even thinking of the movement, Doum'wielle glanced to the north, hoping against hope that she'd see her father flying back on Aurbangras.

But alas, she was alone.

Idiot, the sentient sword said in her thoughts. *Know your place!*

She looked back to the Xorlarrin siblings, and felt like a rabbit looking up at a pair of hungry bobcats. Even that image would be foreign to the dark elves then scowling at her.

Doum'wielle's heart sank as she thought of the rabbits—she loved rabbits!—skipping around the boughs of the Glimmerwood. Perhaps she would see some this day.

More likely, she would never see them again.

"Do you understand?" she heard then, Saribel's voice. She nodded meekly and said, "Yes, Prie—*High* Priestess," knowing full well that if she had admitted that she hadn't even heard Saribel's instructions or admonitions that she was apparently supposed to understand, she would likely feel the bite of the vicious priestess's snake-headed whip.

A disgusted look upon her face, Saribel shook her head and glanced at her equally-disgusted brother.

"I will leave her punishment to you," she heard Saribel say quietly to Ravel.

Ravel Xorlarrin chuckled wickedly at that. "Perhaps I will summon a demon to join in our tryst," he told his sister.

Doum'wielle knew that it wasn't a bluff.

They neared the swift-flowing Rauvin then, with the lead orc riders already picking their way across the rocky debris, the broken stone remains of a shattered bridge. Worgs leaped gracefully from stone to stone, following the familiar path to the north embankment. Several dark elf males paced them on their summoned lizard mounts, and of course the priestesses, Saribel in their lead, would just float above it all.

Doum'wielle just sighed, knowing that she was going to have a difficult crossing with this old and wretched horse they had given her.

They reached the edge of the river, Saribel floating right out, Ravel moving his mount with practiced ease from stone to stone. The remaining drow continued behind and Doum'wielle let them pass. She'd take her time and cross last, then catch up to the group in the fields beyond.

"Smoke in the north!" one of the orcs yelled then, pointing eagerly from his position halfway across the Rauvin. Following his lead, the others began to cheer, for, indeed, a line of black smoke was rising to the northwest, across the perpendicular River Surbrin, in the region of the eastern door of Mithral Hall.

As Bregan D'aerthe had predicted, the battle had begun.

The orcs whooped and urged their worgs forward, eager to join in the murder.

At the front of their line, a lanky orc with one eye missing and a mouth that opened all the way to its ear on one side picked up its pace and began a battle song, spittle pouring over its torn cheek. The orc's ugly lupine mount leaped far to the last stone, ready to spring from there to the north bank of the Rauvin. But when its paws touched down on the stone, the mount and its uglier rider found that the stone was not secure, and indeed, it flipped forward.

Flipped forward and crushed some cleverly hidden ceramic balls.

The worg yelped, the orc shrieked, and all those around grimaced and turned away in a hurry. The area was bathed in bright yellow light, as if the sun had suddenly found its way through the Darkening. The startled worg stumbled and splashed into the swift river, taking its rider with it.

Not far behind, a second orc rider hit a tilted stone in just the right manner to send it levering over, and more light pellets cracked open, bathing the area in still more light. And worse, a vial shattered between the stones, a vial that turned out to be a flask of explosive oil.

The orc and worg went flying in the blast, the rock beneath them lifting into the air and throwing out other stones in a spray like a volley of sling bullets. An unfortunate drow wizard just to the side was cut in half by the spray, and sent flying into the water, his lizard mount disappearing with a dark flash and a whiff of smoke.

A second explosion sounded as the lead orcs leaped to the north bank, and more magical light, stinging and awful, filled drow eyes.

And then they heard the horns, what sounded to them like a thousand horns blowing, and from the north came the charge of the Knights in Silver.

Near the rear of the Many-Arrows train, Ravel and Saribel shielded their eyes from the infernal light. They heard the shouts and the roars and the horns and knew they had to suffer the stinging brightness long enough to fight free. They saw the charge, orcs scrambling to the bank to meet it. The enemy, a full cavalry unit, was closing fast, bows lifted, arrows flying.

Those volleys were not general, the dark elves—all the dark elves—immediately recognized. They were concentrated, and aiming for drow targets.

Ravel winced as a wizard associate, riding up near the front and nearly to the riverbank, found a score of arrows descending upon him. His magical wards deflected the brunt of the barrage, sending arrows skipping every which way with flashes and sparks of purplish light. But then came another missile, spinning end over end, and before it hit, Ravel knew, and so did the poor wizard, that there was no protection from this one.

The young drow mage's wards would not stop Aegis-fang. The warhammer ignited a burst of purplish light, but was not turned, crashing in with bone-shattering force, and sending the young drow mage flying from his seat, twisted and broken, into the river.

Doum'wielle had only barely moved out from the southern bank by that point, just one stride of her unsteady horse onto a flat stone. Khazid'hea screamed out in her thoughts, hungry for blood, and so she drew the sword and urged her horse forward. But this was no agile worg or spectral lizard mount, and the poor nag couldn't begin to find a path, stumbling and hesitating.

Khazid'hea, the hungry Cutter, would have none of it. *Forward, to the fight!* it demanded in Doum'wielle's thoughts.

But the horse would not move.

Dominated by the sword, Doum'wielle slid down from the saddle and leaped to the next stone in line, trying to fashion a path forward. Far ahead, the battle had been joined, she saw, with orcs and their worg mounts interlocked with the larger horses and human riders—mostly humans, at least. To the side, a drow wizard threw a lightning bolt. A second held forth his hand and produced a small pea of flame, a fireball ready to throw.

Doum'wielle grinned, anticipating the blast as she scrambled forward to yet another stone. She nearly fell, though, and slipped down into the water to her waist. Pulling herself back to the rock, she looked forward once more for the fireball.

But the wizard still stood there, some fifty feet or so in front of her, his hand still outstretched, the small flame still burning on his uplifted palm.

Holding that pose, he simply fell over, splashing down into the river, which bubbled and flashed as the fireball exploded underwater. Where the wizard had been stood a diminutive figure, a halfling, holding a bloody rapier.

Doum'wielle blinked. Then it was no longer a halfling, but a drow there, looking much like the wizard who had just tumbled away.

She tried to sort it out, but Khazid'hea didn't care and wouldn't let her care, either, the sword screaming for battle. It drove her forward hungrily, swiftly, recklessly.

Perhaps it was an accident, perhaps more of an intended collision, but scrambling up over the top edge of one triangular stone, Doum'wielle was met not by the closing enemy, but by Ravel and his spectral mount, the drow wizard in full flight back to the southern bank. The crash sent the half-elf twisting over and back, tumbling, Khazid'hea flying from her hand to land in the river with a splash. She saw Ravel leap over her to the next stone to the south. Behind him came Saribel on her disc, and behind her, many of the drow in full retreat.

The river tugged at Doum'wielle, with just her arms on the rock, just her head and shoulders above it. Confused and bruised, she held there, her thoughts swirling and jumbling.

She wanted to cry out for help, for her father, but she could not.

She wanted to pull herself onto the stone, out of the cold water, but she could not.

Desperately, Doum'wielle looked for her sword. She could hear the fighting above, close, even on the rocky ford, she knew. She looked around for her weapon, but it was not there.

She wanted to cry out again, for her mother now, but she could not.

She wanted to cry out for her brother, but she could not.

Her thoughts swirled.

Or not, perhaps, she realized. Her thoughts began to unwind, streaming to clarity. She felt as if she was coming out of a daze, entering reality.

Reality?

Ugly, wretched reality, and she burst out in tears, and cursed herself and saw again the blood on her hands.

She could not bear it. She recoiled from it, retreated to a darker place. And there, Khazid'hea found her and called to her.

Doum'wielle, Little Doe, let go of the stone and ducked under the water, letting the current take her.

Back and forth the battle rolled, like the maw of some gigantic monster gnashing its huge teeth, grinding human, orc, worg, and drow to mush.

They had been outnumbered two to one, and that without counting the worg mounts, which fought with fury. Wulfgar stood on the northern bank of the ford, his horse long dead.

Orcs and worgs came at him, drow hand crossbows and magic spells reached out and slammed him, but the son of Beornegar, his body and face red with blood, would not move aside. He alone held the ford, bottle-necking the enemy force while his companions slaughtered those behind who had already crossed.

No, not alone, he understood, as he saw a drow come up beside an orc rider, saw the orc go flying away, garroted by a leering specter, saw the worg drop flat to the stepping stone, a rapier slid into its brain.

Wulfgar swatted aside the next worg leaping for him, but called out to Regis, seeing a pair of riders rushing in at him from behind. The bar-barian thought to launch his warhammer, but he couldn't as yet another orc jumped in at him, forcing him to defend. He did manage to glance back at his friend to see the halfling-turned-drow spinning around, some flask in his hand, which he threw out and down in front of him, between him and the charging orcs.

The explosion shook the stones of the ford, dislodging riders, and demanded a pause in the fighting even on the field behind Wulfgar. Regis's oil of impact bomb had gone under a stone and blasted it from the river, throwing it and a host of other rocks into the faces of the charging monsters, blowing them away in a gout of smoke and spray.

Another orc came in from the side, but Regis brought forth a hand crossbow and shot the brute in the face.

Victim to the drow sleeping poison, the orc fell to sweet dreams a moment later. But it found those fancies while it slipped under the water.

Another followed, and flew away from the second living snake of the magical dagger, and the third orc coming in behind found itself face-to-face not with the drow that had been standing there, but with a furious halfling wearing a blue beret and holding a magnificent rapier, thin and faster than a striking snake. The orc lost its left eye before it realized that the halfling had struck, and still didn't truly understand as it clutched its throat from the second stab of that beautiful blade.

Wulfgar focused on the orc in front of him, now tightly clenched with him. He twisted Aegis-fang left, bending the orc, then jerked it back to the right with such strength that his enemy went spinning head over heels to the right.

The barbarian called out to his halfling friend, and when Regis turned, Wulfgar saluted him, smiled, and nodded.

He thought to go out there, but he knew that Regis—that Spider Parrafin—did not need his help.

Sometime later, Doum'wielle pulled herself out of the river, Khazid'hea in hand. She gasped for breath, at the end of her endurance. The sword had called her, had dragged her down to retrieve it. Caught in the current, the half-elf had drifted far from the battle, almost to the Surbrin, and now, drenched and freezing, her lungs aching, she crawled onto the field and collapsed into cold darkness.

The drow had fled far to the south. Back to the east, across the Rauvin ford, their enemies had won.

Aleina collapsed into Wulfgar's strong arms, practically falling off her horse into him. For a moment, he feared her dead or gravely wounded, but he felt her grab at him, a deep breath coming to her. She stood stronger then, gathering her thoughts and collecting her remaining strength.

"Four," she said, offering a sly look. "Including a drow."

Wulfgar looked at her curiously.

"How many kills do you claim?" she asked, trying to find some humor in the carnage around her, as if she needed to smile to stop herself from screaming in denial.

Looking around, where a score of their band lay dead and not one had come through unscathed, the barbarian said, "I didn't count."

"Ten," said another, and both looked over to the eastern edge of the ford, where stood Regis, his bright eyes and white teeth shining out through a mask of blood.

Aleina turned to Wulfgar. "You killed *ten?*"

But the barbarian was shaking his head, still staring at Regis. "Not I," Wulfgar said, directing her gaze to his diminutive friend.

"And two dark elves," Regis said with a bow.

Aleina hugged Wulfgar tighter, but glanced around at the devastation behind her on the field. "Our troupe is ended. Yet the fight at the Surbrin Bridge has only just begun."

"We did our part," Wulfgar assured her, his eyes drawn to the smoke and the distant sounds of battle. Drizzt was there, and Catti-brie and Bruenor.

The fate of the Silver Marches was in their hands.

CHAPTER 19

THE BATTLE OF THE SURBRIN BRIDGE

Bruenor and Catti-brie stood on the bank of the Surbrin, watching the approach of a pair of dwarves, male and female, they hardly expected to see at this time and in this place.

"Bah, but ye didn't think we'd be missin' all the fun, did ye?" Athrogate asked when he bounded up to them beside Ambergris.

"Didn't know what to think about yerself," Bruenor replied. "Ain't seen ye in a few days, eh? And yerself," he said to Amber, "why aren't ye with King Harnoth and yer monk friend?"

"Drizzt is with Brother Afafrenfere," Amber answered. "Aye, and we'll be seeing them soon, don't ye doubt!"

Catti-brie and Bruenor exchanged curious looks.

"Aye, and yer boys Wulfgar and Regis been fighting already this day, south where the Surbrin catches the Rauvin," Athrogate explained.

"How can you know that?" a concerned Catti-brie demanded, but she held up her hand, dismissing her own question, and reminding herself of this one's associate, after all.

"So I'm hearin' the plan and laughin' all the while," said Athrogate. "Connerad's out and the smoke's rising!"

"And King Emerus is across the river," said Bruenor, pointing to the west and the main dwarf force from Citadel Felbarr, who were even then preparing their sweep to the south in support of the boys breaking free from Mithral Hall.

"And yerself and yer boys . . ." Athrogate started.

"And girls," Ambergris put in, and she tossed a wink to Catti-brie.

"Aye, all o' them," Athrogate agreed. "Ye're to cut the battle in half, are ye? And to hold that point?" He looked at Bruenor, smile beaming, and all of a sudden he began a riotous laugh. "Bwahaha!" he roared. "Durned if it ain't the craziest plan I've e'er heared!"

"And yet, you are here," Catti-brie said dryly.

"Wouldn't miss it for all the ale in Waterdeep!" the black-bearded dwarf howled. "So ye got a place for Athrogate and Amber Gristle O'Maul on yer boat, good King Bruenor?"

Bruenor and Catti-brie looked to each other again, and shrugged. What did they have to lose, after all, for neither doubted the fighting prowess of this pair, particularly Athrogate and those devastating morningstars he swung around with such ease and aplomb. Their job here with this force of a hundred Gutbusters was to keep the orcs in the large encampment on the eastern side of the Surbrin Bridge from joining in the fight in front of Mithral Hall on the western bank. Who better to hold a choke point than Athrogate, a dwarf as strong as a giant and more ferocious than a cornered wolverine?

"There they go," Amber said, drawing their attention back across the river, where King Emerus and his army began their charge.

"Then here we go," said Bruenor, and he called to Bungalow Thump to begin their most unusual foray. With a determined nod, Bruenor led his three companions to the lead boat.

***

General Dagnabbet looked around hopefully at the progress her charges had made in breaking free of Mithral Hall. The diversion had worked perfectly, the fiery carts and bombs driving back the orcs and creating enough confusion for Dagnabbet to get most of her shield dwarves out of the choke point of Mithral Hall's eastern gate and into some defensive formations at least.

They had broken free, but surely it was to be a temporary and costly thing.

"They'll be here," King Connerad said to her, moving to her side and nodding hopefully.

Dagnabbet nodded back, but her eyes remained on the front lines, where the orc force, so clearly superior to her own, was regrouping, and to the north, where the sounds of a second enemy force could be heard, roaring around the mountain.

And to the Surbrin Bridge, where, already, the lead orc runners from the vast encampments of the eastern bank were making their appearance on the field.

"They better be," she said to her king and friend.

The lines wavered back and forth, dwarves and orcs falling to stone that was soaked under pools of blood.

Then came a roar from the north, and King Connerad, General Dagnabbet, and the other dwarves looked up the western bank of the Surbrin.

As did the orcs, and they were the ones who began to cheer at the sight of their reinforcing brethren.

But a second roar overwhelmed the first, drawing the attention of the combatants again, and this time, the dwarves of Mithral Hall were the ones who knew hope.

A second dwarven army had come, the shield dwarves charging down behind the orcs from the northern encampment, slicing into their ranks. The fight for the second front was on in full.

Dagnabbet and Connerad retreated to a higher vantage point where they could oversee the two fronts, and it didn't take long for the general of Mithral Hall to inform King Connerad that the arrival of King Emerus and his boys wouldn't be enough.

"That's the one camp from the north," she explained. "The small one. The bigger group'll be along soon enough's me guess."

"If them orcs're even needin' it," King Connerad said, looking then to the Surbrin Bridge, its wide lane thick with orc reinforcements swarming in from the east. Beyond the bridge in the eastern fields came a line of monsters that extended out of Connerad's sight, with ogres and giants and goblins rushing eagerly for the battle. That line probably stretched all the way to Felbarr, he realized.

So Connerad was thinking that they would need to retreat back into Mithral Hall, and they were ready for that contingency. He looked to the fight in the north.

"Find us a way to bring them boys from Felbarr in aside us," he instructed Dagnabbet, who was already doing exactly that. "King Bruenor's got to be in that bunch, Moradin watch over him. We'll put a sting on the dogs this day, don't ye doubt, but we're not to fight to the last."

General Dagnabbet wanted to argue, but she could not. They wouldn't win with the influx from the Surbrin Bridge, and if the much larger orc force they knew to be farther north came sweeping down, the dwarven force in the north would be quickly surrounded and obliterated.

She was about to suggest a clever strike to the north, to link with the dwarves up there and bring them fast to Mithral Hall, but her budding plan fell apart a moment later when still more horns began to blow, and a flotilla appeared in the river, a score of small boats, elven boats, sweeping downstream for the bridge.

On the center and lead boat of that flotilla stood King Bruenor Battlehammer, feet spread wide, hands on strong hips, chin tilted defiantly at the enemy standing on the Surbrin Bridge. Athrogate and Ambergris flanked him, with Catti-brie behind, her eyes already closed as she fell into her spellcasting, calling deep into the elemental powers of her magical ring, following the connection to a place of fire.

Bruenor stood rock solid at the prow even as the missiles began to rain down at them. He drew his axe and pulled his shield off his back, and banged his axe on his shield with a drumlike cadence while he sang an old dwarven battle song, one at once rousing and mournful:

> We speak with hammer, axe, and maul
> We call to gods in Mor'din's Hall
> We stand our ground, await our fall
> For then we'll know the grandest feast
> With poking beard and upraised chin
> For though we fall, the clan she'll win
> To die this day for kith and kin
> But kill the ugly goblin beast
> Pile heavy the stones
> To warm me bones . . .

Spears and arrows reached for them from the river's eastern bank, monsters running to pace them so they could continue their rain. The lines of orcs crossing the Surbrin Bridge paused in their charge for the fight at Mithral Hall's door, and instead turned their war whoops and their sights on the flotilla of dwarves being delivered to them where they stood. They too bent back their bows and let fly their spears and javelins.

Those boats nearest the eastern bank took the brunt of the missile barrage, and dwarves growled and cried out, and dwarves fell writhing in pain, or fell into the cold waters to be swept away, or fell dead.

Behind Bruenor, Athrogate glanced over at Amber, neither of them smiling any longer. They still had a long way to go, and under this rain of missiles, would any be alive by the time they threw their grapnels?

But Bruenor held his place and sang all the louder, and many of the Gutbusters took up the cadence, clanging their spiked gauntlets together. Up came Bruenor's shield, picking off an arrow aimed for his face, and a second arrow sank deeply into it as he brought it back in front of him.

The red-bearded dwarf didn't blink.

Athrogate looked to Catti-brie. "Don't ye miss, girl," he whispered, though he was sure she couldn't even hear him, so far into her trance was she.

"Wouldn't that be the wreck of it?" Amber agreed, and Athrogate chuckled—or started to, until an ogre-thrown rock cracked him in the chest and sent him down hard in the boat.

Sitting, the black-bearded dwarf shook his head so fiercely that his lips flapped loudly. He jumped to his feet and hoisted the rock, then turned to the east and heaved it with all his considerable, magically-enhanced giant strength. The heavy missile flew faster and farther than the ogre's throw, to the surprise and demise of one ugly orc, who went flying away under the heavy strike.

Athrogate started to call out his fine throw, but Amber's sudden intake of breath brought his attention back to the south, to the bridge. And Athrogate, too, sucked in his breath and saw their certain doom. The monsters on the bridge had organized now, with ogres hoisting heavy spiked logs.

"This is gonna hurt," Athrogate whispered. The lead boats, including their boat, were nearing the shadows of that bridge now.

But Bruenor was still singing, still banging his shield, which was now holding three broken arrows, with his many-notched axe. He didn't shy away, didn't flinch. He just sang, now his voice as much a growl as a throaty baritone.

They drifted closer. A pair of particularly ugly ogres lifted a spiked log up high.

"Oh, this is gonna hurt," Athrogate said.

And he was right, for Catti-brie's spell was cast then, a line of fire running the length of the bridge, igniting spiked logs, igniting bows and spears, igniting orcs and ogres.

Bruenor stopped banging his shield and grabbed his axe in his shield arm before he lifted a cracked silver horn to his lips and croaked a discordant note. The dwarf reached down with his free arm and lifted a grapnel secured to a thick rope. He let it out a bit and set it spinning, then sent it flying up high for the bridge's stone rail. Over it went, and into the flames, but Bruenor yanked it back quickly, before the fires could catch, pulling the grapnel tight against the wall.

He was the first out of the boats, slinging his shield and axe and leaping high on the rope, the strength of Clangeddin coursing through his muscled arms. Up he went, hand over hand, climbing with ease and with amazing speed, easily outpacing those dwarves on the other boats who were climbing ropes of their own.

Even as Bruenor went over the stone wall, Catti-brie's wall of fire came down. But from it had come a monstrous fire elemental, and that magical beast was already into the battle, slamming an ogre with its fiery fist, sending the brute tumbling.

Athrogate was soon up to the bridge rail, pulling himself over quickly, desperate to join Bruenor, who by then was single-handedly holding back a surging swarm of orcs.

No, not single-handedly, Athrogate realized. The berserker specter of Thibbledorf Pwent was there, warp-stepping from one side to the other, swatting orcs aside with impunity. Athrogate couldn't suppress a laugh as he rolled over the wall, drew his morningstars, and rushed to join Bruenor. An orc flopped atop Thibbledorf Pwent's head, impaled by the long helmet spike. It wasn't yet dead, and the dwarf berserker wasn't doing anything to finish it—except hopping all around, and each jolting movement had the orc writhing and howling in agony.

Up beside Bruenor, Athrogate swatted an ogre, sending it tumbling over the far rail to splash into the river below.

"Bwahaha!" he howled, but he bit it short, seeing the blood pouring from Bruenor's throat.

Bruenor was still singing, or rather, gurgling, and certainly still fighting, though how he hadn't fallen over dead, Athrogate did not know, for surely the wound would prove mortal.

> Pile heavy the stones
> To warm me bones . . .

Over in the west, dwarven cheering was mitigated only by the pained screams and terror of the orcs. King Connerad and General Dagnabbet and their charges saw their famed Gutbusters and the legendary King Bruenor take and quickly secure the Surbrin Bridge, effectively bottlenecking half the enemy forces across the river.

And the orcs saw it, and saw, too, or heard at least, the rout in the north as King Emerus of Citadel Felbarr made his fierce push southward. They all knew it to be Emerus then, as the pennants of proud Felbarr came into view, inexorably closing on the orc force like the jaws of a great wolf.

"Take it to 'em, boys!" King Connerad cried, running the length of the line. "They got nowhere to run, and just enough ground for fallin' dead!"

"Huzzah!" a thousand dwarves cheered in reply.

And the orcs began to die.

For all the cheering and the renewed hope, those dwarves who understood the tactical layout of the armies around Mithral Hall expected that the worst was yet to come. The largest Many-Arrows force was yet to show up on the field, they feared.

What King Connerad's boys didn't know was that the largest orc force was already engaged in battle, far to the north, around the side of the mountain.

Circling up near the Darkening, far above the battlefields, Drizzt chewed his lip nervously. He saw the vast orc force awaken and stretch to the southeast, rolling around the mountain as they rushed to join in the fighting at the Surbrin Bridge, and the fighting now raging north of the bridge, where King Emerus's force had met the earlier orc arrivals from the north.

And Drizzt saw the dark outline of King Harnoth's responding charge, the thousands of shield dwarves of Citadel Adbar rolling down upon the unsuspecting horde. Even from this height, Drizzt could make out the initial shape of the battle. The Many-Arrows force turning southeast was being led by the goblins and orcs, mostly, leaving the larger ogres and giants as the rear guard, as was typical of their tactics.

In this instance, however, with King Harnoth's thousands charging in from the other direction and creating an unexpected second front, that put the behemoths at the front of the battle, and that, Drizzt could see, was not a place they wanted to be.

From this vantage, Harnoth's charge appeared like a black avalanche, and when it hit the darkness of the enemy line, it looked as if it had picked up huge trees to carry forward through the orc morass, as the giants fled just ahead of the collision.

The Many-Arrows horde stopped its southeastern movement quickly and tried to turn around, but from the dark outline of the battle, Drizzt could see that the dwarves had driven into the sea of enemies before any organized defenses or formations could be put in place. By the inevitable point at which the fierce battle became a chaotic jumble of individual struggles, King Harnoth had clearly gained the upper hand.

Drizzt nodded hopefully—despite the fact that his friends were battling at the bridge in the south, this was the most important fight. With that thought, he turned his eye back the other way, and far to the south, Drizzt saw the magical wall of fire brighten the length of the Surbrin Bridge, and he smiled and was afraid all at once. He knew that Catti-brie had come onto the field in all her glory.

"Trust in her," he whispered to himself, the words lost in the wind. He had to do that, to trust in Catti-brie and in Bruenor. His focus had to be here, in this moment, in this situation.

And what a moment it was for Drizzt, flying around on the back of a dragon.

He couldn't wait to get down and into the action, and couldn't wait to see the power of Tazmikella and her sister unleashed on the Many-Arrows hordes—though at the same time, he surely held great trepidations about such power bared. He had thought that the dragons would strike the first blow on the orcs, before Harnoth's legions had joined in with them in the confusion of battle. But no, it was not to be, Tazmikella had informed him.

They had other plans.

Watching the unfolding swarms of the armies far below, Drizzt took heart. He couldn't be sure, but it appeared to him that the flotilla attack on the Surbrin Bridge had been executed well, and that Bruenor's force was still holding strong. His heart leaped when he saw a fireball fly from near the center of the bridge to erupt amidst the hordes of monsters on the eastern shoreline. And through the darkness, he could clearly see a towering fire elemental wreaking havoc at the eastern end of the bridge. Catti-brie still stood strong.

King Emerus's force continued its push south, and King Connerad was holding strong in front of the eastern gate of Mithral Hall.

So far, at least, this battle was playing out exactly as they had drawn it up.

Tazmikella banked sharply, then with one turn flew back for the south and climbed into the lower levels of the Darkening, obscuring the view.

"What?" Drizzt called to her, but the dragon paid him no heed. As they came below the roiling blackness for one instant, Drizzt noted Ilnezhara and Afafrenfere similarly rising into the black.

The drow held on tightly, confused, until the dragon dipped again, and it all came clear with the shriek of another dragon, not Tazmikella or her sister.

The far distant Many-Arrows orcs lifted their arms in a cheer as two white monsters soared through the skies to join in the fighting, flying fast from the south.

Tazmikella and Ilnezhara flew swiftly south to intercept. The white dragons were far below, their focus clearly on the battle as they approached—and Drizzt held his breath. It seemed as though one would fly right across the Surbrin Bridge.

Perhaps the white dragons wouldn't look up until it was too late. The water streamed from his lavender eyes again as Tazmikella gained speed. He had to duck his head low when she began her sudden descent from on high, the wind crackling around her leathery wings. He managed to glance over to see Afafrenfere similarly crouched as Ilnezhara mirrored Tazmikella's dive.

"Hold yer hearts, boys, and hold yer ground!" Bruenor yelled from the eastern end of the bridge, a call that was carried back to the other side, where Bungalow Thump led half the force in defending the western edge. Indeed it was an important call at that moment, for every dwarf on the bridge, and all the monsters on either end, saw the approach of the speeding white dragon and its drow rider, aiming right for the heart of those dwarves that had cut the orc forces in half.

"Girl!' Bruenor yelled to Catti-brie, who was not on the bridge, but rather levitated up beside it, holding one of the ropes that had been thrown over the stone railing. "We're needin' ye, girl!"

Up above the railing, her eyes fixed on the south, Catti-brie was too engaged with her spellcasting to even hear Bruenor's call. She saw the wyrm—it couldn't be missed!—and she knew what she needed to do. All around the bridge in front of her, dwarf priests and priestesses rushed around, casting protection spells on the greatest dwarven fighters, or on any who were close enough. But it wouldn't be enough.

The dragon closed, orc cheers rising. They clearly expected the dwarves to be swept from the bridge. The wyrm soared in low, dwarves dropping to the stone below the railings, and it breathed its frosty, killing breath.

And at that moment, a fireball erupted in the air right in front of the wyrm, and the frosty breath burst through it as a wash of rain and nothing more, and the dragon burst through it, coming out the other side steaming and smoking, its white face red and angry as if it had flown too close to the sun.

The disoriented wyrm didn't even drop its claws to rake free a few dwarves as it flashed over the structure, and instead banked sharply to the northwest, wings beating furiously to gain height.

She had caught it by surprise, Catti-brie knew, much as she had done to the other, much larger white dragon by the cliff wall on the ledge above Keeper's Dale. She had surprised it and she had stung it and she had defeated its pass.

But she hadn't defeated the wyrm—not at all. And now it was aware of her. The woman searched her magical repertoire for some trick that might fend off the inevitable next attack, but her options seemed painfully thin.

"Hold faith and fight on!" Bruenor roared, and the Gutbusters roared in echo. And then they all began to sing:

> We speak with hammer, axe, and maul
> We call to gods in Mor'din's Hall
> We stand our ground, await our fall
> For then we'll know the grandest feast!

But the song didn't hold, broken apart by shrieks and shouts that alarmed the woman, until she turned her expectant gaze to the northwest.

And there she, the dwarves, and the orcs all saw the white dragon turning desperately, trying to be out of the way of a pair of diving copper wyrms.

Catti-brie's heart soared when she saw the silver line of a magical arrow reach ahead of one of those copper-colored dragons, an arrow shot from a bow she had carried for many years.

So excited was she that her next spell came screaming to her lips and tingling from her fingertips, a lightning bolt that crackled to the eastern riverbank beside the bridge buttress, laying low a host of orcs and ogres.

Drizzt fought with all his strength, his body muscles and his legs straining to hold him in place as he leveled Taulmaril at the white dragon, and particularly at its drow rider. He got one shot off, and another, but then threw himself flat and held on for all his life as Tazmikella soared into the white wyrm, breathing forth a magical cloud as she clipped the vulnerable wyrm with bone-shattering force.

Tazmikella spun away, rolling from the impact, and Drizzt held on all the tighter, stunned by the sheer speed of the pass and by the sheer violence of the impact. He felt small indeed in that moment, small and mortal, and caught in the battle between two beings infinitely more powerful than he.

He did manage to turn his head back in time to see Ilnezhara's even more brutal collision. The white dragon, overbalanced by Tazmikella's pass, couldn't properly align itself to mitigate the blow.

Or the acidic breath that preceded it.

Drizzt thought he heard the crunch of bone with the white's wing bent up awkwardly, or perhaps he had just mentally filled in the sound that surely emanated from that crash. Ilnezhara shot by, the white spinning wildly in her wake.

By the time he tore his gaze from that spectacle, Drizzt noted that they were much lower, near the ground, and Tazmikella turned her long neck upward, twisting her spine against the plummet, her great leathery wings catching the updraft and leveling her out. Over the bridge they soared, to cheering dwarves and to a sight—Catti-brie and Bruenor—that warmed Drizzt's heart.

The site brought him back to the present situation.

He took up his bow and strafed the eastern riverbank as Tazmikella soared along. He saw one orc tumble and one giant lurch, but he had no idea how many of his uncounted shots might have scored a hit. It didn't matter anyway. One or two or even ten enemies wouldn't make a difference, but the mere appearance of a death-dealing dragon with a drow rider fighting against Many-Arrows had great effect indeed, on both sides of the battle.

Tazmikella banked west and climbed once more, and Drizzt steadied himself, trying to reorient his thinking to this new and higher level of speed and violence.

Far ahead but closing rapidly loomed the white dragon, somehow still aloft and screeching, perhaps in pain, perhaps in rage. Its movements seemed slower, though, and Drizzt recalled Tazmikella's breath cloud, one not of acid.

Tazmikella climbed northwest, Ilnezhara southwest, flanking their enemy. Both turned sharply in unison, soaring in from opposite directions.

The white met Ilnezhara's charge with a breath of frost, and Drizzt winced for Afafrenfere, but both Tazmikella and Ilnezhara responded with acid spits, burning and biting at their enemy, and at the unfortunate drow riding the white.

For a heartbeat, Drizzt thought the copper dragons were going to crash together against the opposite sides of the white, and the drow cried out in terror, for neither slowed!

But these sisters were well-practiced, and at the same time, they flopped into barrel rolls, Tazmikella going over, Ilnezhara under, and so close that Drizzt nearly bumped heads with the white dragon's rider—a drow he recognized as Tos'un Armgo.

Drizzt had just managed to catch the rhythm of that sudden roll when Tazmikella broke out of it, the momentum so suddenly reversed that the drow ranger slammed his face down on the dragon's shoulders and nearly swooned.

Back to the north, flying level, came Tazmikella, to engage the battered white again. Drizzt tried to shake his dizziness away, tried to put up his bow, but a shriek from behind had him turning back to the south to see another white dragon, far away but flying fast. This one was much larger—bigger than Tazmikella by far, bigger than Ilnezhara by far, bigger than both together, it seemed.

Drizzt forced himself to turn away, to look ahead, where the other white wyrm fluttered on ragged, burned wings, trying to turn aside. It flew at Tazmikella, but Drizzt noted her course and believed she was but a distraction now, diverting the white's attention.

The ranger got off a shot with Taulmaril, the arrow streaking past the wyrm and its rider.

As Drizzt expected, Tazmikella veered back to the east. But then she caught the white dragon, its rider, and Drizzt by surprise as she suddenly reversed direction and leaped more than flew against the white. They became a tangle of raking claws and biting maws, beating wings and slapping tails, turning and rolling and ultimately tumbling.

In the frenzy, Drizzt didn't know if he should draw his scimitars or simply hold on. He saw Tos'un on one turn, the drow burned by acid, his cloak trailing smoke, but with sword in hand.

Drizzt fired off an arrow. He missed his target, Tos'un, but the magical arrow stabbed at the white dragon's flank, though if it even noticed in the frenzy of greater weapons and wounds, Drizzt did not know.

On it went, and now Drizzt could only hold on desperately. Then the wyrms broke the clench, both together kicking out with their hind legs, throwing each other aside.

Tazmikella straightened almost immediately and climbed furiously. Looking back at the new wyrm, much closer now, Drizzt could certainly understand why. He lifted his bow for one last shot, but pulled it back in shock as a much larger missile slammed into the first foe. Ilnezhara drove down upon it from above, full force.

The white dragon went spinning away, Ilnezhara in determined pursuit.

Tazmikella didn't join in, though. The much larger white continued to close in on her.

"Aurbangras!" Arauthator growled. Tiago felt the rumble in his legs as much as he heard the dragon's call. That was Arauthator's son, the drow knew, spinning out with gruesome wounds and with a copper dragon close behind.

"Stay on this one!" the drow warrior cried. "That is Drizzt Do'Urden, the greatest treasure! When he is dead, Lady Lolth will be in our debt!"

The Old White Death swung his head to the left, to watch the flight of his son, and Tiago pleaded desperately. So close! He could see Drizzt on the back of the other copper, directly in front of him, white hair and green cape flying.

It was Drizzt! Of course it was Drizzt!

So close!

"She will gain height and plummet upon your son!" Tiago screamed. "You must catch her!"

Arauthator snaked his great head all the way around to stare his rider in the face, and for a heartbeat, Tiago surely thought his life was at its end.

"You think I care for the fate of Aurbangras?" the dragon said. "He failed, and so he will die." The white dragon's head swiveled back around as he lined up with the fleeing copper wyrm, his great leathery wings beating with tremendous power.

Tiago glanced at the wounded and desperately fleeing Aurbangras, and chuckled at the absence of familial affection; Arauthator would make a good matron mother.

"We will kill this one and its rider, and the other will lead us to her treasures," Arauthator explained.

Tiago held on for all his life as the dragon gained speed with every great pump of his wings. They were flying at a steep angle toward the Darkening, flying upward, but from the mounting velocity, it seemed more to Tiago as if they were diving. At first he thought the copper wyrm would make it into the roiling blackness in the sky above, but now he was not so sure of that.

Neither was the copper dragon, Tiago realized. She turned around suddenly and dived back the way she had come, flying straight for Arauthator.

Tiago's eyes widened with surprise and then with fear, and widened more when a steady stream of silvery arrows came flying forth from Drizzt, soaring down at him and his mount.

Arauthator didn't flinch, didn't turn, and didn't slow, and in a heartbeat he had no time to turn, the wyrms speeding together. Tiago braced and sucked in his breath. He knew he was about to die, was certain he could not survive the collision. He brought his shield up at the last moment, the powerfully-enchanted buckler blocking an arrow that would have laid him low. Then a second and a third thumped against the barrier, and it didn't matter to Tiago. He knew that the crush of the wyrms would surely kill him anyway.

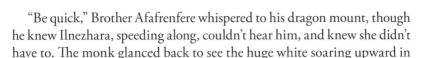

"Be quick," Brother Afafrenfere whispered to his dragon mount, though he knew Ilnezhara, speeding along, couldn't hear him, and knew she didn't have to. The monk glanced back to see the huge white soaring upward in pursuit of Tazmikella and Drizzt.

Up ahead of Ilnezhara, Afafrenfere noted the uneven movements of the badly-wounded smaller white dragon, tattered wings flapping wildly as the wyrm tried to keep level and upright. The white wyrm couldn't seem to turn, for it flew straight for the higher reaches of the great mountain that housed Mithral Hall. On the dragon's back, the drow rider tugged left and right frantically, as if trying to force the dragon to bank this way or that.

He might was well have been trying to move the mountain.

Afafrenfere heard his mount chanting, casting a spell. A couple of heartbeats later, a volley of blue-green glowing bolts of arcane energy shot forth from Ilnezhara, flying faster than dragonflight, swerving around the white dragon's waving tail. But what good would such minor spells be against the power of a dragon? And then they crossed the last expanse to stab into the drow rider.

He winced and hunched, clearly in pain, and looked back, cursing in a language Afafrenfere did not know. He held forth his hand and called upon his own magical powers, and a globe of darkness appeared in the air right in front of Ilnezhara.

The monk ducked reflexively, but he needn't have bothered. The dragon flew through the darkness in an instant, emerging out the other side. Up came the monk, back steady in his seat, and confused that the drow would even bother to attempt something that feeble, until he realized what it was.

It was desperation, blind desperation and a scream against impotence.

The mountain loomed huge now. Up ahead, the white dragon did manage to turn a bit to the right, to the north, and was about to slam head-on into a rocky outcropping. At the last instant, the white just barely lifted up over that jut of stone.

Ilnezhara cut a turn that had Afafrenfere's face twisting under the strain. He kept his gaze aimed at the rocky outcropping, though, and saw beyond it now to the fleeing white dragon, which had crashed into a sloping face of deep snow and skidded along, digging deep grooves and piling the white stuff up in front of its chest, trying to gain some semblance of control. On its back, the drow worked frantically and screamed continually, and so he should. The dragon flipped over the snowbank it had piled, tumbling wildly, and when it came over, no rider could be seen.

Like an avalanche, the white wyrm rolled, spinning around, its wings twisting and snapping and sticking out at unnatural angles. Right to another rocky jut it skidded, crashing against that one hard and awkwardly, and settling there.

"I will finish it!" Afafrenfere yelled to his mount. "Go to your sister!"

In response, Ilnezhara swerved right up near to the cliff, above where the white had crashed. There, the monk leaped for the stone. As Ilnezhara veered up and away, Brother Afafrenfere, infused with the knowledge of Grandmaster Kane, half fell, half ran down the sheer rocky cliff, his hands and feet working in a controlled blur to continually break, and so control, his fall.

He came down onto the snowy slope moments later. He glanced back to a black spot near the first rocky jut, to the twisted form of the drow rider. But the dragon was the greater danger; Afafrenfere paid the drow no more heed and sprinted the other way, toward the twisted form of the white dragon.

But the wyrm wasn't dead and as he neared, the great horned head whipped around and lifted up high, towering over the monk, who looked very tiny indeed.

A collective gasp escaped the orcs and their allies when the white dragon smashed upon the mountain high above.

"Enough, Jarl," Felloki said to his leader.

Jarl Orelson shook his head as he looked around. In front of him, Mithral Hall's eastern gate lay open, but an army of stubborn dwarves would allow no passage. Behind him, his allies had been locked away from the fight. The defense of the bridge would not falter.

In the north, the dwarves were winning.

In the sky, the dragon allies of the dwarves were winning.

Jarl Orelson nodded at the frost giant warrior they called Boomer. "Collect ours," he said, and Felloki nodded grimly and began gathering up the giants of Shining White.

And when they were gathered together around their Jarl, he led them away to the south, their long legs taking them far from the battlefield with every stride, easily outpacing those orcs and goblins who thought to similarly flee.

The war had ended for Shining White, Jarl Orelson had decided.

It was time to go home.

At the Surbrin Bridge, the cheering heightened as the white dragon went crashing into the mountain.

"Hold strong, boys!" Bruenor yelled, and he swatted aside another orc before he crunched yet another's ugly face with his shield as it tried to shoulder him aside.

Bruenor Battlehammer would not be moved.

The dwarves were holding, and the press from the eastern bank was thinning.

All was going as they had planned—indeed, as they had desperately hoped when they had planned.

The cheering reflected that, from all but one.

Catti-brie couldn't take her gaze from the dark sky far above, where the huge white flew into a swarm of silvery arrows. Even from so far away, Catti-brie could see that the dragons were about to collide at full speed, so far above the ground.

"My love," she whispered in farewell.

CHAPTER 20

THE VIOLENCE OF DRAGONS

Half blinded by the acid that had washed over him, battered from the burns and the sheer violence of the dragon collisions, Tos'un nevertheless remained keenly aware that he and his mount were flying at great speed right into a mountain.

And one of the copper dragons was close behind, and if they turned, he would again feel the pain of acidic dragon breath. Still, he tugged and yanked this way and that.

"Turn, you fool!" he screamed continually at Aurbangras, and finally the dragon did manage to swerve—right at a wall.

Tos'un threw his arms up and cried out, but the wyrm went over it. Just beyond, though, Aurbangras hit the snowy slope and went into a fast skid. The dragon reared up, kicking and clawing.

The drow rider remembered a moment in his youth, riding for House Barrison Del'Armgo in a battle against a rival House. His Underdark lizard, running full out, had hit a patch of magically slickened floor. This moment brought him back to that, the mount then, as now, rearing and scrabbling futilely.

And then as now, the lizard caught a lip and flipped over forward. Tos'un instinctively held his seat on the bucking creature—and this time, foolishly.

Aurbangras turned his neck out wide and dipped his shoulders into a roll, slamming Tos'un facedown in the snow, rolling right over him, bending him over backward so fully that the drow's buttocks slammed

288

against his shoulderblades. The dragon kept rolling, but Tos'un did not, other than to unwind weirdly, like a crushed flower trying to lift up once more, before he flopped uselessly to the side.

He knew immediately that many of his bones were broken, and knew too that such a word didn't begin to describe his pulverized hips.

He flopped over to the side and lay there in the snow, and felt strangely calm, with a curious absence of pain or cold—or anything else. He felt disembodied at that moment, as if his eyes had flown free of his body to watch the unfolding drama in front of him. He saw the copper dragon go flying away, saw the robed human come rushing down the cliff.

And he saw the fight, though it couldn't be real, he told himself, because no man could fight like this, no man could resist the kill of the dragon.

Aurbangras breathed a cloud of icy death over where the man stood—or where the man had been standing, at least. Like a striking serpent, the human had leaped to the side, curled and rolled, and avoided the blast completely. And right back in he leaped, as if flying, his feet in front of him to kick the dragon on the flank, and with such power that the wyrm was jolted.

That was not possible.

The wyrm bit, serpent neck snapping the head down. But the man was under it, punching and kicking, flipping and kicking still, and out he came to the side even as Aurbangras dropped straight down to crush him.

Now lower, the dragon took a kick in the face that sent his head swinging the other way, and the man landed on his feet and went right in. Tos'un noted the wound Aurbangras had suffered under one foreleg, the bloody gash in such stark contrast to the white scales. The human noted it too, clearly, for he stabbed there with his hand, fingers extended, driving them right into the gash and pulling back the hand with ligaments and muscle in it.

The dragon roared and bit at him and clawed at him and rolled at him, but the man was always just ahead of every strike. The great tail came sweeping around, but the man was up impossibly high, and the tail went beneath him harmlessly.

And the man touched down, then flew again, running up the dragon's side and back. When the wyrm tried to bite at him, he leaped upon that head, holding fast to a horn with one hand, swinging in against the wyrm's face.

Eye to eye, then fist to eye as the man drove his hand right into that sensitive orb—plunged it into the liquid depths.

The wyrm's shriek shook the mountain. The convulsive snap of the dragon's neck sent the man flying, spinning, though he somehow managed to right himself and touch down in the snow in control.

He stood right in front of Tos'un then, and the drow thought himself doomed.

But no. The enraged dragon advanced, and Tos'un saw its fanged maw right behind the human.

Drizzt saw his doom, the dragons speeding together for a collision that would spell the end of him, and likely of them. He got off one more shot, aimed perfectly for the head of the drow riding the white wyrm, but again that shield came flashing up to block, stealing from Drizzt the satisfaction of slaying Tiago before they both died anyway. He wondered for a moment if this impending doom had been unintentional, an expectation on the part of both wyrms that the other would of course veer aside.

But now it was too late. So suddenly, they were there, together, to crash.

Drizzt cried out, as did his counterpart riding the white wyrm, and reflexively closed his eyes as he braced.

But nothing happened.

The drow blinked and looked around in confusion. How could it be?

He looked back and saw the great white dragon, spinning around, roaring in rage, focusing on Tazmikella, and in doing so, ignoring Ilnezhara, who sped up past the wyrm and spat forth a cloud of gas that engulfed the white and Tiago. And up went Ilnezhara, into the roiling blackness of the Darkening, and so too was Tazmikella climbing again, determined to get into the opaque cloudstuff.

"How?" Drizzt asked, shaking his head. He knew his mount couldn't hear him, and he didn't want to distract her anyway. On came the huge white wyrm, determined to intercept. It was flying quite a bit slower now, Drizzt realized, and he remembered Ilnezhara's breath and the magical properties it exuded.

The drow quickly gauged their respective speeds and the distance left to the Darkening, and he held his breath. It didn't seem to him as if Tazmikella would make it. He looked to the clouds, hoping that Ilnezhara would come forth once more and distract the dogged pursuit.

But she was not to be seen.

Taulmaril thrummed in Drizzt's hands, the drow archer leading the angling white dragon perfectly, putting every shot in line with Tiago.

But the Baenre noble was laughing at him, and Drizzt understood that he had no chance of getting an arrow past that buckler. Tiago was too quick, too agile, and too well guarded, and unaffected by the magical slowing breath of Ilnezhara.

Drizzt thought that he should focus instead on the wyrm, but just shook his head helplessly.

It was too late. The white wyrm had them.

But then it didn't.

It was gone, as if it had simply disappeared. No, not disappeared, Drizzt realized, and then he knew why the dragons hadn't collided previously, as Tazmikella once again cast her spell, a minor teleport that carried her along an extra-dimensional corridor right through the plummeting white dragon's path. And now Tazmikella and Drizzt were clear to the Darkening, and into it they flew, even as the white, far below, began its turn back into a climb.

Tazmikella began to cry out, a short series of high-pitched shrieks, stuttered in length and frequency, and it took Drizzt a few moments to understand that she was communicating with her sister in code, and likely to make sure they didn't inadvertently crash into each other.

For indeed, Tazmikella was flying almost blind, with patchy blackness limiting her vision all around. Ilnezhara's responding shrieks were the only warning Drizzt got before the other copper dragon flew right past, so very close, the black clouds swirling and rolling in her passing.

She was riderless, Drizzt realized, and he swallowed hard and feared for Afafrenfere.

He had no time to dwell on that, however, for another form shook the clouds the other way, a much larger and more ominous form.

Tazmikella rolled over hard to the left and twisted as she went into a straight dive. They plunged out of the Darkening, the world opening suddenly wide below them, but the dragon cut sharply and climbed right back in, even as the white came swirling out.

This was the stuff of nightmares to Drizzt. He didn't dare shoot his bow now for fear of hitting Ilnezhara, for who knew where she might be? Or where the white wyrm might be? For a long while, into and out of the blackness they soared and rolled, dived and climbed, sometimes below, sometimes above.

A great form passed to the left, another to the right, then one above and later one below, and whether it was the white or Ilnezhara, Drizzt could hardly tell.

And so it went, the seemingly endless nightmare.

They came out the top of the Darkening to find the white wyrm waiting. It roared and lunged, and Tazmikella threw herself aside, the dragon's maw snapping just short of her vulnerable neck. They brushed and crashed as they passed and Drizzt barely avoided a wing buffet that would surely have launched him from his seat—then ducked just in time to avoid the cut of Tiago's sword, as the skilled drow managed a passing attack.

Drizzt somehow leveled his bow right before Tazmikella dropped back down into the darkness, and the skilled ranger fired off a trio of arrows.

But Tiago's shield was there yet again. The shots, as fine as they had been, had no chance of hitting the skilled warrior with that magnificent shield.

Back into the nightmare they flew. A cry to the left side told Drizzt that the white wyrm had encountered Ilnezhara, and the pitch of the screech made him believe that Ilnezhara had taken the worst of it.

Or maybe, he realized as Tazmikella calmly swerved and dipped, Ilnezhara was again communicating to her sister.

Out of the darkness dropped Tazmikella and Drizzt, this time dipping lower as she flew out to the left. The swirl of the black clouds above told them that a wyrm was there, barely inside, and Drizzt put up his bow as Tazmikella circled directly underneath.

The drow saw the white scales, and so Taulmaril hummed, silver arrows shooting up to slam at the underbelly of the great white wyrm. They did little damage, but even that was enough to mitigate the mounting frustration Drizzt felt with his inability to get a clean shot at Tiago.

And Drizzt noted something, and he nodded, planning his next shot. That would have to wait, however, as back into the Darkening flew Tazmikella.

The sisters called back and forth, and so they were striking at the white dragon, little hits and nothing more, a quick nip or tail slap and off they spun aside, one after another.

"Sparrows on a hawk," Drizzt whispered, recalling that familiar scene when he watched a pair of smaller and more agile birds chasing some magnificent bird of prey across the sky, away from their nest.

And he would play his role, of course, his bow always ready now, his arrows flying fast whenever he saw the white scales. He shot for the dragon now and not Tiago, not wanting an errant arrow to fly past and knowing that he'd never hit Tiago with that shield anyway.

Patience, Drizzt told himself. He knew that he'd get his chance.

They flew silently then, in darkness, and the hair on the back of the drow's neck stood on end. The white wyrm had figured out the game, he feared from the sudden total silence.

But Tazmikella didn't share his worry. Once more, Drizzt lurched forward and banged his face on Tazmikella's shoulder as the dragon suddenly shot straight up. Out of the Darkening they came, in a sharp bank, and Drizzt turned Taulmaril back, expecting the white dragon to burst out behind them.

The black clouds swirled into a spinning vortex and out came a wyrm, but it was Ilnezhara, not the white, and Drizzt barely held his shot.

Ilnezhara rolled right over and plunged back into the blackness, and now Drizzt did see the white, right at the edge and similarly rolling in pursuit.

And there was the white dragon's belly—there was Drizzt's target—and he let fly once and then again, the arrows streaking in, the second shot skipping across unyielding scales to clip through the leather of the girth of Tiago's saddle.

"Block that," Drizzt whispered with grim satisfaction.

Despite his agony, despite his pulverized hip and his expectation that he was going to die anyway, Tos'un found a measure of satisfaction as his wounded and angry dragon mount hovered over the doomed human.

The maw opened wide, teeth as long as a tall man's leg, and the dragon snapped at the monk, who barely leaped back in time to avoid being bitten in half.

Now he was close to Tos'un, so close that the drow could reach out and grab his leg. He moved to do just that as the wyrm closed in again, but this time when the dragon opened his toothy maw, he didn't bite.

He breathed.

Just before the killing frost descended over Tos'un, ending his misery, he found even his tiny satisfaction stolen from him, for the man in front of him, the man he thought in his grasp and caught by the breath, simply broke apart into floating shards of light, like a thousand tiny flower petals floating down on a gentle breeze.

And the cold settled in, and the drow remained frozen in place, his expression one of abject disbelief.

Fireballs ignited one after the other, half in the Darkening and half below it.

Out came the white dragon, now riderless, roaring in rage. But its movements remained slowed by Ilnezhara's magical breath, and the dragon sisters had each other fully in sight, and had the battlefield precisely as they wanted it.

Once again Drizzt was reminded of the sparrows chasing off a hawk, as Tazmikella and Ilnezhara spun and rolled, under, over, and all around the great white wyrm, biting at it, breathing at it, hitting it with magical fireballs and lightning bolts and magic missiles, and through it all, Drizzt kept up a steady stream of stinging arrows.

At one point, Drizzt heard Tazmikella laugh at her own cleverness—and what a curious sound that was!—when she conjured a wall of stone right in the white dragon's speeding path. The monstrous dragon cracked through it easily enough, sending shards of stone flying and falling the miles to the ground, and truly the wyrm seemed more perturbed than injured.

But that only added to the dragon's mounting frustration, so clearly evident every time it snapped futilely at one sister or the other, invariably behind the flight.

Every breath weapon now came as a cloud of slowing gas, the sisters determined not to let that enchantment fade, determined to keep the superior wyrm unable to catch them. Their bites might sting the white, but its great maw could prove lethal.

Out to the north they flew, over the huge battle raging just beyond the Frost Hills. Suddenly the white dragon simply folded its wings, letting the pull of Toril do what it could not, free-fall, gaining it the speed at last to be away from the nuisance of the copper dragons.

Ilnezhara moved to pursue, but Tazmikella called her back with a shriek.

"The spell of breath is wearing thin," Tazmikella warned her sister as they flew side by side.

"Then stay up high, near the blackness," Ilnezhara agreed.

The three of them, the sisters and Drizzt, watched the great wyrm, a brilliant white speck far below. It came out of its drop, and indeed seemed to be moving with all speed again.

But to the north, speeding for the Spine of the World, where, the sisters knew, the Old White Death made his home.

"So it ends," Tazmikella said.

"You killed his son!" Drizzt said in warning, expecting the white dragon to return with fury.

"Not yet," Tazmikella corrected.

"Arauthator is chromatic," Ilnezhara scoffed at Drizzt, swiveling her huge head so that she was quite—and unnervingly—near to him. "He cares nothing for his son."

"More treasure for him to hoard now, likely," Tazmikella agreed. "Fear not, Drizzt. The wyrm has fled."

"Let us go and finish this," Ilnezhara said, and she banked immediately, swerving back the other way, toward Fourthpeak and the wounded Aurbangras.

He understood the tendrils of murderous coldness filling the air around him, but the sensation was distant and did not hurt him. He understood then the true relationship between his spirit and his corporeal form, just a brief glimpse at the seam between thought and reality, between the physical and the spiritual, between the higher planes and Faerûn.

Brother Afafrenfere hadn't willed himself to such a lightness of being—certainly that had been Grandmaster Kane's doing—nor could he fully understand it or appreciate it. Somehow, some way, he was extraplanar, simply removed from the battlefield and from certain death from the white dragon's breath.

He felt the wounded drow expire—felt and didn't see. He wasn't seeing anything at that time, not in any sense of sight that he had known as a corporeal creature. Still, the reality was as clear to him as if he had watched the drow's spirit exiting the corpse.

He felt light. He felt . . . joined. Joined with everything. No object seemed solid to him, as if he was nothing more than a beam of light through water, where everything, living or inanimate, was simply translucent, and so, incorporeal.

He knew that he was on another level of perception here, and he didn't dare try to sort it out, keenly aware—perhaps it was some mental nudging from Kane—that all of this was quite beyond his understanding, and that trying to sort it out might indeed drive him to madness. Even the beauty in this state, and it was all beauty to Afafrenfere, overwhelmed him to the edge of his sensibilities and threatened to drive him over that edge.

He was guided back to the event at hand by Grandmaster Kane. He sensed the mighty life energy of the wounded white dragon, and stronger still came the emanations from the returning copper dragons.

He felt the violence, as if all of time-space was trembling under the power of three dragons entangled on the mountain slope. He couldn't hear the battle, but its vibrations resonated within and all around him.

Sound began to return, distantly at first, but growing louder, the shrieks of pain and rage, and Brother Afafrenfere knew that he was reconstituting.

His eyes blinked open, the sensation of sight confusing him for a moment until he sorted it out.

In front of him lay the battered white dragon, Ilnezhara perched upon its stretched neck, holding it down. Behind her, Tazmikella chewed into the white's belly, tearing out giant entrails. On her back, Drizzt held on and kept trying to look away.

A long while later, it was over, the white dragon quite dead, and Afafrenfere glanced back to see the drow who had been riding the wyrm all twisted and crushed, encased in the ice from his own mount's killing breath.

"Now, let us finish this," Tazmikella said, her maw and face all bloody and with a long strand of the white dragon's intestine hanging garishly from one tooth.

Afafrenfere shuddered as he recalled the dragon's elf form, so pretty and attractive. This other side of Tazmikella, a level of viciousness beyond human sensibilities, shook him.

He heard her call though and could not ignore her, so he went to Ilnezhara and took his seat. Off they flew, leaping from the mountain with victorious cries that echoed down to King Connerad's forces below, to Bruenor and the Gutbusters on the Surbrin Bridge, and to King Emerus and his charges now pressing the orc force to the field just north of the Surbrin Bridge battle.

Ilnezhara and Afafrenfere soared off to the north to join in the larger battle just beyond the Frost Hills, but Tazmikella and Drizzt headed straight for the bridge. They flew low over the field and low over the dwarves holding strong on the structure.

As they neared the eastern end, Drizzt fired off his arrows. Low came Tazmikella, barely above Bruenor's head, but to the dwarf's laughter and cheering. Her great claws closed around the head and shoulders of the frost giant trying to press through Bruenor's stubborn block.

That frost giant went up into the air and made a most impressive bomb when Tazmikella hurled it into the throng of orcs pressing in from the east.

The minions of Many-Arrows began to break ranks, fleeing from the battle, some running back to the east, others to the north and the cover of the Glimmerwood.

Around came Tazmikella, and she hurried the fleeing monsters along with a blast of acid. Drizzt's arrows nipped at them and cut them down.

"Secured!" Drizzt shouted when they turned back to the bridge to see Bruenor taking most of his force back across to the western edge, leaving only a handful to guard the now-empty eastern ramp.

Catti-brie smiled and waved at the drow and his dragon mount, then turned over the bridge rail and dropped a fireball on the field just to the north, in the midst of the back ranks of orcs battling King Emerus.

"I go to join my sister," Tazmikella said to Drizzt. "Will you stay or come with me?"

"The bridge," Drizzt asked. He wanted to be with Catti-brie and Bruenor then, in this moment of victory.

Tazmikella set him down and sped away, and Drizzt moved up beside his wife and matched her magic with his silver arrows.

The orcs were caught between three forces now, between the Surbrin Bridge and Mithral Hall's eastern door. They had nowhere to run. Many jumped into the River Surbrin and were swept away on icy currents. Much later, rumors came back to Mithral Hall that a handful of the orc swimmers actually managed to crawl out of the river on the other bank.

That handful and the giants of Shining White were the only monsters who got off that field alive.

CHAPTER 21

THE WISDOM OF MORADIN

FIRST THERE WAS THE FRANTIC SCRAMBLE AS HE TRIED FUTILELY TO hold his seat, but the cinch had been cleanly severed, and there was nothing to hold on to.

Then there was anger as he tumbled away, falling out of the Darkening, and watching the copper dragon and that wretched Drizzt Do'Urden flying up into it.

The wind slapping at him fiercely, Tiago still managed to unfasten himself from the ruined saddle, and he shoved it far aside. He even managed to sheathe his sword, and shrank his buckler to its smallest diameter as he held it strapped upon his forearm.

And then a great sense of calm washed over Tiago as he fell from the sky, so removed from the violence of the dragons and the sounds of the armies clashing below. He heard nothing but the wind, its vibrations stealing his every sensibility.

He was simply existing, falling free, his thoughts drawn blank as he took in this grand experience—one grander even than flying around on a great white dragon. He didn't even have the sensation of falling any longer, felt almost as if he was floating, weightless and serene.

He had no sense of time passing, and only when he noted some movement up above by the roiling blackness as the dragons continued their dance, or when he happened to glance below to see the ground much nearer, did such thoughts enter his mind.

The sound from below began to reach his ears, the clash of armies. He was to the west of the fighting, he noted with a glance, far afield of the northernmost, and by far the greatest, of the battles raging.

"Ah, Drizzt Do'Urden," the noble son of House Baenre, the weapons master of House Do'Urden, said, though he couldn't even hear his own voice, really, "so you have won."

Tiago tapped the enchanted Baenre emblem he wore on his cloak, its magic immediately putting him into a state of levitation.

"This time," he finished.

He was still falling from the sheer momentum of his plummet, but slowly, and now the swirling southern spring wind caught him and sent him drifting even farther afield, leaving the battles many miles away, to the north and west, and the empty hilly region in front of the foothills of the Spine of the World known as the Lands Against the Wall.

He could only sigh and hope that Drizzt would survive the fight with Arauthator and the greater battle raging, that he might pay the clever archer back when next they met.

"Soon," he promised himself, at last touching down.

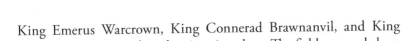

King Emerus Warcrown, King Connerad Brawnanvil, and King Bruenor Battlehammer shared a victorious hug. The fields around them lay littered with dead, and most of those dead were orcs. Copper dragons, allies, flew overhead, returning from the north, their appearance and calls informing the dwarves of the impending arrival of victorious King Harnoth of Citadel Adbar and his legions.

The siege around Mithral Hall had been shattered, the monsters of Many-Arrows sent running, and the dwarven armies were out and free, all three, soon to be joined in a mighty force and singular cause.

At the western end of the Surbrin Bridge, Catti-brie's work had only just begun, as she and the dwarven clerics went to the task of healing the wounded. Drizzt stayed beside her, occasionally running to the eastern end of the bridge, where Bungalow Thump and his Gutbusters were keeping a solid and stoic guard.

But no enemies were coming from that direction, Drizzt believed. The white dragons were gone, but the copper wyrms remained, and would the ferocious dwarves even need that unmistakable advantage?

"It is a good day," Drizzt said to Catti-brie when he returned to her after one such jaunt to the eastern edge of the bridge.

The woman looked around at the carnage, fields littered with bodies, river red with blood, the bridge scarred by flames and burned flesh, the mountain of Fourthpeak showing a gaping hole from the dwarven breakout, and a scar up higher where the white dragon had gone crashing in.

"It was a necessary day," she quietly corrected.

Drizzt nodded and smiled, catching her meaning.

"It is good that we won, and that the white dragons who served our enemies are gone," Catti-brie offered. She looked past Drizzt and pointed with her chin. The drow turned to see the dragon sisters gliding down to them.

"Come, Drizzt," Afafrenfere called from Ilnezhara's back. "There has been another battle this day in the south, where the Rauvin meets the Surbrin. Let us go and learn what we may."

Drizzt turned to Catti-brie.

"Wulfgar and Regis," she whispered, hopefully and fearfully all at once.

Tazmikella set down near the bridge and Drizzt climbed upon her back, and with her permission, pulled Catti-brie up behind him.

"Eh now, where ye goin', elf?" demanded Bruenor, running over to see what the commotion was about.

Drizzt motioned to Afafrenfere, who reached his hand down to the dwarf.

"Ah, but ye're daft if ye think . . ." Bruenor started to grumble.

"A fight in the south!" Drizzt explained, and Tazmikella lifted away. Ilnezhara came close behind, and yes, Bruenor was indeed upon her back, sitting behind Afafrenfere and holding on for all his life.

They climbed high into the sky, the line of the river below them snaking to the south, and soon they came in sight of the fork where the Rauvin River joined the Surbrin. As the dragons drifted down, side by side, the riders came to note the scores of bodies darkening the field north of the Rauvin's rocky ford.

Ilnezhara remained up high, while Tazmikella dived low and sped across, scouting the region. She and her riders saw bows lifted their way from the trees, but before the dragon even veered aside, those bows were pulled down and a huge man came running from the shadows, waving his arms.

"Back! Back!" Drizzt yelled to the dragon, who apparently didn't like his tone, for Tazmikella lifted suddenly, and once more Drizzt went face-down on her shoulders, and poor Catti-brie nearly flipped right over him.

Momentum stolen, the dragon flopped a tight turn and drifted back to settle lightly on the field beside the large human.

Drizzt and Catti-brie were there to give Wulfgar a great hug, and soon, so too was Bruenor, who leaped with joy from Ilnezhara's back before the dragon had even stopped her running landing. The dwarf hit the ground hard, tumbling and bouncing, but came up to his feet without a care in the world as he rushed to leap upon his adopted son.

At the same time, from the trees came Regis, battered but smiling. They were together once more, the Companions of the Hall.

Catti-brie looked to Drizzt. "It is a good day," she said.

Her clothes had dried, but her eyes had not. Overwhelmed, Doum'wielle wandered the fields just south of the Rauvin. At one point, she noted movement to the east, rushing fast to the south.

The drow, fleeing the disaster at the Rauvin ford. They had fled—Ravel's mount had knocked her into the river, and not one had paused to try to help her.

The Moonwood elves would never have . . .

The thought disappeared in a blink, replaced by an overwhelming sense of coldness, colder even than she had felt when first she had crawled from the icy waters of the Rauvin, its wickedly cold waters supplied by the melting snow atop the mountains to the northeast.

This was deeper and more profound, a sensation that the very blood was freezing within her. She stumbled and went down to one knee, holding there, forcing her breath into her aching lungs. Curiously, she noted that she couldn't actually see her breath puffing in front of her face, and that clued her into the reality of this sensation.

Khazid'hea was doing it!

She grasped the sword and cursed it, demanding that it stop, but then she realized that the sword wasn't purposefully imparting the feeling. Her connection to the sword allowed her to recognize that Khazid'hea wasn't creating the sensation, but was experiencing it, and so she was, too, through the sword.

And then she understood, as Khazid'hea understood. The sword had spent decades on the hip of another.

Khazid'hea had felt the death of Tos'un.

Her father was dead.

A moment of grief became overwhelmed by a sensation of utter dread. She looked around as if expecting some enemy, drow or elf, to rush out upon her and lop her head from her shoulders.

She found it hard to breathe.

She wanted to run, but had no idea what direction might serve. Was she to return to Menzoberranzan? How could she? What chance would she have among the drow without the intervening hand of her father and his noble Armgo lineage? Now she was certainly no more than *darthiir*, simple offal to be toyed with and tortured and ultimately murdered.

And Doum'wielle knew that the dark elves would make it hurt. She knew she would be begging for the release of death long before they finally granted her that peace.

She instinctively returned to the north and looked across the Rauvin to the fields and trees beyond. She was a long way from the southern tip of the Glimmerwood, and longer still to the region of that vast forest known as the Moonwood.

But perhaps she could get there, to her old home, to Sinnafein, her mother.

It would be a more merciful death, but no doubt still a death, she thought.

The image of Sinnafein, face twisted by rage, sword up high to deal her the killing blow, washed through poor Doum'wielle. She heard her mother calling out "Little Doe!" but not with affection. Instead, hatred and rage at the murderous child, whose hands still stank with the blood of her brother, Tierflin.

Again hardly aware of the movement, Doum'wielle turned away from the Glimmerwood. There was nothing there for her. She knew that Khazid'hea had spurred her thoughts of doom in her old home and that image of her mother, a fact confirmed by the relief she felt from the sentient blade when she turned away.

But the sword was right, she believed in her heart, and the revelation did not make her question Khazid'hea. Indeed, she turned to the blade for guidance. She had no ideas and no hope.

She found both in Khazid'hea, and as she came to understand the plotting sword, Doum'wielle grinned and nodded.

She didn't need her father. She would survive without him. She would thrive without him.

Perhaps he had been a burden to her with the drow all along. He was Barrison Del'Armgo, but Tiago was Baenre and Ravel was Xorlarrin, both families bitter rivals of House Barrison Del'Armgo.

How much protection had Tos'un truly afforded her? She recalled then the look Tos'un had given her after that moment of ultimate humiliation.

Doum'wielle was done mourning her father.

***

"We got to secure the land on both ends o' the bridge!" King Connerad insisted. "Hold our gains and spread from there!"

"Bah, but Felbarr's still circled," Ragged Dain pointed out.

"Ye canno' be leavin' me folk trapped in another tunnel what might be slammed shut," King Emerus agreed. "Came here to help yerself and yer boys out, and now ye're out, and so I'm callin' ye back to Felbarr to end that siege once and for all time."

"Got more o' me boys on the field than both o' ye together," King Harnoth said, rather imperiously.

Beside him, Oretheo Spikes grimaced, clearly not liking his young king's tone.

"I'll be takin' the force then where me heart's tellin' me to go," King Harnoth said. Indeed, he had near to six thousand on the field, almost twice the number of the combined forces of Mithral Hall and Citadel Felbarr. But while Citadel Adbar was clearly the strongest of the three dwarven citadels, the kings of the other two, particularly Emerus Warcrown of Citadel Felbarr, were far more seasoned in the arts of war. "Hartusk's in the south, and I'm thinkin' it's time we pay the murderin' dog a visit. He ain't got his dragons now, and let's see how his filthy orcs stand against a hunnerd dwarven legions!"

Off to the side of the argument, Drizzt, Bruenor, and the other Companions of the Hall listened.

"Young Connerad will need your support," the drow whispered to Bruenor. Drizzt waited a moment for a response, then tapped the dwarf on the shoulder.

Bruenor brushed his hand away. He hadn't heard the question, and barely recognized the argument roaring on the other side of the campfire. Bruenor's eyes were closed and his thoughts were far away, back in Gauntlgrym and the Throne of the Dwarf Gods.

The problem before him was obvious: they were sadly outnumbered, and any commitment to one battle or another would leave them open in other places. If they went to Citadel Felbarr, what would prevent the army in Keeper's Dale from simply renewing the siege around Mithral Hall? And weren't there far too many orcs and their monstrous allies still scattered around the Upper Surbrin Vale for them to even begin to think of running to the south, to Silverymoon or perhaps even Everlund, in pursuit of Hartusk?

So Bruenor thought of the throne. He heard the call of Clangeddin and saw in his mind the discipline and strength of a dwarven line, and the tirelessness of their march.

He heard the whispers of Dumathoin and considered the many courses they might take, both above and below ground.

He felt the wisdom of Moradin, the understanding of the reactions of his enemies when he executed this or that assault. Where could they hit Hartusk for best effect?

Sometime later, the argument across the bonfire still raging, Bruenor came out of his meditation, blinked open his eyes, and offered a wink to his friends. He turned his attention across the way, to find that Emerus appeared as if he was about to leap over and throttle King Harnoth.

"Me brothers," Bruenor said, as he rose and walked around the flames. "Not the time for fightin'. We got out, and now we're one." He paused and settled his gaze one at a time on the contingents from all three of the dwarven fortresses, on King Emerus, Parson Glaive, and Ragged Dain of Citadel Felbarr; on King Harnoth and Oretheo Spikes and the others of Citadel Adbar; and on King Connerad, General Dagnabbet, and Bungalow Thump of his beloved Mithral Hall.

He ended with an imposing stare that fell squarely over young King Harnoth. "Ye was dead, boy," he said, and those around Harnoth sucked in their breath at the seeming disrespect in that statement.

"Ye was dead until me and me boys pulled ye from it, and ye're knowin' it," Bruenor pressed on. "The orcs and giants had ye in the dale, and not a one o' ye'd've gotten home if it weren't for meself and the Gutbusters and the allies we bringed with us." He looked to Oretheo Spikes and shrugged, and the fierce Wilddwarf could only nod his agreement.

"And yerself wasn't gettin' out," Bruenor said to King Emerus. "Yerself and yer boys were stuck and holding, yer bellies grumblin', yer old and yer young dyin'."

"Is yer point being that we're all owin' ye, Bruenor?" King Emerus dared to reply, and his tone showed that he didn't much appreciate any such implication.

"Nah, I'm just sayin' what was, and askin' ye to trust me now," Bruenor replied.

"Trust ye? What with?"

"I seen the way," Bruenor replied.

"The way?" Harnoth and Emerus asked together.

"Aye," Bruenor said and closed his eyes. He saw them all there in his mind, thousands marching in tight formation. Dwarves had always been known as the toughest of the goodly races, hearty and rough and able to endure great hardships. It was a reputation well earned, Bruenor knew.

But it had become too much of a reputation and not enough of a practice. The gods of old were showing him the way. They could move, all of them, great distances in short order. With such numbers, they could overwhelm pockets of enemies and slaughter goblins, orcs, ogres, and even frost giants without suffering great losses.

Their marches would be inspired and necessary, and so would be without attrition.

He saw it clearly. He believed it in his heart.

"I believe in our boys," he said.

The three dwarf kings exchanged confused looks.

"Mix 'em up and mash 'em all together," Bruenor demanded. "There ain't no Adbar or Felbarr or Mithral Hall now. Aye, not now. Now there's just Delzoun, just dwarf. Ye let me put 'em together, ye let me form 'em up, and ye let me lead 'em while ye ride along beside us."

"Lead 'em where?" King Emerus asked.

"Not knowin' yet," Bruenor replied. He turned to Brother Afafrenfere, who sat off to the side with Sinnafein. "Ye get on yer dragon, monk," he said, "and yerself, elf," he added to Drizzt. "And ye fly all about the lands from the Rauvin Mountains to Keeper's Dale to Dark Arrow Keep. I'm wantin' to know where all them ugly orcs're at, each group and how big."

"Knight-Commander Brightlance has requested that the dragon sisters accompany her to Silverymoon," Afafrenfere replied.

"Aye," Bruenor replied with a nod. "And I'm not arguing that."

The dwarf kings and their entourage grumbled at that. They had argued earlier that the dragons should remain with them to hold their hard-won gains.

"We're not needin' them," Bruenor said, turning a withering gaze upon his peers. "Not when ye get us a map o' the battlefield with our enemies clear to see."

He turned to the kings and met their doubting stares with a look of grim determination. "I seen the way," he told them again. "The ground'll be shaking, don't ye doubt, under the greatest dwarf army Faerûn's seen in a thousand years!"

***

"We don't know," Saribel admitted to a very angry Gromph Baenre. "My husband flew ahead on Arauthator, but we were ambushed and turned back."

"The dragons are gone," Gromph flatly replied. "One lies dead in the snow on the high slopes of the mountain called Fourthpeak. The other is not to be found."

Saribel and Ravel looked at each other with expressions bordering on pure horror. They had lost a dragon? Two dragons? How much did that erase the gains they had found, the glories they had earned? Would they return to Menzoberranzan in disgrace?

For Saribel, the fear went even deeper. What had happened to Tiago, and where did she stand in the ranks of House Do'Urden, or in the family of House Baenre, if he was gone?

"There is nothing left here for you," Gromph explained. "And so it is time to return." He looked to Ravel. "You would be wise to instruct Matron Mother Zeerith's forces to likewise flee to Q'Xorlarrin. The enemies of Many-Arrows have gained the upper hand."

"Warlord Hartusk has assembled a mighty force," Ravel foolishly argued.

Perhaps there was some magical power behind the glare of Gromph, but whatever the reason, Ravel felt his knees going weak under the weight of the archmage's displeasure.

"Do we know of Tiago?" Saribel dared ask.

"It is Aurbangras dead on the mountain," Gromph answered, "and so I expect that the son of House Barrison Del'Armgo has met a most violent end. Arauthator fled to the Spine of the World and his home. Whether Tiago is with him or not, I do not yet know."

Saribel relaxed a bit at that, something that was not lost on the archmage.

"You will be saddened if he has met his end," Gromph said. "How touching. A priestess who cares for a mere male."

Saribel's eyes went wide at that mocking tone, as if Gromph was looking right through her, which, of course, he was.

"Or is it because Tiago is Baenre, and because of him, so are you?" Gromph asked with a chuckle. He turned back to Ravel. "Saribel would care not at all if you were the one missing, you know."

Ravel looked at his nasty sister and shared in Gromph's chuckle. "Of course."

"Gather your entourage at once," Gromph instructed. "I will put the gate to Menzoberranzan right here." He scratched his boot across the ground. "It will not last long, and any who do not pass through the portal are banished from Menzoberranzan for eternity. On my word."

"The Xorlarrins?" Saribel dared ask.

"They can find their own way home. Your old House is one of wizards, is it not?"

With that, the archmage began his casting, and the two noble children of Matron Mother Zeerith glanced at each other and realized that they needed to make all haste in collecting their servants.

As soon as they were gone, Kimmuriel walked out from the shadows to join the archmage.

"So you send them home," he remarked. "And you will join them?"

"My business here is not done," he replied.

Kimmuriel clearly sensed Gromph's unrelenting anger.

"I know what Jarlaxle is doing," Gromph added, staring hard at the psionicist. "I know the source of the . . . aerial force that came against Arauthator and his son."

Kimmuriel stood ready to step far, far away at the first hint of trouble. He wanted no part of Gromph Baenre's wrath.

But . . .

The archmage smiled and arched his white eyebrows, an open expression that invited his instructor to take a look inside his thoughts.

It took Kimmuriel a few moments to fully appreciate that Gromph wasn't upset about Jarlaxle's interference, though he couldn't begin to understand why.

Not out here, at least.

He lifted his hand to Gromph's forehead, using his fingers as an illithid might use its tentacles, to find a bond, a gateway.

It wasn't often that Kimmuriel Oblodra wore an astonished expression.

***

"They will not desert your cause," Jarlaxle informed Catti-brie and Bruenor sometime later. Drizzt and Afafrenfere had already flown from the dwarven encampment on their dragon mounts to begin the survey of the war zone.

"They fear the white dragon will return," Catti-brie reasoned, but Jarlaxle shook his head.

"Arauthator has fled the battle. He has lived for centuries, millennia even, because he is not stupid. He'll not return."

"His son was slain," the woman pointed out.

Jarlaxle shrugged as if that hardly mattered. "White dragons are worse parents than drow mothers, don't you know?"

Catti-brie looked at him curiously at that strange remark.

"Trust me, good lady, Arauthator cares not at all and will not return."

"So we got the dragons now," Bruenor said. "Fightin' the orcs?"

"Helping," Jarlaxle corrected. "I do not expect the sisters to put themselves at risk for the sake of our . . . of your cause. But I expect that simply having them flying about will cause many of Hartusk's allies to reconsider their allegiance. And my dark elf kin have already fled the field. Almost all of them."

"Which battlefield for the dragons, then?" Catti-brie asked.

"Bah, send 'em south," said Bruenor. "We don't need them."

"As I was thinking," said Jarlaxle. "The greatest fight will be for Everlund."

"Aleina Brightlance is returning to Silverymoon now to break the siege and rally the Knights in Silver to Everlund's defense," Catti-brie said. "Wulfgar and Regis have opted to travel with her to bolster her cause."

"Brother Afafrenfere will fly Ilnezhara, and the dwarf Amber has asked to accompany him on Tazmikella," Jarlaxle explained. "Athrogate will go with her. The dragons have agreed."

"What hold ye got on them?" Bruenor asked bluntly.

"It is my irresistible charm, good dwarf."

"And why are ye here?" Bruenor asked. "I'm still not gettin' that, elf. Ye come here to fight against yer own?"

"The powers of Menzoberranzan have achieved all that they set out to do," the drow replied. "It is now a fight between orcs and their allies against the goodly races of the Silver Marches. Do not be too flattered, dwarf, to know that I prefer you to an orc."

"A fine answer," said Catti-brie, "yet your dragons battled the whites ridden by dark elves."

"It is of no concern."

"To you?"

"To you," Jarlaxle corrected. "You should ask fewer questions and accept your good fortune in the spirit it was offered. And you should remember always the conditions I put upon that offer." His expression showed that last line to be more than a casual warning, and indeed it was a threat. Jarlaxle had demanded of Drizzt and the other Companions of the Hall that his presence here in this conflict remain secret, and the reminder now left no doubt that he could take his dragons and leave at any point.

"It is my own curiosity," Catti-brie assured him.

Jarlaxle accepted that with a grin and a bow. "Someday, perhaps, I will satisfy that curiosity."

Bruenor snorted.

"And you are confident that your forces can do what needs to be done before the inevitable return of Hartusk's force?" Jarlaxle asked the dwarf.

"Ye just watch us, elf," Bruenor confidently answered. "And then go do yer kin a favor and tell 'em. They'll know better than to come back here, I'm guessin'."

Jarlaxle had to admit, to himself at least, that Bruenor's boast and confidence intrigued him. From his spying, he had seen the dwarves already falling in line to Bruenor's commands. Their loyalty to their three fortresses had quickly melted away, leaving them a unified and coordinated army. The Wilddwarves and Gutbusters worked in unison, and the squares of dwarves from all three citadels marched as tightly as any groups that had served together for years.

In short, the drow found that he already had come to believe Bruenor's claims, and he was anxious to watch the "hop'n'smack" course Bruenor had outlined—though, of course, Bruenor had no idea that Jarlaxle knew of his plans.

With a tinge of regret, Jarlaxle bid the pair farewell and faded back into the shadows. He wanted to be a part of this more directly.

He fancied himself fighting beside Drizzt, side by side and back to back, and woe to any monsters who came too close!

He thought of Zaknafein, Drizzt's father and Jarlaxle's dear old friend, and the adventures they had shared half a millennium before. How much Drizzt reminded him of Zaknafein . . .

"Someday," he whispered when no one could hear.

CHAPTER 22

THE RITUAL OF THE MARCH

Nine thousand dwarves marched in unison, quick-stepping, trotting, their lines bending and swerving to move through dell and over ridges. They seemed more a force of nature, a living flood, than an army, and so they were.

Dwarf priests had been spaced evenly around the massive force, and they led the song—and indeed, it was more than a song.

Bruenor led it all, reaching back into his memories of the Throne of the Dwarf Gods, which served as a conduit to an ancient dwarven ritual, long forgotten, the Ritual of the March. Dumathoin's whispers brought the words to his lips, and his throaty voice carried them along.

Every dwarf sang, nine thousand voices giving cadence to eighteen thousand boots.

They rumbled and they rambled, the ground shaking beneath their stomping footfalls, and they did not tire—that was the magic, an enchantment that reached into the core of the hearty folk and pulled from them the best they could give.

They rolled over the miles south of Fourthpeak, and along the southern ridge of Keeper's Dale, and just beyond that valley they caught the fleeing orcs' encampment, the one group besieging Mithral Hall that had not joined in at the Battle of the Surbrin Bridge.

Nine thousand dwarves, armed and armored with the finest mithral and adamantine culled from the mines of three dwarven citadels, led by and fighting for four dwarf kings, supported by three hundred elf archers, and with Drizzt Do'Urden and Catti-brie among them, bore down on the orcs.

Outnumbered by more than five to one, caught by surprise at how quickly the vast force had traveled from the Surbrin, the Many-Arrows encampment had no heart for the fight and broke ranks even as the battle began, fleeing every which way, but mostly back to the north.

Drizzt and Sinnafein's elves dogged them every step, shooting them dead, but the dwarves did not.

On Bruenor's call they reversed course to execute their next "hop," and they sang and marched all the way back to the river, then across the bridge to the eastern lands of the Cold Vale and the forces encircling Citadel Felbarr.

They knew where all of the enemy concentrations were settled, in great detail. The dragons and their riders had mapped it all before the march started, and now many elf scouts and Catti-brie's divination guided Bruenor and his peers.

No army, surely not one of short-legged dwarves, had moved with such speed and precision in the memory of men or elves.

Or orcs.

"I am more winded than you," Drizzt said to Bruenor on one of the rare breaks. "I'll need Andahar to pace your forces."

"Sing like a dwarf, elf," Bruenor quipped.

"Bwahaha, but he ain't got the pipes for it!" Bungalow Thump said from nearby, where he sat with General Dagnabbet and King Connerad.

Drizzt laughed at the good-natured ribbing. "Nor can I understand a word you're saying," he replied, and all the dwarves laughed.

"Fifty miles and a fight afore supper," Bruenor said, and Drizzt knew that to be one of the lines of the enchanting song—and an accurate one.

"I'm knowin' why Moradin told me to come back," Bruenor said quietly, so that only Drizzt and Catti-brie could hear.

"Mielikki, you mean," said Drizzt.

"Was Moradin what used her," Bruenor disagreed. "Oh, aye, but I was to do her favor and save yer own skinny bum, but was more than that. I'm knowin' that now. I seen it, and see it still in me thoughts. Dumathoin's whisperin' to me, Clangeddin's giving strength to me arm." He paused and lifted one arm in a flex that accentuated his defined and knotted bicep.

"And Moradin," he said somberly. "Aye, Moradin, he's cheerin', don't ye doubt. Was Gruumsh that sent Obould them decades ago, and now it's Moradin who's putting the dogs back where they belong."

"We'll sweep the Cold Vale," Drizzt said.

"Aye, all the lands from the Redrun to Adbar'll be free of any large bands in just a few days."

"And then?"

"Back across the Surbrin," said Bruenor, grimly, and he was looking more to the northwest and the southwest, where lay the Surbrin Bridge.

Drizzt knew where Bruenor's mind was leading his gaze, knew what was up there. The dwarves held a huge advantage. They didn't have to worry about leaving their flanks or the citadels in their wake vulnerable, for even if Hartusk turned the whole of his vast southern army around, he'd never catch them, nor could he break into Mithral Hall or Citadel Felbarr or Citadel Adbar.

"The Ritual of the March," the drow ranger said, nodding.

"The whisper o' Dumathoin," Bruenor replied with a wink.

"Fifty miles and a fight afore supper," Catti-brie sang in her best dwarven brogue. "A good thing it is that Regis isn't here!"

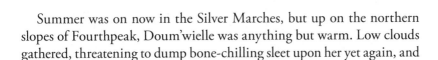

Summer was on now in the Silver Marches, but up on the northern slopes of Fourthpeak, Doum'wielle was anything but warm. Low clouds gathered, threatening to dump bone-chilling sleet upon her yet again, and without shelter, she would have been wise to turn around and quickly descend from the snow line.

But she could not.

Khazid'hea would not let her.

Her breath puffed out visibly in front of her as she trudged along, and often did her feet skid out from under her, leaving her wet and miserable in the melting snowpack, and more than once terrifying her with the thought that she would create an avalanche all around her.

But she did not, and when she came around one rocky jut, her goal was at last in sight.

There in front of her lay the torn and broken form of Aurbangras, the dragon as red with its own blood as white now, and in a pond of red snow and mud.

She tried to give that messy ground a wide berth, but only until she saw the smaller form in front of it.

Then she was running straight through the muck, slipping and falling, but pulling herself up and scrabbling along, and yelling "Father!" with every step.

She got to the broken form of Tos'un and desperately tried to touch him. But the breath of Aurbangras had fallen over him fully, and the ice was thick around the corpse. Scratching futilely until her fingers bled, Doum'wielle finally fell back to a sitting position, gasping for breath, battling her tears.

She had known that Tos'un was dead, of course. The sword had told her, and had even shown her the manner of his death. But now that she was sitting here in front of the body, it became real to her, and so did the dire implications.

She couldn't go back to Menzoberranzan. She couldn't return to her mother and her clan. She had nowhere to go and no hope of getting there.

A jolt of pain stabbed at her like a lightning bolt, and she sucked in her breath and blew away her tears and her dismay and looked down at the source, at her sentient sword.

We will find the course, Khazid'hea promised her, reminding her again of the plan it had revealed to her.

You will be welcomed in the City of the Spider Queen, the sword telepathically promised. *You will do what the son of House Baenre cannot. You will shame him, and so you will be held above him.*

Doum'wielle nodded, trusting the blade.

From the sword, she knew the way to acceptance.

But knew, too, the way to vengeance.

The journey to the Silver Marches had been a long march for most of the Q'Xorlarrin drow, and so it would be a long march home again, they knew. House Xorlarrin, who ruled the new city, was known for its arcane magic-users, but aside from Ravel, who had already gone back to Menzoberranzan with Gromph Baenre, and Tsabrak, who remained at Matron Mother Zeerith's side in the fledgling city, few were adept enough to cast a teleport spell.

So they were doomed to walk, or ride their spectral mounts or summoned discs, a journey they expected would take a month at least.

And every day they remained with Warlord Hartusk's army meant an added two days to their absence from home. The orcs were marching almost directly south now, away from the cave that would take the remaining eighty drow warriors and wizards back to Q'Xorlarrin.

If the battle at the Rauvin River, where a dozen of their kin had been slain, hadn't convinced them to give up this useless war, then surely the departure of the Menzoberranyr drow and the white dragons had.

Do we tell them, or simply leave? the drow wizard Maffizo Vailentarne asked his associates with the silent and intricate hand code of the dark elves.

The ugly orc warlord will not be pleased, an old Xorlarrin warrior named Epricante signed back. *He is only now getting word of the disaster at Mithral Hall.*

The band of half a dozen drow leaders glanced over at Hartusk's main tent, and could see from the shadows cast by the fire within that the burly orc was clearly agitated, up and pacing around briskly. They had marched long into the dark night, through the Moon Pass, and were now almost directly east of Everlund, though with still a hundred marching miles to go. The Nether Mountains loomed over them, directly north, yet another barrier placed between the dark elves and the cavern that would take them to the Underdark tunnels that led home.

And word of the dragons, another offered, and the six nodded. *The whispers from the north hint that Aurbangras might well be destroyed.*

Gather all, Maffizo ordered. *Let us be long from this place before the warlord even knows we have deserted his cause.*

Maffizo looked to the east, where far away, the dim light of the moon could be seen under the eastern edge of Tsabrak's roiling Darkening.

"When the moon's light is stolen by Tsabrak's enchantment," he said to his coconspirators.

The others nodded again and scattered, moving around the clusters of marching monsters to locate the other drow and inform them of the decision and the impending departure. An hour later, they began filtering out singly or in small groups, moving past the campfires of goblins and orcs and other monsters, making their way back to the Moon Pass and Sundabar beyond.

They might have made it through the last lines and into the clear, except for another shadow that appeared in Warlord Hartusk's tent.

"They leave!" said the intruder, who had come in all of a sudden, materializing from nowhere.

The orcs scrambled and fell all over each other trying to fashion some response, but the drow stood impervious. When one of Hartusk's guards hurled a spear at him, he didn't move, and when the spear hit him, it simply bounced away.

"Your dragons are gone, Hartusk," the drow said. "My people of Menzoberranzan have been deceived, and you have been deceived, by the traitors of Q'Xorlarrin!"

A group of orcs closed ranks in front of the warlord, brandishing spears and swords as if they would leap forward and attack. But Hartusk held them back.

"Who are you?" he demanded.

"A messenger from Duke Tiago," the drow replied.

"Whose minions have already fled!" Hartusk said with a growl, and the orcs in front of him brandished their weapons threateningly.

"Because we were deceived!" the drow retorted. "By the dark elves of Q'Xorlarrin."

"Who remain to fight!" growled Hartusk.

The drow smiled at him and shook his head. "No, Warlord Hartusk. They brought you out here, so far from your keep and with long lines of supplies, to see you dead. And now they leave."

With that, the drow shrugged and stepped away, simply disappearing, but not before he reached out to the orc who had thrown the spear at him. A simple gesture of his fingers and that orc flew backward, a wound opening in its chest that replicated the wound his own thrown spear would have made.

And the drow was gone.

The orcs leaped around, expecting him to reappear, but Hartusk slapped them and shouted them to order. "Go and see!" he roared.

"I do so hate the stupid, ugly things," Kimmuriel said to Gromph when he returned to the archmage in a cave far north of the marching orc army and Hartusk's tent.

"They will serve their purpose," the archmage replied evenly.

Kimmuriel nodded, knowing that many Q'Xorlarrin drow would likely die this day. The losses would shame the fledgling city, and would place Matron Mother Zeerith in a very uncomfortable position indeed, so much so that she would inevitably look to Matron Mother Quenthel for support.

And so this grand expedition to the Silver Marches would once again benefit House Baenre. Kimmuriel wasn't surprised by any of that, of course. He had suspected from the beginning that Quenthel's coaxing of soldiers and wizards from Q'Xorlarrin—even enlisting Tsabrak to enact the Darkening, when surely the powerful Gromph would have better sufficed—had been done for exactly this reason. Q'Xorlarrin was never intended to be independent of Menzoberranzan, after all, and Matron Mother Zeerith could not be allowed autonomy from House Baenre.

A few score dead males were nothing to Matron Mother Quenthel, but to Matron Mother Zeerith, with far fewer resources, and fighting to secure Q'Xorlarrin in inhospitable lands—and especially after the damage Zeerith's city had already suffered at the hands of Drizzt and his friends—such a blow could prove painful indeed.

Such a blow might tempt other Menzoberranyr Houses, Melarn or Hunzrin likely, to wonder if perhaps the new city was not as sanctioned and blessed by Lady Lolth as they had been led to believe. It was no secret that Matron Mother Shakti Hunzrin had quietly built up a trade coalition of her own among several of the lesser Houses, and that she had not been pleased by the bold move of House Xorlarrin to establish a sister city in the Upperdark to facilitate trade with the surface.

Kimmuriel stared at the archmage, and wished it was time for another of Gromph's lessons in psionics. Perhaps he could slip into Gromph's mind then, and unravel the mystery of this one, who seemed to be working every faction against one another.

Gromph knew of Jarlaxle's interference, but had not intervened or hindered the mercenary at all. And yet, in sending Kimmuriel to visit Hartusk, Gromph was clearly working in the best interests of Matron Mother Quenthel.

But why?

Dark elves could move very swiftly, even more so when they could conjure spectral steeds and other magical mounts.

But they could not outdistance the relay of calls that cascaded from Warlord Hartusk's camp, back to the north and east, from orc to goblin to ogre to giant.

And so the first battle of Warlord Hartusk's march to Everlund was not against that city's walls, nor against Aleina Brightlance's Knights in Silver or any other raiding band. At the trailing end of his vast army, the word spread that a drow head was worth a hundred pieces of gold and a wagon of slaves.

Fireballs and lightning bolts from drow wizards soon ripped and brightened the night. And fine drow weapons spun and struck and covered the field with the blood of goblinkin and giantkind.

But a hundred giant-hurled boulders went up into the sky, amidst a swarm of orc arrows and spears, and the sheer press of the monstrous forces overwhelmed the forces of Q'Xorlarrin. Some escaped, fleeing into the darkness, but many did not.

Just as Gromph had planned it.

CHAPTER 23

DROW DECONSTRUCTION

Sʜᴇ ʟᴏᴏᴋᴇᴅ ᴛʜʀᴏᴜɢʜ ᴛʜᴇ ꜰʟᴀᴍᴇꜱ ᴀꜱ ꜱᴜʀᴇʟʏ ᴀɴᴅ ᴀꜱ ᴄʟᴇᴀʀʟʏ ᴀꜱ ɪꜰ she were sitting inside them. Through the crackles, she heard the grumbling of the camping monsters, and, now convinced that this was the fire of the leaders of this group, Catti-brie fell deeper into her trance, deeper into the swirling invitation of her magical ring, deeper into her connection with the Plane of Fire.

The bonfire roared high into the night sky, drawing the attention of the orcs and giants all around—attention that had been taken just a few moments earlier by the resonant and rumbling sounds rolling up from the south.

Sounds of chanting, of weapons banging on shields, of the ground reverberating under the stamp of boots.

Some large force was approaching this encampment in the Cold Vale, between the westernmost peaks of the Rauvin Mountains and the Glimmerwood—the same encampment that had driven the desperate King Emerus back into Citadel Felbarr earlier in the year.

Goblinkin and giantkind looked to each other nervously. They knew of the fight at the Surbrin Bridge—some scattered details, at least—and the rumors said that Mithral Hall had come forth.

Was this King Connerad and his charges, then, marching to rescue Felbarr?

The bonfire flared again, and it was not the wind, they knew, nor a sap-filled log exploding in the heat. In a mesmerizing dance, the flames changed hue, turning blue, then red, then orange to white, and the sheer heat of the blaze drove the monsters back.

"What sorcery?" asked Barunga Foestone, the leader of the frost giant contingent and so the leader of this encampment. Barely had the question escaped the behemoth's lips when out of the bonfire came a living giant of flame!

Frost giants yelled for their boulders, and those not near any piles of heavy stones simply grabbed up nearby goblins or orcs and hurled them at the elemental instead.

And in waded Barunga and her fellows, batting the living flames with heavy clubs. One giant rolled away, fire biting at his hair and clothing, and another went down in a tremendous burst of sparks and embers as the elemental connected with a heavy punch solidly into its pale face.

But as great as the frenzy at the fire might be, the sound from the south demanded even more attention. For now the nearest trees of the Glimmerwood began to rustle and shake, and now the song was clear and loud, and infuriating to the goblins and giants, who hated dwarves above all other creatures.

Through the dark trees the stout warriors filtered, and the leaders of the monstrous force called for formations, eager for the fight.

But through the trees the dwarves kept coming, rank after rank, marching in perfect precision, every shield supporting those to either side.

A growing wall of iron and mithral and adamantine.

A growing wall of dwarf.

Where the song had inspired fury, it now elicited fear, for still the bearded folk came, their ranks swelling.

Arrows and spears and boulders flew against the dwarves, but few got through, even the giant-thrown rocks bouncing off the shield wall without causing much harm.

Like a great gray ooze, like the ocean tide itself, the dwarves methodically closed.

No sooner had Barunga Foestone at last put down the elemental with a mighty club smash than a second stepped out from the bonfire.

"Put out the fire!" Barunga yelled at all the monsters around, and she threw herself at the elemental with wild-eyed rage.

Goblins and orcs scrambled at the bonfire from the other directions, behind the elemental, and began kicking dirt at the bonfire, or hooking logs with their weapons and pulling them forth that they could be stamped out.

In short order, a dozen smaller fires burned—along with a few foolish goblins—and Barunga and her charges had the second elemental all but extinguished.

"Now for the dwarves," the frost giant told her fellows.

But not quite then, she and the others learned almost immediately, for from the west came a concentrated hail of elven arrows, centering on Barunga herself, guided by the watcher in the flames, who magically whispered across the fields to her drow husband.

In the south, the dwarves roared and charged, the interlocked shields like a rolling wall of doom. The coordination, the ferocity, the sheer numbers had the minions of Many-Arrows running around in confusion, scrambling to get away.

Nine thousand dwarves yelled "Kneel!" in unison, as was called for in their song, "The Ritual of the March," and so the shield wall skidded as one to bended knee.

And a thousand dwarf crossbows settled and steadied on those shields, and, in time with the call of the ancient song, fired off all at once.

Down went the leading throng of orcs, writhing and falling, and the dwarves began anew their advance, crushing the life from the wounded under stamping boots.

The rout was on, the encampment swept away, the fleeing monsters hounded as they ran by Sinnafein's elves and the silver arrows of Drizzt Do'Urden.

And at the center of it all stood Bruenor Battlehammer, singing, and never had he felt closer to his gods, not even when he had been seated upon the throne in Gauntlgrym.

King Emerus was the first of his peers to find him. Tears streaked the cheeks of the old leader of Citadel Felbarr when he approached Bruenor with open arms, nodding, but too overcome to even speak a word of gratitude.

He wrapped Bruenor in a great hug, and the dwarves all around, dwarves of Felbarr, of Adbar, of Mithral Hall, began a great and continuing cheer.

The Cold Vale was cleared at last, the siege broken, and soon after, the aboveground Runegate of Citadel Felbarr banged open.

They held their feast of victory right there in front of the great gates, and the darkness was stolen under the glow of a thousand bonfires. Dwarves threw goblins and orcs into those flames with one arm, while hoisting flagons of ale with the other, and the dwarfsong echoed from the Rauvins to the Glimmerwood, and followed the elves as they hunted the fleeing monsters and shot them dead or chased them far, far away.

"Drink and eat yer fill, boys!" Bruenor told them, and the word filtered far and wide. "Tomorrow's march'll be straight to sunset through the woods and the next dawn's at the Surbrin, where the boats're waitin'!"

"We'll be crossing north of the bridge?" King Connerad asked.

"That's a hunnerd miles!" King Harnoth put in.

"Far north," Bruenor answered Connerad, offering Harnoth nothing more than a wide grin.

"Straight west, ye're sayin'?" King Emerus asked.

"Ye're taking it to them," remarked Ragged Dain, who knew the region as well as any, and he chuckled and nodded at Emerus as he spoke. "Ah, Little Arr Arr," he added affectionately to Bruenor, "how much ye've grown."

The king of Citadel Felbarr likewise grinned and nodded, when he took a better look at their current position, for like Ragged Dain, Emerus realized that crossing the River Surbrin directly west through the Glimmerwood from their current position would put them closer to Dark Arrow Keep than to Mithral Hall.

"Ye close yer doors tight, me friend," Bruenor said to Emerus. "For we got business to finish, don't ye doubt."

Bruenor put his hands on his hips and stepped away from the others, moving to the northwest. He nodded to acknowledge his daughter, only then coming into view.

"And I'm meanin' to finish that business," he said.

"Dark Arrow Keep," Ragged Dain agreed.

Bruenor nodded, but he was thinking even beyond that coming conquest. His mind's eye went back to a magical throne in a sacred place. A throne he meant to reclaim.

"You are making a terrible mistake!" the drow prisoner roared at Warlord Hartusk. The young male drow strained against the bindings, his back against a wooden post, his arms tightly bound behind it. "I demand—"

A burly orc guard stepped up and slugged the prisoner in the face, jarring him to silence.

It took the drow a few heartbeats to straighten himself once more, and he looked around at the other captives, half a dozen of his fellow drow from Q'Xorlarrin. On the field to the northeast of this gathering, more than threescore dark elves lay dead. They had taken down hundreds of goblinkin and scores of giantkind with them in the battle, but in the end, they were still quite dead, or captured.

Warlord Hartusk walked up beside the impudent prisoner. "You think to play me as the fool," he said with a growl.

"The drow have aided you," the dark elf argued. "We dispatched Lorgru and put you, Hartusk, in power!"

The orc stared at him with bloodshot eyes and a toothy grin.

"Are you saying that I would not be warlord without you?" he said, and truly his voice sounded like the purr of a cat right before it devoured a mouse.

The drow straightened and looked around at his companions, all of them shaking their heads emphatically.

"No, Warlord, of course not!" one called, and got slugged by another guard.

Hartusk stared at the doomed prisoner's eyes and chuckled softly. He glanced back at his nearest soldiers and nodded,. They rushed off, returning a few moments later with a bale of hay, which they began disassembling immediately and placing around the feet of the staked drow. Behind them came more orcs, carrying logs and heavier pieces to burn.

"Have you anything else to say to me?" Hartusk asked.

"Warlord, Matron Mother Zeerith will know of this!" the drow said.

But Hartusk turned away and did not respond. "Burn them, one at a time," he ordered, as the orcs cheered and the goblins leaped up and down with macabre glee, a ruckus that increased tenfold when the torch was put to the hay piles around the prisoner's feet.

Far back of the execution, a handful of frost giants looked on. Jarl Greigor Kundknoddick turned to his favorite courtesan and motioned for her to follow him back to his tent.

He pulled back the tent flap to enter, and the tremendously huge giant guarding it stepped aside.

"You see what I mean?" asked the lone drow in the tent, a most curious fellow with a gigantic, plumed hat and an eye patch over his left eye. He was surrounded by three enormous frost giants, each of whom dwarfed the large Jarl Greigor, and who fancied themselves as three of the legendary ten brothers of Thrym.

"It was predictable," the frost giant leader replied.

"Matron Mother Zeerith Xorlarrin cannot let that stand," said the drow. "She controls a city of dark elves, and Warlord Hartusk will be made to pay."

"Unless she never learns of it," Jarl Greigor said, eyeing the drow dangerously.

Jarlaxle laughed. "I am of Menzoberranzan, not Q'Xorlarrin, and so I hardly care," he explained. "Matron Mother Zeerith's pain is my pleasure."

"Then why have you come to me?" the frost giant demanded.

"I come for Saribel, and the Archmage of Menzoberranzan, who delivered to you the brothers of Thrym," Jarlaxle said, and the huge frost giants all nodded. "We bear some responsibility for your decision to join in Hartusk's march, of course, and would not wish it to end tragically, as we have come to value your friendship, and hope to resume it when this messy business is ended."

"Because you know how it will end?" Jarl Greigor asked with a good measure of sarcasm.

"The dragons are gone, one dead, one fleeing home to the Spine of the World," Jarlaxle said bluntly. "The siege of Mithral Hall has been shattered, all of Hartusk's encampments utterly destroyed. The dwarves are out, Jarl. All of them. Mithral Hall, Citadel Felbarr, and Citadel Adbar. All of them. There are no remaining sizeable forces of Many-Arrows on the eastern bank of the River Surbrin from the Redrun all the way to Citadel Adbar, and none west of the river, either, except those forces arrayed at and around Dark Arrow Keep itself.

"They are out, and the dragons are gone," Jarlaxle said pointedly.

"We have enough here alone to flatten Everlund," Kundknoddick said.

Jarlaxle looked around, then tipped his cap. "Be careful, my large friend," he said, and he rose to leave. "Perhaps Warlord Hartusk will claim victory here in the south, but know that his enemies are many, and they are powerful. If you decide that discretion is the better part of valor at this time, cross the Surbrin south of Mithral Hall and continue to the west to the Spine of the World. The dwarves will not pursue your people. You have my word."

"Your word?" Jarl Greigor said with a snicker.

"Jarl Fimmel Orelson has returned with his minions to Shining White," the drow calmly replied, and the three giants all gasped. "He is done with this battle. He would welcome you and yours to the respite of Shining White."

"You lie!" Jarl Greigor cried, but he was talking to himself.

Jarlaxle had taken a step away and simply slipped out of view, as if time and space itself had warped to deposit him elsewhere.

As indeed it had.

Tiago Baenre arrived at Dark Arrow Keep just as scouts returned with word that a great dwarven force was crossing the River Surbrin, and not far downstream.

There was nothing standing between them and Dark Arrow Keep, so went the whispers. Warlord Hartusk had erred, had gone too far to the south, and the dwarves had come out of their holes behind him.

Tiago knew the truth of the whispers, and knew, too, that the white dragons were lost, and so when other orcs he encountered spoke of copper-colored wyrms flying above Dark Arrow Keep, he understood the dire situation. Indeed, Hartusk had reached too far. Why hadn't he turned around to secure the Cold Vale and the Upper Surbrin Vale, as Tiago had demanded?

Outraged, the drow went right for the command tent, meaning to stride in and tell the commanders to strengthen the defense of the keep's walls and to send runners to recall Warlord Hartusk at once.

He burst into the main chamber of the large circular building, and there his words stuck in his throat and his jaw hung slack.

On the throne sat Lorgru, son of Obould.

Tiago reflexively went for his sword, but a host of orc guards leaped forth, spears leveled his way.

"What are you doing here?" the shocked drow demanded.

"Kill this fool," Lorgru ordered, and the guards came on.

Tiago parried the nearest spears and broke away, speeding out of the chamber. He placed a globe of darkness in the corridor behind him before he exited fully, then walked out as if nothing were amiss, confident that the magical blackness would hold the guards for a few heartbeats, at least.

So he calmly walked off to the side, to the shadows, then sprinted to the picket wall and went over it easily, running off into the mountains.

The drow noble found a perch sometime later, up high and looking back over the rolling hills in the south.

And there he saw the fires of an army of nearly ten thousand ferocious dwarves.

Tiago looked down to his left, toward the fires that marked Dark Arrow Keep.

At least Lorgru would die soon enough, he thought.

"You have outdone yourself this time," Kimmuriel said to Jarlaxle as they watched the dwarven march to the walls of Dark Arrow Keep. Inside the fortress, all seemed calm and quiet, and not a guard shouted, nor did a ballista bolt or a catapult volley reach out to hinder their approach.

"It was my plan all along," Jarlaxle replied.

But Kimmuriel wore a knowing frown. Jarlaxle hadn't even known of Lorgru until Kimmuriel, informed by Gromph, had told him of the deposed rightful heir to the Many-Arrows throne.

"Well, from the time you told me of this one," Jarlaxle corrected with a wry grin, one bolstered by the fact that his elder brother had aided him in retrieving the more civilized orc from exile.

"He did it, elf," a clearly frustrated Bruenor remarked to Drizzt when the high picket walls of the orc fortress towered in front of them.

"They couldn't win against us and they knew it," the drow replied.

"And now them dogs're all running back to their holes in the Spine o' the World, and not to doubt but that they'll be back in time to start the fight anew."

Drizzt stared at Bruenor, who was obviously looking past the orc fortress to the mountain trails beyond.

"We promised Jarlaxle that we would not give chase," Drizzt reminded Bruenor, for indeed the drow mercenary had come to them the night before with news of the desertion. "This is the son of Obould, who has now regained control."

"Still an orc," Bruenor grumbled.

"There will be plenty of orcs to kill soon enough," Drizzt told him.

"Bah!" the dwarf snorted.

"Ne'er have I wanted to tear a place down more than at this moment," King Emerus said, coming over with Connerad and Harnoth to join Bruenor and Drizzt.

"Aye, the place reeks o' death and speaks o' destruction, and suren it's leavin' me cold!" Harnoth agreed.

"Prepare the field afore her gates," Bruenor instructed. "We'll be putting a half-thousand dwarves in there, and all the elves, to greet Hartusk when he limps back home."

"Aye, and the rest of us lyin' in wait," King Connerad agreed.

"Ye think it's really empty?" King Emerus asked, nodding at the high picket wall.

"It's empty," said Catti-brie, who came over to join the gathering. "Or with just a few inside. Those too old or too young, and not quick enough to catch up with the retreat."

"Something to kill, then," King Harnoth said with a growl.

But Bruenor shook his head. "Nah, ye put 'em north o' the place and let 'em go," he ordered.

"Bah!" snorted Harnoth, along with Oretheo Spikes and Bungalow Thump, who were both listening in from the side.

King Emerus Warcrown and Bruenor locked stares, with Emerus finally nodding his agreement. "If any threaten ye, then kill 'em to death," he ordered Ragged Dain. "Ye take five hunnerd and clear what's left o' the vermin. Send 'em runnin' north to their stinkin' mountain holes."

"And we're to take the rest and erase any signs that we come this way," Bruenor informed King Emerus.

Ragged Dain nodded and quickly assembled his force, then rushed for the main gates of Dark Arrow Keep.

They weren't barred. They swung open easily, and in went the dwarves.

Soon after, Ragged Dain appeared back at the opened gate, signaling that all was clear.

The dwarves had Dark Arrow Keep, without a fight.

Without a fight yet, for to be sure, they knew that one would soon be coming their way.

Not far from there, Gromph nodded as he watched the unfolding events in his scrying pool.

"I suspected that Lorgru would prove valuable," the archmage said to the other two dark elves in the small cave chamber. "And so I was right."

"Aren't you always, Brother?" Jarlaxle asked.

"Enough so that I am still alive," Gromph replied.

Jarlaxle just looked at Kimmuriel and shrugged, unable to get his arms around all of this. What was Gromph up to? Why did he care if the dwarves had to fight a terrific battle at the walls of Dark Arrow Keep?

It is about embarrassing Matron Mother Quenthel, Kimmuriel said in Jarlaxle's thoughts, and he looked from the psionicist to the archmage, trying to sort it out. *Or perhaps it goes even higher than her.*

Jarlaxle snorted at that, for who could be higher than Quenthel, who served as the Matron Mother of Menzoberranzan?

Then he figured it out, and he stopped snorting.

He looked at Gromph, only then beginning to appreciate how wounded his brother had been by the betrayal of the Spider Queen. Lolth had gone to the realm of arcane magic, had tried to dominate the Weave itself—and indeed, by all reports, she had made the magical strands encompassing Toril take on the aspect of a gigantic spider web.

Gromph had dared to hope that Lolth's move would elevate his standing, that he, as the greatest drow wizard of the age, as the greatest drow practitioner of the Art, would become more than a mere male in the matriarchal City of Spiders.

That was Gromph's error, Jarlaxle realized, and he nodded knowingly as he considered his brother.

Poor Gromph had dared to hope.

CHAPTER 24

TORN GROUND AND EXCREMENT

Leaving torn ground and piles of excrement in its wake, the massive army of Many-Arrows plodded up the road along the north bank of the River Rauvin, the route connecting the ruins of Sundabar to Everlund. The monsters walked many abreast, a mob more than an army, it seemed, with more than ten full miles separating the leading edge of that catastrophe from the trailing ranks.

Warlord Hartusk was near the front of the army, surrounded by his most trusted and most ferocious orc legions, and so he noted the growing excitement at the front of his march. He understood when word finally carried back to him that they were approaching a settlement, a sizable village on the northern banks of the Rauvin.

"Lhuvenhead," Hartusk's advisor remarked. The warlord nodded, and grinned wickedly. Lhuvenhead was the largest settlement in the Rauvin Vale, a prosperous merchant community.

"We are only two days from the walls of Everlund, Warlord," the advisor added.

"Kill them and capture as many as you can," Hartusk ordered, and the word went forth in eager shouts, and the orcs leading the army launched into a charge, sweeping down upon the village.

But the place was deserted, they found to their disappointment, and no boats remained at the village's disproportionately large docks. Prudence and good planning would have led the Many-Arrows army to leave the village unscathed. As they passed it, it became their land, after all, and with an important and well-designed system of barges and docks that could bring vast supplies down from Everlund in short order.

But these were orcs, and immediate gratification was a far more urgent call to them than wise long-term planning. By the time Hartusk himself arrived in Lhuvenhead, there really was no Lhuvenhead remaining.

There was just a hundred piles of splintered and burning wood and broken homes, and with a mess of jetsam floating down river, splashing and rolling along the forty miles to mighty Everlund.

Warlord Hartusk did not disapprove, even though he was wise enough to realize the waste. His minions needed blood, and none was to be found here, not with every villager long gone—no doubt to Everlund. The orcs needed some release for their violent urges, and so be it.

Besides, Hartusk figured that Everlund itself would be his soon enough.

It was the first day of Flamerule, also called Summertide, the seventh month of 1485. How fitting that this particular village, long known as a pleasant summer respite for the lords and ladies of both Sundabar and Everlund, had simply ceased to exist on this day.

"Press on!" Hartusk ordered his charges, and the black wave of Many-Arrows rolled along toward Everlund, the great gateway to the southlands.

More than an hour later, far back in the line, Jarl Greigor Kundknoddick and his entourage came upon the obliterated village.

The frost giant leader was not amused. He, like Hartusk, recognized the waste, and the opportunity lost. He heard again the drow's warnings in his thoughts.

Would sheer numbers be enough? To conquer, perhaps, but to gain any lasting hold?

Frost giants were not like orcs and goblins and ogres. They did not war for the sake of war, but for the promise of greater riches and power. They preferred beauty to ugliness, and this town was surely ugly.

"The dwarves are out," Jarl Greigor said to those around him. He didn't wait for any answers, and didn't want any.

In truth, he was speaking more to himself than to the others, as he tried futilely to process the information the drow had offered. He had brought his giants into this fray because he hated the dwarves and because it had seemed then that Hartusk's march could not fail. That seemed even more assured when Sundabar had fallen.

Greigor looked to the brothers of Thrym, but they could only shrug and shake their heads.

They had served well in getting him out here, as with his counterpart, Jarl Orelson, to be sure. But that was all they had done.

Jarl Greigor shook his head in reply, and thought again of the great victory at Sundabar, truly the high point of Warlord Hartusk's war. But without the dragons, would that have happened? Without the dragons, and without the surprised dwarves caught in their holes?

A commotion drew Jarl Greigor and his entourage back around the ruins of the village to the east, to view the rear guard of the Many-Arrows force. Dust climbed in the distance and the wind carried cries and screams.

"A battle," one of the other giants, a brutish female named Jierta, remarked.

"Knights in Silver!" an orc confirmed, running by the group. "They have come in great numbers!"

"Silverymoon?" Jierta asked. "They are besieged!"

"So we thought," Jarl Greigor replied. He started away at a great pace to the east, the others running beside him. Soon enough, on a low hilltop, the behemoth spotted the fight.

"Knights in Silver," Jierta confirmed.

Jarl Greigor could only nod in agreement, and wince at the size of the force. Hundreds of armored riders skirmished around the trailing edge of the orc army, firing bows from horseback and running down any monsters who ventured too far from the main throng. Apparently yet another siege had been broken.

"The orcs are organizing," Jarl Greigor remarked, nodding. He could see that the goblinkin were biding their time until the worg riders could arrive. He spotted those riders, nearing the leading edge of the skirmish.

And at last the defensive ranks of the Many-Arrows army broke open wide, a thick stream of orcs and goblins, some riding, most running, stretching out to meet the threat.

Horns blew, echoing off the mountain walls in the north, and the Silverymoon cavalry broke away as one, fleeing back to the north and the foothills of the Nether Mountains.

"We will have them!" Jierta said to Jarl Greigor.

A far greater Many-Arrows force pursued that cavalry and with the mountains looming so near, the riders would have nowhere to run.

The giants ran toward the skirmish, hoping to get into the fray before it was over. They plowed through their smaller allies, trampling many under their huge feet. They lost sight of the battle, or the chase, intermittently, as they rushed through dells and copses of trees, and by the time they neared the area of the initial fighting, all was quiet there.

Not so up to the north of that position, however, where screams of abject terror filled the air.

"They have them!" Jierta cried.

Then came such a roar that the blood drained from the frost giant's face, a monstrous roar—a dragon's roar.

Jarl Greigor Kundknoddick's blue eyes sparkled at that thought. The drow was wrong, just as he'd hoped!

But the screams continued, heightened, and running back from the foothills came the orcs and goblins, desperately falling all over each other.

"A dragon?" Jierta asked her jarl, and the ferocious giantess didn't seem so eager to charge north to join in the fighting.

More than seven thousand Many-Arrows soldiers had swarmed up into the foothills to pursue the raiding Knights in Silver.

Less than one in five returned.

Jarl Greigor motioned to one of his giants, indicating a trembling orc whimpering amidst some of its colleagues. The giant moved over, scattered the standing orcs, and hoisted the sniveling one up into the air, carrying it back to Jarl Greigor by the ankles, and giving it a little shake every couple of steps.

The giant unceremoniously dropped the orc to the ground at Jarl Greigor's feet.

"No, no, I chased them . . . I—I—I had to run," the orc stammered when the imposing Jarl bent down over it.

"A coward deserter?" Jarl Greigor said wickedly, as if he meant to cut the cowardly orc in half on the spot with his gigantic sword.

"No, no!" the orc whined.

"Go back and fight them!" Jarl Greigor demanded, and he grabbed the orc by the collar of its filthy jerkin and yanked it to its feet with frightening strength and ease.

But despite the imposing figure of the mighty giant, the orc shook its head and glanced nervously to the north. "I . . . I can't."

"You cannot?"

"Dragon . . ." the orc said, its voice a whisper. "Dragon."

"Arauthator has returned?" the frost giant asked, but the orc shook its head so violently that it seemed as if it might simply fly from the creature's shoulders.

"Not white. Not . . . ours."

Jarl Greigor looked around at his entourage, all of them now nervously stepping from foot to foot.

"The color of a copper piece," the orc explained.

"This dragon," Jierta demanded, "it aided our enemies?"

"The humans fled in front of us and rode around the dragon without hindrance."

Jarl Greigor tossed the orc aside, and the pathetic terrified creature was fleeing once more even as it hit the ground.

"Our dragons are gone, so claimed the drow, but now our enemies . . ." Jierta started to say, but Jarl Greigor cut her short with an upraised hand.

"Tell the orcs that we will return to Hartusk Keep to lead the northern armies along the northern road to put the dogs of Silverymoon back in their hole," he said. "Have them tell Warlord Hartusk that we will meet him at the walls of Everlund."

The others nodded and ran off, all of them understanding that Jarl Greigor had no intention of doing any such thing. His was not the only frost giant force that had come to the call of Warlord Hartusk, but it was among the most powerful, perhaps second only to Shining White itself, particularly with the three huge brothers of the frost giant god Thrym in their ranks.

Threescore giants broke from Hartusk's vast ranks that day, running north for the Moon Pass and the lands beyond. They would turn west, as they had told the orcs, but not to engage Silverymoon. They were bound for the lands across the Surbrin, west, to the Spine of the World and their icy home.

Warlord Hartusk suspected as much when he heard of Jarl Greigor's departure. If it was true, he silently vowed, he would march on Shining White when he was done with Everlund and Silverymoon.

They were much closer to Everlund now than to Hartusk Keep, and the minor skirmishes against his vast army and the desertion of a few here and there would not deter him. Reports of groups of raiding bands of enemy riders were common—Knights in Silver trapped outside their besieged city, he believed. Nay, such minor inconveniences would not deter him.

Nor would ridiculous rumors of enemy dragons.

⎯⎯⎯⎯⎯⎯⎯ ⧖⧗ ⎯⎯⎯⎯⎯⎯⎯

The army of Many-Arrows pressed on through the dark night, and late the next day, they came in sight of mighty Everlund, settled on the northern bank of the Rauvin River, with two great bridges reaching across the water to the southern road.

Warlord Hartusk nodded grimly. They had to destroy those bridges as soon as they took the city, to prevent enemies from coming up from the great cities in the southlands. Surely the call had already gone out from Everlund.

Nay, this would be no siege, and that very day, Hartusk sent his hordes charging at Everlund's great wall, thinking to knock the city down with sheer numbers.

Indeed, had it been only Everlund there to defy him, his tactics would likely have proven correct and effective, but barely had the first ranks reached the killing grounds before the walls when another force appeared on the field, riding down from the higher ground in the north, horns blowing.

The Knights in Silver.

And this was no raiding group, Hartusk and his commanders knew at once. This was the garrison of Silverymoon, nearly in full.

And with wizards . . . so many wizards.

Fireballs and lightning bolts led that charge, blasting and scattering Hartusk's minions. The warlord and his elite fighters rushed back, calling for a regrouping.

"Kill the fools outside the walls!" he cried, and the great morass of his army began its slow turn.

But then came the two copper dragons, skimming in low, breathing clouds of magically slowing gasses, or spitting acid that melted orcs where they stood.

And the horns blew from the west as well, as Everlund's garrison, too, came forth.

There, between the Nether Mountains and the River Rauvin, just east of Everlund, was fought the greatest battle of the War of the Silver Marches.

On a wider field, Many-Arrows would have prevailed, sheer numbers overwhelming the elves and humans and their allies, even the dragons. But this was no wide field, but a bordered corridor of death.

VENGEANCE OF THE IRON DWARF

Warlord Hartusk was soon in full flight, back to the east, his force chased every mile by the Knights in Silver, who shot their longbows from horseback with deadly accuracy.

Wulfgar lifted Aleina Brightlance in a great hug when he found her on the bloodied fields, not far from Everlund's walls.

The fierce woman grabbed him by his blond hair and tugged his head back so that she could look into his blue eyes.

"We will chase them all the way home," she said. "We will kill them all!"

Wulfgar kissed her passionately and squeezed her so tightly that Aleina thought her spine might crack apart. But she didn't complain, just kissed him even harder, and tugged at his hair, her lust unsated by battle.

They had broken the siege at Silverymoon just days before, the arrival of the dragons and word of the dwarven citadels out and free sending the bulk of the besieging armies in full flight before the battle had even begun.

And now the plan Aleina had proposed to Lord Hornblade, which he had taken to the lords of Everlund with help of a wizard's spell, had worked to perfection.

The fighting wasn't done, Wulfgar and Aleina knew well as they made their way to a quiet and secluded place and made love under the dark sky to the sound of the rushing river.

But that was for tomorrow.

Riding on the back of a dragon, sitting in front of Brother Afafrenfere, Regis could hardly contain his smile. Far below in the east, what remained of the army of Many-Arrows was in full flight for the Moon Pass.

Raiding knights nipped at the stragglers behind, just to thin the ranks as they could, and more importantly, to keep the orcs running.

Many giants remained among the monstrous force, and giants could throw heavy rocks, so the dragon sisters did not engage. They meant to stay up high and allow their mere presence to bring fear to their enemies.

Unless, of course, a sizeable force of monsters turned back to try to catch the pursuing knights.

Then Tazmikella and Ilnezhara would swoop down, alerting the knights of the ambush, to play with the ambushed forces and chase them on their way.

"They'll not stop at Sundabar," Afafrenfere said to Regis on the fourth day, as the Many-Arrows army crossed through the Moon Pass and had the city they had named Hartusk Keep in sight. "They will pass through, with Hartusk hoping that those he leaves behind in the ruined city will hold back the pursuit."

"He knows he's lost," Regis agreed. "He'll run all the way to Dark Arrow Keep!"

"Let us hope," Afafrenfere replied. They both knew what awaited Hartusk's less-than-triumphant return.

The Surbrin Bridge was unguarded, but neither were any of the vast encampments the orcs had set about the place, around Mithral Hall, evident. Hartusk's fleeing army encountered many small bands of fellow orcs in the long retreat, and all of them said the same thing: the dwarves had broken the sieges and the Many-Arrows armies had scattered or had been destroyed.

Just north of Fourthpeak, word came to Warlord Hartusk that a large force was again on his tail, an army flying the banners of Silverymoon and Everlund.

Hartusk was not dismayed by the news. He knew the ground around his home fortress, and that ground had been prepared to ward off an attacking army.

Indeed it had, and those defenses had been improved upon greatly since Warlord Hartusk had departed for the south.

But what Hartusk did not know was that Dark Arrow Keep was now in the hands of four dwarf kings and the combined armies of Mithral Hall, Citadel Felbarr, and mighty Citadel Adbar.

How joyous ran the orcs when at last the tall pickets of Dark Arrow Keep's formidable walls came into view! How great came their cheers, how fast their pace, as they ran for home.

VENGEANCE OF THE IRON DWARF

Several balls of catapulted flaming pitch were in the air before any of the monsters even began to understand the truth before them. It was not until those fiery balls hit and exploded, and created a torrent of flames as lines of shallow-buried oil crisscrossed the field south of Dark Arrow Keep, that Warlord Hartusk understood his doom.

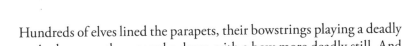

Hundreds of elves lined the parapets, their bowstrings playing a deadly song. And among them raced a drow, with a bow more deadly still. And from their ranks came crackling bolts of lightning, and fireballs, the blue glow of magic lifting up from the spellscarred arms of Catti-brie.

Crack artillery teams of skilled dwarves adjusted the catapults and ballistae—scores of the mighty weapons—and sent their fury raining down upon the Many-Arrows army.

Before the orcs had even adjusted to the shock, from the south came the horns of the Knights in Silver and the garrison of Everlund, accentuated by the roars of a pair of copper dragons.

And from the west, out of the foothills, came the charge of King Bruenor and nine thousand shield dwarves, swarming down like an avalanche on the orc forces, driving them east, to the river.

And all the lines blurred, and the dragons came down low, Ilnezhara dropping a pair of wild-eyed dwarves, Athrogate and Ambergris, into the fray near Bruenor, then flying off to wreak her own savagery upon the monstrous enemies.

Tazmikella, too, came in low, but she didn't pause as her lone passenger, the monk Afafrenfere, leaped down from on high into the midst of a horde of orcs. He landed in a roll and sprang up high out of it, snap-kicking left and right into the surprised faces of a pair of enemies. Almost immediately, orcs began flying away, tumbling and falling as the monk launched into a brutal and unrelenting assault.

And off flew Tazmikella to the walls of Dark Arrow Keep.

In the lone bright spot, the singular force holding the shocked and disorganized hordes of Many-Arrows in any semblance of a fighting posture, was their vicious leader. Bodies piled around Warlord Hartusk, his flaming sword marking the center, the rallying point, of the dwindling but still enormous goblinkin and giantkind forces. Even in the midst of a horrendous slaughter of his people, the orc leader vowed to fight on, and rallied those around him to feats of fury that held the enemies at bay.

His position was not unnoticed.

Bruenor Battlehammer similarly formed the center of the dwarven press, standing tall and singing at the top of his lugs, urging his boys to get to the ugly warlord so that they could at last extinguish his flaming greatsword.

Bruenor heard the flap of great leathery wings before he saw the copper dragon Tazmikella moving up behind him and just above.

"He is an ugly one," Drizzt called down to his red-bearded friend from the dragon's back. Catti-brie sat behind him, her arms around his waist. "I was thinking that perhaps I should go over and put an end to Warlord Hartusk."

"Bah, elf, but ye leave that dog for me!" said Bruenor, and Drizzt smiled wide.

"He was hoping you would say that," Catti-brie said to her father, and before Bruenor could begin to decipher her sly tone and jovial mood, Tazmikella flew past, one great clawed foot reaching down to scoop up Bruenor and carry him away.

All around, surprised dwarves howled in shock, but then, sorting it out, cheered instead.

A soldier from Everlund rolled and squirmed down to the ground, disemboweled by the mighty sword of Hartusk. The orc warlord stood tall, sword upraised in one hand, his other fist upraised as well. He roared in victory and told his minions that the tide of battle would turn.

But before the orcs and others could respond with cheers of their own, a dragon glided in to hover above the great orc, and the monsters around Hartusk cowered and fled.

Surely the wyrm could have killed Hartusk there where he stood, but she did not. Instead, she swooped down lower and deposited her cargo, a dwarf held in one claw, on the field in front of the warlord.

An orc lifted its bow to shoot the dwarf, but one of the dragon's three riders had his arrow nocked first and shot that orc dead with a silver-streaking arrow that launched the ugly archer into the air.

On the ground below Tazmikella, Bruenor Battlehammer straightened and dusted himself off.

"Been waitin' a long time for this," the dwarf said. He adjusted his one-horned helm, then pulled a mug of ale out from behind his burnished magical shield. He lifted it in toast.

"To yer ugly head bouncing about the ground," he said, then drained the flagon with one great gulp.

Hartusk growled and lifted his greatsword.

Bruenor laughed at him and lifted his many-notched axe.

They came together like a pair of raging giants, Hartusk pressing hard with great sweeps of his longer blade.

But Bruenor was hearing the song of Clangeddin then, his arms swelling with strength, his heart lifted in the thrill of battle. Again and again, Hartusk's sword slammed against the shield, but even that mighty weapon in the hands of the powerful orc could not mar the image of the foaming mug emblazoned on the buckler that had twice known the fires of Gauntlgrym's Forge.

The orc's fury played out, the warlord's swing slowing after a dozen-dozen sweeps.

And now came Bruenor, leaping ahead, inside the orc's reach, bashing Hartusk with his axe, denting the warlord's mighty armor and driving him back, step by step.

On one such step back, Hartusk retreated farther and tucked his sword in tight. Then he thrust it ahead powerfully, and roared in victory, knowing that the dwarf could not bring his mighty shield across to block and could dodge neither left nor right.

But Hartusk did not hit.

Bruenor leaped and rolled into the air, his right side thrown back. Spinning a sidelong circuit all the way around, he held there, defying Toril's pull, seemingly floating like a condor on mountain updrafts—or like the dragons watching from above.

Around he went, and for Hartusk, time seemed to slow, agonizingly, for as the dwarf at last came around, that mighty axe led the way, and with his arms and sword extended, with the dwarf above that thrusting blade, Warlord Hartusk had no defense.

The wish of Bruenor's toast had come to pass.

EPILOGUE

H<small>E WEREN'T NO</small> O<small>BOULD, TO BE SURE</small>," B<small>RUENOR SAID AGAINST THE</small> stream of huzzahs and heigh-ho's that came his way. He sat with his peers around a small fire in front of the gates of Dark Arrow Keep.

With Hartusk fallen, the battle had quickly disintegrated into a hodge-podge of small pockets of fighting, and usually with those warriors of Many-Arrows more interested in running away than in fighting.

Many orcs and other monsters did get off that field, indeed, tens of thousands, running north into the mountains.

"Might that they'll be comin' back," King Emerus warned.

"Aye, but we should chase 'em and kill 'em to death," King Harnoth agreed.

"Tear Dark Arrow Keep down, log by log," Bruenor declared. "And float them logs down the Surbrin. Me boys'll take 'em for burning in Mithral Hall."

"Yer boys?" King Emerus said slyly, and he glanced at King Connerad, who looked up at that surprising remark.

Bruenor looked from king to king, then laughed heartily. "Nah," he said. "Connerad's boys. Me place's done here, me friends. I got a road I'm needin' to walk."

"Back to Icewind Dale?" King Connerad asked, but Bruenor shook his head. "I'll tell ye soon enough." He motioned to the side then, noting the approach of Drizzt and the other Companions of the Hall. He knew where they had been, with whom they had met.

"What're ye knowin', elf?" Bruenor asked as Drizzt arrived.

"The orcs will not return," Drizzt replied. "Not soon, at least, and under no king or warlord. Lorgru, the son of Obould, has many of them now under his command, and that one had no designs of conquest." He looked over at Sinnafein as he finished, and the elf nodded knowingly. Lorgru's mercy toward her had started this war, after all.

"He ain't coming back, no matter his designs!" King Harnoth said, and all the others, Bruenor included, nodded at that demand.

Drizzt bowed to diffuse the sudden tension.

"Hartusk usurped the throne from Lorgru, who wanted no war," Drizzt explained.

"And how might ye be knowin' all this, Mister Drizzt Do'Urden?" Ragged Dain asked.

"From a friend."

"A friend?" King Harnoth asked suspiciously.

"A friend who brought dragons," Drizzt replied without hesitation, and that set the young king of Adbar back on his haunches.

The drow started to elaborate, but he stopped suddenly, a curious look coming over him. He looked to Catti-brie first, and his expression gave her pause.

"What is it?" she asked with great concern.

"Drizzt?" Regis added.

But the drow couldn't hear them at that moment. A song was in his head, a spell actually, calling to him. He walked away from the small fire, moving among many campfires, to the curious looks from dwarves and elves and humans.

The Companions of the Hall and many others gave chase, calling to him.

Finally he stopped in the midst of a wide area cleared of bodies and camps. Catti-brie rushed to him, but he lifted his arms to her and motioned her back. The song was loud now in his mind, deafeningly so, urgently so, begging release.

And so Drizzt Do'Urden began to sing. His arms lifted up to the side and hung outstretched. His head went back, his words aimed at the sky above.

To the gasps of the onlookers, Drizzt floated up from the ground. A glow came about him, like faerie fire at first, but then intensifying.

"Drizzt!" his friends shouted—except for Catti-brie, who was crying and laughing all at once, overwhelmed as she believed she had solved the mystery. She had thought herself the Chosen of Mielikki, but how silly that seemed now, considering the drow floating in the air in front of her.

Beams of light shot from Drizzt's hands, reaching up to the Darkening. Subtle and soft at first, they gathered in strength and multitude, and now the flashes came so quickly they couldn't be counted. Into the sky they soared, striking the roiling blackness, and there, fires erupted and lightning flashes shot the night, as the great battle roared.

"Mielikki," Catti-brie said, tears streaking her cheeks, and the sheer glory and weight of the experience drove her to her knees.

Though he was on a hillock far away, Tiago Baenre couldn't miss the spectacle of Drizzt throwing shards of brilliant light up into the sky. The young noble drow ducked behind a bush, its leaves meager to nonexistent, as with all of the flora in the Silver Marches this year. He watched with amazement, and anger.

He grasped the scraggly branches, mesmerized by the mounting display.

"We will have him soon enough," promised a voice behind him, a voice so unexpected that Tiago nearly leaped out of his boots, and spun around with his sword drawn and shield spiraling out to a larger size.

"What are you doing here?" he asked when he recognized the speaker.

"I came to find you," Doum'wielle lied. She had come here to find another, of course, but Khazid'hea had sensed a Baenre House emblem, the residue of Tiago's long float back to Faerûn. For that emblem, like all of House Baenre's marks, had been fashioned of a stone from the Faerzress, the same Underdark region, with its magical emanations, that had granted Khazid'hea its sentience.

"I did not summon you," Tiago barked at her. "Where is Ravel, and my wife?"

"I know not," Doum'wielle answered. "They were chased from the Rauvin ford back to the south. I was cast into the river and washed all the way to the Surbrin. My sword led me to my father, and from there, on the slope of the mountain above the dwarves' home, we came north in search of you."

Tiago looked at her with clear doubt. How could she have known that he would be up here, or even alive? He lowered his sword, and Doum'wielle moved closer.

"You should be glad that I have come, for I can prove to be of great value to you, up here on the World Above," she said, and there was a bit of tease in her soft voice.

"You are worthless, and worthless to me."

"You should rethink that," Doum'wielle said.

"You dare question me?"

"I am not worthless to you, noble son of House Baenre," she said, standing tall. "I can move among the folk of the surface easily, and besides . . ." She moved a bit closer. "I can offer you something the women of Menzoberranzan cannot."

"Do tell," Tiago said when she was standing right in front of him.

"Respect," Doum'wielle said.

Tiago feigned anger at that, and managed a scowl, but Doum'wielle could see that she had gotten through to him a bit, at least, though whether because of the practical benefit she offered or the emotional one, she could not tell.

It didn't matter, she decided. Because she hated him in any case, and needed him to help with her quest, even as he thought she was aiding him in his own.

Even the dwarves were crying soon, all the onlookers on the field overwhelmed by the spectacle.

And the stars peeked through, shining on the Silver Marches for the first time in so many months.

And still it went on, the shards of brilliance leaping from Drizzt to join in the fight. And still he sang, though he felt as if his very life-force was engaged in this perilous struggle now, the Lightening against the Darkening.

It went on through most of that midsummer night, which for the first time in so long became true night once more, with stars and a full silvery Selûne and her Tears bathing the land.

It ended with a whisper, a final, gasping note, and then the spell was broken and Drizzt fell back to the ground and crumpled into a heap. His friends ran to him, thinking him dead and crying to Mielikki.

In the foothills to the west, the normally unflappable Jarlaxle had to slap his hand over his mouth to stop from crying out with laughter. "Brilliant!" he said. "They think it their goddess!"

As the Darkening above fully dissipated, Kimmuriel broke the mental connection he had enacted between Drizzt and Gromph Baenre, wherein the archmage had used the unsuspecting Drizzt as a surrogate for his powerful enchantment, a spell to defeat Tsabrak's.

"I know not what to say," Jarlaxle remarked, shaking his head.

It took Gromph a long time to steady himself after the exertion of that spell, as great a casting as he had ever performed. He opened his eyes and stepped back from the psionicist, closed his huge spellbook, and let his imposing stare fall over Jarlaxle.

"A feint within a feint within a feint, if ever I've seen one," said Jarlaxle, who couldn't remain speechless for long, after all. "All witnessed Drizzt casting the enchantment, and all believed it the power of his goddess flowing through him. The task is far removed from the caster. Brilliant. Why, Brother, you are beginning to remind me of . . . me!"

Gromph arched an eyebrow, and didn't have to utter the threat it signified.

"But surely you understand my confusion, Archmage," Jarlaxle said with proper deference. "Matron Mother—"

"Damn Quenthel to the Nine Hells where devils can play with her," Gromph growled back, and both Jarlaxle and Kimmuriel fell back a step.

"The true Matron Mother of Menzoberranzan sleeps in the arms of Minolin Fey Baenre this day, awaiting my return," Gromph explained. "Quenthel, all of the city, will learn that truth soon enough."

Jarlaxle and Kimmuriel looked to each other with surprise.

The massive pickets of Dark Arrow Keep came tumbling down under the brilliant sunshine of the following day, the dwarves happily carrying them to the Surbrin and tossing them in. Riders had already left for Mithral Hall, and the dwarves at the Surbrin Bridge would be ready to receive the firewood.

The meeting inside the audience chamber of Dark Arrow Keep that day was limited to the four dwarf kings, for this was Delzoun business most serious.

"Mithral Hall's for Connerad," Bruenor asserted as soon as the formalities, including several hearty ales from Bruenor's magical shield, were out of the way. "Even if meself was to stay, it'd not be me place to challenge that what was rightfully and properly given."

"Always'll be a place for Little Arr Arr in Citadel Felbarr!" King Emerus assured the red-bearded dwarf, to a chorus of huzzahs and clanging mugs.

"Bah, but his place is Mithral Hall, and don't ye doubt it!" King Connerad demanded.

"Me place's in the west," Bruenor corrected solemnly, and the flagons drifted lower, and the three kings stared at him somberly. "And I'm hopin' that yerselves, me friends, will afford me the boys I'm needin' to get to that place."

"Gauntlgrym," Connerad said quietly.

"Aye," Bruenor replied. "Damned drow elfs got it, but they ain't for holding it."

"We should be sendin' word to Mirabar," King Harnoth offered. "Aye, and Icewind Dale, course."

"How many boys?" King Emerus asked.

"All ye can spare," Bruenor replied. "It's Gauntlgrym, and the throne's there, and the Forge—ah, but she's the stuff o' legend!"

"There were rumors that ye found it," said Emerus.

"More'n rumors. Found it twice—ye see me shield and axe? Been through the Forge o' Gauntlgrym, and that forge's burnin' with the power of a great beast o' fire. It's all that ye heared, boys, and more, I tell ye."

He lifted his flagon and the others brought theirs up beside it, and the four dwarf kings looked into each other's eyes and hearts, and knew then that Gauntlgrym would be returned to the line of Delzoun.

.:⌢:.